The unthinkable was happening!

Andrew—the smart, witty, creative, articulate man with whom Avery had fallen passionately in love—was cheating on her.

A month ago she'd known their first encounter must have been destiny. Fate. Kismet. It was simply Meant To Be. What difference did it make if they'd never actually met in person? Who cared if they'd never actually spoken to each other? Their cyber relationship was a meeting of minds, a melding of souls, a blending of hearts.

Until now.

Now he was typing nauseating pop-culture-infested lines to some cheap bit of cyberfluff with the screen name Tinky Bell. A brainless ninny who said things like "ur 2 kewl."

The hideous massacre of the English language aside, Avery couldn't believer *her* Andrew was talking about TV shows! He didn't even watch TV!

But the clincher was Andrew using with Tinky Bell the same words that won Avery's heart.

Well, she'd fix Andrew. Not only would she dump him, but she'd give him something to remember her by. Oh, yes. She'd create just the right farewell gift…one he and his precious computer system would never forget.

More delicious "special deliveries" from

ELIZABETH BEVARLY

Express Male (May 2008)
Overnight Male (June 2008)

Recent titles from Silhouette Books

Married to His Business
* The Debutante
† The Newlyweds
Taming the Beastly M.D.
Taming the Prince
The Secret Life of Connor Monahan

† Logan's Legacy
* The Fortunes of Texas: Reunion

ELIZABETH BEVARLY

you've got male

HQN™

ISBN-13: 978-0-373-77276-6
ISBN-10:   0-373-77276-9

YOU'VE GOT MALE

www.HQNBooks.com

Printed in U.S.A.

For Mom, with love.
Because it's been too long since I dedicated a book to you.
Thanks for so many things. You're the best.

Acknowledgments

I have many people to thank for this one.

First, thanks to Liz Bemis of Bemis Web Design for helping me get all the technical jargon and equipment right, thereby enabling me to make Avery the computer whiz and Webhead that she is. Some of the technology and equipment that both OPUS and Avery use I made up myself, but it's okay, because making up stuff is my job. If I did get anything wrong with the real stuff, it's my fault, not Liz's.

Thanks to Wanda Ottewell, my fabulous editor, for helping me buff the rough spots and see the gaps, and make everything in the story nice and neat. Thanks to Tracy Farrell and HQN Books for giving this book such a wonderful home. Thanks to Steve Axelrod for helping me find that home.

I'd also like to thank the incredibly nice, patient, generous David Dafoe, of Pro-Liquitech, whose lovely donation to Turning Point for Autism won him a brief appearance in the book. For more information about all the great things Turning Point does, visit their Web site at turningpoint1.com (don't forget the 1!). It was great fun being able to invite a real person to the party at the Nesbitt estate.

Thanks, too, to good friends (you know who you are)
for daily support and camaraderie and laughter
that goes above and beyond the call of friendship.
Without you guys, I'd be like Avery at the
opening of chapter four.

And finally, as always, thanks to David and Eli, my lifelines.
My life. Without you guys, I'd be lost.
I love you both bunches. Hug. Kiss. Pat.

you've got male

CHAPTER ONE

AVERY NESBITT WAS IN LOVE. Madly, passionately, wildly in love. She was besotted. She was bedazzled. She was befuddled. She was in love as she'd never been in love before.

And it was with a man who went beyond dreamy. He was smart and witty. He was creative and articulate. He was handsome and sexy. He always said what she needed to hear, right when she needed to hear it. He knew her backward and forward, just as she knew him inside and out. And he loved her exactly the way she was. That, more than anything else, had sealed her fate and ensured that her love would last forever. Andrew Paddington made Avery feel as if nothing in her life would ever go wrong again. He was just perfect in every way.

The bastard.

Theirs had been a whirlwind courtship, had come at Avery out of nowhere and swept her into a fantasy worthy of an epic romance. Andrew was in her thoughts and her dreams, in her plans and her performance, in her ego and her id. He filled her days with delight and her nights with pleasure, imbued her with joy that made her downright giddy. And that was no small accomplishment for a woman who was normally pragmatic, cynical and down-to-earth. Although Avery had only met him a month ago, she'd known after that first encounter that their meeting must have been destiny. Fate. Kismet. It was simply Meant To Be.

Bastard.

What difference did it make if they'd never actually met in person? Physical trappings weren't what love was about. Love was a meeting of minds, a melding of souls, a blending of hearts. Besides, they'd exchanged photos, and the ones he'd sent to her depicted him as a sandy-haired twentysomething with the eyes of a poet, the mouth of a troubadour, the hands of an artist and phenomenal pecs. He was an utter, unmitigated masterpiece.

Bastard, bastard, bastard.

Who cared if they'd never actually spoken to each other? Vocal avowals of devotion were as nebulous and inconstant as the wind. Avery had Andrew's love for her in *writing*. In the loveliest prose she'd ever read, words—*feelings*—wrought so tenderly, they would move a despot to tears. After only four weeks, she had a file filled with his e-mails to her and she'd logged every chat-room exchange they'd shared in a special folder titled Snookypie. On those nights when she was alone and feeling dreamy and lovey-dovey, she lit candles and opened a bottle of wine, then read over his words again and again, pretending he was right there in her Central Park West condo, murmuring them into her ear.

Bastard squared.

But now the unthinkable was happening. Andrew was cheating on her with another woman. And Avery was finding out about it just as women did on those bad made-for-cable movies. She'd walked in on him and found him in bed with another woman.

Well, okay, figuratively speaking. What had actually happened was that she'd stumbled upon him online, blabbing away with some cheap bit of cyberfluff in, of all places, a *Survivor: Mall of America* chat room. This after Andrew had assured Avery that he loathed popular culture as much as she did. But what really toasted her melbas was that the cyberfluff he was chatting with, who went by the screen name of—Avery had to bite back her nausea when she saw it—Tinky Belle, was clearly an idiot. But Andrew was *agreeing* with her that the music of Clay Aiken could, if people would just open their eyes and ears and hearts to it, bring peace and harmony to the entire planet.

Bastard cubed.

Unable to believe her eyes, Avery felt around until she located the chair in front of her desk and clumsily pulled it out. Then she nearly missed the surface of her desk when she set her bowl of Cajun popcorn and the bottle of Wild Cherry Pepsi on top of it. She tugged at her electric-blue pajama pants spattered with images of French landmarks and numbly sat down, adjusting the oversize purple sweatshirt boasting Wellesley College as she did. Then she wiggled her toes in her fuzzy pink slippers to warm them, adjusted her little black-framed glasses on the bridge of her nose, pushed one of two long, thick black braids over her shoulder and studied the screen more closely.

Maybe she was wrong, she thought as she watched the rapid-fire exchange scroll by. She shouldn't jump to conclusions. Surely Andrew wasn't the only guy out there in cyberspace who used the handle Mad2Live. It was a phrase from *On the Road,* after all. And there were probably lots of Kerouac fans online. Andrew loved Avery. He'd told her so. He wouldn't cheat on her like this. Especially not with some brainless ninny who said things like, "ur 2 kewl mad."

Please, people! she wanted to shout at the screen whenever she saw message-board shorthand. *Speak English! Or Spanish! Or French! Or German! Or some legitimate language that indicates you're at least halfway literate! And capitalize where necessary! And for God's sake, punctuate!*

Even though she was a computer geek in the most extreme sense of the word, Avery couldn't bring herself to type in anything other than the language she'd learned growing up in the Hamptons. Tony private schools could mess with you in a lot of ways, she knew, but at least they taught you to be well-spoken. That shouldn't change just because your language of choice was cyber-speak.

She watched Mad2Live and Tinky Belle—gag—swap warm fuzzies for as long as she could stomach it and ultimately decided there was no way that this Mad2Live could be Andrew. Andrew would never, ever concede that the *Survivor* series was, as Tinky Belle claimed, "qualty educatnl programing u cn wach w/ the hole famly."

Oh, yes, Avery thought. *It's definitely mus c tv.*

She was about to leave the chat room to visit another—she was, after all, supposed to be working—when Mad2Live posted something that made her fingers convulse on the mouse: *You, Tinky Belle, are a dazzling blossom of hope burgeoning at the center of an unforgiving cultural wasteland.*

Acid heat splashed through Avery's belly when she read that. Because those were the exact words Andrew had used to describe her that first night they met in a Henry James chat room. Except for the Tinky Belle part, since Avery's screen name—at least that night—had been Daisy Miller. There was no way there could be two Mad2Lives on the Internet flirting with women by calling them dazzling blossoms of hope who burgeoned in cultural wastelands. That was Andrew—*her* Andrew—through and through.

After that it was impossible for Avery to ignore Tinky and Mad's conversation. And as she watched the lines of dialogue on her screen roll past, she read more and more from Mad2Live that was pulled verbatim from some of the e-mails Andrew had sent to her. And she should know, since she'd practically memorized some of them.

Had she mentioned he was a complete bastard?

Eventually Tinky bade farewell to Mad and evaporated from the chat room, and Avery watched in astonishment as he immediately began to flirt with another occupant, this one calling herself Deb2000. But Deb wasn't impressed by any of Mad's cajoling, so, obviously disgruntled, Mad signed out of the chat room.

And Avery followed him.

Luckily she had dozens of screen names she used for her work and she could log in to rooms under several that Andrew would never recognize. And luckily, too, she knew the online community better than she knew even her own Manhattan neighborhood. Because the Internet was where Avery worked every single night. And it was where she played after she knocked off work. It was also where she shopped, where she learned and where she socialized. It was where she found her music, her books, her entertainment and her dinner selections.

Hell, she pretty much lived on the Net. And she knew Andrew almost as well as she knew the online community.

Or at least she'd thought she knew him that well. But now she was beginning to think him a complete stranger. Because he flitted from one chat room to another, all of them themed around shallow pop-culture subject matter—everything from Pilates to low-carb cuisine—and in every one of them he waited long enough to identify which of the room's inhabitants were female and which seemed to be the least, uh, bright. And then he chose one and began to work on her in exactly the way he had worked on Avery that first night he'd encountered her. And shame boiled within her when she realized that she had capitulated to his pretty words as easily as had women who thought deep-fried pork flesh was an essential part of good nutrition.

How could he do this to her? How could he think she was stupid? *She?* Avery Nesbitt? She wasn't stupid. She was a criminal genius! Even *Time* magazine had said so! And even if the criminal part was debatable, once a genius, always a genius. How could he cheat on her this way? And be so obvious about it? He *knew* how good she was. He knew what she did for a living and how much time she spent online. He knew everything about her. She'd even told him about her past transgressions, and he hadn't flinched. He'd told her her past didn't matter, that anything that had happened before the day he met her wasn't important because he didn't start living until the day he met her.

Oh, he was *such* a bastard.

Well, she'd fix Andrew. Not only would she dump

him faster than you could say, "*Survivor:* Up Yours," but she'd give him something to remember her by, too. She'd blow off work and stay up all night if she had to to concoct just the right farewell gift.

Of course, being up all night wasn't exactly a sacrifice to Avery, since she pretty much lived her life at night anyway. Nighttime didn't have rules or expectations the way daytime hours did. So when most people were coming home from their jobs and starting to wind down, Avery was rising and revving to go. And when most people's alarm clocks were going off and signaling the beginning of their workday, Avery was pouring herself a scotch and popping a DVD of a *Cracker* mystery into the player and trying to wind down. Unfortunately, she'd never been as good at winding down as she was at revving up.

Because Avery Nesbitt was what some people—those who claimed an ounce or two of compassion—called "a bit neurotic." She was what other people—those who didn't give a damn about compassion—called "totally whack." Hey, what else could you call a woman who lived in her pajamas on the Internet and never left her apartment unless it was to take her cat to the vet, and even then had to load up on half a bottle of scotch just to get herself over the threshold? What else did you call a woman who bought into the tripe men like Andrew Paddington fed to unsuspecting morons?

But Avery didn't care what anyone thought about her these days, any more than she'd cared when she was a kid. She especially didn't care tonight. Tonight and tomorrow night—and all the hours in between— she had other things on her mind. Her gift for Andrew would take the better part of the next forty-eight hours to create.

Fortunately for Avery, she was totally whack and had nowhere else to go.

"HEY, HOW'S IT FEELING OUT there, Dixon?"

"Like Antarctica. Only without all the warm toasti-ness."

"Well, we'll see if we can't get you something closer to Greenland next time you're in the field."

"How many times do I have to remind you people—I'm not supposed to be in the field!"

Because the field was cold and harsh and unforgiv-ing. Even with a laptop and a decent cup of coffee.

Dixon tugged the zipper of his leather jacket higher, curled his hands around a quickly cooling cup of espresso and pulled his backward-facing driver's cap farther down over inky black hair that was badly in need of a trim. But that did little to warm him below the waist, and faded blue jeans, though normally his favorite garment, weren't all that effective in warding off the cold.

Even the cold found in the back of a van that was in-sulated with high-tech surveillance equipment.

He was infinitely more suited to the great indoors, he thought as he switched his attention from the laptop monitor to a television screen that offered a three-hundred-and-sixty-degree view of the area outside the van. Yeah, indoors he could get a hot shower and a hot sandwich and some hot coffee. Life didn't get much better than that. Unless maybe you substituted warmed brandy for the hot coffee and added a hot woman with hot hands to the hot shower. Preferably one with a hot name like Lola or Mimi or Fritzi or—

"Dixon?"

No, that wouldn't work. That was the name he was going by himself these days. It would get way too confusing. So maybe he could just call her—

"Dixon?"

"What?" he said, grinding the words out irritably as his hot shower/hot woman fantasy receded to the back of his brain, leaving him even colder than before.

"You need anything?"

He bit back a grumble at the question that came through the earpiece of his headset. Hadn't he just been thinking about that when the other agent rudely interrupted him?

"No, Gillespie," he muttered into the microphone below his chin to the newly minted OPUS agent who'd been assigned to shadow him—more to keep Gillespie out of trouble than anything else, Dixon knew. "I don't need anything." Except for his usual partner to get back from her leave of absence so *she* could go into the field instead of him, the way she was supposed to. That way Dixon could go back to collecting the information she sent him and find the missing pieces. Indoors. Where he normally worked. Where it was warm.

Because that was standard operating procedure at Dixon's employer, the ultrasecret Office of Political Unity and Security. Agents worked in teams of two, with one in the field collecting information and the other behind the scenes analyzing it. Assimilate, evaluate, articulate. That was Dixon's three-word job description. He was the one responsible for making sense of the intelligence, not the one who gathered it. He was the one who analyzed and scrutinized, calculated and estimated, and then put everything together. He *wasn't* the one who sat on his butt in a cold van waiting for something to happen. At least, he wasn't supposed to be.

"Oh, there is one thing, Gillespie," he said, picturing the other agent in his head. Blond, Dixon recalled. Too blond to be taken seriously, really. His dark blue eyes—cool and sharp and distant—were the only thing that had kept the guy from looking like some gee-whiz, what's-for-supper-Mom, all-American high school football hero.

"What's that?" the other man asked.

"Stop calling me Dixon," Dixon said. "That's not my name."

Gillespie snorted—or something—at the other end of the line. "Yeah, well, my name isn't Gillespie, either, but you have to call me something."

Oh, stop making it so easy, Dixon thought. "I keep forgetting your code name. What is it again?"

"Cowboy," the other man said.

Yee-haw, Dixon thought. He just hoped he could say it with a straight face.

"Besides," Cowboy added, "nobody at my level knows your name. Except for your code name. And you told me never to call you—"

"Okay, Dixon is fine," Dixon hastily amended.

"—that," the other man finished at the same time. "What? You thought I was going to say your code name out loud? Are you nuts? I'm not nuts. From what I hear, the last guy who spoke your code name out loud is still in the hospital. You're a dangerous man."

Damn straight, Dixon thought. And he wouldn't have it any other way. Except that he'd be a dangerous man *out* of the cold. Literally if not figuratively.

The only thing worse than being in the field—where

he wasn't supposed to be anyway, in case he hadn't mentioned it—was being in the field in New York City. Mostly because there were no fields in New York City. Except for those in Central Park, which, okay, were very nice, but they were nothing compared to the rolling green hills surrounding the Virginia farm where he'd grown up. And even though Dixon was currently parked right next to Central Park, he had to be focused on the big tidy building across from it instead. The big tidy building full of outrageously expensive condominiums that only people with more dollars than sense could afford to call their own.

The big tidy building where Daisy Miller lived.

Of course, her name was no more Daisy Miller than his was Dixon. But he'd had to have something to call her, just as he'd had to have something to put on his phony driver's license, in case one of New York's finest wandered by and wondered what a nondescript white van was doing parked in front of a Central Park West address for hours and hours and, oh, look, is that a dead debutante in the back the way there always is on *Law & Order?*

It was a pain in the ass trying to do surveillance in New York City. Yeah, he was good at what he did— quite possibly the best—but it would take an übergenius to clear up some of the audio crap he'd been trying to weed through all evening. Between the lousy weather— which the first week of November was way too early for—and the incessant cell phone use of millions of people and the twenty gazillion satellite channels beaming down from space and the simple proliferation of car and pedestrian traffic, listening in on Daisy Miller's residence this week had been next to impos-

sible. Though Dixon *had* gotten some decent info about
a certain mutual fund when some stockbroker's cell
phone conversation had overlapped with Daisy's frantic
call to the veterinarian about her cat's digestive
problems. Not to mention a very nice tip on the seventh
race at Hialeah tomorrow from some guy named Sal
who seemed to know what he was talking about.

Fortunately except for that call to the vet and a
follow-up the next day—her cat, thank God, was just
fine once it passed that button— Daisy's activity in her
apartment was limited to the point of being nonexistent.
But then, so was her activity *out* of her apartment. In
fact, in the week that Dixon had been keeping an eye
on the place, he was reasonably certain she hadn't left
the building once. And that bothered him a lot on some
level he couldn't even name. Yeah, there was a definite
cold snap going on in the city, and lots of people worked
at home these days, but to not leave one's house one
single time in a full week? Not even to go to a movie
or pick up a gallon of milk or buy a lottery ticket? That
was just…weird.

He wished he knew more about her. Which was a
strange feeling for him, because anytime Dixon—or
anyone else he worked with at OPUS—had wanted to
know more about someone, it had taken less than a day
to find out *every*thing about that person. That was a big
part of his job, after all—to find out whatever he could
about suspicious characters. And thanks to all the sophisticated equipment and arcane networks he had at his
fingertips—not to mention his superior brain—Dixon
never had much trouble doing his job. With Daisy,
though…

She was good. Better than he was, Dixon had been

forced to concede reluctantly. Not only did she have some kind of screening device on her phone he couldn't figure out, but she had a firewall on her computer unlike anything he'd ever seen before—both of them homemade and high-tech and very, very effective. He'd managed to chip a few chinks in the firewall through the course of the week, but only enough to be able to keep track of her when she was online with her desktop. And even then it was more because he'd been able to tap into her wireless server and track her from there. Her 'puter just thumbed its nose at his efforts. And her laptop— forget about it. Luckily for him, she rarely used that. Even so, Dixon hadn't been able to fish any pertinent information out of her computer files. Not even her real name. He didn't even know which apartment in the building was hers, only that she did live in this building. And he'd only been able to trace that much of her because, before this week, he'd been surveilling her online boyfriend, Andrew Paddington, and had inter- cepted some of the e-mails he'd sent to Daisy.

Not that Andrew Paddington's name was really Andrew Paddington, either. Him, Dixon knew well. Too well. And he was a rank bastard. Of course, everyone at OPUS knew Andrew Paddington. Only they all knew him by his real name: Adrian Padgett. And they all thought he was a rank bastard, too. Because once upon a time they'd all believed Adrian was one of them and then had discovered, too late, that he was nobody's man but his own. And a very bad man, at that.

It had been years since they'd heard from Adrian after he went rogue from his position at the Office of Political Unity and Security with millions of dollars in ill-gotten gains and a formerly secret network hanging out to dry. Then suddenly a year and a half ago he'd resurfaced in, of all places, his hometown of Indianapolis. He'd been trying to pass himself off as a legitimate businessman by the name of Adrian Windsor, but there was nothing legitimate about Adrian. If he'd surfaced after years of being underground, it could only be because he was up to no good. OPUS had discovered his activities and deterred him in time to prevent him from doing any real damage, but they'd never quite figured out *what* exactly his activities were leading to, and he'd slipped away before they'd been able to find out. Something illegal, though, that was for damned sure. Because Adrian didn't know how to operate inside the law.

They'd lost track of him for nine months after he'd left Indianapolis, in spite of making him their number-one priority for apprehension. Finally, thanks in large part to the efforts of Dixon and his partner, OPUS had unearthed Adrian again a few months ago, living in New York City…where he seemed to be doing little more than joining online dating services and chatting up young women on the Internet.

Oh, he was definitely up to no good. The bastard. Dixon just wished he knew what it was.

But Adrian's OPUS code name hadn't been Sorcerer for nothing. He could make magic when he wanted to. He could make himself invisible. He could make himself be anyone—or anything—he wanted. And he could mesmerize other people—ordinary, decent, moral people—into thinking they were doing the right thing by helping him out. Other people like, oh…Dixon didn't know…Daisy Miller.

Who the hell was she anyway?

Not that she seemed ordinary in any way. Or decent, considering what Dixon had read in some of the snippets he'd been able to decrypt from her e-mails to Andrew/Adrian/Sorcerer. As for moral, well…the jury was still out on that. Could be she was just another one of Sorcerer's clueless pawns. Or she might be someone as illicitly inclined as he was. Whoever she was, Dixon could see why Sorcerer wanted her. Not just because if she was living here, she had a bundle of money, but if her homemade phone screen and firewall were anything to go by, she also knew a thing or two about communication technology and software. And since Sorcerer's last incarnation had been as a high-level executive for a computer software company in Indianapolis, it was a safe bet that whatever he was up to had something to do with that particular medium.

Although Dixon was fully prepared, and able, to break into Daisy's apartment and bug the hell out of the place if she ever left long enough for him to manage it— and if, you know, he ever *found* it—he hadn't had the opportunity to do so because she never went anywhere. So he'd had to make do with industrial-strength microphones that caught every other damned thing in a half-mile radius, too, and try to filter out what he could. And he'd had to intercept what he could of her online activity through the airwaves. But her firewall made even that hard to do.

Tonight Daisy seemed to be especially active, darting from one chat room to another without even posting in any of them. Not that that was so unusual, since she seemed to be following Sorcerer. Plus, she just spent a lot of time in chat rooms—enough so that Dixon suspected she was a bit neurotic.

But what he'd come to view as her regular haunts were a lot more esoteric than the ones she was visiting tonight. In addition to the Henry James site, she liked the Libertarian Party home page, the Ruth Gordon Fan Club, the Mo Rocca is a Total Babe site, one headed up by the words Love Animals Don't Cut Them into Pieces and Ingest Them, several Magic: the Gathering sites and the Cracker Mysteries site.

That last was where she had declared on the message board that she wanted to have Robbie Coltrane's love child and name it Clem. Dixon had tried to reassure himself that she must have been drinking pretty heavily that night. Somehow, though, that had brought little reassurance. All in all, had he met Daisy Miller at a cocktail party, he could safely say he'd want to keep his distance.

Nevertheless, she was very intriguing. And he couldn't say he hadn't enjoyed some parts of this week. Just not tonight, since it was so friggin' cold and her activity online was so friggin' weird. He was supposed to be on duty until daybreak, when Daisy's activity generally started to ebb, whereupon he'd be relieved by another agent, whose job would be even more boring than his was, because the daylight hours seemed to be the time when Daisy shutdown.

He was about to contact Cowboy and tell the other man he was calling it a night when suddenly, out of nowhere, Dixon got his big break. Because right when he was thinking this was pointless and he might as well pack it in, Daisy Miller picked up her phone and made a call. When he picked up the sound of a man's voice evidently answering the phone at the other end of the line with a cheery, "Hello, Eastern Star Earth-Friendly

Market," he quickly looked up the address on his laptop and saw that it was an all-night market three blocks away.

More satisfying than that, though, was when he heard Daisy—whose voice was very familiar by now—say, "Hi, Mohammed, this is Avery Nesbitt. I need some things delivered."

Dixon picked up one of the more primitive tools he had at his fingertips—a pad and pencil—and listened as Avery Nesbitt, aka Daisy Miller, ticked off a list of essentials that she needed delivered to the very building where Dixon had parked his van. And then Mohammed confirmed that those should go to apartment number— *Oh, yes, there is a God*—7B, right? Yes, thanks, Mohammed, and please charge it to my account, as usual. And add fifteen percent for the delivery boy, twenty if he can deliver it tonight, 'cause I'm really running low on milk. He can? Great. Thanks again, Mohammed, you're the best.

Avery Nesbitt. Dixon smiled at the words he'd scrawled on the pad of paper before him. Not Daisy Miller. And this week, from the market, Avery Nesbitt needed coffee, bread, peanut butter—*the biggest jar you have, please, Mohammed*—Froot Loops, Cap'n Crunch, a box of Chicken in a Biskit crackers, a six-pack of Wild Cherry Pepsi, some of those red-chili pistachios, a mondo bag of M&M's, Sausalito cookies, tampons (she'd said that without an ounce of hesitation) and lots and lots of other stuff that had the nutritional equivalent of a big bag of lint.

Awful lot of caffeine and sugar on her list, Dixon reflected as he read his hastily jotted notes. Evidently Avery Nesbitt lived on nothing but carbohydrates. Which went a long way toward explaining why she stayed up all night, every night, the way she always did. And he found himself wondering what a woman could possibly have to do all night when she was home alone.

"Not playin' Parcheesi, that's for sure," he muttered to himself.

And then he came to the last notation he'd made: *Delivery tonight*. That meant some guy would be bopping down the street very soon with a couple of big grocery sacks from the Eastern Star Earth-Friendly Market destined for Ms. Avery Nesbitt of apartment 7B.

Which gave Dixon an idea he really had no business entertaining.

He contacted Cowboy again, but this time it wasn't to tell the man he was calling it a night. No, this time what Dixon told Cowboy was—

"I'm going in."

"What?" the other man said.

"I'm going in," he repeated.

"You're coming in?" Cowboy asked. "It's that boring?"

"Not *coming* in," Dixon corrected him, "*going* in."

"You mean going in as in…*going in?*"

Dixon smiled. "Yeah. I just a got a nice bit of intelligence and I want to follow up on it."

"So you're going in…where?"

Dixon rolled his eyes. Newbies. "To meet our girl," he said.

"She-Wolf is back?" Cowboy asked, voicing the code name of Dixon's regular partner and sounding very confused. "What's she doing in New York? I thought she went home to Las Vegas to see her mother."

"Not She-Wolf," Dixon said. "Our other girl. Sorcerer's contact."

"Daisy Miller?"

"That's the one."

"But you can't," Cowboy said. "You don't even know which apartment she's in."

"I do now. I told you. I just received some very nice intelligence. And it's from an excellent source." Himself. What better source could there be?

"Then you pass the intelligence along to me, Dixon," Cowboy instructed. "And I figure out what to do with it. Assimilate, evaluate, articulate—that's *my* job. And *you* don't go in until *I* say it's safe. Hell, you don't go in, period, unless you're the field agent."

"But I am the field agent," he reminded the other man, suddenly grateful for that anomaly.

"But you're not *supposed* to be in the field," Cowboy reminded him right back.

"Hey, I didn't ask for this assignment," Dixon said with all the mock innocence he could muster. "But you know how conscientious I am about doing my work the right way."

"The hell you are. You're as conscientious about that as I am."

"And I want to make sure this job gets done right."

"No, Dixon, you—"

"So I'm going in to make contact," he told the other man finally. "I'll let you know what happens when I get back." He smiled to himself. No reason not to mess with the newbie a little. It was so much fun to hear them shriek. "If I come back alive, I mean."

"What?" Cowboy shrieked.

"Wish me luck," he said into the microphone before removing the headset altogether.

Not that that prevented him from hearing more shrieking.

"This is nuts, Dixon," Cowboy told him. "Don't go in there if it's dangerous. You're not even a field agent. You're supposed to monitor the machines and analyze the data, like me. If anyone goes in to make contact, it should be She-Wolf. Wait for her before proceeding any further. She'll be back in a couple of weeks. She's the field agent. You don't know what to do. You don't know proper procedure."

Oh, the hell he didn't. He'd helped write the proper procedure. He'd been an OPUS agent when Cowboy was still fine-tuning his small motor skills.

"Dixon, I'm begging you," Cowboy implored him. But he sounded resigned now. "You can't go in. Please. You don't have permission."

Dixon chuckled as he flipped up the collar of his leather jacket and reached for the handle of the van's side door.

No permission. Right. As if that had ever stopped him before.

CHAPTER TWO

AVERY WAS TOTALLY IMMERSED in creating the code to make her farewell gift to Andrew especially noxious when the doorbell rang and blew her concentration. When she glanced at the clock in the corner of her laptop computer screen, she saw that it was 4:08 a.m. Who on earth came calling at 4:08 in the morning? For that matter, who came calling at all? She hadn't had any visitors to her apartment since…never. That was one of the things that happened when—cue the dramatic music in a minor key—*debutantes go bad.*

Then she remembered the groceries she'd ordered earlier. Duh. She really needed those tampons.

Saving the work she'd completed to her hard drive, Avery rose and made her way to the front door, switching on lights as she went, because she normally worked in the dark. She also launched herself into a full-body stretch, wondering how long she had been sitting still. It hadn't been midnight yet when she'd started working, so more than four hours. Still, she'd gotten a lot done. In fact, she was doing a better job than she usually did for something like this, despite the fact that it had been years since she'd put one of these things together. Funny how productive you could be when someone pissed you off real bad.

Before opening the front door, she peeked through the peephole, frowning when the guy on the other side turned out to be neither Eddie, the usual night delivery guy, nor Mohammed, who from time to time made deliveries himself. Nor did the man out there look like someone who would make his living delivering groceries in the first place. No, thanks to his enormous size— although he was distorted by the fish-eye, he was clearly bigger than the average national monument—he seemed more like the kind of guy who would make his living as a longshoreman. Or a bouncer. Or a wrestler. Or a Mack truck.

Wow, just how bad was the economy, she wondered, if guys who looked like him were reduced to delivering groceries? Maybe she should start visiting CNN.com from time to time and see what was going on outside the walls of her apartment. Not that she really cared, quite frankly, but she was still a citizen of this state, even if she would have preferred to live in a different one. Like maybe the state of altered consciousness. Nice scenery there.

In spite of her misgivings about the delivery guy, Avery figured he must be legit because he was toting two brown grocery sacks with the Eastern Star Earth-Friendly Market logo on them. Pulling herself back from the peephole, she unfastened the four dead bolts and chain that she routinely kept locked in place, then dragged her front door open.

Holy cow. He was even bigger *without* the distortion of the fish-eye, she saw when she glimpsed the man in person. And now he *really* didn't seem like someone who would be delivering groceries for a living. Once she got a better look at his face, Avery decided he was more the kind of guy whose job would involve being onstage somewhere—probably stripping down to his altogether while hundreds of screaming, frantic women stuffed their grocery money into his G-string. He was staggeringly handsome, from his finely wrought mouth to his ruggedly chiseled cheekbones to his aristocratic nose to his oh-my-God eyes.

But somehow Avery suspected the harshness of his features belied good breeding, since she had more than a nodding acquaintance with that—both good breeding *and* harshness. In spite of his tattered attire, he held himself as if he were someone who knew the rules and regulations of proper dress—he just chose not to abide by them. There was a strange mixture of majesty and menace about him, as if he would have been equally comfortable wielding a martini at a high-society function or breaking someone's knuckles as an enforcer for the mob.

It was his eyes, though, that she found most unsettling. An icy, almost opaque green, they made her think of the deepest part of the ocean—where swam the most mysterious, dangerous creatures—frozen over. Instead of repelling her, however, the look in his eyes made her want to draw closer to him. But it wasn't just his good looks that generated such a response in her. It simply had been so long since Avery had experienced the simple pleasure of being close to a man physically. Especially one who looked like him.

"Where do you want these?" he asked without preamble.

Automatically she jutted a thumb over her shoulder. "In the kitchen. Please," she added as an afterthought, nearly forgetting the good manners that had been hammered into her during her years of after-school etiquette and deportment classes at Madame Yvette's School for Genteel Young Ladies in East Hampton. "Thanks," she added with some distraction. Wow. His eyes really were amazing. And the overly long black hair spilling out from beneath the driving cap he'd turned backward on his head only made their color seem that much lighter…and that much darker, too.

But the guy didn't follow her instructions, only stood on the other side of the door gazing back at her. Incisively enough that she began to feel disconcerted, a feeling she really hated. In fact, it had been years since she *had* felt disconcerted, and she'd almost convinced herself she was incapable of feeling that anymore. Along with discomfort and shame and humiliation and all those other things that had once been her constant companions. The realization that this man, simply by showing up at her front door, could rouse even one of them—and so quickly, too, damn him—bothered her a lot.

She was about to snap another order at him when he inclined his head forward and said, "Do you mind?"

"Mind what?" she asked.

"Uh, stepping aside?" he told her. "So I can get through."

Only then did Avery realize that he hadn't come forward because she was blocking his way by standing there stupidly ogling him. Gee, had she felt disconcerted before? That was nothing compared to the mortification she felt now. Especially since she was leering at him again, thanks to the velvety pitch of his voice, a sound that skimmed over her like rough-calloused fingertips on naked flesh.

Oh, yeah. She'd definitely gone too long without physical closeness to the opposite sex if she was thinking a man's request for her to step aside was the equivalent of foreplay. *Good* foreplay, at that.

"Oh. I'm sorry," she apologized, moving to the side. "I… You'll have to excuse me. I was working. My mind is still elsewhere." *Like on how the sound of your voice was making me orgasmic.* "The kitchen is through there," she added, pointing in that direction.

He sauntered past her, and she pushed the front door closed before following. As nice as his front side had been, Avery had to admit that the view from the rear— especially of his rear—was almost nicer. The faded jeans hugged his taut buttocks as snugly as Saran wrap— would that they were as transparent, too—swathing his lean thighs and calves. The leather of his jacket was cracked white in enough places to give it character, his shoulders broad and strong and hard-looking beneath it.

She bit back an involuntary sigh. She'd always loved a man's back more than any other feature, liked how the muscles there were dense and plentiful and elegant and how the skin was smooth and warm and fine. She could have been perfectly content for days lying next to a naked man doing little more than running her open palm over his back. This man's naked back, she was certain, would be spectacular.

When they entered her kitchen, she marveled at how much the room seemed to shrink with his presence. Funny, but she'd always considered the room to be larger than what most apartments in the city claimed. Unfortunately it was also messier than most apartments in the city, cluttered with empty cereal boxes and crumbled pretzel and potato-chip bags and dirty dishes that she hadn't gotten around to putting into the dish-washer. Mostly because she hadn't taken the clean dishes out.

Well, she'd been busy. Working. She had lots of work to do these days. Not to mention she was inherently lazy. In any event, there wasn't even enough clear counter space for him to set down the groceries, so she muttered another apology and waved him toward the door that led to the dining room.

"Just put them on the table in there," she said as she watched him head that way.

Where, she recalled belatedly, she had been working on Andrew's gift, which was still sitting out in the open, where anybody could see it and get her into big, big trouble.

She started to call him back, then decided that if he was delivering groceries for a living, there was little chance he'd recognize what she was putting together on her laptop. So she let him go, crossing her arms over her midsection as she waited for him to return.

And waited. And waited. And waited.

Finally Avery took a few steps toward the other door and called out, "Is there something wrong?"

When she heard what sounded like the shuffling of paper, she bolted toward the dining room in a panic. She halted at the door, however, when she saw the delivery guy down on all fours, scooping up a sheaf of papers that he'd evidently spilled to the floor when he'd set the groceries down on the table.

"Oh, man, I'm sorry," he said as he tried to straighten one piece of paper on top of another. "I knocked this stuff off when I set down one of the sacks. I hope I didn't mess up anything you were working on."

Only when her heart stopped slamming against her rib cage did Avery realize just how hard it had been pounding. Enough to make her light-headed. Though, truth be told, that might have been due to the fact that the delivery guy's adorable butt was facing her, and bent over the way he was, she had an almost uncontrollable urge to go over there and sink her teeth into it.

Hoo-boy, she had to get out and meet some flesh-and-blood men. Though that might be a little difficult, since she was overcome with terror every time she even stepped out into the hallway. As it was, she tipped Billy the doorman to bring her mail up to her every day.

She gave herself a minute to calm down, then joined the delivery guy on the floor, gathering the papers closest to her. "Don't worry about it," she told him. "I was finished with that pile."

It became clearer to Avery why he was working in the job he was as he tried to help her clean up. For every piece of paper she collected, he seemed to lose three, and although he tried to keep them in order as he gathered them, he kept turning them first one way, then another, as if he couldn't tell which way they were supposed to go.

"Here," she said gently, taking pity on him. "That's okay. I'll do it."

He threw her a grateful smile and stood up, and within a few moments Avery had taken care of the mess herself. When she stood, the delivery guy was staring at her laptop, frowning at the lines of code that would be incoherent gibberish to anyone who wasn't familiar with computer programming. He looked over at her and shrugged, smiling an "Oh, well" kind of smile.

"You must be one 'a them computer programmers," he said.

"Kind of," she told him evasively.

"I don't know nothin' 'bout computers myself. 'Cept how to send e-mail. And even then, a lotta times I'll screw it up."

She tried to smile reassuringly. "Well, that's true for a lot of people. It can be confusing."

He nodded enthusiastically. "Sure can." He looked at the screen again, then thrust his chin toward it. "Just what're you doin' there anyway?" he asked.

Instinctively Avery moved to the laptop to protect her work, and even though her visitor clearly couldn't find his megabyte from a hole in the ground, something told her to close the lid and hurry him on his way. Why was he hanging around anyway? she wondered. He'd get his tip from Mohammed when he returned, and she'd be billed for it. That was the way it always worked. Maybe Mohammed hadn't explained that to him yet. This guy was probably new to the job, since Avery had never seen him before.

"Uh, it's just something I'm working on for someone," she hedged, pushing the top down on the computer as unobtrusively as she could. "Look, I told Mohammed to add your tip to the bill, since I don't keep any money in the house," she added.

The comment seemed to invite mischief, and Avery wanted more than ever to get the guy out of her apartment. He seemed nice enough, and Mohammed always did a thorough background check on his employees, but even guys who were easy on the eye could turn out to be anything but easy.

"Thanks for making the delivery so late," she added, hoping that might spur him on.

But he didn't take the hint, only stood on the other

side of the table gazing at her, as if she were something worth gazing at. Which was the most alarming thing of all, because dressed as she was, in her obnoxious pajamas and her least attractive glasses, with her hair in two long braids, she looked like Pippi Longstocking on crystal meth. If he was staring at her, it *wasn't* because he liked what he saw.

"Thanks again," she said a little less amiably. "I appreciate it." When he still made no move to leave, she added, "I'll see you out."

Then she turned to make her way back to the front door, completing the journey without looking back once, and was relieved when the delivery guy followed her. But his pace was slow and relaxed, as if he were in no hurry, and somehow that made Avery want to hurry even more. Although his hands were shoved carelessly into the pockets of his jacket, she couldn't help worrying that there might be something else in those pockets that could be potentially harmful to her. Like, oh…she didn't know…a gun, perhaps. Or a knife. Some rope, maybe. Or duct tape.

Amazing all the dangerous things that would fit easily into a man's jacket pocket, she marveled. Though somehow she suspected his hands would be the most dangerous weapon of all.

He was starting to look menacing again, and it occurred to her how truly isolated she was in her life. She didn't know any of her neighbors and honestly wasn't sure if any of them would respond to an anguished cry in the night. Not that they'd even hear an anguished cry this time of night, because they were probably all asleep, as normal people were at four-something in the morning.

And if something terrible *did* happen to her, who would she turn to in the fallout? Avery hadn't spoken to anyone in her family for nearly a decade, and she didn't kid herself that something like an assault or molestation on her part would change that. On the contrary, were her person to be violated, it would just make the rest of the family that much more determined to avoid her. The Nesbitts of East Hampton were still trying to rebuild their social standing in the wake of their youngest child's exploits. She doubted they'd even send flowers to her funeral.

Her mouth went dry at the thought of her funeral. Or maybe it was because her visitor came to a halt in front of her with scarcely a breath of air separating them. If he did decide to be menacing instead of majestic, he could easily overpower her and no one would be the wiser.

Oh, who was she kidding? He could choose to be majestic, too, and she'd still end up a puddle of ruined womanhood at his feet.

Her heart was hammering hard in her chest again, but surprisingly it wasn't because she felt threatened by him. No, what Avery was feeling was infinitely more dangerous and more potent than fear. What she was feeling was hunger, plain and simple. And it wasn't for the bags of groceries this guy had just delivered. It was for an altogether different sort of package that he had.

Without thinking, she dropped her gaze to the package in question and saw that his jeans hugged him there as intimately as they did elsewhere. And it was a very nice package indeed. When she realized what she was doing, she snatched her gaze back up again, forcing herself to look at his face. But he was smiling at her in a way that told her he knew exactly what she'd been looking at. Worse, he knew she liked what she saw.

"Thanks again," she said as she pulled the front door open and moved behind it. But the words came out sounding breathless and needy and in no way grateful.

"Anytime," he told her as he took a few steps forward. But he halted at the threshold and turned to look at her one last time. Then he lifted a hand to his forehead in something of a salute and smiled at her. "And, sweetheart, I do mean *any*time," he said before leaving.

Avery slammed the door closed behind him with no attempt to be subtle about it, thrusting all four dead bolts into place as quickly as she could and hooking the chain back tight. Then she leaned against it, her arms thrown wide over it, as if her too-slim, one-hundred-and-twenty-pound body could actually hold back two hundred towering pounds of solidly packed male.

Strangely, though, she hadn't taken those precautions because she feared he might come back and ravish her. It was because she was afraid she'd run after him and beg for it.

SHE SMELLED LIKE PEACHES.

That was the thought circling with the most frequency around Dixon's brain thirty minutes after meeting Avery Nesbitt in the flesh. Not the fact that her attire was the sort of thing normally worn by people who'd sustained a severe head trauma. Nor that she hadn't had a qualm about inviting a total stranger into her apartment, never mind that the stranger was carrying groceries she'd ordered—hell, any Tom, Dixon or Harry could have slipped the real delivery boy a Benjamin out on the street and intercepted those groceries to gain entry into her apartment for nefarious purposes. Nor had Dixon been thinking about what a major slob she was. Or about how she'd actually seemed kind of nice, taking pity on the clumsy delivery boy the way she had and cleaning up the guy's mess.

He wasn't even thinking most about how, judging by the collection of letters and numbers and symbols he'd seen on her laptop screen, she was trying to take over the world. No, what Dixon was thinking about most was that Avery Nesbitt smelled like peaches.

And, hey, she might not have been trying to take over the *entire* world. Maybe what she was working on up there was just a sinister little hobby of hers, something she'd keep to herself and not unleash on an unsuspecting planet.

But she was building a monster up there.

And not one of those lame rubber-suited monsters that stomps all over Tokyo, either. No, the beast Avery was building could potentially wipe out life as they knew it from Alaska to Zambia.

Damn, she really *was* good, he thought as he sat in the darkened van and reviewed the episode in her apartment one more time. And now he could really see why Sorcerer wanted to hook up with her. If not sexually— there was still that small matter of her wardrobe—then certainly in a way that was even more useful to Sorcerer.

Dixon hadn't been able to see a lot of what was on the laptop before he'd heard her approaching the dining room and knocked the papers to the floor in an effort to hide his snooping. But even the quick glimpse he'd been able to steal had told him a lot. What Avery Nesbitt was doing in the privacy of her own home was something that could potentially have worldwide repercussions. Because Avery Nesbitt was creating a virus. Not some cute little virus that spread from person to person with a simple *achoo,* but a fast-traveling and highly contagious computer virus that could wipe out any PC it came into contact with.

Even from the little Dixon had seen, there was nothing to rival it. Unless he sat down to dissect and analyze it, he wasn't sure there would be a cure for it. He'd practically fallen in love with her on the spot, so massive was his admiration for her skill. Until he'd remembered that she was a menace to society, wherein his ardor had quickly cooled.

But it had risen to the fore again during that last odd exchange they'd shared just before he'd left her apartment. Okay, so she wasn't what any man in his right mind would call beautiful. In those ridiculous pajama bottoms and that shapeless sweatshirt, he hadn't been able to discern a single feminine attribute. Although she appeared to have a thick, glossy mane of blue-black hair, she'd been wearing it in a style he hadn't seen on any female over the age of twelve. And she'd seemed to select her glasses frames for the sole purpose of birth control. But the eyes behind those glasses…

Oh, baby.

Huge and round and bluer than the sky above. And hungry. They'd been hungry eyes and they'd raked over Dixon as if he were a surf and turf carried to a death-row inmate the night before her execution. He'd nearly burst into flame when she'd looked at him the way she had. It had been all he could do not to respond to that look, just to see if maybe peaches were as sweet in the dead of winter as they were during the torrid heat of summer.

One touch, he'd figured. That was all it would have taken. If he'd touched her one time, the right way, in the right place, Avery Nesbitt would have been his for the night.

Because damn, Dixon was good, too.

He figured she would need at least another day to finish what she was working on, and even then he really did have no evidence to suggest she was planning to put it into circulation. Could be she just had a really bizarre, twisted hobby building computer viruses and then sitting back to admire them.

But he doubted it.

In his experience, people who made viruses only did so for one reason: to send them out into the world and laugh hysterically at all the damage they wrought. And if Avery Nesbitt was involved with Sorcerer, that only made the threat ten times more menacing.

So Dixon had less than a day to find out everything he could about Avery Nesbitt and do whatever he had to do to stop her. He wasn't going to waste a moment of it hanging around outside her apartment building doing surveillance. Not when he'd learned enough about her tonight to uncover *everything* about her. But he needed to be at OPUS to do that, with *his* computer and *his* networks and *his* contacts.

He climbed into the front of the van and turned the key and thought again about the peachy scent of Avery Nesbitt. Then he threw the vehicle into gear and drove away. He glanced once into the rearview mirror as he waited for a signal at the corner to change, at the pale blue glow from a computer screen that was barely visible in the window of what he now knew was Avery Nesbitt's dining room.

She was still at work on her monster. And Dixon was quite possibly the only human being who knew how to stop her.

IT WAS PAST HIS LUNCH hour when he finally took a break, if for no other reason than that he needed to refuel before taking his findings to his superior or he'd get woozy from sheer exhilaration. If Dixon didn't get a major promotion out of this—to nothing less than Exalted Supreme Sovereign of Every Damned Thing There Is—then there was no justice in the world.

Avery Nesbitt was going to be quite a catch.

And Dixon was going to be the one to catch her.

His head swam with his findings as he blindly selected food from the company cafeteria and paid for it. The headquarters for the Office of Political Unity and Security were in Washington, D.C., but the organization had field offices in a handful of major cities: New York, Chicago, Los Angeles, Atlanta and Miami. Dixon normally worked out of D.C., but his search for Sorcerer had taken him and his partner She-Wolf to a half-dozen cities in the past year. He was no stranger to New York, though, having earned his master's degree from Columbia University. Nevertheless, he'd had little opportunity to enjoy himself since his return.

Yeah, he was going to enjoy bringing in Avery Nesbitt for questioning, even if he had to bring her in kicking and screaming.

As he ate his lunch without tasting a bite of it, Dixon connected and divided and reconnected all his discoveries in his brain. She was a fascinating piece of work. But as much as he'd learned about her over the past several hours, he still couldn't get to the core of her—

her motivation. Everybody was motivated by something. Something that had happened to them, or something that they wanted or something that they needed. Motivation defined who a person was. Dixon was no different. He understood his motivation perfectly. But Avery Nesbitt…

He couldn't figure her out.

There had to be a reason for why she had done the things she'd done and there had to be a reason for why she lived the way she did now—which was an odd way to live indeed. But there was nothing in her background that even hinted at what motivated her. It had only made her that much more intriguing to Dixon.

Pushing his tray away with the plate still half-full, he rose and returned to his office to gather up his notes and printouts. He reviewed them one last time to make sure he was prepared, then took the elevator down to the basement, to the office of his most superior superior, the One Whose Name Nobody Dared Say— mostly because Dixon didn't know what his name was. OPUS was, after all, a top-secret organization within a top-secret organization, and everything everyone knew was strictly on a need-to-know basis. But very few knew who needed to know what, including Dixon. There were times when he wondered if the One Whose Name Nobody Dared Say even knew what his own name was.

Usually No-Name stayed nameless in Washington, D.C., since that was where the most superior superiors of OPUS dwelled. But since Sorcerer had been spied in New York, Mr. No-Name had been spending a lot of his time here with the senior agent of the New York office, Another One Whose Name Nobody Dared Say Because

Nobody Knew What It Was Either. Or, as Dixon liked to think of her, *Ms.* No-Name.

Right now, though, he was going to go straight to the top, to the Big Guy himself. He was greeted by Mr. No-Name's secretary, an efficient-looking, white-haired woman dressed in gray flannel, whose name Dixon also didn't know—did she even know the Big Guy's name?—and politely requested an audience with the Great and Powerful Oz. She glanced at her appointment calendar, picked up the phone, murmured a few words into it, then smiled.

"He says you can go right in," she told Dixon before pressing her finger to a buzzer under the desk.

Dixon smiled in return as he passed her, knowing her own warm, outgoing demeanor was strictly for show. If she was like half the secretaries at OPUS, in addition to having a top-secret button under her top-secret desk that opened top-secret doors, she also had a bazooka under there. Maybe a flamethrower. Or even a surface-to-air missile. And, like the other secretaries there, she wasn't afraid to use it and probably had on more than one occasion.

"Sir," Dixon greeted the man sitting behind the big government-issue desk as he entered.

Mr. No-Name was about as remarkable as an insurance claims adjuster would be, wearing a boring gray suit, a boring white shirt and a boring blue tie. His hair was thinning a bit, but no more than that of any other man his age—which Dixon gauged to be somewhere between forty and sixty. In fact, his boss looked like just about every man between the ages of forty and sixty. And he doubtless worked hard at looking average. It wasn't good to stand out when you were a big muckety-muck in a top-secret, bazooka-toting-secretaried organization.

Dixon's superior looked at him through narrowed eyes. "Ah, yes. Your code name is—" He halted before saying it, however, which made Dixon think he really had gotten a bad rep about that code-name business. "Well, what name are you going by now?" the man asked instead.

"Dixon."

"Right. So what do you have to report about Sorcerer?"

Oh, yeah. He was supposed to be keeping tabs on Sorcerer, too, wasn't he? Dixon thought. Funny, but in the wake of Hurricane Avery, he'd all but forgotten the son of a bitch whose ass he wanted to nail to the wall more than he'd ever wanted anything in his life. How odd.

"Actually, sir, there haven't been any new developments with Sorcerer himself."

"Meaning?" his boss asked.

Dixon gazed at the other man blandly. *Meaning there haven't been any new developments with Sorcerer himself,* he wanted to say. Jeez, not everything in the spy business had to be cloak-and-dagger. "What I have to report is something about the woman Sorcerer's been in contact with over the past month."

"Ah. Daisy Miller."

Dixon wasn't surprised that his superior already knew about her. The Big Guy knew everything that went on in the organization. And anything that involved Sorcerer shot especially quickly to the top. "That's the one," he said.

"What about her?"

Dixon took a breath and wondered where to begin. "Well, we have a name for her now. Avery Nesbitt."

His boss sat up stick-straight in his chair. "Nesbitt?" he asked.

Dixon nodded, puzzled by the reaction. His boss seemed to know the name well. "Yeah…" he said.

"Is her father Desmond Nesbitt?"

Dixon nodded, too surprised to speak.

"Of the East Hampton Nesbitts?"

"Well, yeah, she grew up in East Hampton," he said. "But the family has a half dozen other residences, too, all over the world."

His boss nodded. "I know. I know the family."

This time Dixon was the one to narrow his eyes. "You know Avery Nesbitt?"

"Not so much her as her father. But yes, I've met her. Years ago. She couldn't have even been in high school then. Scrawny kid. Long black hair. Big glasses."

It was an apt description for her now, Dixon thought, except for the size of the glasses, which were fashionably smaller. Well, sort of fashionably smaller. Okay, just smaller.

"You're sure Daisy Miller is Avery Nesbitt?" his boss asked.

"Positive."

The other man nodded again. "Tell me what else you have on her."

"Gee, sir, you may know more than I do, if you know the family."

The other man shook his head. "No, as I said, it's been years since I've had any contact with them. Desmond and I were in the same college fraternity. I hear about him occasionally through mutual acquaintances. And of course, everyone heard about that business with—" Again he halted before finishing. "Well, tell me what you've got."

Dixon nodded. "Okay. I'll just hit on the highlights for now and give you my full report at the end of the day. Twenty-nine years old, never married, no kids. Born and raised in East Hampton, New York. Parents Desmond and Felicia Nesbitt. Youngest of three children—she has an older brother and an older sister. Educated at the finest schools money could buy, traveled extensively as a child and teenager. Was accepted to Wellesley College and declared a major in computer science. Attended for two and a half years, but her education was interrupted."

"Right," his boss said.

But the way he said it made Dixon think the guy already knew what had interrupted young Avery's studies. Then again, once Dixon had made the connection, he had remembered the incident himself.

"She was always an exceptional student," he continued, "gifted in both mathematics and language arts. Scored a perfect twenty-four hundred on her SAT, a perfect thirty-six on her ACT. Fluent in French, Spanish and German by the time she graduated high school. Mastered anything computer-related with little effort from an early age. Won a national award when she was fourteen for designing an e-mail program that was then purchased and produced by a company named CompuPax. A few minor behavioral problems in school, but nothing you wouldn't expect from any other exceptionally gifted kid. No black marks on her permanent record. From all accounts, she was the ideal student up until her junior year."

His boss studied him in silence, his fingers steepled together on his desk. "Go on."

Taking a deep breath, Dixon continued, "In her junior year in college, Avery Nesbitt, of the East Hampton Nesbitts, had her education interrupted. Because she earned herself a ten-year prison sentence instead."

CHAPTER THREE

DIXON'S BOSS DIDN'T SEEM surprised by the announcement. "I remember that," he said. "And I imagine you do, too. It's become one of those 'Where were you when' things."

"I remember it now," Dixon said. "But I didn't make the connection at first—it was ten years ago, after all. I couldn't remember her name. But as soon as I read about her conviction, it all came together. I was twenty-nine when it happened and working in decryption. News of her arrest got a lot of buzz around the department. The virus she created was the stuff of legends, and she was just a kid. Even ten years later, no one's figured out how she did it."

Viral Avery. That was how the media had referred to her after the debacle, their too-clever spin on Typhoid Mary. But where an individual would have had to have personal contact with Mary to come down with the bug, Avery had taken out millions with the simple click of a mouse. The college junior had nearly shut down the planet with the computer virus she'd sent out into the world.

At the time of her arrest, she'd claimed it was an accident, that she'd only created the program and sent it in retaliation to a boyfriend who'd jilted her. She'd insisted she'd only wanted to destroy his hard drive and nothing else and that she'd had no idea she'd leave businesses all over the world stalled, scores of governments deadlocked and the Vatican in the dark. For days. By the time it was finally contained, Avery's virus had taken out big chunks of North, Central and South America, Greenland and a good part of Europe, including the Vatican. As for Asia…forget about it.

All told, Viral Avery had cost her fellow man roughly a gazillion dollars in lost revenues, and she'd had people standing in line all along the equator who wanted to string her up for global target practice. Preferably with atomic warheads.

But they'd had to settle for seeing her get slapped with a ten-year prison sentence instead, something that had offended most people because they'd thought it too light a punishment. They were offended even more when two years later she was released on shock probation. Many suspected it had been more her father's dollars and influence that had won her the release than any remorse or trauma on her part. She'd been painted in the media as a spoiled, privileged, snotty little geek who always got her way, thanks to family connections. Before, during and after her release, she was gleefully and thoroughly reviled.

Still, according to her prison records, she had been an exemplary inmate, living quietly and following the rules. And during her trial, the highlights of which Dixon also had studied, there really hadn't been much evidence to indicate she had acted in malice toward anyone other than the boyfriend.

But now she was building another virus, he reminded himself. Within weeks of making the acquaintance of

Sorcerer. And wasn't that just the most interesting co-incidence in the world?

"She's putting together another one," he told his boss.

The other man's eyebrows shot up at that. "She's what?"

"She's building another virus," Dixon said. "I saw part of it myself when I made contact last night. And just that little glimpse told me that it's ten times worse than the one she sent out ten years ago. With technology being what it is now and with a million times more people being connected to the Internet than there were ten years ago…"

He left the comment unfinished, knowing his boss would comprehend the massive repercussions.

"We've got to stop her," the other man said. "We still get calls from the Vatican. Not to mention Greenland."

"Then we better hurry," Dixon said. "Because she could be finished with this thing anytime."

"I'll take care of the paperwork right now," his boss told him. "Get your temporary partner…what's his name?"

"Gillespie," Dixon said. "Tanner Gillespie. Code name Cowboy."

"When's She-Wolf due back?" his boss asked.

"She's had to take an indefinite leave of absence," Dixon said. "Her mother passed away and she has some family matters to see to."

"Right," the other man said. "We'll give her all the time she needs, of course."

Dixon couldn't imagine her needing much. One thing about She-Wolf—she never let life get in the way of her job, never let the personal overshadow the pro-fessional. She was a lot like him in that regard.

"Collect Cowboy," his boss told him again, "and bring in Avery Nesbitt today."

"You sure we have enough on her?"

"We don't need much."

Which was true. Even before 9/11, OPUS had operated outside the rules set up for other government agencies. Since then, they'd been moved under the jurisdiction of Homeland Security, their worth reevaluated, their mission refined, their rules of operation revised. Dixon's boss, he knew, wouldn't have any trouble getting papers signed that would bring Avery Nesbitt to heel.

"Bring her in," the man told him. "Now. We'll have a room waiting for her when you get back."

TWENTY-FOUR HOURS AFTER deciding to send Andrew a farewell gift—not that she wanted him to fare well, of course, hence the farewell gift—things weren't working out the way Avery had hoped. She'd been so sure she could create a virus that would turn his hard drive into tapioca—radioactive tapioca at that—but she'd hit a snag. And snags just didn't happen to her. Well, not since the one that had sent her to prison ten years ago, which, granted, had been a *pret-ty ma-jor* snag. She'd been extremely careful since then not to set herself up for another one. Then again, being genuinely phobic about leaving one's home did rather hinder one in getting oneself into trouble.

And that one major snag ten years ago had only come about because she'd been driven by her emotions instead of her intellect. She'd just been too ambitious with this particular project, that was all. Vengefulness did that to a person sometimes—made them too ambitious. Now she'd have to go back and start over with a virus that was less damaging.

Though this one was very intriguing….

Still, it wasn't as if she could send this thing out anyway. Just *building* another virus would get her in big trouble. If she actually sent it to Andrew, they'd toss her keister back in the slammer and throw away the key for good. Which was why Avery was building it on this particular laptop—it had no communication function whatsoever. It was the laptop she used for off-line gaming. Which was what building this virus was to her—a game. It was physically impossible for her to send it anywhere beyond her hard drive. Unless, you know, she moved it to another computer. Which, *of course,* she would *never* do.

But she'd needed to do *something* to exorcise Andrew from her system—to serve him his just desserts, if only in her own mental bakery. And building him a virus, even one that would never go anywhere, made her feel vindicated. She was a woman scorned and all that, and you should never underestimate the power of one of those. Even the ones who had been effectively spayed in the ol' revenge department.

She studied the lines of code again, backtracking to see where she might have gone wrong. She didn't want to abandon the project completely, because it really was a brilliant bit of work, if she did say so herself. But it wasn't going to function properly the way she had it set up, theoretically or realistically.

Let's see…. If she dropped this command and added a different one instead… Or if she clarified that command a little better… Hmm…

What had she done wrong?

She squinted at the numbers and letters and symbols again, then removed her glasses to rub her eyes. She'd been up for thirty-six hours straight now, her mind completely engaged during the majority of them. She hadn't even stopped working long enough to eat anything since that last bowl of Cajun popcorn. Maybe she needed to take a break for a little while. Clear her head with a nice Starbucks double shot.

Yeah, that's the ticket.

She tossed her glasses onto the table and stood, reaching as high as she could above her head, arching her back to relieve the kinks that had set in. Oh, *man,* that felt good. The sudden activity stirred her cat, Skittles, who had curled herself into a meatloaf shape on one of the other dining room chairs. After mimicking Avery's stretch with one of her own, she leaped down, curling her lithe silver-and-black-striped body around and between Avery's calves. Avery smiled and bent to pick up the cat, cuddling her under her chin and calming immediately at the soft hum of the animal's contented purr.

It was always good to have someone in your life you could count on, no matter what. Skittles was that for Avery. She'd shown up as a stray kitten outside the gates of the Rupert Halloran Women's Correctional Facility during the final month of Avery's term, and after much urging and cajoling from the inmates, one of the guards had brought the scrawny little thing inside for the women to fuss over. They'd decided whoever was the next released would take the kitten with her. Avery had been the winner. In more ways than one. Skittles had been with her ever since.

She strode, cradling Skittles, into the kitchen. It was

still a mess, unfortunately. No friendly little house-cleaning brownies had come by while she'd been working to clean the place up. Dang. Although, speaking of brownies, hadn't she put some Sara Lee brownies on her grocery list? she recalled now. She put down Skittles and padded in sock feet over to the counter, where she had at least cleared a place for the two sacks of groceries, even if she hadn't quite gotten around to unpacking them all yet. Well, she'd needed the space on the dining room table to work and then she'd been too preoccupied by that work to worry about putting away anything but the stuff that needed to be re-frigerated.

She had dug out the brownie tin and peeled back the paper lid from the foil—oh, boy, just the sight of all that icing was enough to send her into spasms of orgasmic chocolaty euphoria—when there was a knock at her front door. She jerked up her head upon hearing it. Two visitors within a matter of hours was extraordinary. It was also very suspicious.

As quietly as she could, she made her way to the front door and leaned forward to peer through the peephole. When she saw who stood on the other side, her heart kicked up a ragged rhythm and heat flooded her belly. Because it was the delivery guy from Eastern Star Earth-friendly Market again, only this time he wasn't carrying groceries.

She told herself to ask him what he wanted but feared she already knew. Hey, a scrawny, ill-favored woman living all alone? Avery knew what an easy mark she was to creeps. Look at what had happened with Andrew. Even if this guy was here for a legitimate reason, Avery didn't feel like answering the door. She had everything she needed, thanks, and preferred to be left alone. She didn't like talking to strangers. She didn't like talking to anybody. She liked keeping to herself and hoping the world—and the grocery delivery guy it rode in on—stayed away.

She started to move away from the peephole, pretending she wasn't home so he'd leave. But he called out through the door, his words stopping her cold.

"I wouldn't do that if I were you, Ms. Nesbitt."

It didn't surprise her that he knew her name. Mohammed would have told him who the delivery was for. But the very nature of her in-home business was to create online security systems for other people and businesses. She'd learned her trade by making her own system—her own life—secure. She'd done everything she knew to do to keep herself safe. It always creeped her out whenever she was identified, regardless of how innocently that identification came. And the fact that the identifier now was standing on the other side of her front door, which was the only way in—or out—of her apartment, made her feel more than a little nauseous.

Pressing her eye to the peephole again, she asked, "What do you want?"

"I want you to open the door, Ms. Nesbitt."

Yeah, she'd just bet he did. "Why?"

"Just open the door, please."

Oh, right. She'd just invite a sexual predator right into her home.

"Not without a good reason," she told him, wondering why she was even bothering. She should be heading for the phone right now to call the cops. Still, she was safe enough behind the four dead bolts and chain. And there *might* be a chance the guy had come here for a perfectly legitimate reason. Maybe. Possibly. In an alternate universe someplace where women *didn't* have to be on guard about their personal safety twenty-four hours a day.

"Because you and I need to have a little chat," he said.

Okay, so much for the Clever Banter portion of their program, Avery thought. Now it was time to move along to the ever-popular Alert the Authorities segment.

"That's not going to happen," she said. "And if you don't leave right now, I'll call the police."

"Peaches, I *am* the police," he said.

Oh. Well. That made a difference. Or rather, it *would* have made a difference. If he hadn't been lying through his teeth. And if he hadn't just called her *Peaches,* something that made her want to open the door just so she could smack him upside the head.

Just to be sure, though, she pressed her eye to the peephole again to see if maybe he was displaying a badge. He wasn't. He was just standing out there wearing the same clothes he'd had on the last time she'd seen him…how many hours ago? She performed some quick mental math…six minus four…drop the three, make it a two…carry the one…and that would be—oh, bugger it, she was too tired for this—last night. His driving cap was still turned backward, his leather bomber jacket was still hanging open over a heavy sweater and blue jeans, and his hands were still stuffed into pockets that could hold anything from chloroform to an automatic weapon.

"Policemen identify themselves right away," she said, still gazing through the peephole. "And they carry badges. And ID. Now go away. Or I'll call the cops. The *real* cops."

His shoulders rose and fell then, as if he were sighing deeply, and he pulled one hand out of one pocket to flip something open. Whatever kind of identification he was trying to show her, it was in a folding case, with some kind of photo and writing on the left side and some kind of badgish-looking thing on the right. She'd have to open the door to get a better look at it. But she wasn't going to do that. Because even through the fish-eye she could tell it was phony as hell. She'd seen police ID before. Hell, she'd seen federal ID before. Up close and personal, too, as a matter of fact. And whatever this guy was holding, it wasn't an ID for New York's finest *or* the feds.

Obviously thinking she'd fall for it, however, he repeated crisply, "Ms. Nesbitt, open the door."

How had he even gotten into the building? she wondered. Billy the doorman must be sleeping on the job. She made a mental note to ask him about it the next time she saw him, then, as quietly as she could, she pushed herself away from the door and took a giant step backward.

Only to hear the man on the other side of her door say, "I wouldn't do that if I were you."

For a single moment Avery hesitated, numerous thoughts circling through her mind. Thought number one: how did he know she was doing anything at all when even *she* hadn't heard herself make a sound? Thought number two: how did he know she wasn't cooperating with his instruction, reaching for the dead bolts to open them, if he *had* heard her make a sound? Thought number three: had he threatened her?

Just as thought number three was forming, she heard the sound of something metallic click against something else metallic and instinctively, she took another quick step back from the door. Then, before she even had time to register what the sound might be, she saw one, two, three, four dead bolts twist open, so quickly that he might as well have had a key to each on the other side. So stunned was she by the sight that she didn't immediately move. Thankfully, though, the chain held the door closed when he pushed it open. Until a small pair of bolt cutters—the perfect size to hide in a jacket pocket—appeared and cut through it as if it was paper. And then the front door was thrown open wide, and the man who hours before had brought her sustenance necessary for life stood framed by the doorway, doubtless with the intention of making that life unlivable for a while.

Her heart pounding, her brain hurtling, Avery turned and ran toward her bedroom, assuring herself she had time to reach it and lock the door behind herself, knowing there was a phone in there she could use to dial 911. That was the only hope she had at the moment—staving off this psycho scumbag long enough for the police to arrive. She didn't expend any more energy to think further than that, channeled all her strength into running as fast as she could in the opposite direction.

It was the couch that did her in. Later she would realize that she should have run around it instead of trying to scramble over it. Because the minute her foot hit the too-soft cushion, her leg buckled beneath her and her body crumpled. When her assailant landed on top of her, he turned her and pinned her effortlessly beneath him, her belly and face pressed into the sofa as he straddled her waist with powerful thighs. Almost casually he gripped both of her wrists in one big hand and shoved them firmly against the small of her back. Then he leaned forward and began to…touch her.

Never in her life had Avery felt so surrounded. He seemed to be everywhere, his free hand moving briskly over her body, sometimes in places that were too intimate to think about. He began at the crown of her head and proceeded downward, over her neck, her shoulders, her back, even her bottom, then lower still when he reached behind himself to run his hand along first one leg, then the other, stretching back far enough to rove over both sock-covered feet. When he moved his hand back up again, over her thighs, he dipped between them, pressing his fingers for only a second against the feminine heart of her. Avery squeezed her eyes shut tight but couldn't quite stifle her gasp.

"Gotta do it, Peaches," he said. "Sorry about that."

And before she had a chance to comment, before she could even open her eyes, he was moving off her. But only long enough to flip her onto her back and straddle her again, this time jerking her hands up over her head. She opened her eyes wide then, ordering herself to catalogue his features, to note any distinguishing characteristics, to take a mental picture so that when this was over, she'd be able to identify him and put his ass in jail. Because eventually this would be over, she told herself. And she would survive it. And then she would do everything she had to do to make him pay.

She had thought he would shy away from her scrutiny, if for no other reason than to prevent her from getting a good look at him. But his gaze met hers unflinchingly, his cold green eyes holding her in place almost as much as his big body did. Again he held both of her wrists firmly in one hand as his other went wandering, down both arms and over her ribs and then briefly but thoroughly over her breasts. Avery closed her eyes again when he touched her, swallowing hard, and she gritted her teeth as he reached behind himself to run his hand down the fronts of her legs this time. This time, though, he didn't venture between them, something that both relieved and puzzled her.

Still straddling her, still holding her wrists firmly above her head, he said ironically, "I won't hurt you."

She snapped her eyes open and glared at him. Too angry to think about her own safety now, she spat out her response. "You already have, you bastard."

Instead of provoking him, however, her charge seemed to deflate him some. His expression, which had been so intense a moment before, suddenly went soft, almost sad. And the hand that gripped her wrists so fiercely loosened a bit. Avery immediately took advantage to jerk one of her hands free, then doubled her fist and punched him in the nose as hard as she could. Taken aback—and hopefully wounded—he released her other hand to bring both of his up to his nose, a gesture that also slackened the legs still encircling her waist.

For one scant, exhilarating second Avery thought she would evade him. She had pulled herself out from beneath him enough to turn her body and claw at the floor, and she was eyeing her escape route—straight for the front door, which, although pushed closed, would still be unlocked—when he recovered himself and jerked her back up onto the couch again. This time when he restrained her, he did it thoroughly, covering her entire front with his own, so that his body pinned hers from shoulder to toe.

"Maybe I should clarify that," he whispered roughly,

his voice edged with steel. "I won't hurt you unless you try to hurt me."

She hurt him? Oh, that was rich. In spite of her having gotten off a decent pop to his nose, he could snap her in two like a matchstick. She knew better than to struggle now. Not only would it be pointless, but it would probably only make him angry. Best-case scenario, he was one of those attackers who got off on a woman's fear, and if she lay quietly and did her best not to show her own, he'd lose interest and be unwilling or unable to perform. Or maybe when he realized why she'd needed those tampons, he'd be too grossed out to perform. Hey, it could happen. Worst-case scenario…

Well. She decided not to think about that.

The best weapon she claimed was her brain, so she would use that. Let him think she was compliant, and when an opportunity presented itself, she would outwit and outmaneuver him and make her escape. She would not, however, succumb to him. She hadn't endured two years in prison without learning a thing or two about survival. Not because she'd needed the skills to survive herself—prison had been surprisingly danger-free for her—but because so many of the other women had needed them before being incarcerated, and they'd shared their expertise with Avery in exchange for computer instruction and other such barterable things.

"What do you want?" she asked quietly, even though she knew perfectly well what he wanted.

"Not what you think," he replied.

She kept her expression bland, determined to show no fear. "If it's not what I think, then let me get up."

He shook his head. "Not yet, Peaches."

She gritted her teeth at the endearment—such as it was. "When?"

He smiled, but there was something strangely unmenacing about it. "When I'm comfortable," he told her.

She didn't want to know how he intended to achieve that.

He said nothing more for a moment, only gazed at her face as if he were the one now who wanted to catalogue features and note any distinguishing characteristics. *Fat chance,* Avery thought. She didn't have any distinguishing characteristics, and her features were in no way memorable. Unlike his own. Even had the situation not been so terrifying, she would remember him.

Now she found herself noticing things other than his looks. Like how he smelled faintly of coffee and exhaust fumes. And how his heart buffeted against her own in a totally calm, completely dispassionate way. She would have thought his pulse would be racing at the prospect of overpowering her and doing his dirty little deed. But he was completely cool and calm and collected. Somehow that only made him scarier.

"You know, you're quite the mystery woman, Avery Nesbitt," he finally said, his voice a soft, velvety purr, his breath warm and damp as it stirred the hair at her temple.

"Not really," she countered shallowly, a little breathlessly. "With me, what you see is what you get."

And, oh, *dammit,* she wished she hadn't said that. If her brain was her fiercest weapon, she might as well concede defeat right now.

His smile told her he was thinking pretty much the same thing. "Maybe," he said. "But I didn't see you before last night. Even though I've been watching you for a while now."

Okay, that really creeped her out. Avery knew about stalkers, of course. But she'd never considered the possibility that she'd be the target of one. How could she be? She never left home. It had been weeks, months even, since she'd left the building, and her destination had been only four blocks away, to Skittles's veterinarian. They'd been gone less than an hour. And Avery hadn't noticed anyone noticing her. Of course, she'd consumed a half-dozen shots of Johnnie Walker before heading out, so she was lucky to have even found the vet's office, not to mention her way home. But Avery could tell when she was being watched. If this guy had been stalking her, she would have known.

"How could you be watching me when I never go anywhere?" she asked. Maybe if she got him talking, kept him talking, she could figure some way out of this.

Instead of answering her question, he posed one of his own. "And why is that? That you never go anywhere?"

She wasn't about to tell him it was because she was afraid to leave her home. *Show no fear,* she commanded herself. *Do* not *let him know your weaknesses.* "I don't have any reason to go anywhere," she said. "I work at home and I work long hours. This is an especially busy time for me, and anything I need, I can have delivered. So I do."

"What about socializing?" he asked.

And she hated to think why. Because if he was thinking she might want to socialize with *him,* he had another think coming. And then he had a poke in the eye coming. And then a knee to the groin.

"I don't socialize much," she said.

"Peaches, you don't socialize at all," he rejoined.

"Unless you count all that bouncing around the Internet you do as socializing. And trust me, there are better ways to socialize than that."

She told herself he couldn't be stalking her on the Net. Not just because she'd done nothing to attract a stalker, but because she had security measures in place on every system she owned that made it impossible for anyone to do that. He was bluffing. Or something. She just wished she knew what the hell was going on.

"Who are you?" she asked.

"What? You don't remember me?" he said. "From the Eastern Star Earth-Friendly Market? After all those steamy looks you threw my way?"

She squeezed her eyes shut tight at the reminder. Oh, God, how could she have ogled him the way she had? Naturally a psycho like him would misinterpret her simple appreciation of his physique as a blatant invitation to come back later and enjoy a slice of what she was clearly desperate to give him. It was almost funny. She'd been cloistered away from the world for a decade—first through mandatory incarceration, then through voluntary seclusion—having scarcely spoken a word to a member of the opposite sex. Now she was about to be violated in the most heinous way, thanks to some chance encounter with a delivery boy.

"I thought you'd be glad to see me again," he murmured. "I thought maybe you'd enjoy…" he grinned lasciviously "…*socializing* with a living, breathing, flesh-and-blood man for a change, instead of a cold, impersonal piece of machinery. And now you're saying you don't even know me? Avery, honey, you're breaking my heart."

"And you're breaking my spine," she muttered,

ignoring the first part of his remark. "Please. I can't breathe," she added.

Something in her voice must have convinced him of her discomfort—though why a man like him would care about her comfort, she couldn't begin to imagine—because although he didn't remove himself from atop her, he shifted his big body to the side some, alleviating the pressure of his weight a bit. In doing so, though, he wedged her body between his and the back of the sofa more firmly, keeping one of his legs draped over hers and one of his hands planted firmly on her hip, so that she was even more effectively pinned than before. Still, at least she could breathe now.

"What do you want?" she asked again.

He hesitated a moment, then told her, "I want to keep you from making a terrible mistake."

Avery narrowed her eyes at him. "What are you talking about?"

"That virus on your laptop," he said.

Her stomach pitched. "What virus?"

"The one you're building," he said. "The one I saw when I was here before. It could send you right back to the slammer, Peaches. Not to mention it's powerful enough to take out half the galaxy."

Avery didn't know whether to feel relieved or more terrified. Maybe he wasn't here to physically assault her. But how did he know about her time in prison? And how did he know what she'd been doing on her laptop unless he had some familiarity with computer viruses himself? And if he had that much familiarity with computer viruses, why was he working as a delivery guy for the Eastern Star Market?

Unless, gee, maybe he wasn't a delivery guy for the

Eastern Star Earth-friendly Market at all. And if that was the case, then who the hell was he? Could his ID have actually been legit? Before Avery had a chance to ask him anything more, he began to speak again, saying things that made her even more confused.

"And that bastard, Andrew Paddington?" he added, sending more fire spilling through her belly. "He's not worth it, Avery. Trust me. That guy is a class-A prick who preys on people like you. Don't get involved in his schemes. Because you'll end up right back in the Rupert Halloran Women's Correctional Facility. And next time not only will you do the full time, you'll earn yourself a bonus stay. And Lana and Petrovsky and Mouse and all those other friends you had inside? They're not there anymore. You'll have to start from square one again, building your posse. And with your lack of people skills, Peaches, I don't think you want to have to do that."

With every new word he spoke Avery felt her panic rise, and it was through no small effort that she managed to tamp it back down again. The last thing she needed right now was to have a panic attack. God, she hadn't had one for months—not since that last time she took Skittles to the vet. She'd begun to think maybe she was coming out of all that. Even in this situation tonight, where panic would have been a perfectly logical and un-derstandable response, she'd managed to hang on and not succumb to an attack. And she wouldn't succumb now, she told herself. She wouldn't. She closed her eyes and inhaled a deep breath, holding it until the fear began to ease.

But how did he know all that stuff about her? she wondered as she opened her eyes again…and immedi-ately began to drown in the frozen green depths of his eyes. Certainly the news of her arrest and conviction was a matter of public record. Hell, it'd been a media circus at the time. But that had been ten years ago. Few people talked about any of that anymore. Fewer still remembered her name. Virtually none of them knew how her life had been in prison or even to which facility she'd been sent. Certainly none knew the names of her closest friends inside, as this man did. And how did he know about Andrew? She'd told no one about him. She'd had no one *to* tell about him.

"Who *are* you?" she asked again.

He smiled that sinister smile of his. "Well, now, Peaches, if you'd looked at my ID, you wouldn't have to ask that question."

"Your ID looks like something that came out of a box of Cap'n Crunch," she told him, ignoring the nickname.

"Oh, and you'd know, since you pretty much live on stuff like Cap'n Crunch."

"Who the hell *are* you?" she demanded for a third time, more forcefully now. Her fear for her personal safety was quickly being usurped by her indignation at having her privacy—and her person—violated. If it turned out this guy wasn't an actual threat to her physical well-being, she was going to bitch-slap him up one side of Park Avenue and down the other.

He eyed her thoughtfully for a moment, as if he were weighing several possible outcomes to the situation. As he did, Avery weighed an outcome he couldn't possibly be anticipating, no matter how much he thought he knew about her. And she was reasonably certain it would be the one outcome that ultimately occurred. For now, though, she contented herself in simply lying limp beneath him, hoping it might lull him into a false sense of security.

It did.

Because he told her, "I'm going to let you up, okay? And I'm going to show you my ID again, and you're going to look at it. And then we're going to have a little chat and then we're going to take a little drive someplace, where you can chat with a few more people, too."

Oh, yeah. No worries here. Whoever this guy was, he'd driven *way* past a false sense of security and was now touring the state of delusion. This was going to work even better than Avery had planned.

She nodded slowly and said, "Okay."

Still obviously wary—he wasn't stupid, after all—the guy began to push himself off and away from her. She waited until he was seated beside her on the sofa, then carefully maneuvered herself into a sitting position, too, at the opposite end. She inhaled another deep breath and pushed both braids over her shoulders.

"Okay," she said again. "Let me see your ID."

He lifted his hands up in front of himself, palms out, keeping one that way while the other dipped beneath his open jacket to extract the leather case he'd held up to the peephole. Gingerly he extended it toward her, and just as gingerly Avery accepted it, opening it to study the information inside.

The badgish-looking thing on the right was a rendition of a badge with a symbol on it, if not an actual badge itself, though it was one Avery had never seen before. And since her incarceration she'd done a lot of research into the various law-enforcement fields of the American justice system. Hey, she'd had some time on her hands. And she'd figured then—just as she did now—that it was always good for one to know everything one could about one's enemies. As a result, she was familiar with some pretty obscure tactical outfits and task forces about which other people had heard very little, if anything at all.

But this badge and its symbol were like nothing she'd ever seen. Although it had the traditional shield shape, there were few identifying marks on it. No numbers or letters at all. A border that resembled a heavy chain wound around the outer edge, surrounding what looked like a lance and a smaller shield at its center.

The left side of the case was considerably more revealing. Or it would have been had Avery believed a single word of the information recorded there. Which she didn't. According to this man's identification, his name was Santiago Dixon and he worked for something called the Office of Political Unity and Security, a bogus-sounding operation if ever there was one. Unless he'd just sauntered shaken-not-stirred out of an Ian Fleming novel, she wasn't buying the name of him or his employer any more than she bought the part where it said his city of birth was Macon, Georgia.

She glanced up from his identification and smiled blandly. "And the reason I should believe this is a legitimate document is because…?"

He smiled blandly back. "Because it's a legitimate document," he told her. "Except for my name and birthplace, naturally. They never put any personal identification on our ID."

"Then what's your real name?" she asked.

He smiled his benign smile again. "If I told you that, Peaches, I'd have to kill you."

"Right."

"No, really," he said. In a way that made her think he wasn't kidding.

"So I'm supposed to believe that this—" she glanced at the ID again "—Office of Political Unity and Security *is* legitimate?"

"Doesn't matter if you believe it," he replied. "It's legit."

"How come I've never heard of it?"

"Peaches, I've never heard of jalapeño-and-Gorgonzola ice cream. That doesn't mean it doesn't exist."

Well, gosh, who could argue with reasoning like that?

"Look, Santiago," she said.

"Please, call me Dixon," he told her in a voice that was the picture of politeness. "Everyone does. Well, for this assignment anyway."

Avery refrained from commenting on that. And before her life had a chance to slip any further into the surreal than it already had, she said, "What do you want? Why are you here?"

"I'll be happy to answer both of those questions," he told her.

"Good."

"Once you and I are in a secure environment."

"Meaning?" she asked.

"Meaning someplace other than here," he told her. Then, very graciously, he further offered, "I'll drive."

She'd really been afraid he was going to say something like that at some point. It was what had caused her to picture the outcome to this situation that he couldn't be anticipating himself, what was going to ruin her day and her week and her month worse than anything else that had already happened tonight would. The only consolation she found in the realization was that it would ruin his day and his week and his month even more.

She folded his ID case and handed it back to him. "I'm afraid that won't be possible," she told him.

He accepted the case graciously and returned it to the inside pocket of his jacket. "I can't wait to hear why."

"Because I'm not going anywhere with you," she said simply.

He expelled a sound that was a mixture of intention and resolution. "Actually you are," he told her. "I was hoping you'd come along peacefully, but…" He shrugged. "Guess it'll just have to be against your will now, that's all."

"That's *all?*" she echoed incredulously. "You're going to *make* me go with you? Against my will? Even though it will be a direct violation of my basic human rights, not to mention my civil rights, not to mention illegal?"

"It won't be illegal," he assured her with total confidence.

"It will be if you don't have an arrest warrant."

"An arrest warrant isn't necessary in these circumstances."

"So then I'm not under arrest?"

"Not exactly."

"Then what exactly *are* the circumstances?"

"Well, for starters, it's a matter of national security."

She almost laughed out loud at that. Almost. Until she got a good look at his expression and realized he was serious. In spite of that, she said softly, "You're joking."

"Actually I'm not."

She gaped at him. "What right do you have to take me anywhere?" she demanded. "I'm still not convinced that this organization you claim to work for even exists."

"You're just going to have to trust me on this one, Peaches. I have the jurisdiction and I'm not afraid to use it."

"You wouldn't dare," she said. But her actions belied her defiant words, because to punctuate the statement she dug her heels into the sofa cushions and crossed her arms over her midsection in a clear gesture of self-preservation.

In response to her actions, he stood, facing her. Avery cowered deeply into the sofa, but he made no further move. Yet. In fact, he kind of looked as if she'd hurt his feelings by being scared of him.

Weird.

"Avery Nesbitt," he said, his voice dripping with formality, "you've been summoned to appear for questioning at the Office of Political Unity and Security."

"Summoned?" she repeated in a voice that was nowhere near as indignant as she had wanted it to be. "By whom?"

He ignored her question and continued in the same no-nonsense voice he had used before. "Should you decline this summons to appear voluntarily, you will be found in violation of three different statutes—"

"Oh, well, that sort of negates the whole voluntary thing, doesn't it?" she said sarcastically.

"—and you will be brought in to the nearest OPUS office for questioning by an agent working for OPUS who is familiar with the charges against you."

"Charges against me?" Avery said indignantly. "What charges? You said I wasn't under arrest! I want to see these alleged 'charges.' In writing."

Again he ignored her and continued. "And since I am such an agent—"

"Says a piece of paper that could have come out of a box of Cap'n Crunch," she pointed out.

"—not to mention exceptionally good at bringing in people who violate statute—" he went on relentlessly.

"Oh, no ego on you, pal, is there?"

"—then that leaves me with no choice but to bring you in for questioning involuntarily."

"I object!" Avery shouted. Mostly because she had no idea what else to say.

"Your objection is noted."

"Oh, well, thank you so much for that measly considera—"

She was never able to finish what she had planned to say because Santiago Dixon—or whoever the hell he was—stepped forward and curled his fingers easily around her upper arms. And that, if nothing he'd said tonight, finally shut Avery up, because where she had expected roughness, he was gentle instead. When he pulled her to standing, it wasn't with animosity but with concern. And when he tugged her away from the couch, that was done gently, too.

And if she hadn't been silenced already, having her body pulled flush against his like that would for sure have done it. Because instead of manhandling her like a criminal, Santiago Dixon held her the same way he might have held a woman he intended to kiss. Her mouth went dry at the realization.

But she didn't have time to think about that. And she didn't have time to notice, either, the way his hard, muscular torso felt pressed against her own soft one or how upon contact her own traitorous body surged forward to meet his. Nor did she have time to marvel at how her struggles this evening with Santiago Dixon were the closest thing she'd had to a sexual encounter for a decade. Her mind was too scrambled, because he wrapped his fingers firmly—intimately?—around her waist. Then she couldn't think at all, because he lifted her off the ground and threw her over one shoulder. Then he started to walk toward the front door. Then he *opened* the front door. And then, with Avery still slung over his shoulder, he walked through it.

Or at least tried to.

But there was one potential outcome for the situation tonight that he hadn't considered, and that moment was when it kicked in.

Santiago Dixon hadn't counted on the fact that Avery Nesbitt was totally whack.

CHAPTER FOUR

IT WAS ONLY ONCE THEY were over that Avery could really get a handle on what happened during her panic attacks. In the calm of the aftermath, she could recall the dizziness, the disorientation, the sheer, unmitigated terror. She could recall how her entire body trembled and perspired, could remember the paralysis of speech and interruption of breath. She could recollect the pain behind her eyes, the insensible workings of her brain, her certainty that she was going to die. Usually when she came out of an attack, she was curled into a fetal position on the floor of the shower stall or in the back of a closet, and she had a towel or article of clothing pressed hard against her mouth. That last, she'd always figured, was an unconscious effort to keep the psychological screaming from escaping through actual cries from her mouth.

But this latest panic attack, she realized as she gradually emerged from the fog, had been different. For one thing, she couldn't remember ever fighting with corporeal monsters during one before. And she couldn't recall ever shouting aloud threats to faceless menaces. Nor had she ever come out of an attack lying spread-eagle on her back, on a bare cot beneath a stark white fluorescent light, her wrists and ankles wrapped in leather restraints. Nor had she ever found herself being stared at from above by someone like Santiago Dixon, who seemed to be as breathless, as terrified and as insensate as she.

So this was a definite first.

"What happened?" she asked when she was coherent enough to manage it.

Before the question even left her mouth, though, she knew. Vaguely she remembered pounding on Dixon's back and yanking at his hair and screaming something about how she would place certain parts of his anatomy into a variety of equipment normally reserved for torture and/or food processing. And also something about lepers and gargoyles. That part wasn't too clear at the moment, so maybe he could help her fill in the blanks later.

But he didn't help her out at all, only gazed at her in wide-eyed silence, as if he couldn't quite figure out who or what she was. Then, *"What happened?"* he echoed incredulously.

She nodded weakly.

He shook his head almost imperceptibly, in clear disbelief. "You just about beat the hell outta me, that's what happened. And you nearly gave my partner a concussion." He jutted a thumb over his shoulder and glared at her some more. "And there are a couple of nurses out there filling out paperwork to enroll themselves in art school."

"Oh," Avery said. "I'm sorry."

His lips parted marginally in surprise, but he said nothing more. His hat and jacket were gone, she noticed, and without them he seemed less menacing somehow. Until she bumped her gaze up to his face again and saw those cold green eyes and the jet-black hair spilling over his forehead. He seemed to be staring straight into her soul. And he seemed to not like what he saw there.

"Really," she tried again. "I am sorry. I don't usually attack people when that happens."

"When what happens?" he demanded gruffly. "Just what the hell was that anyway? You were totally out of control."

She hesitated, not wanting to share any part of herself with a total stranger she didn't trust. Most especially she didn't want to share the damaged part. Not that there were many parts of Avery that weren't at least a little impaired. But he wasn't the sort of person who would understand any of that. He was handsome, savvy, intelligent, confident. He wasn't damaged at all. To try and explain to someone like him what it meant to be terrified of what he would consider nothing would only make her look crazier than she must already seem.

Still, she supposed she owed him an explanation. If nothing else, it might make him stop looking at her as if she were some kind of freak.

"It was a panic attack," she said softly.

"A panic attack," he repeated evenly.

Again she nodded. But she said nothing to elaborate. What else was there for her to say?

He shifted his weight to one foot, hooked his hands on his hips in challenge and flattened his mouth into a tight line. "Peaches, that was no panic attack. That was transglobal, thermodynamic warfare."

She made a face at him. "Oh, stop it with the hyperbole." Although, now that she studied him more closely, she realized there was a big red spot on his cheek. "Look, I said I was sorry," she said again. "It's not like it's something I can control. And usually it's not that bad."

"Just what is it then?"

She sighed. She wished she could tell him. At least in terms that wouldn't make her sound weak and timid and nuts. Unfortunately, over the past several years, Avery had pretty much come to the conclusion that she *was* weak and timid and nuts. Which made her even more reluctant to tell him the truth.

In spite of that, she told him, "I wasn't trying to be coy or uncooperative earlier when I told you I couldn't go anywhere with you. I was telling you the truth. I can't leave my apartment. Not without some serious preparation first."

"What, like you need to make sure you have your wallet and house keys and a token for the subway?" he asked sarcastically.

"No. I can't go out, because…" She sighed, resigned to revealing more of herself than she wanted him to know, because there was no other way to make him understand. "Because I have agoraphobia."

He eyed her dubiously, "Which is what?" he asked. "Fear of the outdoors, right? But you weren't outside yet when you went psycho."

She tried to sit up, remembered that she was strapped down, so fell back against the cot with an exasperated sound. Honestly. Talk about overkill. So she'd roughed him up and called him a leper. So she'd nearly given someone a concussion. So she'd taken a couple of nurses out of commission. Like that didn't happen every day in some boroughs of New York.

She tugged meaningfully at her restraints. "Let me up, will you?" she pleaded. "I'm fine now. I swear."

"What you are is completely whack," he countered. "Has anyone ever told you that?"

"Once or twice," she said softly. Then, more forcefully, "I'm fine," she repeated. She jerked at the restraints again. "Get me *out* of these things. Let me *up*. Please."

Although he obviously didn't believe her, he bent over her and, after a moment's hesitation, cautiously unfastened one of her wrist restraints. But he waited before loosening any more, apparently wanting to take this thing slowly, in case she was still a little, oh, homicidal. After another moment, evidently satisfied that she wasn't going to go all Hannibal Lecter on him again—probably—he carefully freed one of the ankle restraints, too. Then the other. Then finally the last, on her other wrist. Then he took a giant step backward and positioned himself near the door.

Where was she anyway? she wondered as she folded herself into a sitting position on the edge of the cot. It wasn't *quite* a padded cell, but it was a tiny white room, empty save the cot on which she had been restrained, and there was a window in the door for observation from the other side. He'd mentioned nurses, so she must be in a hospital of some kind. God, she couldn't even remember how she'd gotten here.

"What time is it?" she asked.

He flicked his wrist to glance at his watch, returning his attention to Avery in less than a nanosecond. "It's ten after two."

"A.m. or p.m.?"

"It's two-ten in the morning," he said. "You've been

here for about an hour. But it took me and my partner almost an hour to get you here."

Avery nodded, waiting for the panic to rise again, because she wasn't in normal surroundings where she felt safe. Not that she ever really felt entirely safe in her normal surroundings. But nothing happened. She was a bit edgy, to be sure, but who wouldn't be upon one's discovery that one was in a strange place and couldn't remember how one had arrived there? Not to mention when there was a man like Santiago Dixon staring at one as if one had just emerged from a pea pod from outer space?

"And just where is here?" she asked.

"You're in an OPUS facility," he told her.

Well, at least it wasn't Bellevue.

"An OPUS *psychiatric* facility," he clarified.

Oh. So it *was* Bellevue. Only without all the glamour and accountability.

She looked down at her attire, at the loud pajama bottoms and ragged purple sweatshirt. There was a rip in one sleeve that hadn't been there before. One of her socks was missing, and the toenails of her one bare foot were painted five different colors. No telling how that had happened. The lost sock, she meant, since she had painted her toenails herself. One of her braids had come almost completely frayed. She looked at Dixon again, at the mark on his face for which she was responsible. She was lucky they'd only put her in restraints. Any other place would have performed a full frontal lobotomy by now.

Still, she wasn't panicking here. The small, bare room didn't frighten her the way most new surroundings did. And neither did Dixon's presence in it. That had to be significant somehow, but she was too exhausted at the moment to try and figure it out.

"So tell me about this agoraphobia you have," he said.

Avery reached for the unraveling braid and freed what little of it was still intact, then finger-combed her hair as best she could before going about the motions of plaiting it again. "Clinically," she said as she wove the strands back together and avoided his gaze, "it's defined as anxiety about being in a place or situation from which escape might be difficult or in which help may not be available in the event of having an unexpected panic attack or paniclike symptoms."

"In layman's terms?" he asked.

"It means I'm terrified of being someplace where I don't feel safe," she said simply. "And the only place I feel safe is my home. So anytime I have to leave my home, I am literally crippled by fear."

What Avery didn't add was that her agoraphobia had appeared after her release from prison and was a direct result of her incarceration. As bad as it had been to have her freedom revoked, in prison, for the first time in her life, she'd felt oddly safe. Strangely content. There was a strict system and regimen to life inside that had appealed to her. Everything was scheduled and everything went according to plan. Everyone was equal. The only thing that had been expected of her was that she stay out of trouble. And living in a place like that, Avery had felt no desire to get into trouble.

Not as she had growing up in East Hampton, where society's strict rules—which had never made any sense to her—had dictated she behave in ways she didn't want to behave. Growing up in the Hamptons, she had never felt like a worthwhile part of society, and because of that she had rebelled. Constantly. To her family she had always been a troublemaker. Behind bars, though…

As crazy as it sounded, behind bars Avery had felt free for the first time. Free to be herself. Free to say and think and feel what she wanted. Her activities had been curtailed, to be sure. But her mind and her emotions had been liberated. No one had censored her for her feelings or her thoughts or her dreams or her desires. No one had been disappointed by what went on in her head or offended by the things that came out of her mouth. On the contrary, she'd had friends inside, people who liked her because of who she was. And who she was was one of them—a person who wanted the world to work the way it was supposed to, and who had been disappointed by the workings of the world.

Not that there hadn't been bad people in prison. Certainly there were a lot of women at Rupert Halloran who deserved to be behind bars and who were a genuine menace to society. But the ones to whom Avery had gravitated had been like her—victims of circumstance, women who were in the wrong place at the wrong time, women who had gotten involved with men they shouldn't have. They'd understood Avery. Even when they discovered she came from a privileged background, they still understood her. And they liked her. And they considered her their equal. Prison was the only place where she had felt like a useful part of a meaningful society. Maybe it hadn't been the kind of society that society appreciated. But Avery had appreciated it. And she'd been happy there.

Upon her release, though, once she returned to "acceptable" society, she discovered that where before she had felt uncomfortable, now she was genuinely frightened. In fact, she was terrified of acceptable society. Not just of all the rules, but of all the people, too. There were so many people on the outside, and there were so many different ways to go and be and live. Too many expectations on her. Too many societal dictates to follow. Too many choices. Too much freedom. Too much everything.

And Avery was completely alone in the world once she left prison. Her family had stopped speaking to her the minute they learned of her arrest, had turned their backs on her throughout her trial and incarceration. They'd made it clear—through their attorneys—that she would never, *ever,* have contact with them again. She was still entitled to her trust fund—alas, there was nothing they could do about that, since Great-Grandfather Nesbitt had set it up in a way that no one but Avery could touch it after she turned eighteen. But she must take her money and run, her family's attorneys told her, and never return to her family. Because they'd made clear, too, that they weren't her family anymore.

So she took her money—all fifteen million dollars of it—and ran to a condo on Central Park West. There, she could look out her window at society and observe it from a distance, where it was safe, and never have to be a part of it. Little by little, over the years that followed, Avery stopped leaving her apartment. Whenever she needed something, she shopped online and had things delivered. She called Eastern Star Earth-friendly Market, who happily brought her groceries to her front door. The only time she ventured out was if she or Skittles needed to see a doctor. But on those occasions, she began steeling herself for the torment days, even weeks, in advance, shoring herself up to face a ruthless, unforgiving populace, even if only for an hour or two. And then, just to be on the safe side, she got completely snookered before heading out the door. Because the outside world was much too scary, much too menacing. It wasn't safe, the way prison was.

"You're joking."

When she first heard him speak, Avery thought Dixon was reading her mind. Then she realized what he didn't believe was that she couldn't leave home without being incapacitated by fear. This from a man who sported an abraded cheek—never mind who had just released her from leather restraints—after trying to take her for a little ride.

Now, she thought, might be a good time to change the subject.

"Why am I here?" she asked.

Dixon studied Avery Nesbitt in silence, wondering whether or not he should believe her about being terrified of reality. On one hand, she was just flaky enough that he could buy it. On the other hand, she had been corresponding with Sorcerer for a month, and God knew what he'd put her up to.

Still, it was hard to fake the kind of mania that had consumed her when he'd tried to carry her out of her apartment. Dixon was pissed off at himself for how he'd handled that. Or rather, how he *hadn't* handled it. Not just that he hadn't tried any harder to talk to her and explain the situation before resorting to physical removal, but that he'd been so unprepared when she'd gone off the way she had.

But she'd gone off so suddenly and so quickly and with such a powerful detonation, he hadn't known what to do. Nowhere in his investigation of her had he seen any evidence of her having been formally trained in martial arts. Even her prison file had no record of her ever having participated in any kind of altercation. But the minute he'd tried to remove her from her home, she'd attacked. Viciously.

And damn, she fought dirty.

Of course, he'd eventually realized that she was too sloppy, chaotic and desperate to be trained in martial arts. But he hadn't been able to figure out what exactly she *was* doing. When Cowboy heard the commotion coming over his headset, he'd responded to render aid. Between the two of them, they'd managed to wrestle her into a service elevator and then the surveillance van, which Cowboy had parked in the alley behind the building.

But no sooner had they slammed the door shut behind themselves than did Avery go limp in Dixon's arms. Her eyes had remained open and she had been breathing—though rapidly enough that he'd worried she might hyperventilate—but mentally she'd completely checked out. It was spooky how she shut down the way she did.

She'd begun fighting again when he'd tried to remove her from the van. Ultimately it had taken a half hour— and a half dozen orderlies and nurses—to get her into the restraints. They'd said it was for her own safety, but Dixon suspected it was more for theirs. He hadn't left her side once since then. He'd been worried about her, something that frankly had surprised him. He'd wanted to be sure she was okay. That had surprised him, too. Now evidently she *was* okay. So why wasn't he relaxing?

Maybe, he thought, because he was beginning to realize that *okay* for Avery Nesbitt wasn't in any way okay.

He marveled at how anyone who'd just kicked the shit out of him could look so fragile and reserved. Were it not for her ridiculous outfit, she'd even look prim. But what amazed him even more was that he actually found her kind of attractive. In a weird, bohemian, I-really-need-to-be-evaluated kind of way. Though it wasn't necessarily Avery he was thinking needed the evaluation.

Nevertheless, even after all she'd been through in the past few hours, she was surprisingly pretty. That first night he'd been in her apartment, Dixon had thought her eyes only looked enormous because of her glasses. Nobody, he'd thought, could have eyes that big or lashes that thick. But without the glasses her eyes were even larger. There had been times tonight when he'd nearly lost himself in their bottomless blue depths. And when he'd seen how that one braid had come unbound to leave her hair flowing over one shoulder like a shimmering, inky river, he'd found himself wanting to touch it, to see if it was as silky as it looked. Now that she'd rewoven her hair the way it belonged, he felt like a child denied his favorite plaything.

But Avery Nesbitt wasn't a plaything. Quite the contrary. If things turned out the way they were planning, she might be the most powerful weapon OPUS had at its disposal.

"Judging by the restraints," she said, "I'm assuming that I'm under arrest now."

She was perched on the very edge of the cot, her right hand massaging her left wrist where the restraints had been. A pang of guilt shot through Dixon. Seeing her like this, the thought of restraining her seemed silly. She looked like a delicate bird who'd injured its wing, and he couldn't quite jibe the wounded chick with the raging terminator of a little while ago.

Agoraphobia. That's what she said she had. Yet nowhere in his research of her had there been any mention of her suffering from such a condition. Not in her prison records, not in her medical records, nowhere. Either she was lying about it or else she was lying about it. Because OPUS didn't miss things like that. But if she was lying about being agoraphobic, then what had caused her to go off the way she had back at her place? And if she wasn't lying about being agoraphobic, why was she suddenly feeling okay again, even though she wasn't at home? Why wasn't she still throwing a fit or being catatonic or something?

Just what was the deal with Avery Nesbitt?

He waggled his head back and forth a little. "Well, you are under arrest and you aren't," he told her evasively.

She stopped rubbing her wrist and let both hands fall into her lap. "If I'm not under arrest, then I demand to be released immediately," she said levelly. "And if I *am* under arrest, you'll never make it stick, so I demand to be released immediately."

"What makes you think we won't make it stick?" he asked. Mostly because he was sure that whatever her argument was, it was bound to be entertaining.

"You didn't read me my rights," she told him.

"I don't have to," he told her right back.

"Says who?"

"Says the agency I work for."

"Which, as I've said—several times, in fact—I'm still not convinced exists anywhere outside your own delusions."

"Look around you, Peaches," Dixon said. "If OPUS doesn't exist, then where do you think you are?"

"I have no idea," she replied. "Could be the renovated garage of some psychopath for all I know. Some psychopath like—oh, gee, who could I be thinking of?—you."

He didn't rise to the bait. "If you'd studied my ID more closely, you'd have realized it's totally genuine."

She narrowed her eyes at him. "You didn't give me much of a chance to make up my mind about it. You were too busy tackling, harassing and groping me."

"Well, if you'd been a better hostess, I wouldn't have had to tackle or harass you. The groping probably would have happened at some point, though," he added, trying not to sound too smug. "Somehow it almost always comes to that. Whether I'm working or not."

"You searched me illegally," she continued, obviously thinking it best to not dwell on that groping business.

"But it was fun, wasn't it?" Dixon said. He rather liked the idea of keeping the groping topic alive. Though he hated to think why.

"It was illegal," she said again.

"Actually it wasn't," he assured her. "Our rules of operation fall outside the traditional channels for most law-enforcement agencies. Probably because technically we're not a law-enforcement agency."

"You gained entry into my apartment unlawfully," she pointed out.

"It's not unlawful when OPUS is doing it," Dixon told her. "Those untraditional channels again."

She eyed him narrowly. "Does the Libertarian Party know about your agency?"

He shook his head. "Only the people OPUS wants to know about it know about OPUS. Anyone else finds out, they don't live long enough to talk about it."

"I'm going to talk about it," she told him. "I'm going to tell everyone. Starting with the Libertarian Party."

"You go ahead and do that," Dixon told her. "And we'll make you look like a raving lunatic who doesn't know what she's talking about."

"That won't be a problem for the Libertarian Party."

"We'll make it a problem for them."

"Is that a threat?"

"Yep."

"You can't threaten the Libertarian Party."

"Peaches, we can threaten any party we like, be it Libertarian, Birthday, Tupperware or Slumber. And they all forget all about us when we do."

Her jaw set tight, she hissed, "Fascist."

He smiled. "You're cute when you're angry, you know that?"

This time her reply was a snarl. And he hated to say it, but she was even cuter when she did that.

A soft knock on the door made him turn around, and through the wire-reinforced window he saw the round, bland face of Mr. No-Name. Behind him was Tanner Gillespie, who still looked a little shaken from this evening's encounter.

The boss man pushed a series of numbers on a keypad below the doorknob, and the lock released with a soft click. The already small room shrank to microscopic when the two men entered, making Dixon feel crowded and uncomfortable. Avery seemed not to be bothered at all.

Agoraphobia. Right.

"Ms. Nesbitt," Dixon's boss said without awaiting an introduction.

She didn't reply at first, her attention flickering to Dixon instead. He wasn't sure what she wanted from him, so he only met her gaze in return. After a moment, she looked at No-Name again.

"Do I know you?" she asked.

"No," he replied immediately.

"You sure? You look familiar."

"I'm not."

"But—"

Before she could say more, he hurried on, "You're a difficult woman to pin down, Ms. Nesbitt."

"Not really," she said, still eyeing him with wary interest. "I never go anywhere. Well, not usually," she added with a meaningful glance at Dixon. Then to his employer she continued, "I do my best to keep a low profile, but anyone who really wants to find me can."

"Is that why Adrian Padgett was able to find you?"

Her expression turned puzzled at the question. Convincingly so, Dixon had to admit. His boss, on the other hand, looked convincingly skeptical.

"Who's Adrian Padgett?" she asked.

"You might know him better as Andrew Paddington," No-Name said.

Avery glanced at Dixon again, obviously remembering that he had mentioned her online boyfriend earlier tonight, too. "What's Andrew got to do with any of this?" she asked.

Now his boss turned to Dixon, too, giving him a look that let Dixon know the other man was deferring to him. But only because Dixon was more familiar with the particulars of the case. Under no other circumstances would his superior actually *defer* to anyone.

Dixon looked back at Avery. "Where did you meet Andrew Paddington?"

Of course, he already knew the answer to that question, but he wanted to see how honestly she would answer it.

"Online," she told him, surprising him. He had been ready for her to challenge him again and not give him any information at all. "In a Henry James chat room. Why?"

So far, so good, Dixon thought. "And how long have you been corresponding with him?"

She hesitated. "What business is that of yours?"

Dixon ignored the question. Thanks to the OPUS techies at her apartment, who were currently combing through every computer she owned, it wouldn't be long before they knew every detail of her correspondence with and relationship to Sorcerer anyway. But he wanted her to talk about it, too, to see if her version corresponded to what the techies discovered.

He tried a different tack. "Why were you building that virus?"

Had it not been for the two bright spots of pink that appeared on her cheeks, Dixon would have thought she hadn't heard the question. "That's none of your business, either," she said softly.

"It could send you back to prison, Peaches," he said. "It's highly illegal. That makes it my business."

"No, that makes it a matter for the feds," she said. She hesitated only a moment before adding, "And stop calling me 'Peaches.'"

He bit back a smile. He honestly hadn't been aware

he was calling her that. "When it's a matter of national security, it becomes a matter for OPUS, too."

"That virus wasn't a matter of national security," she said.

"It was last time you built one," Dixon reminded her. "Hell, it was a matter of *inter*national security then. We still get calls from the Vatican."

"Not to mention Greenland," his boss added.

Avery expelled a soft sound of capitulation and closed her eyes. Then she lifted a hand to her forehead and rubbed hard at a place just above her right eyebrow. Very wearily, very quietly, she said, "If you want me to explain this, it's going to take a while."

"Peaches," Dixon said—he'd call her that if he wanted to, dammit—"we got no place else to be."

AVERY'S EXPLANATION, WHICH came out over hours of interrogation, corresponded exactly to what Dixon already knew and what the techies found at her apartment. That was his first clue that maybe they'd been wrong in assuming she was working with Sorcerer. His second clue came with the discovery of tons of information on her hard drive about agoraphobia that she'd downloaded from the Net. Evidently Avery was one for self-analysis, self-diagnosis and self-treatment. Except that her self-professed self-treatment on those occasions when she had to leave her apartment seemed to involve large quantities of scotch. Call him an alarmist, but Dixon wondered if maybe it was time to call in an expert. Besides Johnnie Walker, he meant.

Evidently she'd even been telling the truth about not sending out the virus, too, since it existed only on a laptop that had no communication capacity. It would have been impossible for her to send it anywhere from there, and she hadn't saved it to anything but her hard drive. Not to mention the virus itself wouldn't work the way she had it set up. Maybe with a few modifications it would, but Dixon didn't see any way to make it work unless she started over again.

In other words, Avery had built a dud. But that was appropriate, since her boyfriend turned out to be a dud, too.

What ultimately pushed Dixon off the fence and into her camp was the way Avery looked when she talked about that dud, Andrew Paddington. She seemed genuinely hurt by the guy's betrayal. And she seemed genuinely shocked that he hadn't been who he claimed to be. This from a woman who lived her life on the Internet and should know better than anyone how people misrepresented themselves there. That was when Dixon decided Avery was innocent. In more ways than one.

Unfortunately she was OPUS's only tie to Sorcerer, public enemy number one. Which made her their best chance to catch him. Whether she liked it or not. For now, though, Dixon played along with the laughable suggestion that she had a choice in the matter.

So he listened silently as No-Name explained it to Avery. How her beloved Andrew was actually an evildoer named Adrian Padgett who was wanted by OPUS for a variety of crimes. How she was the only known person to currently have a solid, credible, workable connection to said evildoer. How they'd deduced from their investigation that Adrian had deliberately sought her out after stumbling onto her file while working for CompuPax in Indianapolis, a company to whom Avery had sold a software design at the tender age of fourteen. How he was up to no good and needed a computer genius like Avery to help him achieve it. How he was trying to win her over to his way of thinking by luring her into a romantic relationship where he could manipulate her and use her, because that was what Adrian did with every woman he met.

And then more. About how Adrian thought her weak and gullible and completely enamored of him. How he had no idea that she was on to him now, knew who he was and what he had done and that she was cooperating with OPUS. How her relationship with the criminal formerly known as Andrew was OPUS's only hope, *America's* only hope—yeah, play that patriotism card, Big Guy—to prevent the man from committing who knew what kind of international crimes. How it was Avery's civic duty to work with OPUS to bring the son of a bitch to heel.

How in building her virus, however inoperative, they could have her tossed right back into jail. And how OPUS might be persuaded to never mention it to anyone and bury the evidence if she helped them out in this endeavor.

What a guy.

Six hours after Dixon had yanked Avery Nesbitt from her home, her reality, her safety and her life, his boss asked her a question that would change all of it.

"What do you say, Ms. Nesbitt? Will you help us catch him?"

To her credit, Avery didn't even flinch. But it wasn't Dixon's boss she looked at when she replied to the question. It was at Dixon himself. "Yes," she said evenly. "I'll help you. Like I really have a choice." But she added a caveat of her own. "And after you've put this guy away," she said softly, firmly, "I want you people to promise me that for the rest of my life I will be left alone."

"Done," Dixon's boss agreed without hesitation.

And Dixon could see by her expression that, incredibly, Avery actually believed him.

"Can I go home now?" she asked.

"Soon," No-Name told her. "After we figure out our plan of attack. But if you'd like, we can find you a room more comfortable than this one for the time being."

Slowly she pushed herself up from the cot, but when she looked at the door, she went a little pale and sat back down. "I'll just stay here for now," she said. "But I might as well start preparing for the trip home." Again she looked at Dixon. "I'll need a glass, a bottle of Black Label, a bucket of ice and a lemon. I prefer my scotch on the rocks with a twist."

As Dixon waited for Avery to order last call on her own personal happy hour a floor below the one where he and his employer had found a room to chat, he leaned against a wall and silently willed the Big Guy to hurry up and conclude a conversation on his cell phone which seemed—from this end anyway—to consist largely of affirmative grunting. Eventually his superior oinked out a goodbye and disconnected, turning his attention to Dixon.

"Here's how it's going to play out," he said.

Ooh, Dixon was on pins and needles.

"You're going to take Avery Nesbitt back to her place long enough for her to pack some clothes and make any necessary arrangements for leaving town."

Dixon narrowed his eyes at the other man. "Leave

town? Why? I figured Cowboy and I would just keep tabs on her at her place."

His boss shook his head. "Too risky for what we have planned. She has too many neighbors in that building and she's in the heart of the biggest city in the country. We still don't know what Sorcerer is up to, and if we can avoid having her in such a densely populated area, then we need to do that. So Avery Nesbitt's going home."

"Home?" Dixon echoed. "You just said you want her *out* of her apartment."

"No, I mean she's going *home* home," his boss told him. "To her parents' estate in East Hampton."

Okay, now Dixon was really confused. He'd learned from his investigation into Avery's background—and she had confirmed it herself during their recently concluded interview—that she was estranged from her family. More than estranged, actually. The other Nesbitts had severed all ties to her when she was arrested, and she'd had no personal contact with a single member of her family since she was taken into custody. She wasn't welcome at her parents' estate. She didn't want to go there. It made no sense to send her. And Dixon said so.

"It's safer for her," the other man said. "If Sorcerer discovers she's cooperating with us, he'll know where to find her in Manhattan, and I wouldn't put it past him to come after her."

"Oh, and he won't know where to look for her in East Hampton?" Dixon asked. "You can bet he knows as much about Avery as we do. Except for us having found her, too, and having exposed him to her. And even that might not take long for him to discover."

"Which means he also knows that she has no contact with her family," his superior pointed out. "He won't have any reason to think she's staying with them. He won't have any reason to think she's not home. And even if he does find her there, the place is a fortress. Desmond Nesbitt is one of the wealthiest men in the country. He's an even bigger security freak than his daughter is. She'll be safer if she's there," he repeated. "And so will the city of New York."

Dixon didn't buy it. She'd be safest at her apartment with him, since he'd planned to move in with her until they caught Sorcerer. There were too many things that could go wrong by removing her from her natural habitat, not the least of which was another one of those nuclear-holocaust panic attacks. He told his boss that, too.

"She'll be fine," the other man said simply.

She'd be a reeking distillery was what she'd be, Dixon thought. Aloud, however, he only reiterated, "It's too dangerous for her to leave her home, and it makes no sense to insist she do it."

"She's going to East Hampton," his boss stated again in the sort of voice Dixon knew better than to argue with. And before Dixon had a chance to say anything more—not that he planned to say anything more, not with that voice coming at him with both barrels—the other man continued, "Here's what's going to happen. You're going to go home right now and pack a bag for yourself for a week. And you're going to tell whatshisname…your partner now…"

"Cowboy," Dixon supplied.

"Right. Cowboy. You're going to tell him to go home and pack for a week, too. Then you, Dixon, will come back here and get Avery, take her to her apartment and tell her to pack for a week, too."

Oh, that ought to be entertaining, he thought.

"Then you two will rendezvous with Cowboy at the Nesbitt estate in East Hampton. He'll brief the family before your arrival. We'll arrange to have all the necessary equipment sent up, and once you're all settled—"

Like anyone could *settle* Avery, Dixon thought.

"—then you're going to plug her in and watch her go."

Dixon wasn't sure he liked the sound of that. "Sir?" he asked.

"The techs are finished with her computers. Have her take whatever she needs to East Hampton and get her all set up so that she can establish contact with Sorcerer again as soon as possible. Tell her to pick up with him where the two of them left off and draw him out. Literally. She's to arrange a meeting with him somewhere in the city. In person. And then she's to go in to meet him. In person. That's when we'll nab the son of a bitch."

"Now wait a minute," Dixon interrupted. "You never said anything about this. We can't let her meet Sorcerer face-to-face. You yourself just said she's not safe in the city. And that the city isn't safe with her in it. You add a meeting with Sorcerer to the mix, and we're going to have a disaster on our hands."

What the hell was going on? Dixon wondered. He'd been under the impression that yes, they were going to use Avery to lure Sorcerer out from whatever rock he was hiding under, but there was no reason for her to be there for the meeting. That was his job. His and Cowboy's. Or his and She-Wolf's, if she ever got back from Vegas.

His boss frowned at him. "Sorcerer's not going to come out of the woodwork unless he sees her standing somewhere, Dixon. He's too smart for that."

"But Avery's not a trained operative. She's a civilian."

Now his boss looked at him as if he were nuts. Which, considering the words that had just come out of his mouth, Dixon supposed he was.

His boss met his gaze steadily. "And the fact that she's a civilian should concern me because…?"

Right, Dixon thought. Silly him. Far be it from OPUS to let a little thing like an innocent human being stand in the way of getting their man. That was on page one of the official rules. Screw anybody or anything that might potentially obstruct the mission. You learned that the first day of spy school.

"Sorry," Dixon apologized dryly. "Guess I forgot myself."

There was something else going on here, he thought, and his name obviously wasn't on the need-to-know list this time. He knew better than to question his boss's instructions any further. For now. He hadn't gotten as far as he had at OPUS by breaking the rules. Twisting them into an unrecognizable mess had suited him just fine. So far. But there *was* something else going on here. And as long as he didn't forget that, he should be fine.

Avery, though…

Well. Dixon just made a mental note to pack an ice chest and plenty of lemons for the road.

CHAPTER FIVE

IT WAS LATE AFTERNOON by the time Tanner Gillespie, code name Cowboy, real name secret, arrived at the Nesbitt estate. But he knew Dixon was still hours behind him, because his partner had been assigned the unenviable task of rounding up and battening down Avery Nesbitt. Which meant if Dixon was lucky, he'd arrive sometime before the end of the year. If he was really lucky, he wouldn't be maimed or dismembered when he did. And if he was really, *really* lucky, he wouldn't be a yammering, drooling lunatic, either. Tanner was just grateful it hadn't fallen to the newbie agent to tame the Nesbitt shrew. Because not only was he tired of being treated like an amateur, but the Nesbitt shrew was one scary dame. That chick was totally whack.

Although he was a native New Yorker, Tanner had never visited the Hamptons before. Folks from his neighborhood—Queens—just didn't get out this way very much. Go figure. Naturally, though, he'd heard stories of the fabled Hamptons. And he'd seen movies filmed here. And once, in college, when he was working as a bartender in a SoHo club, he'd fixed a Cosmopolitan for a girl who told him she was from East Hampton. Then she'd stiffed him on the tip.

But stiffing people on their tips evidently netted the residents of the Hamptons a tidy income. Because the Nesbitts—like everyone else out here—lived in one big-ass house, to be sure. Tanner rolled his government-issue sedan to a stop in front of it, glancing around to look for a sign that said something about servants using the rear entrance. When astonishingly he didn't see one, he unfolded himself from the car and strode up the half-dozen steps to the front door. But something made him hesitate before ringing the bell. Probably the same something that made him run a quick hand through his blond hair and brush off the front of his charcoal suit. It was the same something that made him also straighten his sapphire-blue necktie and shrug until he was satisfied with the lines of his gray wool overcoat.

Dammit, he wasn't a servant, he reminded himself with a grimace when he realized what he was doing. Not only was he better dressed, but he worked for the United States government, the most powerful employer in the world. Hell, he didn't care how wealthy the Nesbitts were. His Uncle Sam had tons more money than they did. No need to dwell on that pesky trillion-dollar-debt business. No one was perfect.

Still, with a place like this, old man Nesbitt could probably house the entire population of the country. Tanner shook his head as he made a visual sweep of the big-ass mansion, from one end to the other, from bottom to top, as much as he could take in from this angle. He couldn't imagine one family occupying such a dwelling. And the Nesbitts had only raised three kids here, he knew. There had been six growing up in the house Tanner had called home—half of them still lived there—a domicile of only three bedrooms. And only one bathroom until Tanner was fourteen, when he and his father and his uncle Leo installed a second one in the basement.

Since Tanner was the oldest, he'd been awarded the sleeper sofa in the living room when he turned thirteen. He'd happily traded his privacy for a double bed, turning a corner of the family garage into his personal haven, where he could tinker with the cars he loved so much and practice his guitar. He hadn't minded leaving his three brothers to share the "big" bedroom at the back of the house. His two sisters had claimed another, and Tanner's parents had kept the last—and smallest—room for themselves. They'd figured their kids needed more space. And they'd been right. But that was how his folks had always done things. They'd always put their kids' needs ahead of their own.

Which was why Tanner had been perfectly content to take on three jobs after graduating from high school, to put himself through four years at SUNY. He figured his parents had done their jobs by him by the time he left home, had fed and clothed and housed him without ever asking for a nickel in return. And they'd still had five left at home to do the same for. He wasn't afraid of hard work, and sharing a tiny dorm with another guy had been like living in a palace as far as he was concerned.

For seven years now he'd been on his own. And at the age of twenty-four, when a lot of guys were still fumbling their way through college or the want ads, he was in total control of his life. He was more self-aware, more self-assured and more self-reliable than a lot of guys twice his age. He had money in the bank—maybe not a lot, but it was there. And he had a place of his own—maybe just a loft in the Village, but it was his.

And he had a very promising future at OPUS—provided the old-timers stopped doing stuff just to hear the newbie shriek. Who needed a palace when you had all that?

He was lifting a hand toward the Nesbitt's doorbell when he heard the sound of another car roaring up the drive and spun around in time to see a sporty little red Jaguar roadster taking the final turn of the drive with far more speed than was prudent. It spewed a few loose stones as it careened around the circle, then came to a screeching halt behind his boxy black sedan, leaving barely an inch, if that, between the bumpers.

Tanner frowned. It didn't matter if the sedan wasn't his. It didn't matter that the Jag had stopped in time. It didn't matter if it would have cost the driver of the Jag a lot more to fix his car than it would Tanner his. What mattered was that the driver of the Jag had driven that recklessly and edged that close to Tanner's car on purpose. And what mattered was that he had done it with Tanner standing right there watching and with the clear intention of pissing him off.

What mattered was that it had worked.

So Tanner, who'd gone way too long without sleep and who hadn't exactly had a great day to begin with—what with starting it last night being smacked around by the Nesbitt shrew—stepped away from the front door and moved to the place where the porch connected with the top step. He pushed back his overcoat to hook both hands on his hips in challenge and waited for the guy to get out of his car so that the two of them could exchange, if not the phone numbers for their respective insurance agents, which wouldn't be necessary, then a couple of choice epithets, which would.

But it wasn't a guy driving the Jag.

Tanner realized that the minute the driver pushed the door open, because from his higher vantage point he could see a small, black-leather-clad hand doing the pushing, its wrist encircled by a chunky red bracelet. The slender leg encased in smoky black silk that extended from the driver's side was also clearly female. And also long. And slender. Had he mentioned it was long and slender? And on the foot of that long, slender leg was a screaming-red, pointy-toed, spike-heel shoe, which Tanner, ever the astute agent, also concluded was a sign of the driver's gender. As was the black leather miniskirt and red leather motorcycle jacket that also emerged from the car. Not to mention the riot of jet-black curls that topped them all.

He had one brief but *extremely* satisfying glimpse of the woman's backside before she spun around and slammed the car door shut. And then he got an even more satisfying glimpse of her front side. Because the motorcycle jacket hung open over a skintight black top that scooped low enough to reveal…

Well. Suffice it to say maybe he wouldn't have minded so much if her bumper had rammed him after all. Not that that let her off the hook. It just made him turn the reel of his rod more slowly, that was all.

Black wraparound sunglasses obscured the woman's eyes, even though it was cloudy and the accessory was unnecessary. Her mouth, though, was in plain sight, and it was wide and full and really, really red. She smiled when she saw Tanner gazing at her, a dazzling display of white she could have only achieved through a dental professional. Then she slung a little black purse over one shoulder, its handle hooked over a crooked index finger. A shake of her head sent the black curls flying and long, dangly red earrings dancing. But only when he saw the rest of her body get into the act did Tanner's motor well and truly begin to rev.

Carly Nesbitt, he deduced as he watched her stride toward him. Thanks to his file on the family, Tanner knew Avery had two older siblings—a brother named Desmond Jr., age thirty-five, and a sister named Carly, age thirty-nine. Unlike her sister and brother, Carly still lived at home. And unlike her self-employed and quite successful sister and her brother who was second in command under his father at the Nesbitt Corporation, Carly didn't have a job. According to his file, she was active in a number of charities. But her activity seemed to consist mostly of dressing up in brief cocktail dresses and seducing old men into writing fat checks at various society fund-raisers throughout the year. Still, according to one source, Carly Nesbitt had single-handedly raised close to a half billion dollars for various charities in the past ten years.

Judging by the way she looked and the way she dressed and the way she moved, Tanner considered the figure to be a bit low.

Damn, he thought as he watched her approach. A walk like that could stop traffic and start fights. No way would he put her age at pushing forty. *Hel-lo, Mrs. Robinson.*

"Well, aren't you cute," she cooed when she stood at the foot of the steps looking up at him. "And whose little boy are you?"

Tanner frowned. Okay, so maybe there was more than one Nesbitt shrew. Not that he had any intention of taming this one, either. But it was good information to have.

"I'm here to see Avery Nesbitt," he told her without preamble.

The woman's playful smile went bitter cold. "You have the wrong address," she said in a clipped voice. Clipped, too, were her steps as she ascended the stairs and breezed past him toward the front door, never once faltering in the ridiculously high heels.

"This isn't the Nesbitt residence?" Tanner asked coolly.

"This is the Nesbitt residence," she confirmed as she rifled through her tiny purse for her key. "But there's no one by that name living here."

Wow, he thought. The Nesbitts really had turned their backs on their youngest daughter. They couldn't even say her name aloud, as if saying *Avery* would invoke a curse on them forever. Which was weird, because all of them had obviously already turned to stone, so what could be the harm?

"She may not live here anymore," he said, "but she's expected for a visit. Today."

That made Carly Nesbitt's head snap up, and Tanner thought her gaze connected with his. Hard to tell with those dark glasses of hers.

"She's what?" she asked.

"Expected," Tanner repeated. "Here. Today."

"Says who?"

It was as good an opening as any, he thought. Reaching inside his overcoat, he withdrew his OPUS ID from his inside pocket and flipped it open, holding it at arm's length for Carly Nesbitt to read. It was probably best not to get within more than arm's length of her, since he was already detecting a family nature for crabbiness. But instead of looking at the ID, she continued to gaze at Tanner's face. She did at least reach up to remove her sunglasses, something for which he was grateful, since it was easier to gauge when a pit bull was about to strike by watching its eyes. But one look at Carly's eyes nearly made him keel over.

Never in his life had Tanner seen eyes that color before, a mixture of blue and green that defied description. He'd seen a photograph in a magazine once of some Caribbean beach with incredibly blue water surrounding it. Her eyes were kind of like that color. But where the picture of the island had made Tanner feel relaxed and peaceful, looking at Carly made him want to commit mayhem. Preferably while naked.

Her eyes stayed fastened on his as she plucked his ID from his fingers. Normally Tanner hated it when people took his ID from him to inspect it. When Carly did it, though…well, he hated it even more than usual. His fingers itched to snatch it back, but he halted himself, not wanting her to know how much she bothered him. Instead he only watched as her amazing eyes scanned the information on his card.

"Office of Political Unity and Security?" she read aloud. "What the hell is that? I've never heard of it."

"We're a small group," Tanner told her.

"Law enforcement or intelligence?" she asked.

"Yes," he told her.

She narrowed her eyes at him again. "Domestic or international?"

"Yes."

"Hunter or gatherer?"

"Yes."

Now she grinned. "Shaken or stirred?"

He grinned back. "Straight up, baby."

Hoping he looked relaxed—and still wondering why he wasn't—Tanner reached for his ID to reclaim it. But Carly pulled it closer to herself and continued to study it. Without realizing he was doing it, Tanner curled the fingers of both hands into loose fists. Immediately he forced himself to relax, but not before Carly noted his discomfort. And ignored it.

"Tanner Gillespie," she read. "Is that really your name?"

"Any reason why it shouldn't be?" he asked, doing his best—honest, he did—to keep the edge out of his voice.

"I don't know," she said, glancing up again. She smiled at him in the same way she might have smiled at an irritating little terrier who was so overcome with joy to see her that he'd just peed on the floor. "Is this Office of Political Unity and Security one of those agencies where people are assigned code names and have tiny cameras hidden in their tie tacks and carry around disguises in their briefcases?"

"Do you see me carrying around a briefcase full of disguises?" he asked. Probably it wasn't necessary to mention that he did in fact have a code name. Nor did she really need to know about the tiny camera hidden in his tie tack.

In response to his question, she spared a moment to give him a complete once-over, from the top of his blond head to the tip of his black loafers and back again. But as hard as he tried to discern a reaction in her expression—and it bugged the hell out of him that he even cared about her reaction—he couldn't detect a single change in her features.

"No," she admitted. "I don't see a briefcase full of

disguises." Her smile turned indulgent again. "In fact, if it weren't for the suit, I would have pegged you as a Boy Scout selling tickets to the jamboree."

Tanner smiled back, sarcastically he hoped. "Well, golly gee, Ms. Nesbitt, the jamboree's not till summer. But could I maybe interest you in some band candy?"

Her smile fell some. "So you know my name is Nesbitt," she said. "Though I don't suppose that was especially hard to figure out with me heading up to the front door, was it?"

"Yep, I know your name," he confirmed readily. "I know more about you than you probably realize."

It was more than she'd be comfortable with, too, Tanner thought. But unlike some people, he didn't get off on making others feel uneasy, so he'd just keep it to himself. Unless, you know, she asked. In which case he probably could lower himself to making her feel edgy. Why should he be the only one? Of course, there were a lot more interesting ways to put a woman on edge than by saying things to her. There were lots of things he could *do* that would accomplish that, too. Not that he necessarily wanted to do this woman. Uh, do *anything* to this woman, he quickly corrected himself. Probably. Maybe.

"Is that a fact?" she said, smiling the peeing-terrier smile again.

"Yep," Tanner said. "I also know your age. And it's ten years more than the twenty-nine you tell people," he added, leaning in to deliberately invade her space and totally forgetting about that arm's-length business. "That would be your sister who's twenty-nine," he said. "Your *younger* sister. Avery."

Mostly Tanner said all that because…well, just

because, that was why. And it was a good reason, too, dammit. If Carly Nesbitt wanted to compete with him on the annoying scale, he was right there with her.

"And I know your phone number," he continued, "even though it's unlisted and harder to find than mismatched shoes and handbag at a Junior League function. And I know that you've never been married. What I didn't know—before today, I mean—was why. And I know that, in lieu of earning an honest living, you spend your time going to parties where you inveigle men who have more dollars than sense to give you lots of money and make promises for more. For a good cause," he hastened to add.

There. Take that, Ms. Carly Nesbitt of the East Hampton Nesbitts who had doubtless stiffed at least one SoHo bartender in her time.

By the time he finished, her mouth had flattened into a tight line and her eyes had narrowed. "Well, my, my, my. Someone has been doing his homework. And do you know my bra size, too?" she asked caustically.

This time Tanner was the one to give Carly a good once-over, but he lingered over her midsection since, hell, she'd asked for it. Not sure what possessed him to do it, he took a single step forward, bringing his body within inches of hers. And then, since she'd also asked for it, however indirectly, he dipped a hand under each side of her open leather motorcycle jacket. At no time did he touch her body. But he pushed the garment open to give himself a better view of the part of her anatomy to which she had directed his gaze, since, in case he hadn't mentioned it, she'd asked for it. When he finally glanced at her face again, it was to find Carly Nesbitt blushing.

And just like that, he felt the upper hand slip firmly back into his grasp.

"Thirty-six C," he said with confidence as he withdrew his hands and let her jacket fall back into place. "Though it fits a bit more snugly than you'd like, doesn't it?"

Her lips parted in surprise, as if she couldn't believe he'd just spoken to her the way he had. To be honest, Tanner couldn't believe it, either. He wasn't usually a jerk with women. He liked women a lot and he was generally a pretty easygoing guy. But something in Carly Nesbitt brought out the worst in him.

His annoyance with himself compounded when she pulled her jacket closed, her cheeks stained with what he told himself must be anger and couldn't possibly be embarrassment. He started to apologize, then stopped himself. Maybe it would be better if she just went on thinking the worst of him. Because something about her discomfort made him think better of her.

Awkwardly she extended his ID toward him, and Tanner tucked it back into his coat pocket.

"My sister doesn't live here anymore," she said, still not looking at him. "And she isn't expected. Not today. Not ever. Now if you'll excuse me, Mr. Gillespie, my mother and father *are* expecting *me* for dinner."

"They're expecting your sister, too," Tanner said flatly. "She's due anytime. And they're expecting me, as well, since I'm one of the agents assigned to keep an eye on her."

That got Carly's attention again, and she returned her gaze to his. But only long enough to slip her wrap-around sunglasses on over her eyes, after which Tanner saw nothing more of what she was thinking.

"What's she done now?" she demanded.

"Actually she was kind of an innocent bystander in the situation," Tanner said.

"What's she done?" Carly repeated.

"She's helping us catch a very bad person."

That made Carly's mouth twitch. But all she said was, "I see."

Obviously the elder Nesbitts hadn't clued their other children in to what was going on, in spite of having been alerted early that morning to the situation. Tanner wondered why not. Yes, OPUS had rushed this operation into production, but there had still been time for the family to be made aware of what was going on. All of them were in town and all of them had telephones. And cell phones. And e-mail. And PDAs. And BlackBerrys. And every other damned device engineered to keep people hooked up to every damned thing in the universe every damned minute of the day.

But Tanner saw no reason why he couldn't alert Carly Nesbitt to the situation, since she was living in the house where the situation would be unfolding. "My agency has made arrangements with your parents to house Avery here for her own safety while the investigation is under way," he said.

That made Carly chuckle out loud. "Her own safety," she echoed.

Tanner nodded.

"How long will this investigation last?" she asked. "And how exactly did Avery get involved in the first place?"

"I'm not at liberty to discuss the particulars of an ongoing investigation," he said, assuming his no-nonsense OPUS agent voice that people knew not to question.

"Oh, great. *Now* what's she done?"

Well, *most* people knew not to question his no-nonsense OPUS agent voice. Tanner sighed. Slowly, deliberately, he repeated, "I'm not. At liberty. To discuss. The particulars. Of an ongoing. Investigation."

Carly stared at him through the black lenses of her sunglasses and offered not one iota as to what she was thinking. "Fine," she said. "And I. Can't invite. Strangers. Into. My house. Jerk."

With that, she jingled the keys she had by now fished out of her purse, turned her back on Tanner quite literally and let herself into the house. Then—it went without saying—she slammed the door in his face. Leaving Tanner to think something along the lines of how it was going to be a long investigation. Too long, in fact.

And about how maybe he was going to have to tame the Nesbitt shrew after all.

SHE WAS COMING HOME.

That thought more than any other circled around in Carly Nesbitt's head as she pressed her entire body back against the front door. She splayed her hands open wide against it, as if it were going to be not her little sister but the big, bad wolf himself huffing and puffing on the other side.

Then again…

But even remembering Tanner Gillespie's silky golden hair and midnight-blue eyes and those oh-my-God good looks couldn't quite pull Carly's thoughts away from Avery.

There. She'd thought her sister's name even if she still couldn't bring herself to speak it aloud. But even thinking it felt weird after all these years. A decade. That was how long it had been since Carly had seen her sister. Her last glimpse of Avery had been on a television set with the sound turned down low so that no one would know she was watching it. Her parents had forbidden Carly and her brother from watching any coverage of Avery's trial. But that hadn't kept Carly, at least, from seeing every second of it. And when CNN had carried Avery's sentencing live, she couldn't have stayed away from the TV any more than she could have stopped the sun from rising the next day.

She remembered feeling sick to her stomach as she'd waited for the judge's announcement, remembered marveling at Avery's sedate demeanor in the courtroom. Not once in her life had Carly seen her sister express any emotion that wasn't extreme, from exuberance to desolation. There had certainly never been a sedate. Avery had been the talk of East Hampton when they were growing up, unlike Carly, who had always tried to do the right thing and been completely overlooked when achieving it. But then, how could anyone notice her when Avery was just so…out there?

The day her sentence came down, though, Carly would have bet the entire Nesbitt fortune that Avery was wishing she was the one who'd always been overlooked. But what the hell had she expected, sabotaging half the planet the way she had? That they'd let her off with a warning, as her father had done time and time again? That she'd trip away happily to wreak havoc another day, as she always had in East Hampton? Not bloody likely. Not when she'd pissed off the Pope. Not to mention Greenland.

Nevertheless, when the judge sentenced Avery to ten

years in prison, Carly had felt as if someone hit her with a brick. She recalled how her sister's entire body had gone limp at the words, how her attorneys had each grabbed one arm and pulled her back to standing. Carly's little sister. The international criminal mastermind. It had been a coup de grâce to crown the empire of pandemonium Avery had spent her life creating.

After Carly had turned off the TV, she'd done her best to put thoughts of Avery out of her mind. She wasn't a member of the family anymore, that was what their father kept saying. Avery had finally gone too far, had overstepped the bounds of Nesbittdom—which admittedly stretched pretty damned far, Carly knew. They would never speak of her again. That was what her father decreed. He relegated his youngest offspring to the netherworld of slurs to polite society, where also dwelled things like income taxes, domestic wines, Third World countries and the Democratic Party. Just like those heinous things, they would pretend Avery didn't exist. And as had always been the case in the Nesbitt household, Desmond Nesbitt's word was law.

Over the years Carly had done pretty well not thinking about her sister. Holidays were the hardest to get through, but since Avery's estrangement from the family, holidays had been easier in a way, too. Certainly they'd been more peaceful. Ultimately Carly and Desi Jr. had won more of their parents' attention, more of their parents' favor, more of their parents' affection— such as it was. And with Avery gone, the family's social standing in the community had slowly risen again. Once it could be guaranteed that one could invite the Nesbitts to a gathering without incident or embarrassment, more invitations had been extended. And accepted. And enjoyed. Over the years the Nesbitt name had lost its tarnish and turned to silver again. Not that it was sterling yet, not quite. But with Avery out of the picture, it would eventually return to its original peerless status.

Now Avery was coming back. And Tanner Gillespie was going to be keeping an eye on her. Well, wasn't that just like her little sister to command every last scrap of attention?

Avery, who had *always* had to do things *her* way. In preschool, she'd sabotaged the sandboxes, insisting the sand should be allowed to roam free. In elementary school, she'd painted rainbows in shades of gray, declaring they shouldn't be defined by their color. In junior high, she'd run for student council president on the Communist Party ticket, promising to abolish school tuition and open exclusive Brenner Academy to all. And in high school, when all the other girls—like Carly ten years earlier—made their debuts in lovely white designer dresses and diamond-studded tiaras, Avery had shown up for her coming out in basic black. Army fatigues. And tank top. And beret. And combat boots. And a button that said Anarchy is for Lovers.

It hadn't gone over well with their parents.

Or East Hampton in general.

But all of those things had been forgiven. As had the time Avery sneaked onto the Abernathys' property in the middle of the night to "Free the Thoroughbreds!" a movement which—go figure—nobody else in the Hamptons had embraced. And she'd also been forgiven—eventually—for the "Embrace Your Inner Nudist" episode at the Dorseys' Fourth of July barbecue. And also for the Libertarian Party fund-raiser she hosted at home on her eighteenth birthday—without her parents' permission or knowledge…until it was too late—that featured the punk sounds of Shagmore Hiney and the Blisters.

Avery was always forgiven. Until she did the unforgivable.

Nesbitts did not go to jail. That wasn't to say they didn't break the law. Nesbitts had a long history of taking advantage of people, not to mention cheating on their taxes. Such practices had contributed largely to their current social status. There had been other episodes of unlawfulness in the family history, too, but no one had ever been caught. It was even rumored that her great-great-uncle Milton Nesbitt, the railroad tycoon, had killed a man, then married the widow a week later. But that had never been proven, and the man's death had been ruled an accident. Though how having one's trachea crushed by a railroad tie in one's study while one was enjoying a snifter of brandy and a good book could be accidental, no one had ever explained to Carly's satisfaction. These days, no one talked about such things.

But they still talked about Avery.

Why was she coming here? Carly wondered. No matter what kind of trouble she was in or had caused, what reason could there possibly be for bringing her back to East Hampton?

Of course, Carly could have had that question answered immediately if she just opened the door and invited Agent Tanner Gillespie into the house. Oh, right now he might be thinking he couldn't discuss the particulars of an ongoing investigation, but fifteen minutes alone with her and he'd be begging to tell her everything he knew about every case his little spy organization had ever undertaken. Carly just had that kind of effect on men—all modesty aside, since she didn't have any modesty—and she'd had years to hone that skill to perfection. Mostly because none of the men she'd used it on had ever been man enough to handle her for longer than a few months.

It *wasn't* because she was shrill and demanding, as one of those men had told her once. And it *wasn't* because she had nothing to offer a man beyond her obvious physical appeal, as another had said. And it wasn't because she was shrewish or exacting or mean or bitchy or any of those other things she'd overheard herself called in ladies' rooms over the years while she'd sat undiscovered in a stall.

It was because of Avery. Avery was the reason Carly had never married. What man in his right mind would want to marry into a family that had spawned such a creature? Clearly the Nesbitt DNA was impaired in some way if it had generated the likes of Avery. Even if it was a rogue gene floating around somewhere, who wanted to take the chance that it might show up in one's own offspring? Carly didn't blame anyone for not wanting to get too close. She admired her brother's wife for having had the courage to take a dip in the Nesbitt gene pool. Of course, Desi and Jessica had yet to procreate, so maybe the plan was for him to swim upstream for the rest of his life in an effort to spawn. But still, at least Desi had someone to swim with.

Not that Carly hadn't been swimming plenty of times herself. Often with swimmers of Olympic caliber. But she'd never been able to find a man with a really good breaststroke. And none of them had been worthy of putting on a platform and hanging a medal on.

So who did Tanner Gillespie think he was to make her heart race wildly and blood rush to her head? He was a kid. An insolent kid, at that, she thought further, recalling the way he had pushed her jacket open to get a better look at her before announcing her bra size exactly, right down to the tight fit.

And just like that her heart was racing wildly again and blood was rushing to her head at a dizzying pace. Terrific. This was just terrific. Avery was coming home. And she was bringing someone like Tanner Gillespie with her. Carly sighed with something akin to longing and pushed herself away from the front door.

Ladies and gentlemen, she thought as she made her way toward the sweeping staircase that led to the upper floors, *let the games begin.*

CHAPTER SIX

AFTER ZIPPING CLOSED THE suitcase on her bed, Avery flattened both palms against it, closed her eyes and concentrated on her breathing. In. Out. In. Out. Slow. Steady. Deep. And she did what she always did whenever she felt a panic attack threatening and had time to ward it off. She repeated over and over to herself, *I have nothing to fear in this moment. In this moment, there is nothing to fear.* But of course, it wasn't this moment she was worried about. It was the next moment. And then the moment after that. And then the one after that.

Oh, God…

I have nothing to fear in this moment. In this moment, there is nothing to fear.

"How's it coming in there? You about ready?"

Dixon's question snapped her out of her mantra. And out of her panic, too, which was no small feat. Then again, she knew another way to battle her attacks was to focus on something that generated an emotion other than anxiety. And anger especially was a powerful antidote. So if nothing else, Dixon's presence in her life could potentially be the cure-all for her panic attacks.

Gee. For some reason, being trapped in her home for the rest of her life with no contact with the outside world suddenly didn't seem as bad as it used to.

"Avery?"

She expelled a disgruntled sigh. "What?"

"Are you ready to go?" he asked again.

It should have been an easy question. She looked at her overstuffed suitcase, then at Skittles's plush cat carrier, packed for travel with every creature comfort the creature could want. Avery had changed from her mismatched pajamas and sweatshirt into worn blue jeans, a bulky, faded indigo sweater and hiking boots. She'd woven her hair into one fat braid that fell to nearly her waist, perched her glasses onto her nose and fastened three different sets of earrings into the six holes in her earlobes. She was as ready, she supposed, as she'd ever be. Except for one thing.

"Did you fix the Thermos?" she called through the door.

"And I cut the lemon peels into those little curls, yeah," Dixon replied, a clear edge to his voice. "Even though there's an open-container law in this state that could land us in trouble if we get pulled over on the way to East Hampton."

"Especially when no self-respecting cop will buy a phony-baloney Cap'n Crunch ID like yours," Avery muttered.

Dixon ignored her. "Now can we go? I told Gillespie we'd meet him at your folks' house at four, which was five minutes ago. It doesn't look good for the senior agent to fall down on the job, especially when the newbie is still technically in training."

Avery strode slowly to her bedroom door and opened it to find Dixon looming on the other side, and instinctively took a step backward. Good God, the man was big. And he was no less intimidating—or handsome—

now than he had been the first time she'd opened her door to him. Had that actually been less than forty-eight hours ago? she marveled. It felt as if weeks had passed since she'd met him. Today he was wearing more of those snug, formfitting blue jeans, paired with a slouchy heather gray sweatshirt that read, in big blue letters, GWU. George Washington University, she translated. So he'd spent time living in the nation's capital. She wondered how long ago and where he lived now. Not that she cared. But she did wonder.

"Can I have one for the road?" she asked.

He lifted a hand and extended a drink toward her, having already anticipated the question.

"Gee, how can I ever thank you?" she asked as she gratefully accepted it.

"By not becoming an alcoholic," he said tersely.

"Not to worry," she said before enjoying a generous swallow. She closed her eyes as the liquor warmed her throat and spread heat through her chest and stomach. "I only consume more than one drink when I have to go out somewhere."

"How many more than one?" he asked.

She opened her eyes. "Five more than one." But she hurried on, "And since I don't go out more than a couple of times a year—or at least I didn't go out more than a couple of times a year before I met *you*—the only way I'll overdo it is if you hang around in my life much longer."

"No worries there, either," he retorted. "The sooner we wrap this thing up, Peaches, the sooner I'll scoot."

She nodded disconsolately. Unfortunately, to achieve that, they would be returning to the environment that had spawned her. Talk about being driven to drink. Who knew what she would be forced to endure over the next few days? The next few weeks? The next few months? Oh, man, how long was this going to take anyway?

She inhaled another mouthful of scotch and looked at Dixon, this time for a full five seconds before having to look away. Hey, she was getting better at that. "How long will it take to wrap up?" she asked.

"Depends," he told her.

"On what?"

"On how long it takes you to draw your boy Andrew out."

Her boy Andrew, she echoed bitterly to herself. Would that he *had* been Andrew—and hers—she might have actually found someone with whom she could share her life. She'd stopped hoping for something like that years ago, had been resigned to spending her life in solitary confinement. Then, like magic, out of nowhere, Andrew had appeared, and she had let herself dream again. The first dreams she'd enjoyed for a very long time.

She should have known better than to let optimism overtake pragmatism. She'd suffered enough life lessons by now to know that hoping for something didn't mean jack. Andrew didn't exist. His appearance in her life hadn't been magic. On the contrary, if what Dixon said was true, it had been part of some nefarious plan this Adrian Padgett guy was hatching to take over the world. He'd only wanted Avery for her knowledge of computers and viruses and her ability to wreak mayhem on the Net—and the global community. He hadn't wanted her for herself. Now she was back where she'd been before, where she would always be. Alone.

But then why was she surprised? How could she

have believed someone as dreamy and wonderful as the imaginary Andrew could have been interested in her as a woman? As a human being? As anything other than what she continued to be in most people's minds—a criminal-mastermind dissident who could bring down the entire world with the click of a mouse? No way could a man just want to get to know her better because he liked her.

It was laughable, really, the reputation Avery had been saddled with in the aftermath of her college fiasco as a corrupt, antiestablishment, rabble-rousing zealot who wanted to stick it to the system. Even today, she was still the topic of conversation—nay, the *hero*—of corrupt, antiestablishment, rabble-rousing zealots everywhere. But she'd never been any of those things. She'd been a wounded teenage girl whose heart had been broken, and in her hurt and her anger she'd wanted to strike back at the boy responsible. It was the simplest, most basic thing in the world to understand. Instead, thanks to her own carelessness and stupidity, she'd become an icon of the counterculture, a hero to hackers and misfits everywhere, a criminal mastermind who wanted to bring the end of the world as we know it and still feel fine.

Now OPUS wanted her to exploit the reputation she'd never deserved in the first place, the rep she'd spent a decade trying to escape. She'd have to stay in touch with this Adrian guy—who really *was* a criminal mastermind—and pretend she still believed he was Andrew. She'd been told to continue with what she'd thought would be a love affair of epic proportions, but gradually to start talking to him about politics and society and American culture and to voice her distaste for them all. Which to some degree she already had, so that shouldn't be too difficult to make convincing. But she was also supposed to make Adrian think she was the same kind of person he was, so that he would invite her more quickly into whatever he was plotting to do.

And then she was supposed to meet him.

That part of the assignment, more than any other, scared the hell out of her. Not because she would be coming face-to-face with a man who could be dangerous, but because she would have to leave the safety of her home, her life, to do it.

It had been horrible to be dragged from her apartment to a small white room. It would be worse returning to the rambling estate where she grew up. But those experiences were nothing compared to the unmitigated terror Avery felt at the thought of being in the open, where anything could happen. In a small white room she could still feel some measure of safety, still entertain the illusion, at least, that she could see what was coming and be prepared for it. At her parents' house she would at least be in familiar surroundings, and the house would be enclosed. But out in the open, in the city, where there was so much beyond her control, where there were so many strangers and so many things that could go wrong…

She lifted her drink again, her heart rate doubling just at the idea of being outside in the open. She couldn't do it. She wouldn't do it. Not even with a case of Scotland's finest sloshing around inside her. There was no way. She'd tried to explain that to them, but they'd pooh-poohed her concern, assuring her that when the time came for her to meet Adrian, she *would* meet Adrian. Because if she didn't, then she'd be reneging on her part of the deal. And if she reneged on her part of the deal, then OPUS would have no alternative but to renege on their part, as well. They'd report her for building the virus, however ineffective it had been. And that would send Avery right back to prison.

I have nothing to fear in this moment, she told herself rapidly. *In this moment, there is nothing to fear.*

"Avery?"

I have nothing to fear in this moment. In this moment, there is nothing to fear.

"Avery."

I have nothing to fear in this moment. In this moment, there is nothing to—

"Avery!"

"What?"

Dixon set his jaw hard. "It's time to go."

She slugged back what was left of her drink and closed her eyes tight. There was everything to fear in this moment. In this moment, there was everything to fear.

She nodded once and swallowed hard, and made herself focus on the matter at hand. "All right," she said. "I'm ready. Let's go."

DIXON'S BREATH HITCHED in his diaphragm as they rounded the final curve of the long, winding drive that led to the Nesbitt estate and he caught his first glimpse of Avery's childhood home. He came from a moneyed background himself, but he'd never seen anything like this. Not up close, anyway. Not in person.

"It's called Cobble Court," she said as if she'd read his mind.

Sparing a glance at the passenger side of the car,

Dixon saw Avery in profile, her gaze riveted to the looming mansion on the horizon. Her posture was as stiff as…well, a stiff, just as it had been since they'd left her apartment, and her fingers were wrapped white-knuckle around the now-empty thermos in her lap. In spite of her drinking throughout the trip, she seemed stone-cold sober. Fear must be a potent remedy for in-sobriety. Because there was something in her expression that made Dixon think she was even more frightened now than she'd been the night he'd carried her out of her apartment. *Going home* for Avery obviously wasn't the fuzzy, heartwarming condition it was for all those people on the Hallmark Channel. Without questioning why he did it, he eased his foot off the accelerator and the car slowed.

Her expression was the only thing about her that re-sembled the woman he'd met two nights ago. Last time he'd seen her, she'd been a skirmish of color in ugly pajama bottoms and torn sweatshirt, her hair caught in two lopsided braids. A rebel with a really weird cause. Today she was more subdued in varying shades of blue that enhanced the vivid azure of her eyes, her hair plaited into one neat braid. She still smelled like peaches, though, and the source of the fragrance was driving Dixon nuts. She didn't seem the type for perfumes or self-pampering, but the scent of her was nearly intoxicating.

"Yes, my parents live in a house that has a name," she continued in a flat voice. "Only they're not the ones who named it. My great-grandfather named it that when he built it more than a hundred years ago. Not that he built it himself, mind you," she hastened to add. "He paid nonunion workers as little as possible to erect his holy shrine to the almighty dollar. One of those workers even died building this place. Slipped on the roof and fell to his death. And my great-grandfather honored the man's sacrifice by giving his wife and children five whole dollars. One dollar for each child. Wasn't that generous of him?"

Dixon said nothing. As lousy as her great-grandfather sounded, the man probably hadn't been any worse than any other greedy carpetbagger of the day. And it was easy for someone like Avery to spout the cause of the downtrodden and exploited, coming from billions of dollars as she did. He'd been brought up in the rarefied air of the privileged, too—though not the über-privileged, as she had—and he'd had his share of friends who'd shown contempt for their wealth. But had any of them ever offered to give it up? Had any of them delved into their trust funds to ease the burden of the common man? Not likely.

Not that Dixon should be pointing any fingers. He hadn't delved into his trust fund for that, either. Of course, he hadn't dipped into his trust fund at all. He'd worked for OPUS since his graduation from college, in one capacity or another. But it was nice to know the money was there. Still, his family's wealth paled in comparison to the Nesbitts'.

"He was an industrialist, my great-grandfather," Avery went on as they drew nearer to the house.

Dixon probably knew more about the Nesbitt wealth than Avery did, but he let her keep talking. She needed something to occupy her mind, to keep the fear at bay.

"Great-Grandfather Nesbitt was one of those guys who made tons of money doing business," she continued, her voice taking on a kind of singsong quality as the scotch finally kicked in. "He was right up there with Carnegie and Astor and…and…" She waved a hand airily in front of her face. "And all those other guys like that. He made huge, reeking piles of cash by taking advantage of the working man. And he wanted to make sure everyone knew it. So he built this place. And he named it. And he made sure it would always remain in the family and that it would always be inhabited by Nesbitts." She inhaled a breath, released it and concluded in an ominous voice, "World without end. Amen, amen."

"It's a beautiful place," Dixon said with much understatement.

The evening sun was dipping low behind them now, pouring a runnel of red-gold light over the massive Tudor mansion, making it glow like an amber jewel in the early twilight. Behind it, the sky had begun to purple imperiously, ennobling the place even more. The vast lawn was surprisingly hardy for November, and it billowed out before the estate in a seemingly endless wave of—well, there was no way around it—a dark grayish-green the color of currency.

"Eighteen thousand square feet," Avery went on as if she couldn't shift her mind to another topic besides the house. "Twenty-two acres of land. Nearly two thousand feet of frontage on the pond. Ocean views from the back of the house. Seven bedrooms, plus a two-bedroom guesthouse—that, I imagine, is where you and your little friend Gillespie will be staying, since I can't see my mother allowing your kind in the big house."

Dixon was pretty sure she was being sarcastic with that comment, but he decided not to ask.

"Other amenities," she added, "include a guest suite on the first floor, a billiards room, a movie theater, a gymnasium, a wine cellar, an elevator, both indoor and outdoor pools, a lovely pool house, tennis court with viewing pavilion, greenhouse, heated four-car garage and private dock. There are also several whirlpool tubs, a centralized music system, a dozen phone lines and, it goes without saying, a state-of-the-art security system. Some of those are more recent additions to the house," she added in an almost stagelike aside. "Though I'm sure Great-Grandfather would have had them all had they been available in his day. And I'm also sure the house has even more stuff now than it did the last time I was here. My father has always kept up with the latest technology."

Dixon wasn't sure what to say in response to all that. Except maybe *Holy shit.* Finally he decided on, "You sound like a real-estate agent trying to unload the place."

She expelled a soft sound of derision. "Would that I could unload it, I'd be a happier woman." Before he could ask what she meant—not that he didn't already understand—she added, "Fifty million dollars. That's how much it's worth on today's market." She paused before concluding, "Prison never looked as good as it does right now."

Dixon wheeled the car around the cobblestone circle before the house and pulled to a halt in front of Gillespie's car. Behind it was parked an apple-red Jaguar roadster, and behind the Jag was an enormous black Mercedes. Looked like the whole family had turned out to welcome Avery home. Damn them.

He cut the ignition and climbed out, but Avery stayed

rooted where she was. So he circled the car to the trunk, opened it and unloaded the three pieces of luggage within. Avery stayed rooted where she was. He slammed the trunk lid down, made two trips to carry the luggage up to the front door. Avery stayed rooted where she was. He greeted the butler who came out to help, was told that the Nesbitts and Mr. Gillespie were awaiting Mr. Dixon and Miss Avery's arrival in the library and went back to the car. Avery stayed rooted where she was.

In fact, he didn't think she'd moved a single body part since he'd thrown the car into park. Because she still sat stiffly in the passenger seat, her hands gripping the empty Thermos in her lap, her head turned to stare at the house, her lips parted softly, as if she'd been planning to say something but was pulled up short before the words could come.

Gingerly Dixon rapped his knuckles on the window, a gesture that made her flinch but still didn't grab her attention. So he straightened and opened the passenger-side door, thinking that might give her a hint. Avery stayed rooted to the spot.

Great. She was doing that catatonic thing again.

Slowly he bent forward and reached across her lap to unhook her seat belt, but before he could grab it, it zipped back into its holder with a vicious snap. Avery jerked at the sound, blinking this time, and turned her head toward Dixon's, mere inches away.

She blinked several times in rapid succession, and very quietly said, "Dixon."

"Yeah, it's me," he said gently. "We're home, Avery."

She went a little pale at that but nodded. Not sure why he did it, he extended a hand toward her, palm out.

To his surprise, she accepted it, settling her own palm against his. Her hand was damp and cool, but it was steady. She might be holding on by a thread, but she was holding on. He doubted he'd ever understand this agoraphobia thing, but he could tell there was something powerful going on inside her just then. He hoped someday, somehow, she learned how to deal with it.

Still holding his hand, she unfolded herself from the car and stood. She looked not at Dixon but at the house, her gaze scanning it from top to bottom, from left to right, before pinpointing the open front door. She smiled, and Dixon turned to see that the old butler was standing framed in the doorway, his dark suit flawless, his gray hair slicked back, the ghost of a smile playing about his own lips.

"Jensen," Avery said quietly, her smile growing broader.

Still holding her hand, Dixon strode with her to the front steps and up them, halting when she did, a few feet shy of the front door.

"Miss Avery," Jensen greeted her. With very clear affection he added, "It is so very good to have you home."

So Avery had an ally here after all, Dixon thought. The realization made him feel better. Good to know she wasn't entering completely hostile territory. Because even without Avery's obvious reluctance to return to her childhood home, Dixon knew she didn't feel welcome here. Probably that was because she *wasn't* welcome here. Not by anyone besides the butler, at any rate.

The two of them stood looking at each other for an awkward moment, then, clumsily, as if it were an action she wasn't used to performing, Avery leaned forward and gave Jensen a brief hug. Really brief. Like she just ricocheted her body off his and stepped back again. Jensen seemed as surprised to receive the gesture as Avery was to offer it, but he lifted a hand to pat her on the back as she embraced him—only once, though, since that was all he had time for.

"What's the mood like in there?" Avery asked him.

"Not good," Jensen told her. "Miss Carly is here."

Avery's older sister, Dixon knew. He'd read about her in the society rags when he'd been doing his research on the Nesbitt family. In fact, he'd seen almost as many items about Carly Nesbitt's activities as he had about Avery's trial and errors. Interestingly, Carly's reputation in the Hamptons didn't seem to be much better than Avery's, if for different reasons. But where Avery's behavior had cost businesses worldwide a gazillion dollars in lost revenues, Carly's behavior had resulted in the voluntary forking over of a gazillion dollars from some of those same businesses to worthy causes here in the U.S. So it wasn't that corporate America hated losing money to the Nesbitt sisters. They just wanted to be sure they had a receipt for their tax write-offs when it went.

At any rate, there seemed to be as many tongues in East Hampton wagging behind Carly's back as there had been behind Avery's. But where Avery had at least committed a genuine crime to cause her own bad rep, Carly's seemed to have come about because she was notoriously bitchy. So really, who would you rather have at *your* next party?

It was a rhetorical question, naturally. Dixon didn't want *any* of the Nesbitts at his next party.

"Your brother is here, as well," Jensen said. "Along with his wife."

"Jessica," Avery said. "They've been married four years now, huh?"

She knew her sister-in-law's name and the date of her brother's wedding, even though she couldn't have been there for any of the celebration, Dixon thought. Only then did he really start to comprehend what it must be like to be exiled from one's family. To miss milestone events like weddings and births and graduations and funerals. To be absent from holidays like Christmas and Thanksgiving.

And because of her agoraphobia, Avery couldn't go out with friends to celebrate such things, either. Then again, from what Dixon could tell, she didn't have any friends anyway—at least none who weren't online. She must spend her holidays and mark her milestones alone with her cat. And she'd been doing it for eight years.

Dixon couldn't imagine such a thing. Certainly he didn't see as much of his family as most people did, thanks to his line of work. But he had friends and he knew he was welcome at home. He made it home for most holidays. He'd been there for his sister's wedding and his father's memorial service. He received cards and letters and e-mail from them on a regular basis. They talked on the phone. He was emotionally connected to all of them in a way that Avery had been denied.

What would it be like if all that disappeared? How would he feel if his family suddenly decided he was no longer entitled to share their lives? If they decided to pretend he didn't exist?

Pretty crappy, he decided. And pretty pissed.

But Avery just seemed sad. Really, really sad. Maybe by the time ten years passed, sadness was all that was left. But she'd still kept tabs on them, if she knew her sister-in-law's name and how long her brother had been married and the current market value of her parents' home. Interesting, that.

"How are Mother and Father?" she asked Jensen.

The butler smiled a little sadly himself. "Come and see for yourself," he told her.

Inhaling a deep breath, Avery nodded, then turned to look at Dixon. "I'm ready," she told him.

Well, Dixon thought, that made one of them.

CHAPTER SEVEN

NOTHING HAD CHANGED.

As Avery walked through the house where she had lived for the first seventeen years of her life—and from which she had been exiled for the last ten—she realized it looked exactly as she had left it. A creamy-yellow foyer bled into a long marigold hall that bisected the house into north and south wings. The hardwood floor was buffed to a honeyed sheen, and a massive flowered Aubusson spanned the bulk of it. To the right, a sweeping staircase curved up to the second-floor gallery, and to the left, the parlor was awash with varying shades of green. Her mother had always thought rooms should be identified by their colors instead of their functions, so no two in the big house were the same.

As Avery strode through the house with Dixon following, she glanced into each room they passed and was hit by one memory after another. The music room, lush in its random bits of blue, where she and Carly and Desi had learned to play piano from Mr. Willis. The mahogany-paneled living room, which glowed during the day with its floor-to-ceiling windows, its chocolate-colored leather sofa and chairs now bathed in the mellow amber of lamplight. The bloodred formal dining room with its huge Mediterranean-style table and chairs, where her parents had entertained like a feudal lord and lady. On holidays and during parties, the house had come alive.

It felt so strange to be here. Avery had had such a love-hate relationship with Cobble Court. She had reveled in its sumptuous elegance, had marveled at its breathtaking beauty. As a child, she had thought herself incredibly fortunate to call the house home. But as she'd grown up and learned more about the world, when she had discovered how so many other people were forced to live with so little, how many people had terrible homes or no homes at all, she'd begun to feel guilty living here.

Fifty million dollars, she thought again as she drew nearer the library where her family—such as it was—awaited her arrival. How many decent homes could that much money buy for decent people who deserved decent housing? Hundreds, easily. Although her father had never discussed his wealth with his children—he probably didn't even discuss it with his wife—Avery knew what her family was worth. Desmond Nesbitt could give away billions of dollars and still be a billionaire. But he held on to every last penny.

Of course, Avery was worth millions herself. And not just from her trust fund, but from the security business she ran from her home. But she did share her wealth, was a regular contributor to several worthy causes. She knew her father's company, if not the man himself, donated charitably. But it was more for the tax break than it was philanthropy. And she knew, too, that her sister Carly volunteered to raise millions more. Somehow, though, the balance still seemed weighted much too heavily in the Nesbitts' favor.

In spite of her ambivalence about her childhood home, Avery had assumed Cobble Court would always *be* her home. Maybe not as it was for Carly, who continued to live here as an adult—Avery had always planned to have her own place after she graduated from college. But she'd figured she would return for special occasions or when she needed to retreat to the familiar. She had counted on the house being here for her no matter what. It had been comforting to know that if life threw her a curve she couldn't handle, she'd have a place to call home. Always.

But now she was a guest here. Less than a guest, really. Guests were invited. Avery hadn't been. So really she was just a visitor here. And an unwelcome visitor at that.

That was made even clearer as she made her way deeper into the house, because she saw that there was indeed something that had changed in her absence. On the walls and tables where her mother displayed framed photographs of the family, all the ones that had included Avery were gone. Her school pictures. The vacation photos of the family. The portraits of the three Nesbitt children. Something cold and sharp twisted inside her to realize it.

The library loomed immediately ahead, and Avery halted abruptly before reaching it. So abruptly that Dixon, who had been bringing up the rear, walked right into her. She stumbled forward until he reached out and caught her, pulling her back toward himself. But he overcompensated—or maybe Avery was the one to overcompensate—and she tripped backward, falling against him. Hard.

Instead of jerking away from him, though, something

kept her pinned to the spot. Something other than Dixon's hands cupped gently over her shoulders, she meant. Her reluctance to enter the library, she told herself. Her unwillingness to see the family who'd turned its back on her. Anything would be better than that. Even being plastered against Dixon.

Because she was plastered against Dixon. And neither of them was doing anything about it. She felt the press of him from her shoulders to her calves, was more aware of the heat in his big body than her own. She waited for the fear that should have come at being so close to him, braced herself for the inescapable panic, waited for the mental mantra that would keep her calm. But none of those things happened. Instead she heard herself say the strangest thing.

"Dixon, please don't leave me."

The fingers he had cupped over her shoulders skimmed downward, wrapping gently around her upper arms. "I won't," he said. And there was something in his voice that hadn't been there before, something she told herself she needed to identify, something that was gone before she had the chance.

"Do you promise?" she asked softly.

He hesitated not at all before assuring her, "I promise."

She inhaled a deep breath and stepped forward, the action moving her away from Dixon and causing her a moment of panic. But only a moment. Knowing he was behind her, she felt more secure in what she was doing. Kind of. Sort of. In a way.

I have nothing to fear in this moment, she thought as she took another step forward. *In this moment, there is nothing to fear....*

WHY HAD SHE ASKED HIM THAT? Dixon wondered as he followed Avery into the library. Hell, she knew he wasn't going anywhere until this assignment was over. And she'd made it clear she was in no way happy about that. So why suddenly did she ask him not to leave her? And why had she said it the way she had, all soft and quiet and fearful? He didn't have time to think more about it, though, because Avery halted at the library entrance, bringing him to a stop, too.

The library was furnished like the rest of the house, in Early Ostentation. But where the other rooms he'd seen had been color-coded, there was a mix of hues here.

The ceiling and walls were paneled in burled walnut, and the furnishings were leather, the color of ruby port, reinforced with shiny brass tacks. A large fireplace spanned much of the left-hand wall, its mantelpiece crowded by candlesticks, vases and a massive antique clock. The hardwood floors shone with a high gloss, obscured here and there by a scattering of jewel-toned Persian rugs in different but complementary patterns. The far wall consisted of beveled floor-to-ceiling windows that offered a breathtaking view of the expansive back lawn and the pond beyond. With the trees bare, there was a scant glimpse of the ocean in the distance, though during the greener months it would be obscured. From one of the upper floors the view was probably spectacular.

The rest of the library walls were shelves housing all manner of books. Old Man Nesbitt must be a serious collector. Around the perimeter of the room, about a foot below the ceiling, was a metal rod with a ladder attached on coasters. For some reason, the moment

Dixon saw it, a vision erupted in his brain of Avery as a child, hanging from that ladder as she pushed it all the way around the room, long pigtails flying, peals of laughter ringing…until someone—her mother, probably—discovered her and put an end to the play.

As he concluded his inspection of the room, Dixon's gaze fell on Cowboy, who stood in the farthest corner, both hands shoved deep into his trouser pockets. He looked very unhappy. Unless compared to everyone else in the room, in which case he looked downright jolly. A woman stood in the corner opposite Cowboy, and Dixon pegged her as the younger Desmond Nesbitt's wife. Everyone else was parked in the sitting area closest to the entry, as if they were huddling together against a storm that lashed the house outside.

Dixon considered each in turn, testing himself on his knowledge as he went. Might as well start at the top of the Nesbitt pecking order, with the big cock himself—Desmond Nesbitt IV. Upholding the tradition of the big Nesbitt cocks before him, he headed up the multinational, multibillion-dollar Nesbitt Corporation. Desmonds I, II and III had been known in their respective times as industrialists. Desmond IV, however, called a spade a spade—he ID'd himself as a bona fide capitalist and he didn't let anyone forget it. His personal wealth was estimated at nearly six billion dollars. Throw in the corporate assets, and he was one of the ten wealthiest men in America.

This evening he looked every inch the financial despot relaxing at home. At sixty-eight, he was a strikingly handsome man, with the same piercing blue eyes characteristic of all the Nesbitts and a full head of silver-white hair. He was dressed in coffee-brown corduroys, a white dress shirt sans tie and a cardigan sweater the color of a polo field.

Mrs. Desmond Nesbitt IV, née Felicia Hurstbourne, sat beside him, looking every inch the part she played in life—East Hampton Czarina. Although she was five years younger than her husband, she looked older. Her eyes were a duller blue than the rest of the family's— but her hair was as black as her children's, without a trace of gray, leading Dixon to conclude it was colored. It was bobbed at chin length, but she wore it swept back from her face with a tidy leather headband. Like her husband, she looked anything but relaxed relaxing in her home, wearing baggy cream-colored slacks—Dixon hesitated to call them trousers or even pants—and a matching turtleneck, cashmere, he was sure. Plain gold hoops were fastened in her ears, and the hands folded on her lap were surprisingly unadorned, save the massive wedding set that glittered almost blindly on her left hand.

On the love seat, seated far enough apart that it was clear there was no love lost between them, sat Avery's sister and brother, Carly and Desmond V, Desi to most, to avoid confusing him with his father. Carly looked like a tastefully dressed Elvira—if one could consider tasteful skintight leather and low-cut tops. Which Elvira probably would. Desi was a younger version of his father, only with dark hair, right down to the corduroys and cardigan—in his case, though, the cords were the color of a polo field and the sweater was chocolate-brown. His wife, still standing in the corner busily checking titles, had short blond hair, and she wore a straight charcoal skirt and black sweater.

Not the most colorful bunch in the world, Dixon

thought, Carly Nesbitt's red leather miniskirt notwith-standing. And interesting how the immediate family had all gathered together while the outsiders had exiled themselves to opposite corners. He understood, though. The Nesbitts had that effect on people.

Avery took a few steps forward, surprising Dixon when she reached for his hand. He let her take it and followed, widening his stride to catch up with her. She moved slowly but steadily toward the sofa and love seat grouping, eyeing each member of her family in turn. But none of the other Nesbitts looked at her.

Who would speak first? Dixon wondered. Who would throw down that gauntlet? The suspense was killing him....

"'Bout time you arrived," Cowboy said.

Of course. It *would* be the new guy putting his foot in it first.

Cowboy pushed himself away from the wall he'd been holding up and made his way toward Dixon and Avery. His expression indicated he'd been expecting them a *long* time ago. "Shall I make the introductions?" he continued, his voice edged with irritation. "I mean, the Nesbitts and I go *way* back. Almost two hours, in fact." He threw a leering look toward the love seat as he added, "And me and Carly have been together even longer than that."

"Mr. Gillespie and I are *not* together," Carly stated coolly.

Though who she was speaking to was a mystery, since she was gazing straight ahead at no one when she spoke. Still, Dixon figured chances were good that she *wasn't* speaking to her kid sister. Which currently made the Nesbitts zero for four in that regard. Five if you counted the Nesbitt by marriage. Call him crazy, but the odds weren't looking good for a happy reunion.

"I'll make the introductions."

Interestingly, it was the black sheep herself who bleated the offer, another surprise for Dixon. But where Avery's tone was quiet and even when she spoke, the hand gripping his convulsed. She extended her free hand, palm up, toward the sofa. It was trembling, Dixon saw.

"Dixon," she said softly, faltering a little on the word, "this is Desmond Nesbitt and his wife Felicia." She swung her hand toward the love seat, and he noticed it was trembling even more. "And this is Carly Nesbitt and her brother Desi." She dropped her hand back to her side and curled the fingers into a tight fist. "Desi will have to introduce his wife, I'm afraid, since I haven't had the pleasure of meeting her."

Wow, Dixon thought. That had been really polite. Evidently Avery had kept up with her Emily Post during ten years of exile from polite society. Of course, it didn't escape his notice that Avery had assigned no descriptive tags to anyone in her family that might identify them as members of her family. Nor did it escape his notice that no one in the family had jumped up to take exception to that. In fact, no one in the family spoke at all. They didn't even turn to look in her direction.

Dixon was about to say something himself—something like *Oh, for God's sake, people, get over yourselves*—when Carly Nesbitt rose and looked at Avery. She even smiled at her younger sister. Well, it kind of looked like a smile. If she stood a certain way. Like backward. But he decided not to hold it against her—yet.

Instead of speaking to Avery, Carly let her gaze roll

right off her sister—in the same way it might have rolled over a piece of lint on the rug—and rove to Dixon instead. "And who are you?" she asked. "Are you one of Gillespie's little friends?"

Dixon frowned. Okay, he'd hold it against her now. Bitch. He reached into his jacket pocket with the hand Avery wasn't choking to death, and extracted his ID. It took a moment for him to realize that Carly was waiting for him to step forward to hand it to her, and when he did realize that, Dixon stayed right where he was. She sighed a much-put-upon sigh and started to take a step forward, but before she completed it, Dixon tossed the leather case toward her. Oops. Guess he should pay closer attention next time. Caught off guard, Carly's eyes went wide, and she fumbled to catch the ID case. But it bounced off her fingers and landed on the floor a few feet away from her, not six inches from Cowboy's right foot.

She floundered for a second after the fact but quickly recovered her composure. After shaking her black curls from her face, she hooked one hand on her hip and waited for one of the men to retrieve the ID for her. So Dixon and Cowboy, in a rare occurrence of thinking the same way, exchanged identical expressions of bemusement and, as one, turned to gaze back at Carly in silence.

Carly frowned.

Dixon and Gillespie looked bemused.

She dipped her head toward the ID case lying on the floor.

They looked bemused.

She expelled a sound of clear exasperation and strode casually toward Cowboy, bending to scoop up the ID as she passed. Then she continued walking as if nothing out of the ordinary had happened, circling back to the love seat. And Dixon had to hand it to his temporary partner, because Cowboy didn't kick the case out of her reach before she got there, which Dixon couldn't have guaranteed he wouldn't have done himself, had their positions been switched.

"Santiago Dixon?" Carly said incredulously, glancing up from the case she had opened with one hand. "Am I actually supposed to believe that's your real name?"

In response to her question, Dixon released Avery's hand and strode forward, removed his ID case from Carly's fingers, stepped back and took Avery's hand in his again. In doing so he figured he'd acknowledged and replied to Carly Nesbitt, who was a stranger to him, which was more than she had done for her own sister.

He turned to Desmond IV. "Mr. Nesbitt," he said, "OPUS appreciates your cooperation in this matter." Though truly Dixon still didn't know why OPUS had wanted the man's cooperation in this matter. "Gillespie and I will do our best not to disrupt the normal routine of your family while we're here, and—"

"Just why *are* you here?" Carly demanded. "No one's really bothered to explain that to—"

"Not that someone didn't try," Cowboy interjected.

"—us in any way that's made sense," Carly continued as if he hadn't spoken. "And speaking as a resident of this house, which is more than I can say for most of the people in this room, I find the whole thing unbelievably inconvenient. Not to mention potentially dangerous. And also thoughtless. And crass."

"And tacky," Cowboy threw in. "Don't forget tacky."

Thinking it might be best to just ignore *every*one for

now, Dixon directed his reply to the elder Desmond. "With luck, Mr. Nesbitt, we won't have to stay here for more than a couple of weeks. Hopefully it will be less than one. There will be no danger to anyone in your family, and we'll do our best to stay out of your way." He would have assured the elder Nesbitt they'd all be fashionable, too, but remembered how Avery had been dressed the first time he'd seen her and hesitated. No need to be hasty.

Carly completed the three steps necessary to put herself directly between Dixon and her father. Then she fisted her hands on her hips and stated quite baldly, "You're already in our way."

Although he could rectify that by tossing Carly Nesbitt out a window, Dixon instead strode forward until he stood toe-to-toe with her and glared down at her as hard as he could. To her credit, she didn't back down one iota, and in fact seemed to push herself up on tiptoe to get farther into his face. Biting back a growl, he continued on his way *around* her, so that he could look at Desmond Nesbitt again.

"Gillespie and I will need someplace to set up our equipment," he continued. "Preferably someplace quiet and apart from the rest of the family. I noticed a guesthouse as we were driving in," he added, even though he hadn't actually seen the house and was taking Avery's word for it. "That would probably be ideal for our needs."

"Oh, no," Carly said adamantly, spinning around and moving between Dixon and her father again. "The guesthouse is where *I* live. It's *mine* now. You'll have to set up in—" She halted abruptly, clamping her mouth shut tight. She blinked slowly once, inhaled a deep breath and continued, "In…her…old room."

All right, that was it. Dixon had had enough. Obviously the Nesbitts had chosen the wrong daughter to ostracize. How the hell had they gotten the two of them confused? He opened his mouth to put Carly Nesbitt in her place—and that window was looking better all the time—when Avery's brother decided to get in on the action, too.

"The guesthouse is *not* yours," he stated flatly as he rose from the love seat and approached his sister. "It may be where you're living right now, but it doesn't belong to you. The entire estate will eventually come to *me*. Including the guesthouse."

Translation, Dixon thought, once the old folks were rotting in their graves—preferably sooner than later, from the tone of Desmond V's voice—his beloved sister would be hitting the bricks. And, gosh, it just made Dixon feel all warm and fuzzy inside to see such devotion and munificence between siblings, not to mention such love and respect for their still-very-much-alive parents.

"Don't count your acreage before it's hatched, Desi," Carly countered without an ounce of concern. "I've still got my attorneys working on Daddy's will. That bequest-to-the-male-offspring thing that Great-Grandfather insisted on is *so* yesterday. It's only a matter of time before you and I are equal partners in the will. Besides," she added with a smirk, "I'm more man than you'll ever be."

Desmond V went scarlet at the slur on his masculinity. Not that Dixon blamed him. Not that he disagreed with Carly. She was *mucho hombre,* no two ways about it.

"It's *mine*," Desmond V reiterated manfully. Well, kind of manfully. "The big house. The guesthouse. All of it. But maybe if you're nice to me, I'll let you keep living here. Maybe."

That's it, Desi. Don't back down. You go, girl.

Dixon shook his head in amazement. That two siblings could be challenging the will of their still-living parents while those parents looked on without comment—or so much as a sniffle to indicate failing health—was more than a little troubling. But the bickering continued for several minutes without a word from the elder Nesbitts. Clearly it was an old argument, one they heard often. Nevertheless, had the two been Dixon's children arguing about his possessions as if they couldn't wait for his death, he would have dragged them out to the woodshed. And then he would have willed every nickel he owned to Beekeepers for a Tree-Hugging, Whale-Loving, Non-Fur-Wearing Planet.

As Carly and Desmond V carried on, Avery stood silently watching them. Dixon wondered if she'd ever gotten caught up in the sibling battles when she was living here, but decided pretty quickly that she hadn't. For one thing, she didn't seem like the type to care about whether or not she'd end up with the family jewels—especially since Desmond V was in such dire need of them himself. For another thing, he couldn't see her succumbing to such juvenile behavior, in spite of being the youngest of the three Nesbitt offspring.

It was Desmond IV who finally put an end to the squabble. And he did it, Dixon noted, simply by standing up. As soon as he began to unfold himself from the couch, the contentious siblings shut their traps.

"Here's how it's going to work," he announced. "Carly, you'll speak civilly to your brother. Desi, you'll speak civilly to your sister. And you'll both speak civilly and be civil to Avery."

It didn't escape Dixon's notice that the man omitted any mention of Avery's relationship to the rest of them, just as everyone else—Avery included—had done. This was not a well family, he thought. And they did not put the *fun* in dys*fun*ctional, either.

"We've had enough unrest in this house to last a lifetime," the elder Nesbitt continued, clearly confident that no one would mess with him once he started talking. He looked at Avery, then back at his other children. "Whether Avery has been living here or not. And this will be the end of it. Now."

Dixon wished he could believe it. But one look at the other Nesbitt children and he knew better. If looks could kill, Avery would be nuclear fallout right now. The prodigal daughter may have returned. But by the looks of it, she was going to be the fatted calf they slaughtered for dinner.

CHAPTER EIGHT

AVERY KNEW HER FATHER WAS talking, but her head was too full of static for her to make sense of what he said. Something about Dixon and Gillespie setting up their equipment in her old room and assigning Dixon the guest room across the hall from hers and insisting their activities not jeopardize the big party he and his wife were hosting next week. And then something about raging black thunderheads and big hairy spiders and bloody butcher knives and… Oh, no, wait, that was the panic stuff interrupting again. Her father was saying something about putting Gillespie in the guesthouse apartment that Carly wasn't using.

That, Avery suspected, was her father's way of telling his oldest child not to get too attached to the place, because it was indeed intended for Desi, her lawyers be damned. And putting Dixon across the hall from Avery would serve two purposes. One, it would be convenient. And two, it would prevent her parents from having to keep an eye on her.

Avery didn't mind, though. She was strangely reassured knowing Dixon would be so close. So far, he was the only one in the house who'd shown any concern for her. She felt closer to him at the moment than she did anyone in her family. And how bad was that? That someone she'd known a matter of days and with whom she'd shared little more than friction should make her feel more comfortable than the people she had once called her family?

Dixon and Gillespie exchanged a few more words with her father, then they chatted with each other to set up a timetable for when and where and how everything would get done. All the while Carly and Desi circled the wagons. But they created two perimeters instead of one, naturally, neither realizing how much weaker they would be as a result. Or maybe they did realize it and just didn't care. Priorities for the Nesbitts had never exactly harmonized. Or made sense.

When it finally looked as if everything had been settled—at least Gillespie took off to do whatever he was supposed to be doing—Avery figured she could go, too. If she knew *where* to go. Her old room, she supposed, since that was where her father said she would be sleeping. But she suddenly felt as if she shouldn't go anywhere until her host and hostess showed her around.

Telling herself that was silly, she turned to make her way out. But the second she stepped into the hall, she felt panic trying to claw its way in. Fear piled in her belly, terror wrapped around her heart and the demons started tap-tap-tapping at her brain. Her throat closed up, her face went hot and her entire body began to tremble.

And then the world began to collapse on top of her.

Until she felt Dixon's hand on her shoulder and heard his voice near her ear murmuring, "Oh, no you don't. You're not going anywhere without me, Peaches."

His touch and his words jerked her back into her surroundings just enough that she was able to spin clumsily around to look at him. She pinned her attention on his opaque green eyes, making herself think of nothing but their curious color, forcing herself to not succumb to the terror ripping at her insides. He seemed to realize what was happening to her, because his sarcastic smile fell and his expression turned to one of alarm. He cupped his other hand gently over her other shoulder and said very softly, "Don't panic."

She swallowed with some difficulty, but couldn't make herself speak. Her mouth was as dry as soot and not much more useful. Her entire body was numb, immobile. Her brain was a screeching mass of chaos, fear warring with paranoia, anxiety mixing with dread, all of it blending together in a way that made her think she would never pull herself together again.

"Avery," Dixon said, still speaking quietly. "There's nothing to be afraid of."

She saw his mouth moving, could even hear him talking, but what he said made no sense. Nothing to be afraid of? How could he say that? There was *every*thing to be afraid of.

"It's okay," he told her. "No one is going to hurt you. You're safe."

She tried again to speak, failed again to do so. But the fear wasn't quite as overwhelming as it had been before, and somehow she managed to hold it at bay. She continued to focus on Dixon's face, on his strangely beautiful eyes and the way the green turned smoky gray at their center.

"Avery," he said again even more quietly than before. "You're all right, sweetheart. Don't be afraid. I'm here."

By the time he spoke those last two words, she was

beginning to come out of it. The terror ebbed, the dread slunk away and the panic gradually receded. Little by little, reality returned, and she saw the long hallway of her parents' house stretching before her. But where it had seemed interminable before, now she saw the end of it—the front door leading outside, which was no safer than where she stood right now.

Then she realized that wasn't true. Where she stood right now was indeed safe. But not because it was familiar. She couldn't quite say why she felt safe here, and really, she wasn't completely at ease. But she could function now. She could manage. She could look away from Dixon's face and see her parents, her brother and sister and Tanner Gillespie all staring back. At some point during the last few minutes she had twined her fingers in the front of Dixon's sweater, viciously enough that her fingers ached. Now she released him, absently brushing her palms over the garment to smooth the wadded-up fabric. But he caught her hands in his and pulled them away from his body, so she jerked herself the rest of the way free and dropped her hands to her sides.

"I'm sorry," she said hoarsely.

"No problem," Dixon replied just as softly.

No one said anything more for a moment, then Avery's father took a step forward. "What the hell was that?" he asked.

She opened her mouth to tell him, not sure how to explain the panic attacks she'd never had when living at home, but Dixon spoke before she had a chance.

"Nothing," he told her father. "Just a little disorientation trying to figure out which way to go. Understandable, since she hasn't set foot in this house for ten years."

And somehow, the way he said it, he made it sound as if he was also telling her parents they ought to be ashamed of themselves for that. Avery told herself she was just imagining it, that she was confused in the aftermath of her near panic attack, that Dixon had only said what he did to hurry things along so they could get everything set up and go to work.

But her father seemed to have heard the same thing she did, because he replied in a surprisingly gentle voice, "Well. She's here now. Time enough to reacquaint herself with everything."

She told herself he wasn't including the family in that *everything*. But at least he didn't sound angry.

Another awkward silence ensued, as if no one knew what to say or do or feel. Avery included. She wished she could just shrink into a little ball and disappear, or that she would wake up and discover the past few days had been a dream. She wanted to be back at home, seated in front of her computer, flirting and chatting with Andrew—an Andrew who was real, not some heinous scammer—living her life as well as she could manage. Maybe hers hadn't been the greatest life in the world, but neither had it been awful. Well, not too awful. Not usually.

For now, she wanted to hide in her old bedroom and try to bar the door against the emotional upheavals that would be coming for her. Tears, for sure, because they were right on the verge, but she couldn't quite tell yet what was causing them. Could be anger. Could be fear. Could even be sadness. Because all of those were cartwheeling inside her.

And there were other things, too, things she hadn't expected. Guilt for one. Shame for another. And embarrassment. That last, perhaps more than all the others, was probably what was motivating her right now. Embarrassment that Dixon had been a witness to how little her family thought of her. Embarrassment for her weakness that had nearly brought on another attack. And the fact that she cared so much about what Dixon thought of her told her more about herself than she wanted to admit.

Looking at him now, Avery realized she wouldn't be granted the escape she craved. Her family murmured uneasily among themselves and one by one dispersed, and Gillespie excused himself from the group to get settled in his room. But Dixon stayed where he was.

He said nothing until everyone else had left. Then, "You didn't have any dinner," he said. "You wouldn't let me stop on the way up."

Which was true. Because there was just something about going catatonic in a roadside diner that played havoc with a person's appetite.

"Neither did you," she reminded him.

"Then we both need something to eat."

"I'm not hungry," she said, turning toward the stairs. She tried to walk away, but he caught her wrist gently in his fingers. If she'd tugged hard enough, he probably would have let her go. But she just couldn't rouse the strength to manage it. Sighing softly, she turned to face him.

"I'm hungry," he said. "And I don't like to eat alone."

"Dixon, I—"

"Come on, Avery," he said. And there was something in his voice that made her want to accept his invitation. "You're going to need all your strength to face what's ahead," he added. Then he smiled. "And now that I've met your family, so will I."

She relented after that, unable to help the small smile that curled her lips. "Okay," she said. She gestured half-heartedly over her shoulder. "The kitchen's that way."

She turned and began to walk in that direction, assuming he would follow. But he didn't. This time he strode side by side with her, as if he knew precisely where he was going, too. He said nothing more as they covered the short distance to the back of the house, but he halted just inside the kitchen, giving it a good once-over.

"Wow," he said when he completed the survey.

"What?" Avery asked.

She looked at the kitchen, too, trying to see it for the first time, but it looked exactly the same as she remembered it, right down to the brushed-aluminum appliances. Granted, the Nesbitt kitchen probably claimed a few more appliances than the average home—the two-hundred-and-fifty-bottle wine cooler, nearly full, for instance, and the under-the-counter TV—but still. The cherrywood cabinets and hardwood floor weren't so unusual. Even if there were about two dozen more cabinets and a couple hundred more square feet of floor than the normal suburban home. And, okay, the dozens of pieces of copper cookware hanging from the ceiling were maybe a bit more than the average family cook needed—or could afford. It was still just a kitchen.

Dixon only shook his head in response to her question and headed straight for the double-doored Sub-Zero refrigerator on the other side of the room. "You know," he said as he opened it and began to inspect its contents, "you'd feel a lot better if you didn't eat so much crap."

"I do *not* eat crap," she said defensively, wondering when he'd turned into the diet doctor. "And I feel just fine," she added.

"Hey, I eavesdropped on your most recent grocery list," he reminded her. "You eat nothing *but* crap. Here's *your* food pyramid," he said, turning around, the fridge door still open behind him. He made an L shape out of the thumb and forefinger of each hand and pressed them together to make a triangle. "At the top, in that little bitty space? That's where anything remotely nutritional is. Your pineapple upside-down cake, say. Or chocolate-covered raisins. One level down comes dairy, which in your case would be yogurt-covered pretzels and sour-cream potato chips. Next to that is your protein group. For you, that means candied almonds, and lots of 'em. Next level, instead of fruits and vegetables, you've got the three Cs: cookies, candy and caffeine. And that big space at the bottom?" he said. "That's your crap quota. News flash for you, Peaches," he added as he dropped his hands and turned his attention back to the refrigerator. "Cheetos are *not* a significant source of calcium."

She narrowed her eyes at him. "And your point would be…?"

His back still turned to her, he replied, "That you're out on the Net often enough. Don't you ever visit any Web pages that focus on health and nutrition?"

"And the reason I would do that is because…?"

He turned again and met her gaze flatly. "Because you're sick."

She gaped at him. "I am not."

"One word, Peaches—agoraphobia."

"That's not a sickness. It's a phobia."

"It's not normal."

"But it's not a sickness."

"It's not healthy, either."

As much as Avery wanted to argue with that, she couldn't. So she said nothing.

"Haven't you read about how the things you eat can affect your frame of mind?" he asked.

"Yes," she admitted reluctantly. "But just because somebody writes something down doesn't make it true." Even though in this particular case, she conceded to herself, they were probably right.

Naturally, he ignored her protest. "According to some studies," he told her, "overindulgence in sugary foods, carbohydrates, caffeine and alcohol can contribute to panic and anxiety disorders. You need to ease up on those and add more protein and vegetables to your diet. And while you're at it, make sure you get enough vitamin B."

Avery narrowed her eyes at him. "Since when do you know so much about it?"

He lifted one shoulder and let it drop, a gesture that vaguely resembled a shrug but not quite. Even more interesting than the unconvincing shrug, though, was the fact that his gaze, which had been fixed so intently on hers, suddenly skidded to the side. In fact, he turned his back on her again and began picking through the overstuffed fridge without seeming to look at anything it held.

"I did a little reading on the Net before I came to pick you up," he said, his voice absent now of all the confident swagger it had held. Also very interesting.

"Why?" Avery asked.

He continued to avoid looking at her as he said, "I just didn't want to get the shit kicked out of me again, that's all."

She felt her face grow warm at that, and her own gaze scuttled to the other side of the room, where she saw that Jensen had deposited Skittles's cat carrier. The door was open, but Skittles was still inside, tucked into a tight ball, looking very frightened.

I'm right there with you, sweetie, she thought as she rose and made her way over to the animal.

She plucked the cat's food dish and water bowl from the bag beside the carrier and went about feeding and watering her, then cooed softly until Skittles emerged and warily sniffed at her food. Avery stroked her slowly as she ate, and eventually the cat began to purr softly. Would that she could acclimate herself as quickly, she thought.

"Look, I said I was sorry about what happened that night," she told Dixon. But she said nothing more. What else was there to say?

"I'm not looking for an apology," he said.

She looked up at him, but he still had his back to her, rifling through the contents of the fridge. "Then what are you looking for?"

"Something healthy to eat."

"You know what I mean, Dixon."

He expelled a restless sound. "Just that maybe you could…you know…feel better if you wanted to, that's all."

He couldn't possibly be suggesting what he seemed to be suggesting. In spite of that, she asked incredulously, "Oh, so I *like* having panic attacks and being terrified to leave my own home?"

He began to pull some things out of the refrigerator and set them on the counter, but as he worked, he told her, "No, Avery, it's not that."

He was calling her by her given name more frequently, she noticed, and she couldn't quite stop the little ripple of pleasure that wound through her every time he did. Like now. Immediately she tamped the sensation down and stuffed it into the very back of her brain. She did *not* want to feel pleasant around this unpleasant man.

"Then what are you trying to say?" she asked.

He pulled a few more things out of the fridge to join the others on the counter, then turned to look at her, setting his jaw hard and staring at her face. She wasn't positive, but she was pretty sure he growled at her. Which went a long way toward illustrating why she didn't want to feel pleasant around him.

"How about an omelet?" he asked. "That's what I'm trying to say. Lots of protein. You've ingested enough sugar over the past few days to make Willy Wonka hurl."

"Okay," she said, obviously surprising him with her acquiescence. Not that he should be surprised. She'd say anything to drop the subject.

She watched him as he moved about the kitchen, marveling at how comfortable he seemed to be. Not just being a man in a room traditionally deemed feminine, but being a newcomer to an unfamiliar environment. He did what needed doing, with whatever tools he had at hand. She envied his ability to switch gears so effortlessly.

"Santiago Dixon isn't your real name, is it?" she asked as he worked.

He hesitated before replying but didn't look up. "No."

She strode to where he stood, halting a good five feet

away from him, but leaning her hip against the counter where he worked. "Will you tell me what your real name is?" she asked.

This time he hesitated not at all. "No."

It was going to be a boring conversation if he kept up with the one-word answers. She tried a new tack.

"You know everything about me, don't you?"

"Yes."

So much for the new tack. She tried again.

"I mean, you know how I grew up, where I went to school, everything about my family, what I do for a living, all of it."

"Well, I know you're self-employed and that you work from your home. And I know you run a computer security business called Invulnerable, Inc. Which is a name I find fascinating on several levels." Before Avery could ask him what he meant by that, he continued, "But I'm still not sure I understand everything Invulnerable, Inc. does." He paused in his work and turned halfway around to look at her, finally meeting her gaze. "Yet."

Without awaiting a comment, he extended a hand upward and, barely having to reach, pulled down a sauté pan from the assortment of copper cookware hanging overhead. He set it atop the stove with a negligent clatter and lit the burner, tipped a bottle of olive oil briefly over the pan, and tossed in a little salt. He cracked a half dozen eggs one-handed into a crockery bowl, then deftly diced to pieces half an onion and two cloves of garlic.

Amazing, Avery thought. He obviously took good care of himself and had been doing it for a while. For the first time she wondered about his marital status, but somehow decided immediately that he'd always been single. She didn't know how she knew that. She just did. What was weird was how happy the realization made her.

"The only reason you don't know what my business does is because the OPUS guys rifling through my computer files weren't able to access the best stuff," she guessed.

"Yet," he repeated as he chopped up a red pepper and snagged a green one for the same treatment.

"You could just ask me yourself," she ventured. "You could ask me now and then you wouldn't have to wait."

He finished with the green pepper and reached for a yellow one, quickly slicing it, too, into little pieces. She wondered where he he'd learned such skill with a knife…then decided she was probably better off not knowing. A few sprigs of fresh rosemary joined everything else he'd hacked to bits, then he lowered the flame on the stove and dumped the mixture into the now sizzling pan.

He stirred as he spoke, and Avery watched the play of muscles against his sweater with every move he made. *Man, he's built,* she thought. A strange ripple of pleasure wound through her as she watched him work, and it took a moment for her to recognize it as desire. Which was the last thing she needed—wanted—to be feeling for this man. She dropped her gaze to the floor.

"So," he said. "What is it *exactly* that you do for a living at Invulnerable, Inc?"

"Lots of things, actually," she said. "I design firewalls and virus-detecting software for both personal and business use. I maintain a couple of Web sites and networks where I post updates about viruses that may be making the rounds on the Net and what to do if one gets into your system. And I'm a viral bounty hunter."

He arched his eyebrows at that. "You're a what?"

She smiled. "A viral bounty hunter," she repeated. "Sometimes when someone unleashes an especially nasty virus on the world, the software and PC manufacturers will put a bounty on that person's head. If I can find out who and where they are and provide evidence that they're the person or persons responsible for the outbreak, then I'm paid a bounty for the information."

He smiled. "Nice irony there."

She smiled back. "Among other things."

"Yeah, I guess in this day and age, that could pay pretty well."

"It's not bad," she admitted. "But it's not the bulk of my income by any means." Then another thought struck her. "How do you think this Adrian Padgett guy found me? I mean, it's not just my job to keep people and businesses safe. It's a way of life for me. I don't even market some of the security programs I've developed, because I don't want anyone to be able to study and decrypt them. That's the stuff I keep for myself. And I stay pretty anonymous on the Web. How did Adrian put it all together and figure out who and where I am?"

"Yeah, well, that's the big question, isn't it?" Dixon said as he reached for the eggs and began to whisk them. "We think he first stumbled on your name while he was working for CompuPax. That software you designed for them when you were fourteen had to have piqued his interest, such a young computer whiz and all. When he looked for more information on you—hell, he could have just Googled you and found a lot of hits about your conviction—he discovered the near-global destruction you accomplished when you were nineteen."

"But that was an accident," Avery interjected. "I genuinely didn't know my own strength."

"Even so, he's got to be looking at you like you could design anything. Some mass weapon of destruction, even if it's just a computer virus or whatever it is he's looking to do. You nearly shut down the planet ten years ago. Imagine what you could do now, with your smarts and today's technology and the massive number of people online. You really could shut down the planet if you wanted to. And we think that's why Adrian tapped into you."

Tapped into you, Avery echoed to herself. As though she was a resource instead of a human being. Then again, if what Dixon was saying was true, that was exactly what Adrian Padgett considered her to be.

"As for how he found you," Dixon continued, "well, his code name wasn't Sorcerer for nothing. He's got smarts, too. The guy could do anything. He was the field agent on his team when he was with OPUS, but he still knew how to operate all the equipment and had access to all the networks. I imagine he still has some way to stay connected, even if it's not a legal one. I just wish I knew how he's stayed one step ahead of us. It's scary how that guy seems to always know what's going on before we do."

That wasn't the only thing that was scary about him, Avery thought, recalling that they wanted her to meet with him out in the great wide open. Though the great wide open scared her even more.

She decided not to think about it right now.

"On the flip side," Dixon said, "how do you conduct business if everything is so secret with you?"

"Businesswise, I'm not a secret," she said. "Invulnerable has a Web site, and anyone can access me through there via e-mail. I also have a toll-free number. I don't have to advertise much because I get lots of word-of-mouth clients. But I keep my name out of it. As far as anyone is concerned, I have lots of employees and departments and the CEO is some computerwhiz recluse who keeps a low profile."

He smiled. Again. "But it's all you?"

She smiled back. Again. "It's all me."

"Busy woman," he said, turning back to the omelet.

"Hey, I got nothing else to do," she said. And although she meant it as a joke, for some reason it sure didn't sound like one. So she hurried on, "Now that you know about my business, you know everything there is to know about me." Not that that comment did anything to lighten her mood, either.

It wasn't a question, which Dixon seemed to realize because he said nothing in reply. He only tended to his culinary creation on the stove, which smelled wonderful. Her stomach rumbled in spite of her assurances that she wasn't hungry, and suddenly she was hungrier than she'd been in a long time. She also felt more comfortable than she had in a long time. Talking to Dixon had distracted her enough that she had been able to forget about her situation for a little while. And for that she was reluctantly grateful.

She was surprised at how little it bothered her that he knew so much about her. On the contrary, there was something kind of liberating about it. There was no point in trying to hide anything from him. Lying would be useless. She didn't have to make an effort to impress him, nor did she have to worry about what he might think of her if he found out about the things she'd done.

"But I don't know anything about you," she told him.

And that did bother her. A lot. What bothered her more was how very much she did want to learn about him.

But he seemed to interpret that as a statement and not a question, too, and he didn't reply to it, either. And, okay, so maybe it was a statement and not a question, thanks to that pesky punctuation, but her intimation was there, even if his intimacy wasn't.

Why did she care anyway? she asked herself. It wasn't as though the two of them were going to be friends. They weren't even acquaintances, really. They were two people who, by sheer mischance, were forced to work together to catch someone they both knew from different times and places. Once OPUS had Adrian Padgett, bad guy extraordinaire, Avery and Dixon would never see each other again. She should be doing her best *not* to learn anything more about him than she had to.

"So where did you learn to cook?" she heard herself ask. And what she wouldn't have given in that moment for a brick to smack herself upside the head.

But Dixon surprised her by actually responding to her question this time. "From Mrs. Fegenbush, who cooked for my family when I was growing up."

"Your family has money then," Avery guessed.

"Not like yours, Peaches," he said, still cooking. "Not like yours."

"You're lucky then," she told him.

"Maybe," he agreed.

"I'm betting your family wasn't like mine, either," she said.

"No," he replied simply, returning to the one-word answers again.

"Then you're lucky about that, too."

He did turn around to look at her then, his expression cold. "My father died seven years ago," he said. "I wouldn't call that lucky."

"I'm sorry, Dixon," she said softly. "I didn't know. Of course that wasn't lucky." And although she told herself not to pry, that everything in his voice and his posture told her that this was a subject best left alone, she heard herself asking, "How did he die?"

"He was murdered," he said flatly. Before she had a chance to comment—not that she really had any idea what to say—he quickly added, "And that's all I'm going to say about that."

Translation, Avery thought, *don't push your luck.*

"I'm sorry," she said again, more quietly this time. But she forced herself not to repeat any of the questions circling in her head. Why had his father been murdered? Who had killed him? Had the killer been caught? Had it had anything to do with Dixon's line of work? Did he blame himself for it?

Surely not, she told herself. Why would she even wonder about such a thing? Still, murder. That had to have compounded his grief over the loss of his father even more.

He said nothing more as he finished cooking, then evenly divided the omelet onto two plates, which he carried to a small butcher-block table in the far corner of the kitchen. Avery took a seat at one of the two ladder-back chairs beside it, then waited for Dixon to return—which he did, with an open beer for himself and a glass of milk for her.

"Beats the hell out of Cheetos," he said as he set the glass down beside her plate.

She wanted to object, wanted to go to the fridge to find a soda or get up to brew a pot of coffee, but she made herself say with almost genuine-sounding gratitude, "Thank you."

"You're welcome," he told her as he folded himself into the chair opposite her. "Now clean your plate, Peaches," he added as he lifted his fork. "We've got a big night ahead of us."

CHAPTER NINE

HER BEDROOM HAD CHANGED a lot, Avery saw when she and Dixon pushed open the door an hour later. She supposed that shouldn't surprise her. When a family banished one of its members, they naturally would want to exorcise that member's spirit from the house, starting with that member's bedroom. Still, she couldn't help thinking this newer version of her bedroom was perfect for her. Because it was clearly a guest room now.

The earth tones provided a nice gender-free color scheme, and the furnishings were completely asexual—a sleigh bed, tallboy, armoire and dresser of mahogany. They housed a variety of unremarkable knickknacks, a few she recalled being stored in closets when she'd lived here. Likewise, the landscapes on the walls were some her mother had banished to the attic when Avery was a child, deeming them of too inferior quality to be displayed. So what her bedroom had become in her absence was a storage space for Nesbitt cast-offs that no one was supposed to see.

Oh. She'd been wrong. Her bedroom hadn't changed after all.

"My father may have called it my room," she told Dixon as he closed the door behind them, "but there's nothing of me here anymore. My mother totally re-decorated the place."

"Gee, I can't imagine why," Dixon said wryly as he looked around. "I mean, a woman like her not appreciating a Che Guevara poster over the bed? What's up with that?"

"Over the desk," Avery told him.

He looked puzzled. "What?"

"My Che Guevara poster hung over my desk, not my bed."

He narrowed his eyes at her, clearly trying to decide whether or not to believe her. "I was, uh… I was kidding about that, Avery."

"Well, I'm not. Che Guevara was over there," she said, pointing toward the far corner of the room. "Over my bed I had a poster of Ralph Nader. And on the closet door," she added, turning in that direction, "I had Russell Means."

"Oh, well. In that case, I *really* can't imagine what your mother was thinking."

"She's a Republican," Avery said.

She scanned the room again, shaking her head. "Man, there's not one thing of me left in this entire house. I honestly didn't realize until now just how much they hate me."

"They don't hate you, Avery," Dixon said softly.

Somehow she managed a chuckle for that. But it was an anxious sound, not a happy one. "Oh, please. You saw what happened downstairs. You saw how they feel about me. They can barely look at me. They can't even say my name."

"They don't hate you," he said again. "They're hurt, Avery. Not just because of what they think you did to them, but because of what they did to you. Give them time."

She set her jaw firmly. "They've had ten years, Dixon," she said.

"They need more."

She said nothing in response to that, mostly because she wasn't sure whether or not she wanted to give them—or herself—any more time. It had been ten years. And nothing had changed. The only reason she was here now was by government decree. And that had only come about because she'd gotten herself into trouble again. So there were a few more things that hadn't changed: her inability to exercise good judgment when it came to men. And her inability to manage her anger when those men pissed her off. And her enormous talent at embarrassing her family with the results.

"Okay, so they redecorated," Dixon said when she didn't reply. "It's nothing a little nitro and acetylene wouldn't take care of."

She chuckled again, and this time there was a touch of genuine good humor in the sound. "Thanks, Dixon," she said.

"For what?"

"I don't know. For trying to make me laugh. For helping me stave off a panic attack. For fixing me something to eat. For standing up to my family when I couldn't do it myself. I appreciate it."

He gazed at her in silence for a moment, started to speak, but was interrupted by a brief knock at the door. Without awaiting a reply Gillespie entered carrying two cases of what looked like computer equipment with him. More sat in the hallway outside.

While he and Dixon went to work unpacking it all,

Avery returned to the kitchen for Skittles, and by the time everything was up and running, her room was looking more like her again. Not just because the cat immediately made herself at home on the bed, curling against one pillow into the bowling-ball shape she preferred for serious sleeping, but because some of what the two agents unpacked belonged to Avery. They told her the OPUS geeks had even fixed it so that it would appear that she was connecting from her Central Park condo instead of her parents' house in the Hamptons. Adrian would have no way of knowing anything was amiss.

But although she searched all of Andrew's old haunts—even the distasteful pop-culture chat rooms where he'd gone slumming for morons—he seemed to be nowhere. Either he was checking in late tonight or he wasn't going to check in at all. Nor did she have e-mail from him, which wasn't really unusual, but neither was it normal. Still, he'd been the last one to send something, so she was the one who owed mail to him. It did made her uneasy, though, that she couldn't find him. Though it might simply be the fact that she was working with Dixon on such an assignment to begin with that made her feel that way.

By midnight, the time when Avery was usually just getting into her groove, she felt like nodding off. And that was saying something for a chronic insomniac. "You know," she told Dixon as she pushed her glasses up onto her head and rubbed her eyes, "I always figured spy work wasn't as glamorous as they made it out to be in James Bond movies, but I figured it would be at least a little more exciting than watching my fingernails grow."

She was sitting on an overstuffed ottoman in front of her computer, which she'd placed on one of the night-stands—strangely her mother had decided a desk chair would be out of place in a room that had no desk. Dixon sat on the floor, leaning against the bed, where he was leafing through the contents of a fat file folder. "Sometimes it's actually more exciting than a James Bond movie," he said. "But more often it's like this."

"So what made you want to become a spy?" she asked.

"What can I say?" he told her, still reading. "Ever since I was a kid, I've dreamed about traveling around the world and catching bad guys and decoding secret messages and working with high-tech gizmos and drinking martinis shaken-not-stirred and being shot at and camping out in frigid surveillance vans and posing as a grocery-store delivery boy and getting the shit kicked out of me by women half my size with whom I've tried to be perfectly reasonable."

Oh, no, she thought. He wasn't going to slip in that comment about being shot at and then divert her attention with that last remark about herself. She'd apologized enough. "You've been shot at?"

"Yeah, I've been shot at. More than once, as a matter of fact."

"Wow," she said with much understatement. "Have you ever as a matter of fact been hit?"

"Yeah."

"More than once?"

"Hey, believe me, once was enough."

"Where were you hit?"

That finally made him look up. "Why do you care?"

"I don't know. I just…" She stopped herself before

finishing the statement. Not because she didn't know what she wanted to say. But because she realized then that it was precisely because she *did* care. About him. About a guy who had forcibly entered her home and scared the hell out of her. A guy who had jerked her into a dangerous situation that she had no business being a part of. A guy who could be abrasive, overbearing, cocky and completely full of himself.

A guy who'd fixed her one for the road before she'd even asked. A guy who'd held her hand when she confronted her family. A guy who'd cooked her dinner when no one else had even asked—or cared—if she wanted something to eat. A guy who had promised no harm would come to her during her participation in this…whatever the hell it was.

"I don't know," she said again, even though she suddenly knew perfectly well. "Prurient interest, I guess."

But he still didn't answer her question, only turned his head to look at the computer screen in front of her, as if he found it infinitely more interesting than he found her. Which, of course, he did. Because that computer was hooked up, however intricately and however ephemerally, to the person he wanted most in the world to find. So Avery turned back to look at the monitor, too, telling herself she was more interested in its connection to Adrian Padgett than she was in Dixon's answer. Because once they found Adrian and once they caught him, she would be free of this insane task and free of Dixon—and the confusing feelings she was beginning to have for him—for good. Then she could go back to her miserable little life and be happy.

"In the shoulder," she heard him say from behind her. "I was shot in the shoulder once."

She turned to look at him again, but he was still gazing at the computer screen. "Left or right?" she asked.

"Left."

Her gaze fell to that part of his body, which, thanks to where he was seated, was nearly touching her own thigh. "When did it happen?" she asked.

"About four years ago." But he continued to look at the monitor, not Avery.

"Do you have a scar?"

"Yes."

"Does it still bother you?"

"Sometimes."

"Did they catch the guy who shot you?"

"No."

"Do you know who it was?"

"No."

Although she told herself she knew better than to ask, Avery went for broke and said, "Will you tell me your real name?"

"No." The word came swiftly, quietly and with complete conviction.

"Oh," she replied in a very small voice.

He spared a quick glance at her face, then returned his attention to the monitor. "Look, it's nothing personal," he said in the clipped, indifferent tone of voice he'd used when interrogating her the day before.

"Yeah, I know," she said dispassionately. "It's totally professional. You can't tell me your real name because it could jeopardize your identity and the security of your mission, yada yada yada. Whatever the hell that mission is. Other than bugging the hell outta me, I mean."

"No, it's not even professional," he told her, still not looking at her. "I just don't tell anyone my name, that's all. The only people who know it are the ones who are very, very close to me."

"You actually let people get close to you?" she asked, not quite able to mask the sarcasm that tinted the question.

He looked at her again, narrowing his eyes at her. Those eyes that were such a strange icy shade of green. But instead of going cold at the sight, Avery suddenly felt heat rushing through her body. God, he was so gorgeous. How could a man who looked like that be in the sort of profession he was in? She would have thought they'd want someone ordinary-looking and nondescript for a job like his, so that no one would be able to remember seeing him. One look at Dixon and you'd never forget a single detail. He was just that well put together.

"Well, if you won't tell me your real name," she said, assuring herself her voice did *not* suddenly sound shallow and thready, "then will you at least tell me your code name?"

"No." The word came even more swiftly, even more quietly and with even more conviction than before.

"Why not?" she demanded. "Gillespie told me his code name. And I've heard you call him Cowboy since we arrived." Though, for the first time it occurred to her that Gillespie had never addressed Dixon by any name other than Dixon. Despite that, she added, "Everybody in your stupid organization seems to call each other by their stupid code names. Why won't you tell me yours?"

"Because nobody who learns my code name lives to talk about it," he said plainly.

Her eyebrows shot up at that. "Because you're so deep undercover and it's so top secret that they can't afford to let word get out?"

"No, because I beat the hell out of anybody who says it."

Now Avery narrowed her eyes in confusion. "Um, why?"

"I have my reasons."

She wanted to ask what they were, but one look at his expression and she knew better. So instead she asked, "How do they decide what code name a person gets? I mean, if I were an OPUS agent, what would my code name be?"

He seemed to give that some serious thought. Finally with a grin, he said, "If I was naming you, I'd give you the code name Badger."

"Badger?" she repeated distastefully. "Oh, come on. You can do better than that."

He shook his head. "No, it would be Badger. The code name always has to have something to do with the personality or some character trait of the real person."

"And you think I'm a badger?"

"Peaches, it's what you do best."

She made a haughty sound. "Then I'll come up with my own name." She, too, gave it some serious thought, then hit on exactly the right one. "Garbo," she decided. "That's what my code name would be."

"How do you figure?"

"Because I vahnt to be aloooone," she told him, hoping he'd get the not-so-subtle hint.

Now his smile became wry. "A gentle reminder, Peaches—you've been alone for the past decade."

"Then Garbo is perfect for me," she said. Suddenly,

though, she didn't like the name nearly as much as she had when she proposed it.

He growled something unintelligible under his breath, then, "Let's talk about something else, okay?" he said.

"Fine," she replied tersely. "What do you want to talk about?"

He met her gaze levelly. "Tell me about your time in prison."

This time Avery was the one to reply swiftly, quietly and with utter conviction. "No."

"Oh, come on," he said.

"No," she said again.

"Please?"

"Why would you care?" she asked point-blank.

In response he echoed her reply to his similar question. "I don't know. I just…"

There was no way his reasons could mirror her own, she told herself. No way could he care about her, even in the vaguely interested, not-really kind of way she cared about him. Still, they were both bored and needed something to pass the time….

"All right, here's the deal," she said. "Until Adrian comes online, I'll answer one of your questions about my life in prison for every one of my questions you answer about your job. Fair?"

"Fine. But I get to go first."

Yeah, yeah, yeah.

"Was it horrible?" he asked, going right for the main event.

She knew her answer would surprise him, but she told him truthfully, "No. My turn."

"Wait a minute!" he interjected. "It's not your turn yet."

"Sure it is. You asked a question, I answered it. Now it's my turn to ask you one."

He opened his mouth, closed it, opened it again. Then he grinned smugly. "You asked me a question earlier that I answered," he reminded her. "About why I wanted to be a spy. So now it's my turn again."

"Uh-uh," she protested. "We're still one for one. It's my turn." And then, before he could get in another word, she asked, "Where did you grow up?"

He narrowed his eyes at her again. "What's that got to do with being a spy?"

"I told you it's not your turn to ask a question," she said.

"Tough. Neither of us seems to want to play by the rules."

He had a point. Not that she was surprised by it. "Earlier tonight you mentioned having grown up with a cook," she said. "To me, that indicates you come from a moneyed background. True?"

"Is that your question?" he asked. "Or is the other question the one you want me to answer?"

"Do you know any other punctuation marks besides a question mark?" she asked.

"Do you?" he countered.

Evidently not, she thought. But then, that thought had ended with a period. When she was talking to herself, she did just fine. It was only Dixon who made her feel questionable.

"Okay, no more games. Let's just chat, shall we?"

He curled his lip back in distaste. "I hate chatting."

"I hate being bored. We're even."

He expelled a sound of resignation. "I grew up in Charlottesville, Virginia," he said. "My parents raised Thoroughbreds. Satisfied?"

Not by a long shot, she thought. She couldn't imagine Dixon having grown up in such a pastoral, genteel setting. What had led the Virginia farm boy into a life of intrigue and espionage?

"My mother sold the farm after my father died," he added when she didn't reply, "and she moved into a condo in D.C.—Georgetown."

"I've never been to Virginia," Avery said, wanting to skirt the subject of his father's death as much as she could, "but I knew at girl at Wellesley who was from Richmond. I hear it's a beautiful state."

"It is that," he agreed, his voice still sounding a bit flat.

"So do you have brothers or sisters still living there?"

"One sister," he said. "Younger. She and her family live in D.C., too, not far from my mother. She works for the State Department."

"Sounds like you're a political family," Avery said.

"Runs in the blood," he confirmed. "My mother was an attaché at the Norwegian embassy when she met my father. And before and for a little while after they married, my father was in the same line of work I'm in now."

She could tell he immediately regretted the revelation, because he twisted his mouth into a tight line.

"Your dad was a spy, too?"

"Yeah."

She understood then why Dixon didn't want to talk about his father's death. "He died in the line of duty, didn't he?"

Dixon nodded. "But he was called out of retirement for it. He shouldn't have been working. But OPUS insisted he was the only one who could do the job."

"And was he?"

"I could have done it," Dixon said with complete confidence. "But I was fresh out of training and I'd never been in the field. They wouldn't hear of it. They lured my father back instead."

"And somehow you feel responsible for his death," she guessed.

He shook his head. "No, I know who's responsible."

And suddenly Avery did, too. "Adrian Padgett," she said softly.

He nodded. "Yeah. Adrian Padgett."

"You want to talk about it?"

"No."

She knew better than to push him. In an effort to change the subject, she told him, "Prison really wasn't as bad as you might think."

She wasn't sure, but when he looked at her this time, he seemed to be grateful. "How so?" he asked.

It was only fair, Avery thought. He'd shared a little of himself when he talked about his father, however vaguely. The least she could do was share something of herself, too.

"Growing up here," she said, driving her gaze around her still-luxurious room, "I never felt comfortable."

"Hey, no offense, Peaches, but sleeping under a Ralph Nader poster would put me off my lunch, too."

"I'm not talking about the room," she said wearily, striving for patience. And also tamping down the urge to smack him.

"Yeah, well, having met your family, it still doesn't surprise me."

She smiled at that, albeit a bit sadly. "Actually that wasn't the worst of it, either. For the first part of my life

I got along fine with all of them. I figured everyone lived the way we did. In a huge, beautiful house with two swimming pools and horses in the stable and servants to take care of all the menial tasks. Everyone I knew lived like that, so that must be the way of the world, you know? Even when we traveled, we visited people or places that were like home. I never had any reason to believe there was another way to live."

"Then when did it become uncomfortable?" he asked.

"I can't really give you an exact time, but as I got older and learned more about the world outside my own reality, I gradually started to realize that very few people lived the way I did. We'd go into the city and I'd see homeless people and run-down neighborhoods. Or I'd watch the news and read the paper and see that most people lived lives entirely different from my own. Little chinks of ugliness started to open up in the great white wall around my life. And I started wondering what made me so special that I got to live the way I did when other people had to live the way they did."

"And what did make you so special?" Dixon asked.

"Nothing," she said with a small shrug. "A happy accident of birth, that was all."

"You should have felt relieved," he told her.

"I felt something else instead," she said.

"What?"

"Guilt."

He studied her a moment in silence. "You know, a good therapist could help you work through that. And luckily for you, you could afford a good therapist."

She smiled. "Listen, I saw some of the best of them when I was a teenager. My parents insisted. They couldn't figure out why I was so unhappy and rebellious when I was living the sort of life anyone else would have envied."

"And it didn't help?"

Avery lifted her shoulders again and let them drop. "Not really. I just couldn't accept it, Dixon, that I had so much…*so much*…and others had so little. For no good reason."

"Maybe God just decided to smile on you."

"God doesn't pick favorites."

"Maybe you did something good in a previous life that you're being rewarded for in this one."

"Nobody's that good."

"Maybe it's your karma. You radiate goodness, so goodness returns to you."

She only rolled her eyes at that one.

"Yeah, okay, that was pushing it," he said. "So maybe it was just a happy accident of birth. So what?"

Avery said nothing in response to that. Mostly because she still wasn't okay with it. These days, she still lived a privileged life. She still had a lot more than most people did. And yes, she still felt guilty about it. But she also knew she could give away every penny she had and there would still be millions of people who went without. Until the day came when *every*one who was in a position to do so gave away much of their wealth, the fortunes of people would stay unfairly disproportionate. Avery's generosity could only go so far.

"So it was another happy accident," she said, "that made me realize what was really important. That was the one that sent me to the Rupert Halloran Correctional Facility."

"You think that was luck?" he said.

"Yeah, I do," she told him. "Good luck, at that."

"How do you figure?"

"Prison was totally egalitarian," she said. "Nobody had any more than anyone else. We all had to work. We were all expected to follow the same rules and the same schedule."

"Hey, you're talkin' like a commie now, Peaches. You can get in trouble for that."

She smiled. "I guess it was kind of Communistic. In a good way."

"No good can come of Communism, missy."

His silliness soothed some of her tension and made it a little easier for her to talk about that two-year period of her life. Not that remembering prison had ever caused her any grief. But she didn't usually like to talk about it with other people because they never understood why she hadn't been miserable there.

"I felt like I had a purpose in prison, Dixon. Does that make sense?" she asked.

"Not really," he told her. "I mean, you worked as a seamstress, right? Sewing pillowcases for a mail-order linen company."

"Yeah, but it was honest work," she pointed out. "I earned my own way. No one gave me anything just because I was Avery Nesbitt, of the Hampton Nesbitts."

"And that's important to you?"

"Hell, yes, it's important to me," she said. "Aren't you proud of what you do for a living?"

"Damn right."

"Your family was wealthy, right?"

He nodded.

"You probably have a trust fund or some kind of inheritance?"

"Both, actually," he told her.

"Yet you don't rely on them for your income. You have a job. A dangerous job, at that. And one I doubt is making you a rich man."

"Yeah, but those government benefits are killer," he said.

"So are some of the people you deal with on a regular basis," she reminded him. "But you do this because it gives you a sense of purpose and makes you feel worthwhile. Like you're an important part of the world, right?"

He seemed uncomfortable with her assessment. "I guess…"

"That's what I always wanted, too," she told him. "To feel important. Or at least worthwhile. I never got that growing up here. I never felt valued or valuable. But when I was at Rupert Halloran, I did."

He expelled an incredulous sound. "Yeah, people went to bed at night feeling more comfortable because of the pillowcases you made."

"Hey, when you've had a long, crappy day at work, it's a pretty major thing to be able to go to sleep with a smile on your face," she told him indignantly. "The pillowcases I stitched together gave people pleasure. Made them smile. Made them feel better. How often have you done that for anyone?"

He dipped his head forward. "Okay, I guess you have a point."

"I just wanted to be important to someone, Dixon," she said, hating the pleading tone in her voice but having no idea how to mask it. "In whatever small way I could."

"And putting together pillowcases for total strangers while being locked up made you feel that?"

She nodded, fighting back tears that came out of nowhere. What the hell was that all about? "Yeah," she said. "It did."

Dixon studied Avery from his seat on the floor and marveled at what she had just revealed. She'd felt more significant locked up behind bars and performing meaningless manual labor than she'd felt living in a palatial home as a member of one of the wealthiest families in America.

No wonder she'd been in therapy.

Now she was looking at him as though she was going to start crying, and if she did that, he was going to feel like a complete heel, not to mention he'd have no idea what to say or do next, and please, for God's sake, don't let her throw herself into his arms and start sobbing uncontrollably, because then he'd really lose it, and dammit, why couldn't he have just kept his mouth shut for once in his life?

But she didn't start crying. Instead she looked away, turning her attention to the computer screen.

"He's not going to show tonight," she said.

But her voice was thick when she spoke, and he saw her swipe a finger under her glasses to rub her eyes. She pretended it was eye strain, but Dixon suspected she was trying not to cry. He told himself he was grateful. The last thing he wanted on his hands was a weepy woman. Never mind that Avery didn't seem the type for that. Never mind that she had a good reason to feel weepy. Hell, he'd felt like crying himself since meeting the Nesbitt clan.

"What makes you think he's not going to show?" he asked.

"He's always online by now if he's going to get

online. Unless he's using a new screen name I don't know about. But even then I'd be able to find him. Or unless he's using a different computer."

"And if he was using a different computer, it would mean…what?"

"Could mean a lot of things," she said. "That he bought a new 'puter. That he's accessing the Net from a Wi-Fi café because he's out of town or something."

"That he knows your working with us, so he's starting to hide his tracks," Dixon said.

"Possibly," she conceded without flinching. "But why would he suspect something like that?"

Damned if Dixon knew. But Sorcerer had a way of knowing things that was downright mystical at times.

"It's only been five days since I spoke to him," Avery said. "That's not all that unusual. He does seem to travel a lot for his work. Or something. And there were a couple of nights there when I wasn't online myself, since I was too busy being manhandled and interrogated by a government-sponsored goon squad. Occasionally I have so much work to do myself that I don't talk to him for days."

Dixon tried not to take the "goon squad" comment personally. He had, after all, been working without an official partner for a couple of months now, which made him a lone goon.

"Could be he and I just missed each other tonight," she added when he said nothing in reply. Rebuttal. Retort. Whatever. "We can try again tomorrow night."

"And what if he doesn't show then, either?"

"Then we try again the next night," she said.

"And if he doesn't show then?"

She eyed him warily. "Why are you worried? Are

you afraid he's suspicious? Or is it that you don't think I'm attractive or exciting enough for him to be interested in me anymore? Not that he was ever really interested in me in the first place, if what you've told me is true. He just wants me to build him a nice virus or something to take over the world. It had nothing to do with my feminine charms, right?"

"Avery…" Dixon began. But what could he say? She was right. Adrian had never been interested in her as a woman. Only as a big computer brain. If he'd found someone else who could help him complete whatever nefarious plans he was hatching, he'd drop her faster than chili through a Chihuahua.

"Yeah, well, here's a news flash for you, Dixon," she said, sounding indignant now. "Maybe you don't think I have much to offer a man, but some guys out there actually look for more in a woman than a pretty face and round heels. Some guys actually *like* it when a woman's brain is as full as her bra."

Unbidden, a memory rose in his head of lying atop Avery on the couch in her condo while he searched her that first night. He hadn't intended for there to be anything more to it than a quick check for weapons. Dixon had searched women before and never felt a flicker of anything other than caution. But he'd be lying if he said he hadn't noticed the curves and swells and valleys beneath his fingers and just how nicely Avery did fill her B cups. Still, her brain was quite a bit fuller than her bra. What was odd was that Dixon liked that, too.

Not that he normally went for brainless women. But neither was he especially turned on by supersmarts like hers. He had no problem conceding that she had the edge on him when it came to understanding and designing and using technology. But where he'd normally feel competitive in such a situation—regardless of the gender of the other person—with Avery he felt grudging admiration. And he found himself wanting to learn more. About her brain *and* her bra.

It was a troubling thought. But not an unpleasant one.

"Peaches, you have no idea what I want in a woman," he finally said. Of course, suddenly *he* wasn't entirely sure what he wanted in a woman, either. But that was beside the point. The point was he was starting to have thoughts about Avery Nesbitt that he really shouldn't be having. Not to mention that he really didn't want to have. Therefore, there was only one thing left to do about it.

Flee.

"Well, if you think he's not going to show," Dixon said as he leaped up from the floor, "then that's good enough for me."

Avery stood, too, clearly confused by his reaction. Which only made sense, since Dixon was surprised by it, too. In fact, so was the cat, who growled something low, jumped down from the bed and slunk beneath it. Would that Dixon could escape so easily, he thought as he watched the cat's flight with something akin to envy.

"O-okay," Avery said as he bent to collect the pages that had spilled from his file as he'd hastily risen. "We'll try again tomorrow night."

He nodded, thinking that by tomorrow night he'd be in a better position to work anyway. It had been a long day, coming on the heels of another long day and another long day before that. He was in an environment that was alien to him, one he hadn't had a chance to scope out in advance. He was mostly on his own, since Avery wasn't an agent and Cowboy was just barely. Another day would give him a chance to get some rest, to acclimate himself to his surroundings and the situation.

Yeah, that had to be what was wrong with him, he thought as he looked at Avery again. At the huge, incredibly blue eyes behind her geeky glasses and the long, silky hair she wore in that frustrating braid and the soft, womanly curves beneath her shapeless clothes.

Long day, he told himself again. Really, really, really long day. And strange situation. Really, really, really strange situation. That had to be it. Had to. And it was also why he only managed to mumble a quick good-night to her and not another word as he exited. Nor did he look back a single time once he left the room. Not that he didn't want to.

But because he didn't dare.

CHAPTER TEN

TANNER GILLESPIE ROLLED over in bed to see the glowing blue numbers on his travel alarm clock informing him that it was a little past 5:00 a.m. Earlier than his usual waking time of five-thirty, but he was sleeping in a strange bed, so that wasn't surprising. Hell, he was sleeping in a strange room, in a strange place, surrounded by strange—to put it mildly—people, so it *really* wasn't surprising. And since he hadn't logged more than a few nanoseconds of sleep, that additional twenty or thirty minutes would have been welcomed.

Then again, how was a man supposed to sleep in a room that had been decorated for Louis XVI? Even in the dark Tanner could see the gilt on the lush furnishings glistening. The walls, he recalled, were a deep velvety blue, the puffy sofa and chairs a rich Fort Knox gold. The bed was even more overstuffed than the rest of the pillowy furniture, one of those mattress-on-a-mattress things that was supposed to make sleeping easier. And it might have worked, had it not been piled high with all kinds of pansy froufrou like tasseled pillows and ruffled…stuff. His testosterone had been seeping from him little by little ever since he walked through the door.

There was only one thing a bed like this was good

for, he thought as he folded his hands behind his head and gazed at the canopy—a *canopy,* for God's sake—overhead. Tumbling a too-expensive woman and introducing her to the joys of the working-class man.

Naturally Tanner was thinking of one too-expensive woman in particular. And of one working-class man in particular, too. But it was the woman who really occupied his thoughts. A woman with rich black curls and Caribbean-blue eyes who just so happened to be sleeping a couple hundred feet away from him. He'd heard Carly Nesbitt come to her room a little after one o'clock—hell, he'd been awake, what else was he supposed to do but listen for her return?—and he'd immediately started picturing her going about her end-of-the-day rituals. Locking the door behind her—since, hey, there was some lowbrow, low-income, lower-class lowlife sleeping right across the hall—then arching her lithe body into a leisurely stretch and kicking off her really high heels. Then, in his mind's eye, she'd walked toward the bathroom and started the shower, hot, steamy water gushing down over slick black tile.

Not that he had a clue what her place looked like—he was, after all, a lowbrow, low-income, lower-class lowlife who would never be invited inside—but he'd had a vivid imagination since he was a boy and he wasn't afraid to use it. And after Carly Nesbitt had started her shower, she'd peeled off her little black top and reached behind herself for the zipper of that red leather skirt to tug it down, down, down, exposing the creamy flesh of her back, the skinny strap of a black lacy bra and skimpy black panties. And then black garters. Attached to black stockings. Hey, it was Tanner's fantasy. He'd dress her—and then undress her—

however he damn well pleased. Not that black lacy stuff was outside the realm of possibility, all things Carly Nesbitt considered.

After stepping out of the skirt, she'd settled one foot on a chair and unhooked the first smoky stocking one fastening at a time, rolling down the filmy silk over inch after inch of milky skin. Then she'd done the same for the other leg before unfastening the garter belt and tossing it aside. The black brassiere had followed, spilling perfect, ample breasts topped by wide, rosy nipples. She'd hooked her fingers into the waistband of her panties, turned her back on Tanner's mental eye and wiggled out of them, revealing a full, flawless, incredible ass. Then she'd stepped under the jet of the steamy shower and reached for the soap.

Tanner groaned as he rolled over in bed again, his waking boner surging higher. Hell, no wonder he hadn't slept last night after thinking about all that. But *why* had he been thinking about all that? He didn't even *like* Carly Nesbitt, so why was he fantasizing about her being naked and rosy and naked and wet and naked and hot and naked and steamy and naked? Oh, right. Stupid question. Because she had a body that wouldn't quit. Whether or not he liked her was immaterial.

Still, sex with Carly Nesbitt? He could safely say that wasn't on his to-do list anytime this century. Not unless, you know, anything vaguely resembling an opportunity presented itself.

Doing his best to push aside the rampant thoughts, Tanner jackknifed up in bed stark naked and scrubbed two hands through his insomnia-rumpled hair. The reason he awoke at five-thirty was so he could stop by the Y on his way to work and catch a few laps in the pool. He'd packed his trunks for this trip, just in case he had the chance to do likewise here. But as far as he could tell, there was no Y in the Hamptons. Kinda unnecessary, he supposed, when anyone who wanted the use of a gym here just installed one in their own home. The Nesbitts, he knew, were no different. Old Man Nesbitt himself had told both Tanner and Dixon they were welcome to use any of the facilities as long as they were staying here…provided no one else was around. So that must mean the Olympic-size swimming pool at the back of the big house was included…provided no one else was around. And at 5:00 a.m., it was a safe bet no one else was.

He thought again about Carly Nesbitt and her underthings and all the things she had under them. And suddenly a few dozen laps in a cold swimming pool sounded like a very good idea. Of course, with his luck since arriving at the Nesbitt estate, that pool was probably heated, something Tanner definitely did *not* need at the moment. Nevertheless, the physical exertion would do him good, two nanoseconds of sleep notwithstanding.

His mind made up, he rose to brush his teeth and don his Speedo.

CARLY COULDN'T REMEMBER the last time she'd been awake at five-thirty in the morning. Except for those occasions when she was returning home after partying all night. But she couldn't recall ever *waking* at such an hour. Not even when she was going to school.

So now she had another reason to resent Gillespie's invasion of her home—not that she needed another reason to do that. Still, the little riser-and-shiner had been anything but quiet when he'd left his room a little while ago—the *guest* room, she hastily corrected herself—to go only God knew where. Her curiosity getting the better of her—it *wasn't* because she actually cared—she'd risen from bed to look out the window and had watched him cross the foggy, ill-lit yard to the pool entrance on the side of the big house.

Swimmer, she'd deduced. Liked to get in those early-morning laps. Health-conscious lad. But then, he was still young. He didn't know any better. He didn't realize that no matter how hard you tried to fight it off, age still found you. And it didn't treat you particularly well, either. It was the beautiful people like Tanner, too, who seemed to be hit hardest.

Not that Carly cared.

And to prove it, she'd gone straight back to bed with every intention of going back to sleep and forgetting all about Tanner Gillespie. Unfortunately, instead of forgetting about him, she'd suddenly seen him bathed in a spotlight at the very center of her brain. Wearing nothing but swimming trunks. His wet hair slicked back from his finely carved features. His smooth, powerful chest crisscrossed by slowly undulating runnels of water. His attire making more prominent his already outstanding, uh…manhood.

Which was when she'd realized her sleeping was done for the night.

Dammit. What was the matter with her? Why couldn't she stop thinking about him? He couldn't be more than twenty-five or -six. Biologically speaking, she was old enough to be his mother. She was normally attracted to men twice his age. Men who had prospects. Men who had maturity. Men who had careers. Men who had money. Tanner Gillespie wasn't seasoned yet. He couldn't know what it was like to be knocked down and have to pick himself up again. He couldn't have traveled much, was barely out of school, couldn't know anything about life. As cocky and confident as he seemed, he was probably clumsy and self-conscious in bed. What could she possibly find sexy about all that?

Okay, so he was gorgeous. Big deal. Yes, Carly knew people considered her shallow, but she really wasn't the type of woman to go solely for looks. She liked men with depth. Men with style. Men with smarts. Men with spice. She liked *men*. That was the point. Men with lines on their faces and gray in their hair and thoughts in their heads and checkers in their pasts. Not some fresh-faced, squeaky-clean, gee-whiz, all-American boy.

But then, maybe that was the attraction right there, she thought. His cleanness. His artlessness. His innocence. Not that she thought for a moment Tanner Gillespie was innocent. But neither did he seem to have learned all the games men and women played when they reached a certain age. Or maybe it was a certain social standing that demanded the politeness of behavior Carly usually encountered in others. But Gillespie didn't have that, either. He was completely out there—there was no artifice in him that she could see, and he didn't give a damn about polite behavior. His blatant inspection of her yesterday had been unlike any reaction she had ever received from a man. Oh, she'd been ogled plenty of times. But never so obviously. And never in a way that had made her feel so…exposed.

And the way he'd spoken to her. No man had ever dared speak to Carly the way Gillespie had. Not to her face. Oh, she knew about the boorish and crude things men said about her behind her back. But that was just it. Men were always ever so polite, ever so amiable when they were in her company. Tanner wasn't. Not polite. Not amiable. On the contrary, he had behaved toward her in the same way he would anyone else who challenged him. And maybe that, more than anything else, was why he was commanding so much of her attention.

She looked at the clock again, then at the window, lighter now than it had been when she'd watched him stride across the yard. The sun was coming up. The night was ended. The servants would be stirring now, getting the day ready for the Nesbitts.

Not asking herself why she did it, Carly rose, too. Although she didn't normally swim during the colder months, she knew exactly where her suit was, and it was readily accessible. More to the point, she knew where Tanner Gillespie was. But was he accessible, too? And why, she wondered, did she want so badly to know?

HE DIDN'T NOTICE SHE WAS there until he'd finished his final lap—and Carly couldn't help noticing that he had a *very* nice stroke—and was hauling himself out of the pool. By then she had been watching him for a good ten minutes, noting how his powerful arms sliced effortlessly through the water, how his nimble body moved gracefully forward, how focused he was on his task. Despite the humidity in the cavernous room and the condensation streaking the glass that surrounded the pool like a giant ice cube, she felt her mouth go dry while she watched him.

He swam to the side where she stood and pushed

himself up out of the water, his biceps bulging with the action, his forearms anchored firmly on the tile edging the pool. Then he was standing and stretching an arm out for the towel he'd draped over a nearby chair, something that gave her a wide-open view of his nearly naked body, and her brain suddenly went dry, too.

She was helpless to stop the little sound of disquiet that bubbled up from someplace deep inside her, and any hope she'd held that he hadn't heard it fled when his head snapped up and his gaze fell upon her. For one scant scintillating moment, neither of them said a word. They only looked at each other as if each was equally surprised to see the other. Then Tanner's gaze shifted, dropping lower, over the flaming-red maillot bathing suit that scooped low over her breasts and was cut high above her thighs. She'd shed her shoes and outerwear while she'd watched him swim and had left it folded neatly on one of the tables poolside. The suit wasn't exactly modest, but neither was it blatantly revealing. Nevertheless, when his gaze found hers again, she could tell he'd liked what he'd seen. A lot.

But his voice was disapproving when he said, "You get lost on your way to Grandma's house, Red? Maybe you shoulda left some bread crumbs to follow."

"You're mixing up your fairy tales," she replied evenly. "Which surprises me, because it couldn't have been that long ago that your mommy was reading them to you."

He frowned, his blue eyes going absolutely glacial. But he offered not a word of rebuke. Which didn't surprise Carly, unfortunately. She was excellent at leaving men speechless. Somehow, though, she'd expected better of Gillespie. Ah, well. Good to know early on that he'd be an easy mark. Still, it wasn't going to be nearly as fun now.

Although she knew it wasn't wise to push a man after impugning his masculinity, she couldn't quite keep herself from adding, "Oh, don't pout, Gillespie. Even if you do mess up your fairy tales, I still think you're plenty grim."

Just to show him that he and his broodiness didn't scare her one whit, she slung her towel over her shoulder and walked right toward him. Smiling, she never once broke her stride, walking past without saying another word, content that she'd gotten the last one rather handily.

Until his fingers snaked around her wrist with lightning speed and he tugged on her hand. Hard.

She had no choice but to stumble backward, catching herself just before she would have tumbled face-first into him. Tanner dropped his hands to her waist before she could pull away, pinning her to the spot without a care for how she might react to his manhandling. Then he dipped his head low, until scarcely a breath of air separated their faces. His wet hair hung over eyes that seemed even bluer with the pool behind him, giving him a faintly menacing look. Water beaded on his forehead, and she watched, fascinated, as one slow trickle streamed from his left temple to his cheekbone to his jaw. God help her, all Carly wanted to do was lean forward and lick the errant drop from his skin. Her heart hammered hard against her breastbone, but she did her best not to show an ounce of interest. Or fear.

But then, she didn't fear Tanner, she told herself. She didn't. No, what she felt for him in that moment was infinitely more hazardous to her health than fear.

"Don't push me, Carly," he said softly. Evenly. Certainly. "I'm not one of your old guys who'll be so grateful for a glimpse of skin or a flirty little smile that I'll open my wallet and let you plunder at will. I have a different reaction to a woman's skin and her smiles. And it doesn't involve my wallet. Though there could be some opening and plundering." He smiled wickedly. "If you're lucky."

Her heart rate doubled at that, but she gave her head a careless toss—at least she hoped it was careless—and muttered as nonchalantly as she could, "Oh, get over your bad self already." But the words came out quiet and breathless and in no way confident.

His smile broadened, and he dipped his head closer still. Close enough that she could see a faint rim of dark green circling the blue of his irises, close enough that she could smell the clean chlorine scent of him, close enough that she could feel his body heat radiating against her. Even more softly and certainly than before he said, "I don't think I'm the one who needs to get over my bad self, sweetheart."

And for that, more than anything else, Carly decided he was going to have to die. Slowly and painfully. Preferably by her hand. Bad enough she was responding to this little upstart the way she was. Worse that he was so aware of her condition.

"You're nuts," she said. "If there's anything *I* need to get over, it's your flaming great ego."

He chuckled. "Yeah, well, takes one to know one, doesn't it?"

She ignored the comment and told herself to move away from him, to dive into the pool and swim off the strange restlessness that had come over her this morning. For some reason, though, she couldn't make herself move. Her body hummed where he touched her, even with the fabric of her bathing suit hindering any skin-to-skin contact. And although a good inch separated them, she could almost feel the vibration of his heartbeat slamming against her own. Not trusting herself to move away from him, Carly remained rooted in place.

He loosened his grip on her waist but didn't release her. Nor did he withdraw so much as a millimeter. "Look," he said, "trust me when I tell you that I'm no happier to be here than you are to have me. So maybe we should just both stay out of each other's way while I'm here. What do you say?"

She started to tell him she was *not* going to have him and would be delighted to stay out of his way but quickly changed her mind. For the first time in her life Carly felt almost evenly matched by a man. Almost. And she honestly wasn't sure what to do about it. Where she had initially found Tanner Gillespie to be an annoying little boy toy, now she was beginning to think he might be something more. She just wasn't sure what yet. All she knew was that she was having a reaction to him unlike any she'd had to another man, and she was curious to see how it would play out.

Probably nothing would come of it. He didn't seem to like her any more than she liked him. But maybe, just maybe, the next couple of weeks wouldn't be as irritating or cumbersome as she'd first thought. A younger man might offer an interesting diversion for a woman like her. He might even know a few things men her age or older didn't.

A girl could hope, after all.

When she didn't immediately reply to his question, the hands holding her waist clenched tighter again. Though whether Tanner was thinking about pulling her close to kiss her or chuck her into the pool, Carly couldn't have said. When she looked at his face again, she realized he didn't know what he wanted to do, either.

Interesting. Very interesting.

Since he didn't seem to know what to do next—poor boy—she decided to do it for him. Cupping her own hands over the ones he still held at her waist, she pushed herself upward until she was nose to nose with him. "Am I supposed to be afraid of you, Gillespie?" She easily removed his hands from her waist and shoved them back down to his sides, where they stayed. "A man who can't even find the best parts of a woman who's dressed in a way that should show him exactly where to look? Call me crazy; but I'm not impressed."

And with that, she spun around and made her way to the edge of the pool and dived in. As she broke through the water and began to freestyle her way to the other end, she didn't spare another look—or another thought—for Tanner Gillespie.

She didn't need to. One thing she'd learned after two decades of dealing with men—young or old, experienced or not, they were all essentially the same. They were driven by one thing and one thing only— their cocks. And Carly Nesbitt was an excellent driver.

Tanner Gillespie was going to be a pushover.

TANNER WATCHED AS CARLY Nesbitt strode away from him, shaking his head at the picture she created. Damn. She'd looked downright luscious in skintight leather and clingy black, but in a screaming-red swimsuit...

mmm, mmm good. To be really crass about it and reduce her to a food metaphor. Which he had a habit of doing with especially luscious women. So sue him.

He wasn't surprised when she didn't spare him a second glance—or thought. Women like her were totally predictable. Utterly sure of themselves and their ample charms, certain they were God's gift to men. And, it went without saying, they were right. Like any gift, though, Tanner wasn't about to decline the offer. He only wished he didn't have to do this on her turf, since that put him at a bit of a disadvantage. The über-wealthy had too many polite-society rules to follow, and Tanner was only familiar with the one about not chewing with your mouth open. A woman like Carly Nesbitt, who'd been pampered and spoiled and coddled from birth, could learn a thing or two about real life in the place where Tanner grew up.

Ah, well. He was a man accustomed to adapting. And he was a fast learner. Lucky for Carly, he was a fast teacher, too. She had no idea what she was in for.

But he couldn't wait to show her.

CHAPTER ELEVEN

FOR THREE DAYS AND NIGHTS following the first there was no contact from Sorcerer, nor were Dixon and Avery able to locate him online. Dixon noted that Avery reverted to her usual habit of sleeping during the day, though he couldn't have said whether that was because of their late hours on the computer or simply because she wanted to avoid her family as much as she could. He suspected it was the latter. Not that he blamed her. He slept during the day, too. Cowboy kept opposite hours, monitoring the equipment in his room during the day, looking for signs of Sorcerer from the lists of handles he used and chat rooms he frequented that Avery had supplied OPUS. But the other agent didn't have any more luck than she and Dixon had. It was as if Sorcerer had disappeared from the planet—or perhaps had discovered somehow that they were looking for him.

Either way, he stayed quiet. And Dixon did his best not to show his concern that this assignment might wind up being one big bust. Avery was more upbeat, certain there was a reasonable explanation for Sorcerer's absence. By that fourth night, however, Dixon could tell she was becoming a little anxious, too.

So, as had become their habit, they spent much of the

evening engaged in some semitense banter to stave off the monotony. Though Dixon made sure the banter was light and insubstantial. He still didn't know what had possessed him to share as much of himself with Avery as he had that first night, why he'd told her about his father. He *never* talked about that. With *any*one. He'd tried to tell himself it was a lack of sleep and the strangeness of the assignment, but he'd finally had to admit that there was just something in Avery that sparked something in him he wasn't used to feeling. And he did his best not to think about it.

But every night when he saw her, something inside him just…opened up. He couldn't think of any other way to describe it. It was as if a part of him opened to greet her. To invite her inside. To visit with her. Be with her. It was the damnedest thing. But the feeling was with him whenever he was near her.

Like now.

Only now it was stronger. Because where she was seated as she always was—on the ottoman in front of her computer—he had moved from his usual position on the floor to sit immediately behind her, in an effort to watch what she was doing. He was as close to her as he'd ever been, save that delirious night in her home when he'd been forced to pin her to the couch. Because she preferred to work in the dark and because he sat so close, he could see the bluish light of the monitor reflecting off her little black glasses and her long black hair, woven—as it had been since her arrival at her parents' house—into a single braid that tumbled down the center of her back to nearly her waist.

As was her habit, she wore clothes that were maddeningly loose and unfeminine, heavy socks, grubby

blue jeans and an oversize plaid flannel shirt. And
Dixon didn't want to think about why that bothered
him so much—aside from the fact that it mirrored his
own clothing exactly. What he wouldn't have given to
see her just once looking like a woman. He called
himself every manner of sexist for thinking that way—
not to mention stupid—but there it was all the same.

What he noticed more than anything about her,
though, was that intoxicating peachy scent of her, an
aroma whose origin he had yet to identify but which
continued to drive him crazy. It made no sense. He'd
been with women who smelled of the most expensive
perfumes, women who wore ridiculously fluffy lingerie,
women who celebrated their femaleness with the most
feminine clothing money could buy. Yet it was Avery
Nesbitt, brainy tomboy computer geek, who was front
and center in his thoughts lately.

Obviously the boredom was making him crazy.

Tonight the lack of activity seemed to frustrate Avery
even more than it did him. Of course, it might not be
Sorcerer's lack of activity that was bothering her the
most. Her family had been exceptionally annoying over
the past few days. Dixon had witnessed enough aberrant
familial behavior by now to send Freud himself into a
push-up bra and thong underwear. Dinners especially
had been a Nesbitt psychosis fest. Happily Desmond V
and his wife had only been present for one, otherwise
Dixon would have had to listen to yet another tug-of-
war over the guesthouse and numerous other family
possessions.

But even without the brother present, Carly Nesbitt
always seemed to find someone to spar with—though
Gillespie seemed to be her favorite for that. Not that

Dixon didn't understand, because he found the guy to be pretty irritating, too. Nevertheless, he supposed he should be grateful he and Gillespie—not to mention Avery—were even included in the family dinners. He'd half expected to have to stay in his room while Jensen the butler brought him a TV tray filled with tepid water and scraps of bread.

Mostly the Nesbitts continued to pretend Avery wasn't there. And through it all, Avery remained stoic, even passive. Truth be told, her response annoyed Dixon even more than the family's behavior did. She never fought back. She never showed any reaction to the things they said—or didn't say—or the way they treated her. She just pretended there was nothing wrong with the situation as it was.

What had happened to the woman who had popped him in the nose that night at her apartment? Where was the kicking and the screaming, metaphorical if not literal? Where was her defiance? Her damned spirit? It was as if walking into this house had stripped her of everything that made her Avery.

Except at night, he amended now, when she was trying to lure out the man who had played her for a fool. On those occasions, the dauntless, crafty, spirited Avery came into her own.

And Dixon told himself it didn't bother him that she exhibited more life when she was dealing with Sorcerer than she did with him. He told himself he preferred it that way. She should care more about Sorcerer than she cared about him. Because Sorcerer was the one she needed to draw out, not Dixon.

"He's here."

Avery's two very softly spoken words yanked Dixon

out of his thoughts and into the action—where he needed to be, where he preferred to be. He snapped forward in his chair until his face was immediately beside hers, nearly touching her.

"Where?" he asked.

"He's signed in as Mad2Live. It's his favorite handle. He's making it easy for me to find him. But right now I'm signed in under a name he won't recognize as me."

"Then he doesn't know you're watching him," Dixon said.

"No, he doesn't. But he knows I use other handles for my work that he wouldn't recognize. So he could suspect I'm online. He'll e-mail me at an address I sent to him alone if he wants me to meet him. Or he'll hope I'm watching for him and IM him."

"Check your mail at that address," Dixon told her. "Don't contact him with whoever you're being right now."

She signed out and in again under another name. The little flag on her cyber mailbox popped up, punctuated by a cheery female voice announcing, "You've got mail!"

"Coochie and Snookypie," he muttered incredulously when he recognized their two names from earlier e-mail exchanges he'd intercepted between the two of them. "You know, for two intelligent people, you and Sorcerer sure are weird."

"Welcome to the world of cyberdating," Avery said. "There's a lovely anonymity here that allows you to say and do things and even *be* things you might not otherwise say or do or be."

"Like a twenty-six-year-old guitarist/songwriter/ poet/animal-rights activist and Libertarian party member named Andrew Paddington," Dixon said, knowing that was the phony persona Sorcerer had presented to Avery.

"Yeah," she replied quietly. "Like that."

He read over her shoulder the e-mail she opened from the phony songwriter Andrew Paddington and the genuine bastard Adrian Padgett. But there was nothing helpful in it, only a brief announcement that he'd been out of town, touring with his band and trying to make a few bucks to cover rent, but he'd be online tonight if Coochie—*Coochie?* Dixon still couldn't jibe her as such—wanted to hook up.

No sooner had he read the sig line, however—a quote from Jack Kerouac designed to make the poster of said quote look anticonsumer in a capitalist world, so ironic in light of the fact that Sorcerer wanted to consume the entire world—an IM window popped up with a message in red text from Mad2Live that said, Hi, Coochie!

Dixon feared he might be genuinely sick, but fortunately Avery kept her Snookypies to herself. Because she only typed a blue-lettered response that said, Hey, you. Where've you been?

There was a momentary pause at Sorcerer's end for typing, then another line appeared in the IM box: I could ask you the same thing. Where have YOU been?

"What do I do?" she whispered, her voice edged with alarm.

"Answer him," Dixon told her, keeping his voice calm, even though heat had coiled in his stomach and blood was surging through his veins.

"Oh, right," Avery said. "Tell him that I've been out of touch because I was arrested?"

"You weren't arrested," Dixon told her.

"The hell I wasn't."

"Now is not the time," he said, his voice edged with warning.

"Then what am I supposed to tell him?" she hissed.

She was beginning to panic, and that was the last thing they needed right now. So he extended his arms around her, reaching for the keyboard, and began to type himself.

I'm sorry, he wrote. I've had a lot of work this week.

You work too much, came Sorcerer's reply.

His arms still around Avery, Dixon typed, It was a job I got at the last minute. Client needed it finished right away. It's consumed my life for the past five days.

Can you chat now? Sorcerer wrote next.

Sure, Dixon typed back.

Avery was filled with dread when she saw the question Andrew—or rather Adrian—asked, and the way Dixon answered it without consulting her first. She just hoped this "chat" he wanted would be one of their innocent exchanges that touched on the events of their daily lives and didn't turn into one of the steamy interludes she had once enjoyed so much they could bring her to the brink of orgasm. And not just because it would sicken her to have to pretend to be turned on by a man who'd been lying to and misleading her, either. The last thing she wanted was to end up in the virtual bedroom with Andrew/Adrian while Dixon was looking over her shoulder, close enough that she could feel his warm breath on the back of her neck and smell the clean soapy fragrance of him. His arms skimmed along the length of hers as he typed and his shoulders brushed her back. If she leaned even the tiniest bit to one side, she could rub her cheek against his and see if his skin was as warm and rough as it looked.

Oh, yeah. She really needed to avoid any kind of sexual encounter with Andrew—Adrian, she corrected herself—online tonight. Because it would be way too easy to take it off-line with Dixon instead.

"What now?" he asked when Adrian said nothing more.

"We go to our room," she said.

"You have a chat room for the two of you?"

Avery nodded as she pushed Dixon's hands away from the keyboard to type in the URL. Adrian was already there waiting for her when she signed in. They began with the usual catching up, each filling in the other on what had been happening during their time apart. Only this time Avery knew they were both lying. Adrian, as Andrew, told her about driving to Pittsburgh and Cincinnati and Louisville and Nashville to play some gigs and how great it was to be back in Philadelphia again.

Dixon had told her Adrian was living in New York City, and Avery had wondered since then just how close he may have gotten to her, physically. Did he know where she lived? Had he visited her building? She told herself he couldn't know her whereabouts because she had too many security precautions in place. But Dixon had found her. Maybe not easily, but he had. Could Adrian have located her, too?

It didn't bear thinking about. Because if Adrian knew where she lived, and if he'd scoped out her place, he might have known she was being surveilled even before she found out about it herself. He might know she'd been taken into custody. He might know she was working in concert with the agency trying to bring him down. And if he knew all that, and she drew him out, and he came looking for her or for Dixon…

I have nothing to fear in this moment, she told herself as panic splashed into her belly. *In this moment I have nothing to fear….*

"Avery." Dixon's voice sounded softly in her right ear, punctuated by his warm breath on her neck. "You need to answer him."

She looked at the screen and saw what Adrian had typed most recently: I want you, Coochie. Tell me you want me, too.

Oh, God, she thought. He wanted sex. This man who was a total stranger to her. This man who was corrupt and vicious and dangerous. He wanted her to tell him how much she needed him. How much she wanted him. How much she loved him. While Dixon was looking on.

"I can't do this," she whispered roughly, dropping her hands from the keyboard. "I just can't."

"You have to," Dixon told her. "He's expecting it. He'll get suspicious if you don't."

"I can't," she said again. "I can't pretend I'm turned on by him and I can't make love, even virtually, to a stranger."

"He's not a stranger," Dixon reminded her. "You've been doing this with him for weeks."

"Not him," she said. "I thought he was someone else, someone I cared about. And I can't do this now."

"You have to," he said again.

"Dixon, I *can't.*"

"Well, I'm sure as hell not gonna do it."

In spite of his protest, he leaned forward again, reaching both arms around her to place them over the keyboard. When he did it this time, he thrust his entire body forward so that his chest pressed into her back and his arms were aligned with hers and his legs were spread open alongside her own, his thighs pressing intimately into hers. And for one brief incredibly wonderful moment, his rough jaw brushed lightly over her cheek. Avery felt more than the warmth of his breath now. She felt the heat, the humming life, of his body, too. And she smelled him, the Ivory soap he'd bathed with that morning, the spicy shampoo he'd used on his hair, the potent scent of his own distinct masculinity.

And it was almost more than she could bear.

So long, she thought as her eyes fluttered closed. It had been so long since she had been physically close to a man. Ten years. That was how long it had been since she'd touched a man. That was how long it had been since a man had touched her.

No, not ten years, she remembered. Because Dixon had touched her that night in her apartment. Touched her intimately, too, when he'd searched her. But that night she'd been unable to respond with anything but terror. Tonight there was no fear. At least, not the kind that had been there before. She hadn't known what was going on that first time, hadn't known who he was or what his intentions were or where he would take her. Now she knew what was happening. Now she knew where he could take her. And she wanted more than anything for him to take her there.

She forced herself to open her eyes, to return her attention to the computer screen. And she saw that Dixon had typed something in for her and that Adrian had replied to what he'd said. But Dixon hadn't moved away from her when he'd finished. His chair was still scooted up behind her stool and his body was perched right on its edge. His powerful thighs were still pressing into hers, his chest was still pushed against her back and his arms still rubbed along her own. But as much as she noticed the nearness of his body, she was focused more on the words that had scrolled down the screen.

Tell me what you want, Dixon had last typed for her.

I want your mouth on me, Adrian had replied.

Oh, God…

"Answer him," Dixon said, his voice sounding even closer now than it had before. He dropped his hands from the keyboard, grabbed both of Avery's and placed them where his had been. "I got you this far," he added. "But you have to be the one to do the rest. Tell him what he wants to hear."

"I can't," she said again, more breathlessly this time.

"You can," Dixon assured her.

And she realized that she could, because Dixon's nearness made her want all the things that Adrian wanted, too. If she could just think about Dixon instead of Adrian, think about the feel of his body against her own…his smell…his voice…his everything…

Taking a deep breath, Avery began to type.

She remembered what Andrew liked and she remembered he liked to read about it in coarse, raw language. So that was what she used for Adrian. Her fingers fumbled on the keys a few times as she began to describe what she was doing to him, but she recovered and continued as well as she could.

Now my hands are on your belt, she typed. Unfastening it, pulling the leather through the buckle very slowly. Watch the leather as it glides through the buckle. Now see my hands on the snap of your jeans.

I'm undoing it, Andrew, and pulling down the zipper. I can see your big cock surging up as I unzip you and I put my hand inside to touch you. I palm the head and drag my fingers down your shaft. It's so hard and long. I can't wait to put it in my mouth. Your zipper is completely undone now and your cock is free. I'm lowering my head to it now, sucking you into my mouth....

She heard Dixon's breathing coming from behind her, harder than it had been before, and she wondered if it was because he was getting as turned on as she was by what she was writing. Normally at this point in her conversations with Andrew she'd be touching herself, giving herself some small pleasure to help ease her frustration and make her enjoy the experience more. But with Dixon behind her, that was impossible. Her panties had grown damp and her breasts were tender and expectant, and her inability to satisfy herself the way she wanted to only multiplied her desire and her need and her passion. Adrian's occasional comments—coarse and raw—enflamed her even more with the explicitness of what he would do to her when she was finished with him. Little by little, Avery began to breathe more raggedly, too.

You feel so good in my mouth, she typed. You taste so hot. So alive. I'm sucking you harder now, do you feel it? Pulling you deeper into my mouth, curling my tongue around the head of your cock. I feel your hand between my legs now, rubbing me, making me even wetter. Put your finger inside me....

She made her descriptions more graphic, more crude, more explicit. Heat shuddered through her, uncoiling in her belly to spread between her legs and over her breasts. She opened her mouth to breathe harder, battling the urge to reach behind herself for Dixon, to move his hand to the places she wanted so desperately to touch herself. So fierce was her need for him that for a moment she actually felt as if he were touching her, as if he'd slipped an arm around her waist and curled his fingers beneath her breast.

And then she realized she wasn't imagining it at all. He really was touching her, was cradling the lower swell of her breast in the deep V of his thumb and forefinger. A frantic little sound escaped her, but she didn't let herself turn around. Instead she kept typing, kept telling Adrian all the ways she wanted to pleasure him, all the things she wanted him to do to her. And as Dixon read over her shoulder, his hand drifted lower, along her rib cage, over her belly, down to her thigh, between her legs.

She cried out at the contact, so exquisite was his touch there. As he pressed his hand hard against her, Dixon groaned, dipping his head to her neck, rubbing his open mouth along the sensitive column of her throat. He looped his other arm around her waist, pulling her body back toward him, covering her breast over her shirt with one big hand. His other hand pushed harder against her damp center, making her cry out again, and it was all she could do to punch her thumb against the power button on the computer to shut it off.

She didn't want Adrian. She wanted Dixon. And she wanted Dixon now.

Turning off the computer the way she had left them in total darkness, but that only made it more arousing. She felt his hands at the bottom of her shirt now, feverishly working to unbutton it, so she moved her own hands to the top, working her way down. They met at her center, and once the garment fell open, he jerked it down over her arms and cast it aside, covering her breasts with both hands over her bra. She surged forward as he pressed his mouth to her neck again, and reached behind herself to thread her fingers through his hair. It was so soft, so wonderful. She'd forgotten how silky a man's hair could be, the sensual way it felt twined around her fingers. With one deft motion he unfastened the front clasp of her bra and cast it, too, to the floor. And then his hands were on her again, bare flesh to bare flesh.

It was glorious. He palmed her breasts with much enthusiasm, once, twice, three times, four, then caught her nipples between thumb and forefinger, rolling them gently before covering her with his hand again. One hand dipped lower, following the same route he had charted before, this time pausing at the waistband of her blue jeans. He fumbled for a minute with the buttons of her fly, then his hand was dipping inside the soft denim and pushing under the elastic of her panties, threading through the soft hair between her legs. Then lower still, to the damp folds of flesh that had been aching to be touched.

Avery spread her legs wider, granting him fuller access, and he responded by scooping his hand beneath her, slipping one long finger deep inside. She gasped at the extent and immediacy of his entry, bucking her hips forward to deepen the penetration, only to have him withdraw his finger and slide it in again. Over and over he thrust into and out of her, and Avery gasped at the ripples of pleasure that rocketed through her with each new push.

Good. It felt so good. So incredible. So extraordinary. So much better than when she did it herself....

Her orgasm seemed to go on forever, but eventually the little quakes inside her subsided. She felt a momentary pang of regret, then remembered that she and Dixon were just getting started. He wasn't even undressed yet—something she intended to remedy right away.

He didn't seem surprised when she rose and turned to face him. But he obviously hadn't expected her to turn on the bedside lamp, because he squinted at the intrusion of the light, however scant. His gaze settled on hers for just a second, then dropped lower, to her naked breasts and her unfastened jeans. When he looked at her face again, his pupils had expanded to nearly eclipse the green irises.

For a moment, he said nothing. Then in a hoarse whisper he told her, "Come here."

She took one step forward, all that was necessary to bring her between his legs. He lifted his hands to her waist, splaying them open over her sensitive flesh, raking his thumbs lightly over her bottom ribs. She closed her eyes and curled her fingers into his hair, sighing when she felt him press his mouth to her bare abdomen. He traced her navel with his tongue, rubbed his open mouth along her flat torso, then pushed his hands into her blue jeans and began to pull them and her panties down.

When he reached her ankles, she stepped out of her clothes, amazed at how little inhibition she felt being naked with him while he was still dressed. She'd always insisted on the man undressing first, had liked the feeling of being in control. With Dixon, though, she didn't care. This time he could be in control. Next time she could be—

Well. She wouldn't think about next time. She had him this time. And this time she intended to enjoy him. Somehow, it was enough.

He cupped his hands over her naked hips and pulled her toward himself, positioning her in a way that told her he wanted her to straddle him. She roped her arms around his neck as she sat astride his lap, threaded her fingers through his hair again, then leaned in to cover his open mouth with hers, capturing his tongue in an effort to consume him. She felt his hands open wide over her bare back, then move lower, cupping the curves of her derriere and squeezing hard.

Impatient and wanting to touch him, too, Avery moved her hands to the collar of his shirt and jerked hard to open it, ripping a few buttons completely from their moorings. She pushed the garment over his shoulders and tossed it to the floor, kissing him and kissing him and kissing him, until finally her naked skin connected with his.

It was a magnificent sensation, hot flesh rubbing against hot flesh. Avery had always loved sex. Reveled in it. She'd forgotten how narcotic the experience could be. As a teenager, she'd never been able to understand the inhibitions of her friends. Not that she'd been promiscuous or careless about sex—she'd been in college before she'd gone all the way with a boy. But from the moment she'd discovered physical closeness with the opposite sex, she'd seen no reason to be coy. She'd loved touching. She'd loved cuddling. She'd loved caressing. She'd loved tasting. She'd loved the sheer closeness of another body alongside her own. And once she did discover the joy of coupling, she'd wondered how she would ever live without it.

But she had lived without it. For much too long. And now…

Oh, *now*…

"Now, Dixon," she said aloud. "I want you inside me now."

And without waiting for him to respond, she scrambled out of his lap and onto the floor, kneeling before him as she fought with the zipper of his jeans. The moment she pulled the heavy fabric open, he sprang forward, fully erect. She took a moment to marvel at the size and power of him, then she dipped her head forward and drew him into her mouth. He uttered a sound like a wild animal, then cupped one hand over the crown of her head. Avery rose up on her knees and pushed her head lower, drawing as much of him into her mouth as she could, savoring every inch. He tasted alive and male and potent, and although she took her time with him, it wasn't enough. Not nearly enough.

"Oh, God, Avery," he groaned as she intensified her attentions. "You keep this up, I'm not going to last much longer."

Reluctantly she pulled back, not wanting things to move too fast. She'd waited ten years for a night like this and intended to enjoy every moment of it. She may never have another like it again.

She rose from her knees and moved to the bed, grabbing the corner of the spread and pulling it back. She did her best to look sensual as she climbed atop it, giving him a good view of what, all modesty aside, she knew was a very nice ass. At the center of the bed, she turned to face him and curled her legs beneath her, then brought her braid forward and loosened the rubber band that held it at the bottom. Little by little she unbraided it, until her hair cascaded over her shoulders like an ebony river. And then she fixed her gaze on Dixon's, hoping he wouldn't be able to resist.

Silently he stood, and she caught her breath at the sheer size of him. Half-naked, he somehow seemed even bigger than when he was clothed. Dark hair spanned his chest, his jeans gaped open and his hard rod stood at full staff. He looked primitive and untamable and hot. She could scarcely believe she was about to make love with such a man. Just the thought of it nearly brought her to climax.

"Peaches," he said softly as he came to a halt by the side of the bed, "I didn't exactly come here expecting a party. If you know what I mean. I don't have a condom."

"It doesn't matter," she told him. "My cycles run like clockwork. I won't get pregnant."

"What about STDs?" he asked. "I get checked every year on the government's dime, but…"

"But you're not sure you can trust me to be clean, right?" she asked matter-of-factly.

He said nothing. Which pretty much amounted to an affirmative.

She didn't want to tell him the truth, that she hadn't been with anyone since before she went to prison. That it had been ten years since she had been with a man. But how could she lie? She was relentlessly honest with men. It was one of her worst vices.

"It's been a long time for me, Dixon," she finally said. "I mean, a long, long time."

"How long?"

"Since college," she said.

His eyebrows shot up at that. "You haven't had sex for ten years?"

"Look, could we talk about this later?" she asked. "Just know that I'm healthy, all right? Trust me. The way that I trust you."

She'd meant about the whole health issue when she said it, but as the words left her mouth she was astonished to realize that she did indeed trust Dixon. Wholly and completely. In every sense of the word. At least in that moment. At least for now. And really, when all was said and done, *now* was all Avery had. It was all she'd ever had. Later would take care of itself. Now, though, Avery wanted...

Well, she wanted too much to even begin to list it all. But most of all, she wanted Dixon.

She wasn't sure when he decided to trust her, too, or even if he decided to trust her at all. He must have decided to have sex with her, though, because he hooked his thumbs into the waistband of his jeans and pushed them down. His eyes never left Avery's as he stepped out of them and kicked them away, then joined her on the bed, lying alongside her, facing her, covering her hip with one hand.

She smiled as she placed her hand on his chest and urged him to lie flat on his back, then levered one leg over him to straddle his middle. Dixon took his cue from there and, smiling back at her, settled both hands on her hips. Slowly she moved her body forward until her calves were hugging his rib cage and her knees were nudging him under his arms. He pressed his hands more insistently into her flesh, pulling her forward even more. She gripped the headboard behind him and, with one final motion, brought herself to the place they both wanted her to be. Dixon lifted his head from the pillow, moved it between her legs and gently began tonguing her tender flesh.

Her eyes fluttered closed as he tasted her, her grip tightening on the headboard with each stroke of his tongue. Vaguely she registered the movement of his hands from her hips to her bottom, his fingers delving into the elegant line bisecting it. He urged her forward with one hand, and as he penetrated her damp canal with his tongue, he gently dipped a finger inside her from behind. She gasped at the double penetration, then sighed, feeling full and complete and very aroused.

For a long time he savored her, consumed her, pleasured her with his finger and his tongue. Before she could succumb to another orgasm, though, he withdrew from her, moving her gently backward over the length of his hard shaft. Rising up on her knees, Avery brought herself down over him, sighing with pleasure at the slow, thorough penetration. He was so big, she'd wondered if he would hurt her. But he filled her perfectly, the gentle friction of him moving inside her generating a deep sense of satisfaction. Up and down she moved her body, her pace leisurely at first, then gradually quickening, then slowing again.

During one of the slow times, Dixon gripped her hips again and lifted her off him, twisting their bodies until he was kneeling behind her. Avery positioned herself on her hands and knees, but he gently urged her head and shoulders down to the mattress. He entered her from behind, easily, thoroughly, sliding hard and deep, so damp was she from her arousal.

The crispness of the sheet felt rough against her sensitive nipples, so she covered her breasts with her hands as he joined his body with hers, bringing herself even more pleasure. Again and again Dixon bucked his hips against her, claiming her body with his own. Little by little his movements quickened until he reached a feverish rhythm, when he withdrew from Avery completely and turned her so that she lay on her back. He gripped one of her ankles in each hand, spreading her legs wide, then knelt before her and pushed himself inside her again. For long moments he thrust in and out of her that way, Avery tangling her fingers in the sheet beside her and groaning for more. Just as she was about to crest, he stopped and withdrew, folding himself over her, his body pressed into hers, bracing both muscular forearms on the mattress near her head.

"I want to watch you while you come," he said raggedly.

And she very nearly did right then.

But he hesitated when he seemed to realize just how close she was, smiling at the control he held so capably. With another slow push, he was deep, *deep,* inside her again. After that, things became a little hazy for her, so lost was she in the sheer ecstasy cartwheeling through her. She cupped her hands behind his neck as he drove himself harder, spreading her legs wide and tilting her hips upward to encourage a deeper penetration still. Again and again he thrust inside her until they were both panting and grunting on the verge of detonation. At the same time that an explosion of white heat erupted at her center, she felt his body jerk to a halt, felt his heat spilling inside her, mingling his essence with her own.

They were one in that moment in every possible way—physically, spiritually, sexually, emotionally. And even if that moment only lasted a moment, it was more than Avery had had in a long time. It was more than she'd ever had, really. Because in that moment, she very nearly loved Dixon. And even if that only lasted a moment, too, she would hold on to the memory forever.

But the night was still young, she thought as he collapsed against her. Really, they were only just beginning….

CHAPTER TWELVE

ON DAY FIVE OF WHAT TANNER had come to think of as not his Hamptons *Idyll* but his Hamptons *Ordeal*, he wrestled with his necktie and tried to think of a proper analogy for dinner with the Nesbitts. Old Man Nesbitt kept insisting that the meal was a formal affair, and as such, everyone was required to dress for the occasion. But over the past week Tanner had come to think of it more as, oh…what was a good analogy? Hmm…let's see…. Okay, he had one. Dinner with the Nesbitts wasn't so much a formal affair as it was a colonoscopy performed with a hacksaw. Without anesthesia. In the dark. By an orangutan. Though, now that he thought about it, even that was preferable to spending another evening sitting across the table from Carly Nesbitt while she and the rest of her family gave bitterness a bad name.

The only reason Tanner continued to take his meals with them was because a man had to eat, and he'd discovered that the average cost of lunch in the Hamptons was roughly eighty billion dollars. And Tanner was saving up his money for something special—a lifestyle. So he'd just go for the free eats the Nesbitts offered and he'd deal with the indigestion that came from sitting across from Carly later.

Of course, indigestion wasn't the only thing Carly had been giving him the past few nights. She'd also given him a hard time. And she'd given him the once-over. Several times, in fact. And she'd given him some steamy looks, too. But those he hadn't minded so much. Nor had he minded her giving him an eyeful, which she'd also done at least once during every meal, usually by reaching *waaaaaaaay* down the table for a salt shaker instead of asking someone to pass it, which would have been the polite thing to do. Even Tanner, with his working-class manners, knew that. But had she done the polite thing, then she couldn't have leaned *waaaaaaaay* over in the low-cut dress she invariably wore and do the impolite thing she liked doing even better: flashing the guests.

Or maybe it was just Tanner she liked flashing. She always seemed to wait until everyone else was caught up in some other activity—usually quarreling or nit-picking or grumbling, more favorite Nesbitt pastimes—before she put on her little peep show. And gosh, but he was just so touched that she'd single him out that way.

And yeah, okay, so maybe that was another reason he kept joining the family for dinner. So sue him.

He'd meant it that morning by the pool when he'd told her the two of them should just stay out of each other's way. And he'd done his best—honest he had—to follow his own advice. He'd kept to his room, planted in front of his computer, trawling for leads or information about Sorcerer, analyzing and reanalyzing what little they did have on the guy, monitoring Avery's comings and goings on the Net until Padgett finally showed his face.

And how bad was that, that when the guy finally, *finally,* showed up, Avery's computer went down for no apparent reason? And right when things had been getting steamy, too, Tanner had been sorry to see when he went to prepare the transcript first thing next morning. Not that he was into voyeurism or anything, but… Well. Suffice it to say he'd never be able to look at Avery quite the same way again.

Still, had she and Sorcerer been able to, uh, consummate their, uh, whatever it was they had, then maybe they could have moved on to an exchange that would have furthered the assignment. It had been nearly a week since they'd set up shop at the Nesbitt estate, and so far they had nothing more than a brief, unfinished dialogue with their quarry that helped not at all. At this rate, Tanner would be spending the rest of his life sleeping in a room that looked as if it belonged in a high-class brothel and staring down Carly Nesbitt's shirt.

Not that there was anything wrong with that.

True to form, when he seated himself at the Nesbitt dinner table—which he'd noted that first night was roughly the size of Delaware—he saw that Carly had once again squeezed herself into a tiny little dress, this one the color of a sailor-take-warning sunrise. Or maybe it was the color of a sailor's-delight sunset. Tanner would have to wait and see how he felt by evening's end. In any event, it was a cross between hot-pink and flaming-red, and it set off more than a few sirens in his head. Not to mention other parts of his body.

"Ms. Nesbitt," he greeted her as he had every evening—with a touch of sarcasm for flavor—then folded himself into his seat.

"Gillespie," she replied easily, dispensing with any sort of formal address in an effort to make him feel, he was sure, like a slug.

Tonight there seemed to be even more tension in the

air than usual. That could have been because the younger Desmond Nesbitt and his wife were present, but the tension seemed to come more from Dixon and Avery's end of the table than anywhere else. Although Avery hadn't arrived, Dixon was sitting in his usual place next to hers on the other side of Tanner, at the very end of the table. But where the other man had seemed reasonably comfortable in the arrangement before, chatting amiably if not deeply with everyone else— particularly Avery—tonight he was looking at no one. And no one was saying a word to him, either.

Odd, Tanner thought. Not that he'd found Dixon to be the most gregarious guy in the world, but he had seemed to warm up some since their arrival at the estate. Tonight, though, his expression was as dark as the black federal-agent suit he wore and his mouth was flattened into a hard line. Certainly he had plenty to be pissed off about, having lost Sorcerer last night. But they could try again this evening. There was no reason for him to look as if it were the end of the world.

A flash of pink—a soft, rosy pink this time, as opposed to the anatomically correct Georgia O'Keefe pink Carly was wearing—caught Tanner's eye, and he looked up at the entry to see… No, it couldn't be. That couldn't possibly be Avery Nesbitt, whose concessions to "dressing for dinner" had so far consisted of baggy man-style trousers and even baggier man-style shirts, wearing a pink sweater set and slim gray skirt. She looked like…well, Mrs. Nesbitt. Only not as frigid. Probably that was because Avery wasn't wearing her hair in that long, tight braid down her back she normally favored and had instead woven it very loosely and pulled it forward over one shoulder.

She actually looked kind of pretty, Tanner thought. She also looked nervous about something. Of course, nervous was pretty much her natural state, but she, too, seemed to have relaxed some since that first evening at her ancestral home. Even at dinner, when her family seemed to be at its worst, she was always able to stay cool. Tonight, however, she was obviously edgy.

He started to return his attention to Carly, who made him feel edgy and nervous—in a good way—but his gaze halted on Dixon before completing the journey. Wow. Had he thought the guy was glowering before? Man, he'd had no idea. Because Dixon's dark expression had become downright black. And the reason for it, Tanner also saw, was Avery's arrival. Or maybe it was her appearance. Or maybe it was both. In any event, it was Avery Dixon was looking at when his scowl turned into a grimace, Avery who was clearly the source of his discomfort. Or maybe it was displeasure he was feeling. Or even dislike.

She seemed to sense his turbulence, because what had been an almost smile playing about her lips went flat and she hastily dropped her gaze to the floor. She didn't turn around and bolt from the room, though, which was what she had looked ready to do. Instead she strode over to the table and took her seat next to Dixon. But she kept her body turned away from him, toward the place where her father sat, and Dixon likewise turned away from her.

And suddenly Tanner found himself wondering if maybe, just maybe, the computer shutting down the way it had the night before, *when* it had the night before, hadn't been such an accident after all.

Well, well, well. So Dixon could be as professionally unethical as the next guy. The next guy being Tanner, of course, whose thoughts about Carly had been anything but professional since his arrival, never mind ethical. Or moral. Or decent.

As if his thoughts set her into action, she suddenly spoke up, saying tartly, "My God, she *can* show some fashion sense when she wants to. Of course, that outfit was *more* fashionable twenty years ago when Mother bought it." Then, a little too sweetly she added, "Oh, but it looks good on *her.*"

"I didn't know we'd be dressing for dinner when I packed," Avery said quietly without looking up. "I didn't bring enough clothes. I found some in the closet in my old room. I didn't think anyone would mind."

Carly opened her mouth to say more—and knowing her, it would be something really mean, Tanner thought—so he cut her off with, "Carly, just what do you call that color of your dress? It reminds me of something I saw at the scene of an especially grisly murder. Guy's head got ripped right off his shoulders. It was amazing."

Of course he was only kidding about that. Tanner had never been at the scene of a grisly murder. The color actually reminded him of a woman's pudendum. But he didn't think that made for polite dinner conversation. At least, not in the Hamptons. Not even when he used a word like *pudendum.*

Carly snapped her mouth shut and she narrowed her eyes at him, just as Tanner had hoped she would. He loved it when she did that squinty thing. It meant he'd really pissed her off.

"The designer called it 'pomegranate,'" she said coolly.

"Well it's like no granite I've ever seen," he told her. "And I worked construction while I was in college, so that's quite a compliment."

"It's not—" She expelled an exasperated sound,

another reaction Tanner enjoyed, then finished, "Oh, never mind. You're too provincial to understand."

Yeah, and you're lovin' me for it, he thought. "Ooh, provincial," he said. "That makes me sound so French."

"No," she said. "It makes you sound so annoying."

He grinned. "Well, then, I think you're pretty provincial yourself, Ms. Nesbitt."

Dinner passed as it invariably did—awkwardly—until the guy in the monkey suit brought around coffee and pie. Well, not pie, since that was too plebeian. But it was something with fruit and what vaguely resembled a crust, so pie was what Tanner would go with. Old Man Nesbitt lit his usual cigar without offering one to either him or Dixon or even his son, then leaned back in his throne to survey his subjects at the dinner table.

"How is this…thing with Avery going?" he finally said.

Although he hadn't directed the question to anyone in particular, Tanner was pretty sure he was talking about his and Dixon's assignment, since, well, the other *things* with Avery were too entrenched in the family tradition of shunning to be going anywhere anytime soon.

He waited for Dixon to answer, since he was the senior operative, not to mention more knowledgeable about the particulars, but nothing was forthcoming from that end of the table. When Tanner turned his attention in that direction, it was to discover that the reason for that was because Dixon had left. Funny, but he hadn't even noticed. Of course, Carly had been doing that leaning *waaaaaaay* over thing to get the cream for her coffee, so Tanner probably should have been grateful he even remembered his own name.

"We had a major development last night," he told Desmond IV, turning back to look at the other man.

Although he wasn't sure, he thought Avery gasped when he said it. But when he glanced at her, she was staring down into her coffee. With *a lot* of interest. A bright spot of pink had appeared on the cheek that Tanner could see, though, and it gave him pause.

"What kind of development?" Desmond IV asked from the other end of the table.

Instead of replying, Tanner kept watching Avery. She lumped one, two, three…wow, six spoonfuls of sugar into her coffee, then stirred it furiously enough to send some sloshing over the side. She didn't seem to notice, though, because she was reaching for the sugar bowl again.

"Your daughter hooked up," Tanner said, using the phrase deliberately to see if she would—yep, she did—flinch visibly in her seat. "Online," he clarified, noting how she predictably relaxed, "with the man we've been looking for. Unfortunately we had a computer glitch before we could move forward much. Which is weird, because your daughter has nothing but state-of-the-art equipment."

Avery looked up, meeting Tanner's gaze unflaggingly. He knew then without question what had happened last night. That Dixon and Avery had hooked up, too. Off-line. That they'd been as turned on by the dialogue she was having with Sorcerer as Tanner had gotten reading it after the fact. Probably more so, since they'd been together at the time it was happening and they'd been, you know, together at the time it was happening. Judging by what he'd seen so far at dinner tonight, Avery was handling what had happened better than Dixon was. She also seemed to be taking it more seriously than Dixon was.

Surprising, Tanner thought. And not a little interesting.

"But she can try again tonight," he said aloud. "Maybe with better results this time."

Although he wasn't positive, he thought maybe Avery nodded once at that.

CARLY WAS BORED. SHE DIDN'T want to hear Tanner talking about his little spy mission with Avery. She wanted to hear more about how he was noticing her dress. Even if he didn't flatter her, she could read between the lines. She spoke Plebeian surprisingly well—and she spoke Man even better—even if she didn't care for the lifestyle. Plebeian *or* Man. And strangely since meeting Tanner, she'd been more curious about both.

But he just kept droning on about what he and Dixon had been doing since their arrival and how now they'd finally made contact with whatshisname—the guy who wanted to take over the world, yawn, as if that was any great gig—and how things should start happening now and how they shouldn't have to remain at the estate much longer, blah blah blah blah blah…

Finally her father interrupted—thank God—telling Tanner, "I'm going to have to ask that you curtail your activities Saturday night."

"Why?" Tanner asked. "By Saturday night we could be making major progress. That's still four nights away."

"Saturday night Mrs. Nesbitt and I will be entertaining a hundred and fifty people in our home for our annual November open house," her father announced. "I don't want any disruptions."

"There won't be any disruptions," Tanner told him. "Dixon and Avery and I will stay out of your way."

There was a moment of cumbersome silence, then Carly's father dropped a bomb. A thermonuclear warhead to be exact. Because he said, "Avery will be at the party."

"What?"

The outraged exclamation came not from Tanner but from Carly, who didn't even realize she had offered it until every eye at the table was suddenly focused on her. Including Avery's. What was weird, though, wasn't how she reacted to her father's statement. What was weird was how she reacted to seeing the hurt expression on her sister's face.

Embarrassed. That was how Carly felt in that moment. Not for her sister but for herself. And ashamed, too. But again, not for Avery.

Before she could ponder that conundrum, Avery said, "Don't worry, Carly, I won't do anything to embarrass you or make you ashamed."

Too late for that, Carly thought.

"Because I won't be at the party," Avery added decisively.

"Yes, you will," their father said even more decisively.

"No. I won't," Avery reiterated.

Wow, Carly thought. She'd never seen her sister defiant. Rebellious, sure, constantly when she was a teenager. But not once had she spoken back to their father with such open challenge. Whenever he'd come down on her for some infraction, she'd just stayed silent, then gone her own way. Not once had she faced him down.

"Yes," their father said again, "you will."

Avery said nothing for a moment, then finally, "Why would you even want me there?" she asked.

This time their father remained silent, meeting Avery's gaze from the head of the table as if he were trying to put into words something that was very, very important. It was their mother, though, who finally clarified things.

"Because you're here," she said simply. "And there will be a number of people who want to see you while you're here. Making an appearance is the least you can do."

No, Carly thought. The least Avery could do was not show up. What was going on here? For ten years her parents hadn't even allowed anyone to mention Avery's name. Now suddenly they demanded she be at a party where *all* of their friends and family would see her? Just how much burgundy had been in the coq au vin tonight?

"And there will be none of your shenanigans," their father added. "While you're under this roof, you'll behave in a fitting manner. You'll attend the party Saturday night, just as you would have when you lived here. But this time you will refrain from executing any of your childish pranks. You're not a child anymore, Avery," he added. "You will behave as politely Saturday night as any other guest."

Carly wondered if her father noticed, as she did—and as Avery doubtless did, too—that he had just referred to his daughter as a guest. Probably not. But wouldn't everyone at the party be surprised when they saw this particular guest? Carly hadn't realized until now just how bad her little sister's timing was. As usual. Naturally she would return after a ten-year hiatus just when her parents were throwing their biggest party of the year. They should change the theme of the event from Some Enchanted Evening to Some Misguided Offspring. Because that was what everyone would be talking about now. God only knew what Avery would do this time to get the neighborhood tongues wagging.

Before she even completed the thought, Carly knew it was wrong. Avery had been so quiet since her return. There was none of the spirit in her now that had been there when she'd lived at home. Carly wasn't sure if that was because of two years of prison or ten years of estrangement from her family or simple maturity at work. But her sister was past a time when she'd demanded all the attention. Now she seemed to want nothing more than to disappear.

Carly told herself she should be happy about that, that there was nothing she'd wanted more when they were young than for Avery to go away. Now that felt wrong. Avery felt wrong. Carly had ridden her little sister mercilessly since her return, had deliberately struck at all the places where she knew Avery was most vulnerable just to get a rise out of her. She didn't mean anything by it. That was just her way. Carly always struck at people where they were most vulnerable just to get a rise out of them. She liked unsettling people. Liked being an irritant. She liked being a reminder that things weren't always easy. Mostly, she supposed, because things had always come too easily for her.

But Avery hadn't fought back, even though she should have by now. Before, she'd always been equipped for Carly's attacks. Now she seemed defenseless. And Carly kept attacking anyway.

Not because she was mean, though, she realized now. Oh, she could be mean as hell when she wanted to and had been on many occasions that warranted it. But with Avery she hadn't been trying to punish. Only now was she beginning to understand that. She had simply been trying to bring her sister back.

But Avery didn't seem to want to come back. And Carly couldn't understand why.

"Dixon and I may still have to work that night," Tanner said, pulling her out of her troubling thoughts, "but if we do, we'll stay out of everyone's way. You won't even know we're here."

His announcement should have relieved Carly, but instead it bothered her. A lot. She'd kind of counted on having Tanner at the party. In fact, she'd kind of counted on *having* Tanner at the party. Or at the very least right afterward.

Evidently she was going to have to adapt the time-table.

"Avery will be at the party," her father said again, this time in the tone of voice that brooked absolutely no argument. "And so will you and your partner, Mr. Gillespie," he added in the same tone. "I want all of you where I can keep an eye on you. That way I know no one will be creating any trouble."

Oh, that's what you *think, Daddy....*

Tanner seemed to understand that her father's word was final, because he said nothing more about it. Which was fine with Carly, because she had plenty to say herself.

Starting with, "Well, if you'll all excuse me," and ending with rising from her chair and leaving the room.

It may have been a speech of only a half dozen words, but its repercussions were awesome. Because Carly hadn't even taken a half dozen steps down the hall before she felt Tanner coming up from behind her. Exactly where she wanted him most. But she kept on walking as if she didn't notice him, because...

Well. Because she was Carly Nesbitt.

"Oh, Ms. Neeesssbiiitt," he sang out as he caught up with her.

He cobbled his stride to hers, but there was a bounce to it that was altogether unlike him, so she knew he was going to be in a frisky mood. Which was fine with her. She was feeling a little frisky herself. For lack of a better word.

"Where ya goin'?" he asked in the same playful voice.

Good God, he was so adorable. Though there was something in his eyes that prevented him from being precious. Really, it prevented him from being adorable, too, she thought. But she had to keep him in perspective or she might just—

Well, she just had to keep her in perspective, that was all.

"I thought I might go to the library to look for a good book," she told him. "There's not much else to do tonight."

"Maybe I'll go with you," he said. "Maybe I'll look for a book, too."

"Don't you have to work?" she asked, pretending she couldn't have cared less about his answer. Because she couldn't have cared less about his answer. Really. She couldn't. Honest.

"Eventually," he told her. "I have a little time to kill before then."

"Mmm," she replied noncommittally. She wondered how much time was "a little." Then again, she'd brought men to their knees in seconds. Which was another place she wouldn't have minded having Tanner.

"Well, I guess I don't mind if you tag along," she told him.

He took her at her word and affixed himself to her side as she made her way to the library. And he was still affixed to her side when she entered the library. And as she took her time perusing the titles in the library, one by leisurely one, scarcely seeing any of them because he kept himself so damned affixed to her side. And he was still affixed there when she finally chose a book from among the thousands her father owned, not really paying attention to its title, either, since—had she mentioned?—he was totally affixed to her side. And he was still there when she began to flip through the book, still not seeing it, and when she closed it with the decision to take it with her, not caring what it was.

In fact, Tanner never moved more than an inch away from her the entire time she was in the library. But he never touched her, either. Nor did he speak to her. He only stood beside her gazing at her, smiling faintly, as if he found her amusing. Which bothered Carly, since she had planned on being the one to be amused by him.

Damn. She hated that he kept turning the tables on her. Even if she did kind of like the way he did it.

"You seem to want to tell me something," she finally said, even though she'd sworn she wouldn't be the one to break the silence.

She told herself his faintly amused smile did not turn smug. "Actually I want to ask you something," he said.

She widened her eyes in mock surprise. "Oh, my goodness. How exceedingly polite of you."

He ignored her sarcasm. "Looks like I'm going to be needing a date for this party your old man is insisting I attend Saturday night."

"That's not a question," she pointed out, ignoring the flutter of nervousness that tickled her belly. Honestly, she hadn't felt nervousness since…never. No man had ever made her feel nervous. She was too certain of them. No way would a little upstart like Tanner Gillespie make her feel that way.

He dipped his head forward a bit in what might have been his silent way of saying, *Touché*. Or not. "So who are *you* going to be bringing to the party, Ms. Nesbitt?"

She turned to lean back against the bookcase and clutched her book to her chest. Though *not* because she suddenly felt as if she needed some kind of barrier between them or something. She expelled a long, thoughtful sigh and said, "I've not made up my mind yet."

He took a single step to his left that brought his body immediately in front of hers. And even though he still wasn't touching her, the flutter of nervousness in Carly's belly exploded into full-fledged excitement. Funny, but she couldn't remember ever feeling that where men were concerned, either. Mostly because she'd never met any exciting men.

"You have that many suitors knocking down your door, have you?" he asked mildly.

She uttered a wistful sound and told him, "Yes, I'm afraid I'm that in demand."

He curled an arm over her head, propping it against the bookshelf, something that brought his body closer to hers, though still he wasn't touching her. Dammit.

"Guess that's what happens when you're that demanding," he murmured.

"I'm not demanding," she said, telling herself her words did *not* sound breathless. "I ask for only one thing where men are concerned."

He smiled again, but all amusement was gone. "And what's that?"

"Worship," she said without hesitation.

He laughed out loud at that, a soft, sexy sound that came from somewhere deep inside him, a place that Carly would have loved to know more about. "What a coincidence," he said when he finished. "I love being worshipped. Have your people call my people. Maybe we can set something up."

Grateful for the book she was clutching against herself, since it hid the erratic pounding of her heart, she said, "You think a lot of yourself, don't you, Gillespie?"

He nodded slowly, his gaze never leaving hers. "Yeah. As a matter of fact, I do."

"And why is that, I wonder?" she asked.

He leaned in closer, flattening his other hand against the shelf beside her face. But still he kept a breath of air between them, so although she could feel his heat, she couldn't feel his body. And that was something she decided they needed to remedy.

"Bet you'd love to find out, wouldn't you?" he asked, his voice a mere whisper.

Indeed she would. In fact, she wanted so badly to investigate this thing that was radiating between them, she said, "I'm sorry, but I have plans tonight."

He dropped his gaze to the book she was gripping so tightly her fingers were getting numb. "I'll say you do," he told her. But when he looked up at her again, he was smiling again.

She found his reaction curious, so she, too, glanced down at the book in her hands, really seeing it for the first time. Its cover was facing him, but its title was reproduced on the back. And it was with no small amount of embarrassment—damn, that was twice in one night—that she read the words printed there.

Lady Chatterley's Lover. Oh, dear.

"Is there something I should know, Ms. Nesbitt?" Tanner asked, still smiling.

This time, though, Carly smiled back. "Actually there's something *I* need to know, Gillespie."

"What's that?"

"How long did you say you have before you have to go to work?"

He smiled with supreme confidence at that, moving one hand toward her face to strum his fingertips lightly over her cheekbone. Heat flared in Carly's belly at first contact, spreading like wildfire through her body when he turned his hand backward to skim his knuckles along the line of her jaw, across her lower lip and down to her throat. He touched her cautiously, curiously, as if he wanted— no, intended—to get to know every inch of her. Intimately.

Not much caring where it landed, Carly tossed the book onto a nearby chair. Then she threaded the fingers of one hand through his hair, cupping the other lightly over his nape. Little by little he lowered his head to hers, and little by little she pushed herself up on tiptoe to meet him halfway. When their mouths connected, it was the most seductive, most delicious sensation Carly had ever felt. Tanner kissed her as if she were the secret to his happiness, kissed her as if he intended to make her very happy, too. He brushed his lips lightly over hers once, twice, three times, four, then traced her plump lower lip with the tip of his tongue. As he kissed her, he grazed his fingers lightly down the length of her bare arm, electrifying every inch of her flesh along the way. He wove the fingers of his right hand with the fingers of her left, then brought her hand up to his mouth to treat it to a series of gentle kisses, too.

Something inside Carly came apart as she watched him, and, unable to help herself, she withdrew her hand from his and raked her fingertips across his mouth, too. So soft. So warm. So incredibly sexy. The things he could probably do with that mouth…

She leaned forward and kissed him this time, and this time neither of them stopped. Tanner slanted his mouth over hers, first one way, then the other, as if he wasn't sure which he liked best. But Carly didn't mind, because she was trying to make some similar decisions. Hand cupping his shoulder? Palm cradling his jaw? Knuckles skimming along his throat? Fingers tangled in his hair? Oh, why not just enjoy them all?

As she did, she challenged him for possession of the kiss, turning her own head and opening her mouth to invite him inside. He entered eagerly, tasting her deeply, his breathing growing heavier and more frayed every time his tongue penetrated her mouth. Carly fisted the fabric of his shirt in both hands, then splayed her fingers wide over the broad expanse of his chest, pressing her palms against him as she dragged her hands higher, over his shoulders and back into his hair.

Tanner tore his mouth from hers and moved it over her jaw, her throat, the sensitive skin of her bare shoulder. She tipped back her head as he went, her own breathing coming in rapid, ragged breaths now. She felt hungry, impatient, needy. Never in her life had she wanted anything the way she wanted Tanner in that moment.

He traced her collarbone with his lips, then his tongue, then dipped his head lower, to the place where her warm skin met the top of her dress. Carly stilled when she felt his hot breath there, then looked down to see him lift a hand toward the bright pink fabric to tuck his long middle finger inside. He glanced up at her face once, not really asking permission but more, she thought, to give her advance warning. When she smiled, he inserted another finger into her dress and then slowly, gently, he began to pull the fabric down.

Beneath it was the filmy pink lace of a demicup bra, certainly no match for someone like Tanner. Instead of pushing that garment aside, too, though, he pressed his mouth to the bare flesh peeking out of the skimpy cups. And when he did, it was with such sweet tenderness that Carly went weak all over.

Not sure she would be able to keep standing much longer—and glancing over to see that the library doors were still open and that anyone might walk in and catch them anytime—she cupped her hands over Tanner's shoulders and pushed herself away from the shelves. When he looked up, puzzled, she tipped her head toward the entryway.

"This isn't the place," she said softly.

His eyes were dark with his passion, and they never left hers as he rearranged her dress and put everything back the way it was. Well, almost everything, Carly thought. She wasn't sure she'd ever be the same after this.

"Maybe it's not the place," he agreed, "but is it the time?"

Without hesitation, she nodded. "Past time, really. But you're going to have to tell me your real name," she added breathlessly when he began strumming his fingers over her bare shoulder again.

"Why?" he asked.

She lifted her hand to his hair again, weaving it

through her fingers once more. Something told her she would never get enough of touching this man. Very softly she told him, "I'll need to know what to call you in the throes of passion."

He arched one eyebrow and smiled. "Then, Ms. Nesbitt, I suggest we find a secluded place where we can...rendezvous. Then I'll tell you everything I want you to do for this covert assignment."

She grinned back at him. "Well, then, Agent Gillespie. Your secluded place or mine?"

CHAPTER THIRTEEN

DIXON KNEW HE'D BEHAVED like a jerk when he fled the dining room the minute dinner was over without saying a word to Avery. At the time he'd told himself he was in a hurry because he had a lot to do, that he was overly preoccupied by thoughts of what lay ahead that evening with regard to Sorcerer. But as he'd left the room—oh, all right, as he'd stomped out like a big baby—he'd had no choice but to admit that what had him more preoccupied than anything were thoughts of Avery.

And that had been true even before she'd come into the room looking more beautiful than he'd ever seen her looking.

He sighed heavily as he rose from his bed in the room opposite hers and tugged viciously on the necktie that dinner with the Nesbitts dictated. If this assignment went on much longer, he was going to wind up in tighter restraints than the ones they'd had Avery wearing. Five days he'd been here. It felt more like five months. She'd survived seventeen *years* in this place. Hell, it was a wonder she wasn't psychotic.

He stripped off the rest of the dark suit he normally only wore for official government business and hung it haphazardly back in his closet. His room, like Avery's, had been furnished with guests in mind, in bland neutrals with few personal touches. Still, even with his very limited knowledge of such things, Dixon suspected the heavy antique furniture would have brought in six figures at auction.

He shook his head in wonder. For such wealthy, tasteful people, the Nesbitts had some of the emptiest souls he'd ever met. And hell, he should know, since, after his little performance down in the dining room, he wasn't exactly a model of amiability.

He'd been more than a jerk tonight, he told himself as he tugged on a pair of jeans and a Washington Capitals sweatshirt. *Jerk* was a word you used for someone who was stupid and thoughtless. What he'd been downstairs was far worse. He'd been… Hell. He didn't want to put a name on what he'd been tonight. Because there was nothing bad enough to label himself, even in his vast cache of profanity.

Coward. There. That was a start. But he'd been a coward before tonight because he'd spent the entire day trying to avoid Avery. He hadn't known what to say to her after what happened last night. Mostly because he wasn't sure what *had* happened last night. Other than some of the most explosive, exhaustive, X-rated sex he'd ever enjoyed. But after that last time they'd come together, around four in the morning, when she'd fallen asleep in his embrace, her silky black hair wrapped around both of them, her slender arms roped loosely around his waist, Dixon had experienced a moment of terror unlike anything he'd ever felt before. Carefully, so as not to wake her, he'd dislodged himself from beside her and silently returned to his own room.

He told himself he'd done it to avoid an ugly morning-after scene. He never spent the night with women for that very reason. He didn't know why he always assumed the morning after would be ugly. He'd never hung around for one to find out. But there was something about the thought of going to bed with a woman in the evening and waking up beside her in the morning that smacked of domesticity. And if there was one thing Dixon was not, it was domestic. He was a feral creature and he intended to stay that way. Home, to him, was a minuscule apartment in Georgetown where he spent a few months out of the year—though none of them consecutive. He had the place because he needed a home base, if not a home per se. He traveled constantly in his work, wherever OPUS sent him. Eighty percent of his life was spent somewhere other than that anything-but-permanent address in D.C. And he wouldn't have it any other way.

Avery, though, was a woman for whom it was virtually impossible to leave home. Her Central Park address was permanent in every sense of the word. It was the only place she felt safe, where she lived, worked, played, everything. The last thing she wanted was to go anywhere.

But even that wasn't why he had avoided her all day. He'd been involved with women in the past he should have steadfastly avoided, often for only a few days. It wasn't a temporary involvement with Avery that had made him bolt from the dining room earlier. It was something else entirely he feared happening with her. Something that wasn't temporary. Something that went beyond involvement.

But even *that* wasn't the worst of it. Last night Dixon had completely forgotten about the assignment. No, worse than that. It wasn't that he had forgotten what he and Avery were supposed to be doing. It was that he had stopped caring. He'd wanted something more than he had wanted to catch Sorcerer. He'd wanted Avery. To the exclusion of everything else. Including the job.

And that, he knew, was the most abominable offense of all. Not that he'd wanted Avery. He was only human, after all. Reading what she was writing to Sorcerer as she was writing it, being so close to her, feeling her heat, hearing her ragged breathing, inhaling the intoxicating scent of her… No man in his right mind would have behaved any differently than Dixon had last night. But he had wanted Avery more than he'd wanted to catch the man responsible for his father's death. Last night, for the first time in years, Dixon had lost sight of what had made him wake up day after day after day. He had forgotten what motivated him. He had forgotten his father and his need to avenge his father's death. And for that he wasn't sure he would ever be able to forgive himself.

Of course, that was no reason for him to lash out at Avery. It wasn't her fault he had wanted her as much as he had. On the contrary, unlike Dixon, she *had* been doing her job last night. Even though she hadn't wanted to. Even though she'd been offended by what she had to do. She'd done it because she knew it was her duty. It was he who had fallen down on the job, he who had been weak and unfocused.

He lifted a hand to his forehead and rubbed hard. Christ, what he'd been reduced to in one week's time. Sneaking around. Avoiding people. Shirking his duty. Forgetting his mission in life. If this was what he was like after a week in Avery's presence, what was he going to be like by the end of the assignment? Because even though they'd made contact with Sorcerer, they were going to have to reel him in slowly. Especially after losing him so easily last night. Dixon was confident he and Avery could manufacture some excuse for her disappearance from cyberspace that would wash. But it would still take time to build up Sorcerer's trust in her enough to draw him out into the open.

Dixon sighed heavily, muttered a ripe epithet under his breath and told himself to get to work. But the hardest work that lay ahead, he realized then, didn't involve Sorcerer at all. Because it wasn't Sorcerer's trust Dixon was worried about.

AVERY RETURNED TO HER ROOM after dinner feeling more foolish than she had ever felt in her life. Which was saying something, since there had been innumerable times in her life when she'd felt foolish.

How could she have been so stupid? How could she have thought last night with Dixon had been anything more than what it was—two people having sex because they were too turned on not to. Hell, they didn't even like each other. How could she have woken up that morning thinking anything had changed between them? How could she have felt giddy and bubbly all day at the simple prospect of seeing him again? How could she have allowed herself to feel hopeful and buoyant and happy that her life may have taken a turn for the better?

How could she have dressed for dinner in a way she had thought would please him, when she hated to wear clothes like that?

Her face flamed to even think about what she had done and her stomach rolled with self-loathing. She was such an idiot. Dixon had probably left the room so quickly after dinner because he'd had to go somewhere and laugh himself silly. Working with him after this was going to be unbearable.

As quickly as she could, she jerked off her mother's cast-off clothing and hung it back in the closet—in the very farthest reach, where she wouldn't see it again. Then she pulled on her grubbiest blue jeans and the rattiest sweatshirt she'd brought with her. She tore the ribbon—a *ribbon,* for God's sake!—out of her hair and threw it in the wastebasket, then ruthlessly braided her hair without even paying attention to whether or not it was straight.

She fired up her computer but didn't go online. Dixon had forbidden her from doing so without him present, and for some reason she still felt obligated to abide by his edict. Because he held her future in his hands, she told herself. If she disobeyed his instructions, he could send her back to jail. It wasn't because she cared that he would be disappointed in her if she broke the rules.

Oh, God, what had she become? There had been a time in her life when she'd reveled in breaking the rules. When she'd been driven by a consummate need to be her own person, and if the rest of the world couldn't handle her, then bugger 'em. What had happened to that person? she wondered. Had it been two years of prison that had broken her? Ten years of alienation from her family? Eight years of self-inflicted solitary confinement? Countless years of anxiety and panic attacks? What? When had she stopped caring about herself? When had she stopped liking herself? When had she stopped wanting to be herself?

The moment those questions unrolled in her head,

Avery realized why she had awoken that morning overcome by happiness. It wasn't because anything had changed between her and Dixon. It was because something had changed in her. She had liked herself this morning. And she had cared about herself, too. For the first time in a long time. Knowing Dixon liked her enough to make love to her—or at least have sex with her—had made her think maybe she was worthwhile. And how bad was that, that it took a man's interest in her to make her think she had some value? She really was a broken shadow of her former self.

Her epiphany was cut short by a quick trio of raps at her door. Dixon, she knew before even opening it. Who else would it be? Of course, he was only here because the two of them had work to do. Long work that would last almost until morning. She had to endure hours alone with him, pretending nothing was wrong, before she'd be granted some small measure of privacy again.

She swiped both hands over her face, as if that might physically remove any expression she was wearing, but her stomach roiled with anxiety as she gripped the doorknob hard and turned it. As she opened the door, she waited for her anxiety to escalate into panic at seeing him again. But really all she felt was sad. And tired. And hopeless.

"Come on in," she said by way of a greeting. Maybe if she just pretended nothing was wrong, he'd take his cue from her and go along with the charade.

He was silent as he entered and closed the door behind him. And he remained silent as he pulled up his usual chair behind her usual stool and sat down. Avery, though, couldn't quite make herself move toward him and instead retreated to the far side of the bedroom, where she switched on a light. Dixon looked surprised by the gesture, which wasn't surprising, since she had always insisted on working in the dark, as she did at home. But he still said nothing, only glanced meaningfully at his watch, then back up at her.

"It's still early," she told him. "He won't be online yet."

"How do you know?" he asked. "Things ended so unexpectedly last night that he might—"

He halted abruptly and closed his eyes, as if he couldn't believe he'd said what he had. But Avery strangely was grateful for his gaffe. Maybe it would be better to clear the air.

"We should talk about that," she said.

He nodded resolutely, then opened his eyes. "Yeah, we should. Have you decided what you're going to say to Sorcerer to explain your sudden disappearance?"

"No, I meant we should talk about what happened between you and me last night."

"We had sex," he said flatly.

This time Avery was the one to nod. "And that's all it was," she said emphatically.

Her remark seemed to surprise him even more than her turning on the light did. So what the hell, she went for broke.

"It won't happen again," she told him.

That remark seemed not to surprise him at all. It also seemed to piss him off. Not that she cared.

Nevertheless, he sounded agreeable enough when he replied, "Sounds like we're both on the same page then. Let's get to work."

Gee, Avery thought, it was just so great when two people could talk like grown-ups and get right to the heart of a matter without having to wade through a lot of pooh-pooh.

"Let's get to work," she echoed.

And with that, she crossed the room and took her seat, clicking on the icon to go online. She left the lamp on, however, eschewing the darkness tonight, and decided not to think about why. She only allowed herself to think about the matter at hand—finding Adrian Padgett ASAP so she could get Dixon out of her life. ASAP.

It didn't take long to find him. Especially since it turned out he was already on the Net looking for her.

What happened to you last night? he IMed her within seconds of her signing in. You disappeared just when things were getting good.

Power went out in the building, Avery typed, knowing it was a legitimate excuse because it had happened once before. Not when they were in the middle of sex, but when they'd been having a regular conversation. Super said this morning it was because of construction up the block again. I missed you, too.

Maybe we can pick up where we left off, Adrian wrote.

Oh, great, she thought. No way. Not again. Can't, she told him. Woke up feeling like crap this morning. I think I'm coming down with something. I'm sorry, Andrew—I'm just not in the mood.

"He won't go for it," Dixon said. "You're going to have to give him a better excuse than that."

"It'll be fine," she assured him. "There have been times in the past when he wanted sex and I didn't, and it didn't bother him at all."

There was a lengthy pause, wherein she assumed

Adrian was typing something very long. But when his text finally appeared, all it said was, Poor Coochie. And she couldn't help wondering if maybe Dixon was right. Maybe he really didn't believe her. Maybe he was suspicious.

She waited to see if more would be forthcoming, but there was nothing. So she took her cue from what Dixon had told her during her initial briefing for the job and what Tanner Gillespie had told her that afternoon. Knowing she was supposed to draw Adrian into a discussion of politics and her unrest with the way the government did things, she added, Besides, after reading the paper today, I don't feel like doing much of anything. Except maybe blowing up the entire planet.

Dixon made a sound behind her as he read what she'd written, and she didn't think it was one of approval. Well, tough, she thought. She didn't care if she was hurrying things along too quickly. She was sick of sitting here night after night in a hostile environment that was becoming more hostile with each passing day. Even after nearly a week here her family still abhorred her and were still barely speaking to her. And now things with Dixon, which had begun to feel kind of nice, had taken a hit from which they would probably never recover. She wanted this thing over. She wanted to go home. *Home* home. To her Central Park condo. And then she wanted everyone in the world to leave her the hell alone.

There was another lengthy pause from Adrian, where she thought he must be typing something of biblical proportions. But once again his reply was brief: How so?

She hesitated, too, before replying, choosing her words carefully. What? You don't read the paper? You don't see it all around us?

See what? he typed back, quickly enough this time that she knew he hadn't hesitated at all.

It's everywhere you look, she wrote. The economy here, the war over there, the xenophobia and intolerance everywhere. It sucks, Andrew. The world really is going to hell in a handbasket. And I, for one, am just about ready to help it on its way.

Avery, you're exaggerating, he wrote back.

No, I'm not, she told him. And then she went off on a riff that covered every crooked world leader and every pocket of political unrest and every economic scandal and every global disaster she'd read about in the past month.

"Too much too soon, Avery," Dixon said from behind her. "You're going to spook him. He's going to wonder where the hell all this is coming from all of a sudden."

"I won't spook him," she said. "He'll totally buy it. And he'll totally come around. Watch this."

She concluded her diatribe with the coup de grâce: Sorry, Andrew. Didn't mean to go off. Must be PMSing.

"You're not PMSing," Dixon said. And he'd know, wouldn't he?

"Yeah, but that's the beautiful thing about PMS," she told him. "We women can do whatever the hell we want, say whatever the hell we want, be as bitchy and nasty as we want to be and then blow it off by telling you guys we're PMSing. And you buy it every time, hook, line and sinker. Suckers. Just wait."

Sure enough, although Adrian started off by pooh-poohing her assertions, with a little cajoling he began to concede that maybe Avery had a point and maybe they should talk more about it.

They were off, she thought as she settled into her

chair for the long haul. Once she and Andrew had started talking in the past, their conversations could last for hours. Before, she'd never noticed the passage of time. Tonight, though, she would mark every second.

Because Dixon had leaned forward behind her again to get a better look at the monitor. Close enough that she could feel his heat and hear his breathing and smell the clean, masculine scent of him. Close enough that she would be profoundly aware of him for the remainder of the night. But where before she had told herself he was off-limits, never quite believing it, now she knew for sure that he was.

"See?" she said as her dialogue with Adrian began to pick up speed. "I told you he'd believe me about ev-erything. Including my not wanting to have sex," she couldn't quite keep herself from adding. "Maybe most men think sex is more important than anything, but Andrew—I mean, Adrian—never minded putting it off for another time. Now he and I can spend the rest of the evening bad-mouthing the government," she added dryly. "It'll be great."

Dixon said nothing for a moment, long enough that she began to think he wouldn't reply. Then, "Yeah, well, maybe it's not Sorcerer you're talking to after all then," he finally muttered. "Because that guy's libido is legen-dary."

Would that it wasn't Adrian Padgett at the other end of the exchange, Avery would be a happier woman. OPUS had given her a look at some of the data on him, if only enough to aid her in her efforts to draw him out. Had she not been convinced of the organization's findings fairly early into the game, she never would have gone along with the assignment. Maybe her reasons for wanting to catch the son of a bitch were different from Dixon's, but her determination was just as strong. Now even more so. Because the sooner they caught Adrian Padgett, international bad guy, the sooner she could go home.

And the sooner she could start forgetting about Santiago Dixon.

FOR THE THREE NIGHTS THAT followed, Avery and Adrian talked politics. Only on one occasion did the dialogue turn toward the sexual, and on that occasion, when Dixon told her she'd better go through with it because otherwise Adrian would get suspicious, she'd made him leave the room, telling him he could read the transcript later. And although he balked at first, ultimately he capitulated. Probably, Avery thought, because he didn't want a repeat of that first time any more than she did.

Still, the only way she'd been able to get through the session was to pretend it was Dixon at the other end of the line and to remember what it had been like with him. To imagine that it was him she was stroking and tonguing and loving. After it was over, she'd wondered if there would ever be a time in her life again when she could enjoy anything remotely sexual without thinking of him. She'd even gone so far as to worry he might have ruined her for other men. But then she'd told herself she was being silly. She knew full well there wouldn't be other men. Not for a woman who was as whack as she.

By the end of that third night, Adrian seemed convinced of her antiestablishment tendencies. Because just as Avery was about to start winding the conversation down, he wrote something very significant.

I was going to surprise you, but now I've decided I can't wait to tell you. I'm going to be in New York next week. The band got an unexpected gig in the Village.

Avery's eyes widened as she read the announcement, and she flexed her fingers to halt their trembling before replying, No way! Where?

A club called Duke's, he told her.

Never heard of it, she wrote. But, hey, I don't get out much, right? she added. Andrew knew, of course, that she suffered from agoraphobia and that she never went anywhere.

I was hoping you might get out for this, he told her. It would be great if you came to hear us play.

Andrew, I can't, she immediately replied. You know that. I'd love to hear you play, but it's impossible. I'm sorry.

Not even my being in New York could change your mind?

No, she told him without hesitation.

"Tell him you'll be there," Dixon said from behind her. "Ask him what day and what time."

"He'd know I was lying," she said without looking back. "He knows how bad I get. He knows about the panic attacks. He knows I can't go anywhere." Then she put voice to something that was worrying her, but something Dixon ought to know. "I think he's testing me."

There was a small hesitation, then he said, "What do you mean?"

"I think maybe he's kind of suspicious and that this is his way of finding out if I'm trying to trick him. If I said, 'Yeah, sure, I'll be there,' then he'd know I was agreeing too quickly and he wouldn't contact me again. I have to be true to form here, Dixon. I can't agree to meet him in a public place. At least not right off the bat. He knows I can get out for emergencies and really big stuff if I have enough time—and scotch—to prepare myself. But if I just jump right up and say I'll meet him somewhere, it won't ring true."

Come on, Avery, Adrian had typed by now. You can come for me, can't you? I might never be in New York again. We'll finally be able to meet face-to-face.

She purposely waited a moment to reply, then said, Maybe. Let me think about it. Next week is awfully close. But I don't want to come to a club. It's too crowded. There are too many people. If we meet, and I do mean if, it would have to be somewhere else.

Don't you want to hear me play?

I'd love to, Andrew. But not in a club.

Then where?

I don't know. I have to think about it. You know me. You know I have trouble with this stuff.

You have to face your fears someday, Avery.

And why did that sound so ominous? she thought as she read the words. It was very like something Andrew would have said to her. In fact, Andrew probably had said it to her before. Suddenly, though, the suggestion seemed so sinister.

Maybe, she typed back. Though she deliberately kept it vague as to whether she was referring to facing her fears or meeting him.

Thankfully he didn't push any further. They chatted for a little while longer, then parted amiably, and Avery signed off.

"What if he tries to call you on the phone?" Dixon asked, as if he were just now considering the possibility.

"He can't," she said. "He doesn't have my phone number."

"You didn't give him your phone number?"

"Of course not. Or my address, either. There's no way he can find out where I am."

Dixon said nothing for a moment, as if thinking carefully about what she said. Then very quietly he told her, "He's awfully good at what he does, Avery. How can you be sure?"

She sat up a little straighter in her chair, confident of what she said next. "Because I'm better at what I do, that's how."

He nodded slowly, but she didn't think he was as strong in her conviction as she. "Why didn't you give him your phone number or address?" he asked.

"Oh, please. I might have been stupid enough to fall in love with him, but I'm not so stupid that I'm going to give my phone number or address to a man I met on the Internet and have only known a month."

Dixon narrowed his eyes at her, then shook his head slowly, as if he just couldn't figure her out. Yeah, well, that made two of them, Avery thought. Because she couldn't get a handle on him, either.

Especially after he said quietly, "You're not stupid at all, Avery."

Yeah, right, she thought. Whatever. But the big icy chip on her shoulder melted just a little at the way he said it.

As was always the case, neither of them seemed to know what to say to the other after she'd signed off for the night. They'd spent their days avoiding each other since the night they made love, something that had been easy after spending their nights awake, working. Avery slept during much of the day and spent the rest of her time reading or playing computer games, just as she did at home. Skittles usually kept her company—though somehow the cat's company wasn't quite as pacifying as it used to be—purring from her place on the bed or following on those few occasions when Avery left her room. Occasionally, when she felt certain no one was around, she ventured down to the kitchen for something to eat or out to explore parts of the house that had once been havens to her but which now felt intimidating. She visited with Jensen and spoke with a handful of other servants who had been in residence when she was a girl.

Sometimes she stood at the big windows gazing out at the grounds and at the pond and the ocean beyond, wondering if maybe she had the nerve to go outside and look around. Stroll through the garden and down the boardwalk to the beach, as she had done so many times when she was a kid. Walk along the beach so she could feel the cold wind on her face, taste the salt that limned her lips, listen to the forsaken cries of the spiraling gulls, watch the little sandpipers as they hurried, hurried, hurried over the sand to God knew where. But panic would begin to seize her just thinking about it, and she'd have to step away from the windows and hurry back to her room. Mostly during the day Avery just kept to herself. The same as she did when she was at home.

Now Dixon mumbled something about reviewing the transcripts, and she said something about being tired and wanting to go to bed. She was lying, though. It was nearly four o'clock in the morning, but the last thing she wanted to do was sleep. She was too keyed up from her conversation with Adrian, too terrified at the prospect of having to meet him. Never mind that she'd be surrounded by OPUS agents when she did. She'd be outside somewhere. In the great wide open. Where anything could happen. Where anyone could hurt her. Where she had no idea how to manage her fears.

"Dixon?" she said as he opened the bedroom door.

He turned, looking surprised that she'd called out to him. "Yeah?"

She hesitated only a moment before asking, "Do I really have to meet him? Can't I just set something up and let you guys do the rest?"

He studied her in silence for a moment, but she didn't think it was because he was trying to make a decision. He knew as well as she did that she was going to have to go through with it. The big muckety-muck at OPUS that first night had made that clear. She wasn't even sure why she'd asked about it.

"I wish I could tell you that would be okay," he said. "But Adrian knows what you look like. Once he sets up a meeting, he's not going to come out of hiding until he sees you there. So, yeah. You have to do it."

She nodded, since that was the answer she had expected. But she still didn't know how she was going to go through with it. True, she hadn't suffered a full-fledged panic attack since that close call the night of her arrival. She supposed that was because the house was familiar enough to her subconscious that it didn't feel endangered here. But she didn't kid herself that she'd seen the last of them. She'd gone months between them before, had even had times where she thought they were behind her. Then something would happen or she'd have to go outside for some reason, and they'd start up again.

Safety was the key. Security. That was what really made the attacks stop. Feeling safe. Knowing she was secure. Being familiar enough with her surroundings and the people within them that she didn't fear reprisal or abandonment should an attack occur. Despite the presence of OPUS agents nearby, she knew she'd be meeting Adrian alone when the time came. She would have only herself to count on. That was what scared her most of all. Because these days, the last person on earth Avery could count on was herself.

CHAPTER FOURTEEN

ONLY WHEN THE SUN CRESTED over the trees outside did Avery realize it was almost bedtime. She wasn't sure how long she'd been standing in front of the arched window in the living room—the floor-to-ceiling window, the biggest window in the house—but it had been full dark when she'd entered still troubled by thoughts of having to meet Adrian Padgett. When she'd first moved to the window, the grounds behind the house hadn't been visible beyond the dimly lit patio outside. Her stomach had clenched at even that scant view, but she'd forced herself to stay where she was. Little by little the sun had crept over the earth, bringing more and more of the yard into view. And with each new scrap revealed, Avery had had to battle another flare of panic, until she'd been so focused on fighting her anxiety that she'd stopped noticing the dawning day.

Now she saw the sun hanging over the trees, bathing acre after acre in mellow morning light. A fine mist rose from the grass, giving the yard a shimmery, otherwordly appearance. It was radiant and delicate and ephemeral against the sharply defined backdrop of black, sullen, winter-set trees looking wholly out of place yet completely a part of the environment. Funny, she thought, how something so fragile and fleeting could make an otherwise stark setting so beautiful.

A small sound from behind her made her spin around quickly, and so preoccupied had she become with her thoughts that it took her a moment to remember where she was. When she saw her father standing at the entry, she remembered. Remembered more than she wanted to, really, but that had been something of a problem since coming here.

He was dressed for work in one of his pinstriped power suits, a mug of steaming coffee in one hand, a still-folded copy of the *Wall Street Journal* in the other. She'd seen him looking like that countless times when she'd lived here, virtually every day. Never, though, had she seen him looking uncertain, the way he did now.

"I was just leaving," she said as she started for the door. She wished there was another way out, some deus ex machina trapdoor that would swallow her whole and spit her out amid a new bit of scenery like an angry ancient god. But the angry god was barring her way, and she'd have to walk within arm's length of him to pass. Ah, well, she thought. It wasn't as if she hadn't had to face up to him a million times before.

But instead of stepping aside to give her a wide berth, which she had expected him to do, her father tucked his newspaper under one arm and reached out his hand, almost, almost, touching her arm. He halted just before making contact, but even that small gesture was enough to make her hesitate before pushing past him.

What made her stop completely was her father's softly uttered, "Avery, wait."

She closed her eyes at hearing him say her name, so infrequently had she heard it since coming back. When she opened her eyes again, her father was looking right at her, full on, as if seeing her for the first time. So. She wasn't quite invisible after all. Still she said nothing. Mostly because she had no idea what to say.

Her father shoved his hand into his trouser pocket, but he didn't look away. "How is this…this thing you're doing for the government…going? Are you making any progress?"

It was the sort of thing she could see him saying to one of his vice presidents or corporate drones. In spite of that, she was able to conjure a small, almost genuine smile. "I'm not supposed to talk about it," she told him.

He nodded, a jerky, jarring motion that let her know he was every bit as uncomfortable at the moment as she was. "Of course. Your room then," he quickly added, as if he needed to have some topic, however inconsequential, to talk about. "Are you comfortable there?"

As comfortable as a guest could be, Avery thought. Aloud, though, she said, "Yes. It's fine. Thanks."

"Your mother redecorated in there," he said unnecessarily.

This time Avery was the one to nod. "Yes, she did."

"She wasn't sure what to do with your old things, so she put them in storage. In the attic."

Avery wasn't sure what to say to that, so she only nodded again.

"You can take them home with you when you go, if you want."

"Thanks."

"But if you'd rather—"

He stopped speaking before completing the thought, and Avery wondered what he had been about to say. He'd probably been about to offer to ship everything to her, then reconsidered. Why go to all that trouble and expense, right? They were Avery's things. She should be the one to cover the cost and inconvenience of moving them. Funny thing was, she wasn't sure she really wanted her old things back. She wasn't the young girl who had thumbtacked revolutionaries to her walls and listened to the music of anarchist bands. Extremism was for people who lacked the maturity to reason things out. Avery hadn't been extreme for a long time. Not that she came close to sharing her parents' views and politics. But neither did she discount them so completely as before.

Give and take. Shades of gray. More or less. The other hand. They were phrases that used to be absent from her vocabulary. Now she saw their need. She wondered if the rest of her family ever would.

"It's okay," she told her father. "They can stay in storage. I don't need them anymore."

He opened his mouth to say something, seemed to think better of it, closed his mouth again, then opened it once more. "Your mother," he said, "she really didn't want to make the changes. And I didn't, either. But after a while, your room just became too much of a…"

Again he didn't finish what he had started to say. But Avery got the gist of it. *A liability,* that's what he had been about to call her room. Or the equivalent. Her room became too tacky for the rest of the house. It offered too many reminders of the Nesbitt black sheep and how much she had embarrassed the family. Appearances and all that. It wasn't as though they'd actually needed another guest room.

She lifted one shoulder and let it drop. "It's your house."

Again her father opened his mouth and again he

closed it before finishing. The exchange was growing more uncomfortable by the minute, but for the life of her Avery had no idea what to say to conclude it. She was about to just bolt without another word when her father changed the subject again.

"This man you're working with," he said. But he added nothing to enlighten her as to just what he wanted to know about Dixon.

"Dixon? What about him?" she asked.

"Is he… I mean, he's not… There's nothing… You're not…"

"He's fine," she hurried to say when her father looked as if he would be slipping over into babbling. "I mean, he's not the most gregarious guy in the world, but he's good at what he does. His job, I mean," she felt it necessary to clarify for some reason.

"So there's no danger?" her father asked.

"You're all perfectly safe," she told him.

Her father hesitated only a moment before asking, "And you, Avery? Are you safe, too?"

Something in his tone of voice made something inside her…shift a bit. She wasn't sure how else to describe it. Just that something inside her that had been sitting off-kilter seemed to tilt a little and fall into a more comfortable place. "It's okay," she told him. "I'm fine…Dad."

And only when she said that last word did she realize she had been as guilty as her family of not naming names. She couldn't remember the last time she had called her father *Dad,* even when speaking of him in the third person. Worse than that, she couldn't remember the last time she had embraced him. The last time she had told him she loved him. Even when she was living at home, seeing him every day, before she fell out of his reasonably good graces, she hadn't been able to express how she felt about him. Or her mother. Or her sister or brother. She couldn't remember any of them hugging or expressing love for each other. Other families told each other how important they were to each other, she thought, told each other how they felt about each other. The good feelings, she meant, along with the bad. But the Nesbitts had never seemed comfortable expressing affection. Anger, sure. Jealousy, you bet. Resentment, no problem. But love? It wasn't a language any of them spoke.

Including Avery.

"Dad, I—"

"Avery, I—"

They spoke as one and halted as one, and this time neither of them seemed inclined to finish whatever they'd wanted to say. Avery, for one, wasn't even exactly sure what she'd wanted to tell him. And now suddenly she just wanted to be alone.

No, not alone, she realized then. She wasn't sure where she was supposed to be. Where she wanted to be. She still didn't feel comfortable with her father. But she didn't want to be by herself, either. No place felt right. Except maybe…

"I should turn in," she said, not sure why she said that, either. "It's been a long night."

Her father—her dad—still seemed to want to say something, but he only nodded again, with a bit less jerk and jarring this time. "Get some rest," he told her gently. "I'll see you… Your mother and I will see you at dinner tonight. Desi and Jessica will be coming, too."

The whole family, in other words, Avery thought. For the first time in years, though, the very idea didn't generate panic.

ONLY ONCE IN HER LIFE HAD Avery ever asked her sister for help. She had been in the third grade at the time, struggling with a language-arts teacher Carly had had herself in the third grade, an odious Mrs. Pearson who'd adopted the elder Nesbitt daughter as her pride and joy and designated the younger as a thorn in her side and a boil on her butt. Mrs. Pearson had daily made clear her disappointment with Avery for not being as clever as her older sister or as articulate as her older sister or as talented as her older sister, until Avery had been so overcome with frustration, she'd begged Carly to help her win the woman over.

"What can I do to make Mrs. Pearson like me?" nine-year-old Avery had asked her sister when Carly came home for Thanksgiving her first year in college. "What can I say or do that will make her like me the way she liked you?"

Carly had given the question much thought that night at the dinner table, and finally she'd told Avery, "Mrs. Pearson adores peanut butter truffles. Go to the chocolate store and fill one of those gold boxes with peanut butter truffles and leave them on her desk with a note. She'll remember you forever."

Mrs. Pearson, thanks to a severe peanut allergy, had ended up in the hospital for nearly a week. Avery, in turn, had ended up first in the principal's office, then in summer school, where she'd had to retake the entire semester after Mrs. Pearson threw her out of class. She'd never asked Carly for anything again.

Until now.

Because like Cinderella, Avery had nothing to wear to the ball. Or rather for the party her father was throwing at the house tonight, the party which she was expected—nay, which she'd been ordered—to attend. Her reason for coming home might not exactly be a Hallmark sentiment—unless it was for a sympathy card—but while she was living here, she was, as her father had told her, expected to behave in a fitting manner. Never mind that her behavior had been anything but fitting when she lived here for real. She wasn't a child anymore, her father had reminded her. Not that Avery needed any reminding of that. So tonight she would attend her parents' party as an adult woman. And she would behave as politely as any other guest.

Any other guest. That phrase, more than anything else her father had said to her that evening at dinner, remained most fresh in Avery's mind. He couldn't have made it any clearer that even after ten years she was no longer welcome here. Not that that surprised her. Nor did it hurt her feelings. Not really. But only after her father had described her as a guest had she realized she had been nurturing a hope—however small—that she might be able to bridge the vast chasm that had lain between her and her family for a decade. And only then had she realized how very much she'd wanted to build such a bridge. That awkward communication with her father in the living room might be one very small, very tentative step. Maybe.

As a teenager, her father's warning of a few nights ago would have roused her righteous indignation that she was expected to behave a certain way simply because polite society dictated such a thing. But now

Avery only felt sad. She was too tired for anger. Too tired for righteous indignation. Since Dixon had jerked her out of her normal life, she'd been using all of her energy to stay focused on the assignment, to stay sane, to keep from falling apart. All she wanted was to get through the evening with as little trouble as possible. To accomplish that, she intended to be insignificant and un-remarkable. She would blend. She would fade into the woodwork. Which actually wouldn't pose much of a problem. Her family didn't want her. Her friends didn't remember her. Dixon didn't like her. No one would notice her anyway. Provided, of course, she looked like everyone else.

So she would consent to her father's edict and make an appearance at the party. And she would remember her manners—what few she'd managed to cultivate over the years—while she was there. Not because she felt she owed her father anything. But because she just didn't have it in her anymore to make waves. She didn't even care that she had to ask Carly for help. Whatever it took to get through the night ahead, Avery would do it.

Lifting a hand toward her sister's door, she rapped hard four times. The door opened quickly enough to surprise Avery, but Carly looked even more surprised, as if she had been expecting someone else. But then, what reason would Avery have for being here?

"I need your help," she told her sister without preamble. Then she added softly, "I'm sorry to bother you."

Carly didn't say anything at first, and for a moment Avery thought her sister might slam the door in her face. Instead she lifted her arm and braced it against the jamb in a way that suggested she was trying to decide whether or not she was in the mood for visitors.

Where Avery's choice of dress for relaxing at home was sloppy and cut-rate—yellow-and-black-plaid pajama bottoms and a black sweatshirt emblazoned with the logo for her company—Carly looked as if she were ready to go out for a formal luncheon in a stark white scoop-neck cashmere sweater over a short, stark white cashmere skirt.

"What do you want?" she asked.

Strangely the question didn't sound rude. She genuinely seemed to want to know what it was that Avery needed. Nevertheless, an image of Mrs. Pearson's swollen face swam up in Avery's memory, and she had to tamp it back down again.

"I was wondering if I could borrow a dress to wear tonight," Avery said quietly. "I didn't pack anything… fitting," she deliberately said in echo of her father's words, "for a party."

Not that she even *owned* anything appropriate for a party, Avery thought. Why bother when even the idea of attending a party turned her into a stark raving loony?

"I'm not surprised you have nothing that fits," her sister replied, deliberately misconstruing what Avery had said. "My God, you look like you're twenty pounds lighter than you were when you lived here. Eat a cookie, for God's sake."

Avery closed her eyes and sighed hard. "Never mind," she said, turning away. "Forget I even asked."

She must have been crazy to think Carly would help her. Or help her without first making her beg. She'd just figure out something else to do for the party. Maybe her mother would have something. Of course, her mother chose the sort of clothing women had worn during the Eisenhower era. Still, it wasn't like Avery was trying to impress anyone, was she? Who cared if she looked like Mamie Eisenhower? Dixon wouldn't be looking at her anyway.

And damn her for even caring about that.

As she started to walk away from Carly's door, she prepared herself for the slamming of it. Never do quietly what one could do extremely, that was Carly's creed. For all the criticizing she'd done of Avery's activities when she'd lived here before, Carly had never been one for demurring. But her outrageous acts had all been condoned by Hampton society—spreading gossip, assassinating character, partying till all hours, coming home drunk, sleeping with anything that wore pants, that kind of thing. So it was Avery who had been ostracized. Go figure.

But she had barely completed one step when she felt Carly's hand on her shoulder, heard her sister say softly, "Avery, wait."

She stopped dead in her tracks and slowly turned. It was the first time Carly had called her by her name since she'd come home. Even more significant, she hadn't sounded angry or repulsed when she did it. She sounded like…a sister. Or at least what Avery had always imagined a sister should sound like. She and Carly had never been close. Not just because of the age difference but because they'd had nothing in common. Nevertheless, as a child Avery had often fantasized how it would be to have a big sister who showed her how to apply mascara and told her how to talk to boys and took her shopping for her first bra. But Carly had been too busy with her own life to notice Avery. And Avery had felt too overshadowed by her beautiful, glamorous sister to ever think she might be open to an overture.

When she looked at her sister now, Carly was smiling at her. Maybe it wasn't the doting-big-sister smile Avery had hoped for twenty years ago, but neither was it the harsh, sarcastic smile she had seen so often since her return.

"You really aren't my size," Carly said.

"You never buy your size," Avery countered, recalling how Carly preferred to squeeze herself into her clothing in much the same way that a meat packer crammed pork into a paper-thin casing.

Carly studied her in silence for a moment, as if she were sizing Avery up. In one way or another. Finally, "I have an old green thing that might work on you," she said.

And oh, didn't *that* sound like just the dress for Avery?

Her sister punctuated the announcement with another one of those almost-sisterly-but-not-quite smiles, so Avery braved a small smile of her own in return. "Thanks, Carly," she said. "I'd appreciate it."

"It should fit you fairly well. I only wore it once. Come on in."

Wow, Avery thought. Carly had almost sounded considerate when she spoke that time. Her sister said not another word, though, as she strode across the sitting room to the bedroom at the back, leaving Avery to decide for herself whether or not she wanted to follow.

This part of the guesthouse, like the big house, hadn't changed much. The walls were a darker, richer, more twenty-first-century shade of cobalt instead of the robin's-egg-blue Avery remembered, but the Empire furnishings were the same. Carly had added a few personal touches in the form of photographs and books and plants but little else. Avery wondered if the living quarters on the other side of the guesthouse had been updated, too. And she wondered how Tanner Gillespie was surviving, living so close to the virago that was her sister.

Avery couldn't quite help smiling at the thought. Probably, she decided, Tanner Gillespie was doing just fine.

Taking the initiative, she followed her sister into the bedroom. Here, quite a bit had changed. Where before the room had been elegant and gender-neutral, Carly had turned it into an unquestionably feminine domain. The walls had been painted the color of cinnamon and the noble Aubusson had been replaced by an exuberant Oriental that mingled the fertile colors of a spice cabinet. The bed was covered in embroidered Moroccan silk reminiscent of a desert sunset, then piled high with a dozen pillows garnished with beads and tassels and brocade.

Funny, she thought, but Carly had never seemed the type to go for the sheikh fantasy. Then again, it was doubtless Carly who was the chieftain here.

"It's back here somewhere," her sister said as she rifled through the contents of her closet. "I got it to wear to the party after the Davenport christening. Their yacht, not their kid," she clarified. "I don't think they ever got around to christening him. Ah. Here we go."

She withdrew an opaque, zippered garment bag, something that told Avery the dress wasn't such an old green thing after all. Now that she thought about it, if Carly had even kept it, it must be a nice piece of couture.

The fact that it was packed so carefully meant she intended to hang on to it for some time. Avery wasn't sure what to make of that—that her sister would lend her something she actually liked. So she decided, for now, to make nothing of it at all.

She started to reach for the dress, not really caring what it looked like, just grateful to have something that would be in keeping with the rest of the crowd. But as her fingers were about to close over the hanger, Carly pulled it backward, out of Avery's reach.

Oh, great. Keep-away. They hadn't played that since Avery was a toddler. Back then, the pubescent Carly had delighted in making her little sister cry.

"You're going to need shoes, too," she said. And without a bit of rancor, too. "And jewelry. I remember you never cared about fashion or the proper accessories when you lived at home." She drove her gaze over Avery's sweatshirt and pajama bottoms. "Gee, just a shot in the dark, but I'm guessing you haven't changed much there." Again, though, there was no malice in her tone, only bland observation.

"No," Avery said. "I still think it's silly to spend thousands of dollars on clothing and jewelry when the same amount of money could go toward buying affordable housing for deserving people. I'm kinda wacky that way."

Carly ignored the jab, something else that surprised Avery. "And you need to cut your hair," she said. "That lovely-long-locks look went out with… Well. Actually that lovely-long-locks look was never in to begin with. I could get you into my salon this afternoon if you want."

The offer was staggeringly surprising. Carly had never offered Avery anything. Period. There must be a hidden camera somewhere and a television audience laughing uproariously right now.

"I, um…" *Don't know what to say,* Avery thought to herself. Except maybe, *Who are you and where's the pea pod from outer space that's holding my sister hostage?* Then again, did she really want to know? This alien Carly was kind of pleasant.

Just what had gotten into her? Avery wondered. Why was she being so nice? Yeah, there was still a little bit of an edge to it, but she wasn't being mean. Not like before. Not like always. What was wrong with her that she wasn't being nasty?

"No, that's okay," Avery finally said, declining the offer of Carly's stylist. It had taken her over an hour—not to mention three scotches—just to work up the nerve to walk from the big house to the guesthouse. "I'll be fine."

"Oh, that's right," her sister said, sounding in no way concerned. "You can't go out in public without feeling some kind of crippling paranoia or something, can you?"

"It isn't paranoia," Avery said. Well, not clinically anyway.

But Carly just waved a hand airily in front of herself. "Whatever. Okay, fine. I'll make him come here."

"No, Carly—"

"That's all right. You can thank me later."

"But—"

"And I think I have some shoes that will be fine. I know you're not my size there, either," she added before Avery had a chance to object, "but a little Kleenex in the toe, and you'll be fine."

Oh, sure, Avery thought. Until she tried to dance or some—

She stopped herself before even completing the thought, astonished to have something like that even occur to her. Who was she kidding? As if she'd really be dancing with anyone tonight. No, she intended to just find a nice quiet corner of the room and plant herself there for an hour or so—long enough for her father to see her and content himself that she'd shown up and was behaving herself—then fade completely out of sight.

"And we'll figure something out for the jewelry," Carly was saying. "Don't worry, Avery. By the time I finish with you, no one will ever suspect you were once the black sheep of the family. You'll be as snow-white as the rest of us. Baa baa."

And although Avery told herself that was exactly what she wanted—at least for tonight—she suddenly felt sick to her stomach.

SHE WAS STILL FEELING THAT way some hours later as she stood in the gallery overlooking the party below. Because she was inescapably reminded of another time she had found herself in a similar situation. The autumn of her coming out, thirteen years ago. Then, as now, Avery had hovered in the shadows, hugging the wall and peering through the slats in the gallery railing, where no one could see her. Then, as now, she had tried to gauge the mood of the crowd below with little success and had wondered what her reception would be when she finally made her appearance—with even less success. Then, as now, her stomach had been knotted with nerves, and her mouth had been dry as parchment. Then, as now, she had been shaking in her boots.

Except that she wasn't wearing boots this time. Instead of rebelling against convention by dressing in the black combat gear she had worn for her debut, Avery was rebelling against expectation this time and wearing something perfectly appropriate. The old green thing Carly had offered her had turned out to be a simple emerald-green cocktail dress fashioned of exquisite watered silk that, although none too tight, still managed to hug her curves from the strapless bodice to the fitted hemline just above her knees. It was the most modest garment she'd ever known Carly to own, but where her sister had made it daring by what would have been a snug fit and too-short hemline on her, the dress fit a smaller Avery almost perfectly. And instead of the enormous, outrageous, sparkly crystal necklace and chandelier earrings that Carly said she usually wore with it, Avery had donned a simple pearl choker, earrings and bracelet.

Her newly shorn hair skimmed her shoulders, but Carly's stylist had pulled the front part back and caught it in a pearly clasp. Avery had thought the style would be too childish, but the finished product actually looked surprisingly sophisticated. And once Carly had talked her into removing her glasses and leaving them behind for the night, Avery had realized that the green of the dress somehow made the blue of her eyes more vivid and she'd decided maybe Carly was right.

Avery really wasn't bad-looking when she was cleaned up.

It was just too bad her new and improved exterior could only go so far to rectify what lay underneath. Inside Avery was no different. She still felt awkward, still felt unwelcome, still dreaded the evening ahead. Anxiety and panic danced at the very edges of her brain, just waiting for an opportunity to dart past her fragile barriers. In spite of her uneasy truce with Carly, Avery was filled with apprehension. A new appearance could only do so much. Inside she was still an ex-con, still a black sheep, still a social pariah, still an agoraphobe.

And she still had feelings for Dixon she would rather not have.

Damn. She'd really hoped she could go without admitting that to herself for a little while longer—like, say, the rest of her life. Denial had served her nicely since that feverish night the two of them had spent together. Well, except for the morning after, of course, when she'd woken up half thinking she was in love with the guy. Okay, maybe more than half, she made herself confess. But since he'd made it clear that he didn't share her feelings, denial had been her best and truest companion. She'd assumed that denial would be her date to the party tonight, too. Alas, it was looking like a no-show.

Story of her life.

But she wouldn't think about that, she told herself. She wouldn't think about Dixon or what had happened that night in her room or how he had shunned her at dinner or how she felt about him. And she wouldn't think about Adrian Padgett or having to set up a meeting with him or going out into the big, wide world of the unknown. She would empty her mind and go on autopilot and she would move through the crowd below as if it didn't exist. She would go straight to the bar and ask for a scotch—straight up, double, if you please—and then she would retreat to a far corner of the ballroom and stay there. She would drink her drink—and a few more besides—and she would look for her parents. Then she would lift her glass to them both to show them that she was here and she was behaving. And then she would escape to her room.

Simple plan. No problemo.

She would not look for Dixon, she further instructed herself. She would not constantly scan the crowd for a mere glimpse of him. She would not speak to him. Would not dance with him. Would not acknowledge his existence in the workings of the universe. And she would not think about what her life would be like without him once this assignment drew to a close.

She took a deep breath and approached the stairs.

I have nothing to fear in this moment, she assured herself as she went. *In this moment, there is nothing to fear….*

CHAPTER FIFTEEN

DIXON STOOD NEAR THE sweeping staircase that spilled into the massive Nesbitt ballroom, scanning the crowd, feeling impatient and trying to remember the name of the man he'd been speaking to for ten minutes. It was nothing personal. The guy was pleasant enough. Dixon just had his mind on other things, that was all. Like, for instance, how he felt like an idiot in the rented tux he and Gillespie both had been instructed to wear to this party upon pain of death. Or, at the very least, upon pain of being browbeaten by Carly Nesbitt at dinner every night for the remainder of their stay if they *didn't* put the damned things on.

Dafoe. That was the man's name. David Dafoe. Like the writer, only with a different first name. And not a writer. Dixon had been talking to him about his beverage business—see, he had been paying atten-tion—and trying hard not to think about how badly he himself wanted a beverage. Preferably a double bourbon, straight up. Instead he felt the hairs on the back of his neck stick straight up. He spun quickly around, and although he had no idea where to look, his gaze flew immediately to the top of the steps, where he saw a woman who looked very much like—

"Ms. Avery Nesbitt," Jensen the butler announced from his perch on the top step, just as he had announced every guest that evening.

But where the other guests had warranted little more than the occasional nod and/or smile of recognition and/or acknowledgment from the crowd below—if that much—Avery's appearance was met with total and complete silence, and every eye in the room fell upon her.

The reaction was enough to make Dixon have a panic attack. He couldn't imagine what Avery must be feeling just then.

He waited to see if she toppled down the stairs like a Slinky. Or if she cried out something like "Property is theft!" or "Better Red than well-bred!" or "Viva Guevara!" Or if she lobbed a cream pie in the general direction of her father. Or even if she just stuck out her tongue at everyone present and said, "Neener neener neener." But she did none of those things.

Instead she strode gracefully down the steps without paying attention to anyone. And she looked incredible doing it. She was dressed in a way he'd never seen her dressed before, wrapped in a fine, filmy fabric that appeared at turns green and turquoise, depending on how she moved under the lights. Her hair, that glorious mane of inky silk Dixon had found so intoxicating during their lovemaking, had been cut shorter by a foot, but somehow the way the tresses danced on her bare shoulders only made her more feminine, more beautiful.

Because she truly was beautiful. Only now did Dixon really see that. Though it wasn't the outer trappings that had done it. She'd been beautiful that first time he saw her, too. He'd just been too blind to see it. Now, though… He closed his eyes and opened them again, thinking he must be seeing more than was actually there. But on second glance, Avery still looked elegant and refined, she still made her way gracefully down the stairs, she still looked beautiful.

And she still wasn't panicking. Which was ironic, because Dixon could feel panic deep in his belly, clawing its way to get out.

"Friend of yours?" he heard David Dafoe ask.

Until that moment, Dixon had completely forgotten he was standing in a crowded room. He'd been aware only of Avery and himself. And he'd been aware of them in a way that wasn't exactly appropriate for a man standing in a crowded room.

He turned to his dark-haired companion with the neatly trimmed mustache and beard. "I wouldn't say that," Dixon replied absently. Because he hadn't considered Avery a friend since meeting her. He'd considered her…something else.

"Girlfriend?" Dafoe asked.

"God, no."

"Oh, so it's someone you'd rather not see here at all," Dafoe said.

"No, that's not it, either," Dixon told him.

"Oh."

The single-word response, uttered by someone else, was the perfect response, Dixon had to admit. Frankly he couldn't think of much else to say himself besides *Oh*. Because as he watched Avery descend the stairs, taking each one with what he knew must be painful care, his brain turned into pudding. And not even tapioca, which at least had a little substance and nutritional value. No, his brain went right to the instant variety. Store brand. Stirred with a fork. Then spilled on the floor. And stepped in. No thoughts entered or left his brain. There was just sheer, unadulterated response.

Of course, that response was so flagrant that thinking about it would have caused him to spontaneously combust, so it was just as well he couldn't think. But Avery commanded every scrap of his attention, and Dixon willingly surrendered it.

Little by little the crowd began to stir again around him, after it became clear that Avery wasn't going to use the party tonight as a vehicle to either a) humiliate herself or her family beyond the pale or b) humiliate herself or her family beyond the pale. But Dixon couldn't make himself look away. David Dafoe started talking again, but damned if Dixon heard a word of what the man said. Which was a shame, because he was a very nice man.

He just wasn't Avery.

Excusing himself from the conversation as quickly as courtesy allowed—oh, all right, he just blew the other guy off with a hasty "Gotta run, Dafoe"—Dixon strode straight for the stairs Avery was nearly finished maneuvering, arriving at the last one the same time she did. But she was looking at her feet—though whether to aid her navigation of the steps or because she was too terrified to look at the crowd, he couldn't have said— so she didn't see him until she was literally toe-to-toe with him. When she saw his feet opposite her own, however, she glanced up. And he saw immediately that, contrary to her seemingly calm condition, she was indeed terrified and close to coming apart.

"I need a drink," she whispered.

Dixon nodded, but instead of steering her to the bar, he took her hand in his and led her toward a door on the opposite side of the room that exited into a smaller sitting area. A handful of people had congregated there to escape the noisy throng in the ballroom, but it was a considerably less threatening environment.

"No, Dixon, I said I need a drink," Avery repeated as he guided her in that direction.

"You don't need a drink," he said. "You just need a smaller room."

"No, I—"

"I'm right here with you, Avery," he told her quietly, pulling her close. "And I'm not going anywhere."

"But—" she tried again.

"Just trust me," he told her.

"But—"

"Trust me, Avery."

"But—"

"Please."

That single, softly uttered word seemed to be more powerful than any other cajoling or bullying he'd attempted with her since meeting her. Even more powerful than that first night at her condo, when he'd lain atop her to keep her from bolting. With one simple *Please,* he managed to calm her, sway her and win her over. So obviously his mother had been right. It really was a magic word.

Avery said nothing more, but nodded. She followed as he threaded his way through the hordes of guests, pushing her body against his when the crowd thickened and grew noisier at the center. Automatically, he wrapped an arm around her shoulders and drew her closer, dipping his head to hers so that he wouldn't be towering over her so much. He felt her go tense beneath him and stroked her bare arm lightly with his fingers in an effort to soothe her. Strangely, the more she relaxed at the gentle caressing, the more Dixon tensed.

Her skin was so soft beneath his fingertips. And with her body pulled against his the way it was, he was surrounded by the scent of peaches. She smelled the way she had the night he met her, the way she had the night the two of them had made love. But where those occasions had both been born of desperation, even fear, tonight Dixon felt…

Well. He had to think about that for a minute, because he honestly didn't recognize the warm, wistful sensation seeping through him. Tenderness, he finally decided. He was amazed that he was able to recognize it, having never felt it before. But that had to be what it was. Because it was unlike anything he'd ever felt for a woman. And it was wrapped up with a lot of other feelings he didn't normally have for the opposite sex. Admiration. Affection. Intimacy. Respect. A desire to protect her, even knowing she could fight for herself.

Not that Dixon dismissed or disliked women. On the contrary, he generally took them very seriously and liked them very much. His partner was the strongest human being he'd ever met, male or female, and he was deeply devoted to her. But his feelings for Avery were so different, so varied and so numerous. He just responded to her on so many levels, in ways he'd never responded to women before.

He knew she was still scared and frantic, and maybe that was what had brought on his sudden urge to take care of her. But she was strong enough, too, he knew, to combat the fear that would have paralyzed her as recently as a couple of weeks ago. Maybe she hadn't won the battle yet, but neither had she succumbed to it as easily as she had before.

The moment they left the ballroom and entered the small parlor, he guided her to a window and pushed it up to allow in the cold night air. He sat her on a love seat beneath it and said, "Breathe. Slowly," he added when her first few breaths were little more than shallow gasps.

She nodded and did as he instructed, closing her eyes and inhaling a deep, level breath. She held it for a moment, then released it slowly, then drew in another in much the same way.

"That's it," he told her. "You're okay, Avery. There's nothing here to hurt you. Nothing to be afraid of. You're just fine."

She opened her eyes, fixing her gaze on his face. She really did look different tonight, he thought. Not just in her mode of dressing but in the rest of her, too. Her glasses were gone, but her eyes still looked huge. This time, though, it was because they were shadowed by silvery powder and darkened with mascara. Her mouth was made fuller by the presence of dark lipstick, her elegant cheekbones defined by a dusky blush. He couldn't understand the presence of cosmetics. Her skin was already flawless, and her eyes and mouth had already wreaked havoc with his senses. Now that her features were so much more prominent…

Well. *Havoc* was way too tame a word for what was being wreaked inside him now.

"You cut your hair," he said, not sure why he'd chosen that moment to remark on it, and bothered by the disappointment he heard in the comment. It was none of his business what she decided to do with her hair or her face or any other part of herself.

She must have picked up on his tone of voice, because her expression fell. "You don't like it?"

"No, I think it's great," he said. But even he thought his enthusiasm sounded phony. "Just…" He lifted one shoulder and let it drop. "You look different, that's all."

She seemed horrified by the remark. "Different?" she echoed, sounding crushed. "But I wanted to look like everyone else."

"Why?" he asked, confused. From what he knew of her—which was a lot—Avery Nesbitt had never been one for conformity.

"Because I didn't want anyone to notice me," she said.

Dixon couldn't help smiling at that. "Tough luck, Peaches. That's not going to happen. You'll be a standout no matter what you do."

She said nothing for a moment, then very softly remarked, "You haven't called me that for a while."

"Called you what?" he asked, puzzled.

"Peaches."

He honestly hadn't been aware of doing it just then. Strangely, it didn't bother him to realize he had. What was even stranger was that he identified it for what it was— a term of endearment—and that didn't bother him, either.

"And you don't seem mad at me for calling you Peaches," he said.

She lifted one shoulder and let it drop, something that brought Dixon's attention to the creamy expanse of naked flesh exposed there. Okay, now he was bothered.

"Maybe I don't mind being called that anymore," she said.

And maybe someday, Dixon thought, he'd find out why she smelled like peaches.

No, he immediately told himself. He would never find that out. Because in a few weeks his time with Avery would be over. With luck, she'd be making physical contact with Sorcerer in a matter of days. With a little more luck, OPUS would have Sorcerer behind bars right after that. With a lot more luck, Dixon would forget all about having ever made Avery's acquaintance. Which, now that he thought about it, was the strangest thing yet. Thinking about not having Avery around, he suddenly didn't feel lucky at all.

"You really are a standout, Avery," he said, surprising himself further. He'd intended to change the subject. "Don't try to be like everyone else, no matter how they try to make you feel. You're special. Don't let anyone ever make you think you're not."

Her expression changed not one whit when he said it, but her eyes seemed to go darker somehow, deeper, more expressive. And it was with no small astonishment that Dixon realized there were tears welling in her eyes. Before he had a chance to say anything—not that he had any idea what the hell he was supposed to say—she was turning her back on him. He watched in silence as she swiped a finger under first one eye, then the other, listened in more silence as she sniffled a couple of times. But he had no idea what to do.

Since Dixon had met her, Avery Nesbitt had been a bundle of contradictions. She would fight off an attacker twice her size but could be emotionally shattered by a simple step over her threshold. She was as fearless as a wolverine but panicked when she looked out a window. She was smart enough to develop software no one else could even conceive but was suckered by a man she met online because he treated her with kindness. She thumbed her nose at society but wanted desperately to be a part of it. She'd made clear her disdain of him, then turned to him with the most incendiary passion he'd ever known with a woman. From day one he hadn't been able to figure her out. She'd been as alien to him as she would have had she come from another planet.

But not tonight.

Tonight, finally, Dixon understood Avery completely. Because tonight, for the first time, he saw her for what she was—human. No, it was even more basic than that. Tonight Avery Nesbitt was a woman. And Dixon, God help him, didn't know what to do. Which was completely unlike him. Usually he knew exactly what to do with women. And rarely had he hesitated to do it. The fact that his reaction to Avery was just the opposite—that he didn't know what to do and he wanted to hesitate—made him question everything about what made him a man.

Well, except maybe one thing. Because that thing suddenly stirred to life in a way that had never happened in a public venue.

"Hey," he said softly as he reached a hand toward her.

But she must not have heard him, because she kept her back turned and said nothing. She didn't seem to be sniffling anymore, though, so that was something. He wished she would turn around so he could see if she was all right. Aw, hell, who was he kidding? He wished she'd turn around so he could see her, period. He hesitated again before touching her, but only for a moment this time, then curled his fingers lightly over her bare shoulder.

She tensed at the contact, and he immediately realized his mistake. Not that she might not welcome his touch, but touching her that way, he was reminded of the last time they had touched—skin to skin. And it made him want to be that way with her again. Now.

Later, he told himself. He could think about that— and maybe do something about it, too—later.

He'd thought the clerk at the tuxedo rental place was nuts, fixing the handkerchief in his breast pocket with such a gaudy flourish, but now Dixon was grateful to the guy. Ripping the scrap of silk from its resting place—with considerably less flourish, alas—he squeezed her shoulder a little more firmly, then reached past her with his other hand, offering her the handkerchief without comment.

She accepted it without comment, too, but instead of dabbing at her eyes or blowing her nose, she twisted it nervously in her fingers. At least she'd stopped crying. But it would help if he could figure out what had caused her tears in the first place. Had it been the crowd? The noise? His physical manhandling of her, however well-intentioned, in leading her through the guests? Or had it been, as she'd told him, her failed desire to fit in? Just what had set Avery off this time?

And why was he scared it was something *he'd* done?

"Are you okay?" he asked.

He moved to stand in front of her and cupped both hands over her shoulders this time. But still she didn't look at him.

"Avery?" he asked again, "Are you okay?"

Finally she nodded. Once. Quickly. But it was something.

"You sure?"

She nodded again, putting a little more effort into it this time. And then she really went all out and answered, "Yes."

"Can I get you anything?" he asked. "Water?" he quickly clarified. She really needed to start reevaluating this scotch remedy of hers.

"Just stay here with me for a minute, Dixon, okay?"

A minute? he repeated to himself. Did she honestly think he had any intention of leaving her side for the rest of the evening?

But he only told her, "No problem."

By now the music had kicked up again in the ballroom, so what few people had been lingering in the parlor trickled out to dance. When Dixon looked up, he saw that the two of them were pretty much alone. Knowing that would make her feel better—which was weird, because it made him feel more uneasy—he pressed his hands gently against her shoulders and slowly pivoted her around.

"Everyone's gone," he said. "You can breathe a little easier now."

"Says you," she replied in a voice so quiet he wasn't sure he was even meant to hear her.

"I thought that would make you feel better," he said.

She expelled a soft sound that might have been a sigh and turned back around to face him. "What would make me feel better is being home. *My* home," she added emphatically, as if that needed clarification. "With *my* stuff."

Dixon smiled at that. "Sorry, Peaches. But the only thing here right now from that life is me."

Her eyes met his when he said it, and she caught the corner of her lower lip in her teeth, as if she were giving major consideration to something. The only thing Dixon could give consideration to was how much he wanted to nibble that lip himself. And then maybe nibble her neck, too. And then maybe he could move lower and nibble her shoulder. Then lower still, so he could nibble her—

"Thanks, Dixon," she said, her soft words sending all his plans up in a puff of smoke. Okay, a puff of steam.

"What are you thanking me for?" he asked.

She held out the handkerchief to him. "Nothing. Everything. Just…thanks."

She was back to confusing him again, back to being a bundle of contradictions. But for some reason he didn't mind it so much now.

"You're welcome," he said, even though he had no idea why.

Then he said something he understood even less, something he was sure he would regret in the morning. But he couldn't stop himself. Feeling as if he were standing by helplessly as two trains went hurtling toward each other, he heard himself say, "Dance with me, Avery."

Avery was certain she must have misunderstood. Dixon couldn't possibly have just asked her—no, told her—to dance with him. He must have said something else. Something like *Glance at me, Avery.* But then, she was already looking at him, so it couldn't have been that. So maybe he'd said *Prance with me, Avery.* Of course, Dixon didn't exactly seem like the kind of guy who went for prancing. Maybe it had been *Go to France with me, Avery.* Not that that made one whit of sense. Or perhaps *Fence with me, Avery.* Yeah, that must have been it. They'd done such a good job of verbally sparring since meeting. He must want to go back to doing that again.

Unbidden, a memory erupted in her head of something else the two of them had been good at. But she doubted he was asking her to burst into flame with him again, either.

"What did you say?" she finally asked.

He smiled in a way she had never seen him smile before. As if he were genuinely happy about something. "I said dance with me. The music's nice. Maybe it'll take your mind off of things."

Oh, no, she thought. *No, no, no, no, no.* Dancing with Dixon would put her mind *on* things she had no business thinking about. "I can't," she told him. She glanced out at the crowded ballroom, where scores of people were swaying across the dance floor, and she knew she couldn't have headed out there even if she did want to dance with Dixon. Which she didn't, of course. No way. "There are way too many people out there," she told him. "Let's just stay in here."

"Okay," he said. But instead of sitting down to pass the time, he swept her into his arms and began to dance her around the small room.

"Dixon," she objected halfheartedly. Likewise halfhearted were her efforts to extricate herself from his loose embrace.

"What?" he asked as he continued to dance toward the other side of the room.

What was she supposed to say? *Leave me alone? Let me go? I don't want to dance with you?* That would have made her a liar. So she only sighed heavily and settled her hands gingerly on his shoulders and allowed him to lead her around the room. Which didn't take long since it was so small, so Dixon immediately began another circuit.

"I didn't realize you enjoyed dancing so much," she said as their bodies moved fluidly from one place to another.

"I hate dancing," he replied without hesitation.

"Then why—"

"I have no idea," he said. "So let's talk about something else."

His suggestion resulted in dead silence from both of them. But each continued to meet the other's gaze unflinchingly as they danced around the room. More than once Avery stepped on one of Dixon's toes—she'd never been a very good dancer even back when she'd had an occasional opportunity to dance—but not once did he mutter a sound of complaint. Each time it happened, he only pulled her a little closer, tightened the arm he'd wrapped around her waist and slowed the pace. Naturally that only made Avery more nervous, and when she was more nervous, she stepped on his toes more often. It was a vicious cycle.

But not too vicious.

By the time the slow number segued into an even slower one, Dixon had pulled her close enough that her body was pressed intimately into his, and she had moved her hands from his shoulders to link them behind his neck. She could feel the soft brush of his silky hair over her fingers and the gentle thumping of his heart against her own. Not sure why she did it, she placed her head against his shoulder and closed her eyes, inhaling the distinct, vital scent of him that had become both unsettling and comforting to her over the past week. Tonight, though, it was the latter. As turbulently as the evening had started off, at the moment she felt almost totally at peace.

She couldn't remember the last time she had felt like that. Not even at home, living her usual life. Not even back when she'd been living here at her parents' estate. Peaceful had never been one of those states Avery was able to achieve. At least, she hadn't thought it was. But something about Dixon, something about being close to him, made her feel as if nothing in the world would ever go wrong again.

Which was crazy, because since he'd entered her life, everything had been wrong. And soon she would have to complete a task that would put her at risk as she'd never been before. He should represent nothing but danger and adversity to her. He should make her feel frightened and anxious. Instead he made her feel untroubled. Content.

"Dixon?" she said softly.

"Hmm?"

"Will you ever tell me your real name? I mean, years from now, when I'm thinking back on all this, telling my grandchildren about it," she added, even though someone whack like her would never be a grandmother, "will I be able to think of you as something besides 'Dixon?'"

He said nothing for a moment, and she was afraid maybe she'd taken too much advantage of the mellowness that had settled over them. She didn't know why she'd asked him his name again, only that for some reason it seemed very important just then that she know it. His silence went on for so long, though, she began to think he would pretend he hadn't heard her. But she knew he had. Because his body had gone tense as she'd concluded the question.

Then, very, very quietly he told her, "Oliver. My name is Oliver. Oliver Sheridan."

Warmth spread through her that he would share something so intimate with her, but she didn't let herself attach any more significance to it than that he was simply telling her his name because she had asked. It wasn't the kind of name she had expected, but somehow it seemed totally appropriate.

She lifted her head from his shoulder and smiled. "It's a nice name," she said.

He lifted one shoulder and let it drop. "It's okay, I guess."

"How about your code name?" she asked. "Will you tell me that?"

He narrowed his eyes at her but didn't seem angry. "Don't push your luck, Peaches," he told her.

"Okay, Oliver."

"And don't call me Oliver. For this assignment, I'm Dixon."

"And after this assignment?" she asked. Boy, talk about pushing her luck….

Instead of answering her, he placed his hand behind her head and gently urged it back onto his shoulder. Avery didn't mind. She kind of liked having it there.

"I'm sorry about the panic attack earlier," she said.

"What panic attack?"

He was right, she realized. It had never turned into a full-blown attack. "I think that's the first time I've been able to handle one without a drink," she said. She lifted her head from his shoulder and smiled at him again. "Must be because of your intoxicating personality."

She waited for him to smile back, but he only met her gaze intently for a moment, as if he were thinking very hard about what he should say. "You're going to be fine, Avery," he finally told her. "Really you are."

Instead of feeling reassured by his reassurance, Avery felt the tranquillity that had been seeping through her evaporate. Her smile fell and something cool and unpleasant slid into her belly. Dixon's voice sounded conclusive. Final. As if he were already telling her goodbye.

She tried to inject a lightness she didn't feel into her voice when she said, "Yeah, I know. I should just stop picking at my scabs and get over it, right?"

Dixon did smile then, shaking his head very slowly. "Peaches, your scabs healed a long time ago. What you can't seem to quit doing is showing off your scars."

She was about to ask him what he meant by that, but a man's hand appeared on his shoulder. When Avery looked past it, she saw Tanner Gillespie talking instead. Next to him stood Carly, with her arm looped affectionately through his. And there was a faint smudge of lipstick near his mouth that was the exact same color as hers.

Well, my, my, my. Wasn't it just a big night for revelations? Suddenly Avery understood why her sister had softened up so much over the past few days.

"I've been looking for you all night," Tanner told Dixon, his voice tight, his expression grim. "You need to phone home," he added. "Now."

Dixon went rigid at the announcement. "What's up?"

"It's She-Wolf," Tanner said.

"She-Wolf?" Avery and Dixon said as one. Avery because the two words confused her, but Dixon obviously recognized them well.

"Who's She-Wolf?" Avery asked further, swiveling her gaze between the two men.

"My partner," Dixon said. But something in his voice

told Avery the woman was a lot more to him than that. "What's wrong?" he asked.

Gillespie shook his head. "The Big Guy wouldn't give me details. He only told me that you and I need to go to code black."

"Code black?" Avery echoed, even more confused. Then she bit back a nervous giggle, suddenly feeling like a Bond girl, an idea that was too funny for words.

"I know," Carly spoke up, reading her mind. "Doesn't it make you feel *so* shaken-not-stirred? Like you just entered Casino Royale? I told Tanner we need code names, too, you and me."

"I already have one," Avery told her. In fact, she had two. But suddenly she was rather liking Dixon's better than her own. She didn't want to be Garbo anymore. She didn't vahnt to be aloooooone. "I'm code name Badger," she told her sister with a smile.

Carly chuckled. "It's perfect. So who shall I be?"

"Do you *mind?*" Gillespie interjected tersely. "This is official business we're on here."

Carly made a face and waved a negligent hand at him, then looked at Avery again. "I'll be code name Vixen. What do you think? I think that's totally appropriate for me."

"Keep it up," Gillespie said, "and you'll be code name Roadkill."

"Look, folks, could we settle this code-name business later?" Dixon asked. "I need to know what's happened to my partner."

Avery's lifted spirits sank again. She just wished she knew what else She-Wolf was to him.

"Like I said, you need to phone home," Gillespie repeated.

"That means he needs to call headquarters," Carly whispered loudly to Avery in a not-so-subtle aside. "Isn't that cute? They even have code names for stuff like that. 'Code black' means they have to hide their whereabouts from everyone except the guy in charge."

Black was also the color of the look Dixon threw Gillespie, Avery noted. "You're telling a civilian our business?" he demanded.

Tanner's arms flew out to his sides. "What can I say? She just has a way of making me do these things."

Carly grinned smugly, then blew on her fingernails and buffed them on her little black dress. "Like I said. Vixen. I could be a real asset to your organization." She leaned toward Avery and added in another one of those conspiratorial whispers, "I know Tanner's real name, too." Then, as Dixon looked horrified by the revelation—not that he had any right, Avery thought—Carly moved her fingers to her mouth, mimicked the locking of her lips with a tiny key, followed by the throwing away of said key and smiled with much satisfaction.

Dixon closed his eyes, shook his head slowly, then opened them again and fixed his gaze on Gillespie's. "What's She-Wolf got to do with our going to code black?" he asked, ignoring both women now.

Gillespie said nothing for a minute, as if he were afraid of what might happen when he said what he had to say. Finally, though, he said, "She-Wolf is missing."

"Missing?" Dixon repeated incredulously. "How the hell can she be missing?"

"Actually it's worse than missing," Gillespie said. "According to the Big Guy, She-Wolf has gone rogue."

"Rogue?" Dixon asked, even more incredulous than before.

Gillespie nodded. "Yeah, rogue. She's armed, Dixon, and she's dangerous. And OPUS is reasonably certain that she's going to come looking for you."

CHAPTER SIXTEEN

TANNER'S FAVORITE BAR IN the whole wide world was buzzing with action, even on Sunday night at ten o'clock. The chunk of nondescript brick squatted on the corner of a fairly busy intersection in Queens, its blue-and-red-neon sign proclaiming it simply Ed's. The place was exactly as it had been the first time he'd entered it almost four years ago, on his twenty-first birthday with his father so the old man could order Tanner his first—legal, anyway—beer. His younger brother Stu worked here as a bartender now, and his sister Lily was a waitress, so Sunday nights at Ed's were almost like coming home.

So much for going to code black, Tanner thought as he pushed open the door to the place for Carly to precede him through it. Instead of packing up their gear Saturday night, as they'd been instructed to do, Dixon had insisted he needed another twenty-four hours at least to take care of some business.

Tanner immediately had suspected that the business Dixon needed to take care of had nothing to do with their current assignment and everything to do with his rogue partner. His suspicion had become confirmation when Dixon told him to take the night off because he and Avery could manage without him. They could manage, Tanner thought, because they wouldn't be looking for Sorcerer tonight. At least Dixon wouldn't. Avery would doubtless sit alone in her room doing that thing she did to draw Sorcerer out, while Dixon manned the equipment in Tanner's room, trawling for information about She-Wolf.

Tanner told himself he should be more concerned, that he'd probably be dragged down, too, if Dixon got caught disobeying orders. Somehow, though, he couldn't bring himself to be too concerned. Like Dixon, he was confident there was more to She-Wolf's situation than the Big Guy was letting on—operatives that good didn't go bad that fast, and they'd offered no solid evidence that She-Wolf had committed any crimes. Dixon was a big boy. He knew what he was doing. And—for now, at least—Tanner was his partner, and partners watched each other's backs. So he'd take tonight off and let Dixon do whatever he had to do. And, hey, who better to spend a night off with than Carly?

Although Ed's hadn't changed in the brief time Tanner had been away from the place, tonight he felt different coming here. For a minute he couldn't put his finger on why. Then, with no small amount of astonishment, he realized he was nervous about bringing Carly here. But whether he was anxious about how she would see the place, or how the place would view her, he couldn't have said.

Probably it was a combination of both. Bringing a girl to Ed's was the closest Tanner came to bringing a girl home to meet Mom. What was strange was that Carly was the first woman Tanner had brought here. He'd met women here on a number of occasions—both for the first time and for a date. Once, on an especially drunken New Year's Eve, he'd *had* a woman here, in a bathroom stall. But he'd never physically brought one with him before. And maybe that was causing some of his nervousness, too. That it would be Carly Nesbitt, of all people, he wanted to bring here was more than a little weird.

But since that night in the library, when he'd called her on the Lady Chatterley thing, the two of them had been enjoying quite the sexual alliance. To put it politely. What they'd really been enjoying was some of the downest and dirtiest and most incredible sex Tanner had ever had. Whether it was in her room or his, they'd spent not a single night apart. And there had been some afternoons and mornings they'd not spent apart, either. In fact, over the past week, he'd had more sex than he'd enjoyed during the previous six months. And he'd had it in places he never would have imagined a person could have sex. Frankly, he would never look at a grand piano the same way again.

The moment the door to Ed's swung open, Tanner was hit by a blend of cigarette smoke, beer on tap, raucous laughter and raw guitar. As he followed Carly through the door, he tried to see the bar for the first time, the way she would. Fake wood paneling formed the walls on all sides that weren't front window, and scarred red linoleum covered the floor—what you could see of the floor anyway. Neon signs for virtually every brand of beer—American only, thankyouverymuch—dotted the walls, and most of them, Tanner was impressed to see, were working at at least seventy-five percent. Ed had done some sprucing up.

The population of the bar was almost perfectly

divided male and female, but most of the people present were couples. Ed's wasn't the kind of place where you usually went to meet people, Tanner's own habits notwithstanding. It was the kind of place where you went to hang with friends you knew well. He'd wager Carly was the only one here tonight who hadn't been here at least once before. It was a neighborhood pub, and the people who came here were neighbors. Certainly none of them was slumming from the Hamptons.

He hoped Carly wasn't, either.

She'd overdressed for the place but not by a lot. Where most of the women wore jeans and sweaters and the guys were dressed in jeans and flannel, there were a few people who'd come from Sunday dress-up events of one kind or another and still wore nine-to-five type clothing. Ties were loose, of course, and heels discarded. But Carly, in her black leather skirt and bright blue cashmere sweater—okay, that could be a problem…if, you know, anyone actually recognized it as cashmere—didn't stand out much. He'd anticipated her wardrobe selection, however, and had dressed to complement her so she wouldn't feel out of place. Instead of his usual jeans and flannel, he'd donned gray cords and a navy blue sweater. Preppier than he liked, but what the hell.

The things he did for women. Man.

"Busy place," she said over the din.

"Actually it's just getting warmed up," Tanner told her. "By midnight the joint will be jumping."

"Even on a Sunday?"

"Even on a Sunday. People in my neighborhood don't care if they feel like hell when they go to work on Monday, 'cause for most of them, that only improves the job."

"Interesting," she said, still not looking at him.

Though he couldn't be sure if she was talking about the people or the place. But he was heartened by the fact that she didn't make the comment scornfully or sarcastically. She was just stating a fact. He supposed a place like this and the people in it would be interesting to someone like her. He'd bet good money Carly Nesbitt had never stepped over a class line in her life. But from the Hamptons to Queens, she'd had to leap over quite a few. Blue blood versus blue-collar. Had to make for a combination that was, well, interesting.

"What are you drinking?" Tanner asked.

It was a rhetorical question, naturally. Ed would rather stick needles in his eyes than mix up something with a name like cosmopolitan or appletini. If a beverage wasn't some shade of brown, you weren't going to find it at Ed's.

Carly opened her mouth to reply with what was probably her usual drink of choice, then, smart woman that she was, looked around the room and back at Tanner. "Just a shot in the dark, but I'll bet I'm having a beer."

He smiled and nodded. "Good choice. Got a brand in mind?"

She looked at the signs on the walls. "Oh, gee. Something domestic, I think."

"You got it," he told her.

He started to leave her where she was, then thought better of it. Already she had drawn some eyes. And not all of them male. Two of them belonged to Tanner's sister Lily, who was making clear both her curiosity and criticism. He hadn't told anyone in his family about Carly, of course. And until a few days ago, he hadn't thought he would ever tell anyone about her. But Lily knew, like everyone else at Ed's, that Tanner didn't show up here with women on his arm. If he was with Carly now, it was a clear statement of intent. He just wished he knew what his intention was. Maybe he ought to ask Lily, since she seemed to know.

"Come with me," he told Carly, curling his fingers over her wrist and pulling her close. "I don't want you to get lost."

She grinned. "Wow. That's like totally opposite what you told me that first day we met."

He grinned back, but circled her waist with his other arm as he propelled them carefully through the crowd. "Nah, you just weren't listening that first day."

"I was listening," she told him. "But you were using a language I didn't understand."

He gave her a little squeeze. "Sweetheart, I would have thought you spoke body language better than anyone."

She bumped her hip against his. "Well, you speak it in a dialect I never heard before."

"And you're not likely to hear it again, either," he told her with supreme confidence.

"Rather sure of ourself, aren't we?"

"We are."

By now they had made it to the edge of the bar, and Tanner called out to the nearest bartender, a woman he'd known since second grade. "Brenda! Two dark drafts!"

"Comin' right up, Scotty!" she replied as she reached overhead for two pilsners.

He cringed when he heard his real name shouted with such familiarity. Not because it had been a while since anyone had called him that, but because he'd always hated the name. No amount of insistence that people call him *Scott*—not *Scotty,* as he'd been called throughout childhood—had worked. To everyone in his neighborhood, he would always be Scotty. It was yet another reason why he'd wanted to join an organization that would provide him with a new identity.

"*Scotty?*" Carly echoed from his side. "They actually call you *Scotty? And you let them?*"

"It's a childhood nickname," he muttered. "A term of endearment."

"I like my term of endearment for you better," she said, leaning in close to whisper that very term in his ear, arousing him on the spot.

"Call me that in front of my family," he murmured back, "and my mother will wash your mouth out with soap."

As Brenda filled the glasses with deep-amber brew, a half dozen other people at the bar greeted Tanner, including his brother Stu, who was working the far end. Tanner pointed him out to Carly, identifying their relationship, then indicated his sister Lily, who was making her way toward a nearby table with a tray full of drinks. When Stu saw his brother standing on the other side, though, he nodded to Brenda to switch places with him, and it was he who served up Tanner's order.

At twenty-three, he was a darker, slightly shorter version of Tanner who had just started law school at Columbia. Tanner's folks were incredibly proud. Not just of Stu but of all their kids. Lily was finishing up her last year at CUNY with a major in sociology, and Tanner's sister Megan was embarking on her freshman year at Syracuse. Ginny and Tiff, the twins, were juniors in high school, but with their smarts, there were already colleges fighting to get them. Tanner's generation was the first to make it to college, and the fact that they were all paying for it themselves—or with academic scholarships—only made the accomplishment that much greater.

When Stu saw Tanner turn to hand one beer to Carly, he smiled knowingly at his brother. But the smile fell when Carly turned fully around to accept the drink, and the temperature at the bar dipped a good fifty degrees.

Damn, Tanner thought. Was it that obvious she was so far above him socially? And did it really matter that much if she was?

When Tanner slapped a ten onto the bar to pay for the drinks, Stu reached out ostensibly for the money but grabbed his brother's wrist instead. Pulling Tanner close so he could speak low, Stu said, "Tell me you just met her and didn't bring her here with you tonight."

Tanner's brows arrowed down at the distaste in his brother's voice. "What if I did, Stu?" he asked, his voice edged with warning.

Stu dipped his head forward in acknowledgment. "Okay. Then tell me you didn't bring her here because she's special."

Again Tanner was surprised by his brother's obvious and immediate dislike of a woman to whom he hadn't even said hello. Between Stu's comments and Lily's expression, Tanner figured he was two for two in the family disapproval rating.

All he said in reply, though, was, "Stu, have I ever brought a woman to Ed's before?"

His brother shook his head.

"And is this not Sunday night, a night when I know that at least a third of my family will be here?"

This time Stu nodded.

"Do the math, Stu."

His brother eyed him steadily for a moment, then said, "Can't."

"Why not?"

Stu met his gaze unflinchingly. "Doesn't add up, dude."

With that, Stu released him and withdrew, sliding the tenner with him. His expression was one of challenge, as if he were waiting to see what Tanner would do now that he'd made clear his disapproval of his big brother's choice of women. In fact, the last time Stu had looked at Tanner like that, it was because he'd just taken the old man's straight razor to the tires of Tanner's Stingray when Tanner had gotten one for Christmas and Stu hadn't. Tanner had kicked his brother's ass that day, up one side of Flatbush Avenue and down the other.

So it was going to be like that, was it? he thought. Evidently it wasn't just blue bloods who felt entitled to be snobs.

This time Tanner was the one to lean across the bar, crooking his finger at his brother in the internationally known sign language for "Get your ass over here, you little prick."

Stu hesitated for a moment—obviously he hadn't forgotten the ass-kicking he'd received on Flatbush Avenue—but he moved to the edge of the bar again and leaned closer to his brother. Sort of. And where what Tanner really wanted to do just then was smack Stu upside the head, all he did was take the ten spot out of his brother's hand and stuff it back into his pocket.

"This round's on you, Stu," he said. "Don't forget to tip yourself. Not that you deserve it for the lousy service." He started to pull away and return his attention to Carly, who, he noted, had a very curious expression on her face. But he held up one finger to her in a just-a-second kind of way and turned around to face his brother again.

"And don't forget that time I kicked your ass on Flatbush Avenue, either," he warned his brother. "Carly is with me. And she's special. Get used to it."

But Stu wasn't the cowering seven-year-old he used to be. More was the pity. Because instead of being intimidated by Tanner's warning, he only sneered and said, "Not only is she a rich bitch, but she's probably only five or six years younger than Mom."

"Actually, Stu, she's only three years younger than Mom."

And with that, Tanner spun around and gave his brother his back. That was all Stu deserved right now. Later, though, Tanner intended to give him an ass-kicking that would make Flatbush Avenue look like cotillion class.

NEVER IN HER LIFE HAD Carly felt the way she did standing behind Tanner at Ed's, eavesdropping on his conversation with the man who was his little brother. Not so much the fish-out-of-water thing. That feeling was no stranger. Though she had to admit, the water at Ed's was a lot different from the water in the Hamptons. No, it was the Mrs. Robinson thing she didn't recognize.

Funny, but she honestly didn't feel older than Tanner. That first day, sure. He'd looked every inch the Eagle Scout. But since meeting him and talking to him, he'd seemed to grow older. Plus, she didn't feel thirty-nine. She'd decided somewhere in her late twenties that she was as old—mentally and emotionally and psychologically, anyway—as she was ever going to get. At some point, they'd each crossed a line in the other direction, until they were roughly the same age.

And really there were times when Tanner even seemed older than she. He had more confidence and was more comfortable with himself than most men she'd met who were much older. Although his life experience wasn't up there with her own, he'd been taking care of himself since he'd gone off to college at seventeen. Carly, at thirty-nine, still lived at home. She'd never taken care of herself in her life.

After listening to his brother's comments, however, she was reminded that there was indeed a significant difference in her and Tanner's ages. She remembered cultural and social milestones that had happened a full decade before he was born. They'd grown up listening to different music, watching different TV shows, seeing different movies. The social history he remembered started much later than the social history she recalled. As a couple, they'd be killer at Trivial Pursuit. But romantically…

She just hadn't anticipated a problem, that was all. Tanner obviously hadn't, either. His family, however, did see one. Or at least one family member did. Still, Carly knew from experience that families tended to band together on things, regardless of how each individual actually felt. But in her experience, it was the father who stipulated where the chips would fall, so maybe the brother was an anomaly.

Or maybe the father—and the rest of the family— would feel the same way.

But then, why did she care? It wasn't as if she and Tanner planned to have anything more than a good time together, right? It wasn't as if she would have any contact with his family beyond this evening, right? Of course, having just eavesdropped so shamelessly on his conversation with his brother, she got the impression that Tanner's having brought her to this place tonight was tantamount to his declaring to the world that he had dibs on Carly Nesbitt, nyah nyah nyah nyah nyah.

In which case, she should be pissed off. She didn't *do* dibs. Men knew better than to become proprietary toward her. At least, other men had known better. Then again, Tanner probably knew better, too, but he'd become proprietary anyway. Instead of pissing her off, though, it made her feel…well, kind of aroused, truth be told. Maybe it wasn't so bad to have a man feeling proprietary about one. Provided one also felt proprietary toward the man. And it was with no small amount of astonishment that Carly realized she did indeed feel proprietary toward Tanner. She had dibs on him, too. Nyah nyah nyah nyah nyah.

So evidently there would be a problem, since his family obviously felt a bit proprietary toward him, too. At least, they did when they didn't approve of the woman who had dibs on him.

He turned from the bar and jerked his thumb toward the other side of the room. "Air's nicer over there," he said.

"After you," she told him.

Not because she was trying to be polite. But because he had such a cute butt and she loved watching him when he walked. She followed him to the far side of the bar, where the music was louder but there were fewer people sitting down, since most of them had fled to the dance floor. A couple at a tiny table in the very back was standing to put on their coats, so Tanner quickly usurped their table. He helped Carly out of her jacket, then shed his own, hanging both on a hook affixed to the wall. When she sat down in her wobbly chair, she saw that the table was sticky with bottle rings and scarred from cigarette burns and crudely carved profanity. The bar was smoky and humid and loud, not at all the sort of environment Carly normally enjoyed. But Tanner was here.

Truly, it was just enchanting.

She waited for him to sit down opposite her, then asked point-blank, "Does it bother you, the difference in our ages?"

He had been lifting his beer to his mouth, but his hand stilled as she completed the question, and he lowered it back to the table. "You heard what my brother said."

"I did," she told him. "So does it? Bother you?"

He grinned at her, and she released a breath she hadn't even been aware of holding. "Why would that bother me?"

She shrugged. "It seems to bother your family. A lot."

He lifted his beer again, and she knew he was completely unconcerned about his family's reaction. "They don't know you," he said before enjoying a sip.

"You don't know me, either," she told him.

He grinned even more broadly at that. "Oh, I know you pretty well, Carly. Probably even better than you know yourself."

She told herself she should be offended by the comment. Instead she was intrigued. "How so?"

"For one thing, I know you're not nearly as bitchy as you act."

"Says you. I'm a raging bitch. Ask anyone."

"Knows me," he countered. "I don't have to ask anyone. They might call you a bitch, but they don't realize you act the way you do because you want to have a reason for why people don't like you. This before you even give them a chance to like you."

"There's nothing in me *to* like," she said simply. It was a statement of fact, not a poor-poor-pitiful-me whine. Carly knew what she was. And she didn't try to be anything else. Nor did she blame anyone else for being the way she was. She'd put her baggage on the train a long time ago and bid it farewell. These days, she didn't carry around anything more than would fit in an elegant little evening bag. Comb. Compact. Lipstick. Breath mints. Okay, and a minor Electra complex. Hey, they were in fashion this season. All the girls she knew had one.

"Oh, I don't know about that," Tanner said.

She had to backtrack a bit to figure out what he was talking about, then remembered she had told him there was nothing in her to like.

"Well, I'll grant you there is one thing to like about me," she conceded. "But it's the same thing men have always liked about me." She glanced down at her torso. "Okay, the same *two* things men have always liked about me."

Tanner enjoyed another swallow of his beer. "News flash. Men usually get beyond the physical thing eventually. If a woman lets them."

"I haven't let you," she said.

"Sure you did. That first day. With one look."

"What look?" she asked, genuinely wanting to hear the answer. She'd always thought she was extremely good at hiding herself from people. "I don't have a look."

"Yeah, you do," he said. "But a man has to be awfully good at what he does to see it."

"Ah," she said, understanding now. "He has to be a spy."

Tanner shook his head. "No. He has to be good at what he does."

She narrowed her eyes at him for a minute, having no idea what he was talking about. But little by little it started to make sense. Tanner was right. It had nothing to do with his being a spy. When it came to being a man, nobody did it better.

"What happens if your family keeps not liking me?" she asked.

"I think they'll like you. If you let them."

"But what if they don't?" She needed a serious answer from him on that. Because for the first time in her life Carly felt serious, too.

Tanner looked over at the bar, where his brother was pulling a beer for someone and his sister was loading drinks onto a tray. Then he looked back at Carly again. "If they don't, then it will be their loss."

"You're sure?" she asked. And somehow she hoped he realized she was asking about a lot more than his family's approval.

He smiled. "I've never been more sure of anything in my life."

Carly nodded at his response. Then she smiled, too. It was nice to know they were on the same page.

CHAPTER SEVENTEEN

UNTIL HE MET AVERY, THERE was only one person in the world whose presence Dixon could sense whenever she came within a one-hundred-foot radius. So when he returned to his room from Cowboy's shortly after midnight on Sunday night, he knew immediately that he wasn't alone. He also knew it wasn't Avery who was with him.

"She-Wolf," he said just loudly enough for her to hear him.

She stepped out of the darkness where he wouldn't have seen her until he turned on a light—when it would have been too late for him had he been anyone else. She was only a shadow against the pale moonlight filtering through the window behind her, but Dixon knew better than to turn on a light, in case anyone was outside watching the house. And of course, he knew there was someone outside watching the house.

"You're under surveillance," she said quietly, as if she'd read his mind. Which wasn't outside the realm of possibility, since they were both prone to such a thing after having worked so closely together for so many years. "You have been since yesterday afternoon. They knew you'd be the first person I'd look for."

"Luckily you had no trouble staying under their

radar," Dixon said. Really, he wondered why OPUS even bothered. She-Wolf was legendary at the organization. She'd eluded some of the most arcane, hush-hush spy networks on the planet. She sure as hell wasn't going to get caught by the one whose workings she knew backward and forward.

"Yeah, lucky," she echoed quietly. "That's me."

"Where the hell have you been? And what the hell is going on?"

When Dixon had telephoned his boss last night, he'd been told his partner had, to put it in pop-culture terms, gone over to the dark side. She'd been out of touch with OPUS for days, ever since an especially explosive exchange with none other than He Whose Name Nobody Dared Say. Dixon had been told she'd tried to kill the other man. Somehow he'd managed to keep his laughter in check. There wasn't an operative in OPUS who hadn't wanted to murder the Big Guy at some point. But that it should be She-Wolf who finally tried it? Not bloody likely. She was too smart. And too cool. As often as Dixon had seen her in extreme situations, he'd never known her to lose control. It was kind of scary, really, how little emotion she showed. But that was doubtless what made her so good at what she did.

His boss had told him, too, that if Dixon saw She-Wolf, he was to take her into custody and notify them immediately. And that for the remainder of their assignment he and Gillespie were to take Avery into hiding at an OPUS safe house and continue their quest for Sorcerer from there. Nothing else was to change, especially in light of their having come so close to drawing their subject out. But he and Gillespie were to close up shop in East Hampton immediately, so as not to put the

Nesbitt family at risk while a rogue agent was at large, looking for her partner.

Dixon had told his boss he would need at least twenty-four hours to break everything down because he'd known it wouldn't take any longer than that for She-Wolf to contact him. He didn't know why she'd been marked the way she had, couldn't imagine what she had said or done to generate this kind of reaction within the organization. And he wouldn't accept any excuses or explanations unless they came from her.

She took a few steps forward, away from the window, into a slice of moonlight that flowed over the floor. Dixon caught his breath at the sight of her. A petite woman to begin with, she looked even thinner than the last time he'd seen her. Her hair, normally a rich fall of platinum-blond, looked dull and unwashed, swept back from her face—mostly, anyway—in a bedraggled ponytail. Her features were pinched and pale, and her eyes, usually vivid blue, looked flat and gray in the moonlight. Over the years he'd seen her dressed in just about everything for the job, from elegant evening gowns to black commando camouflage. But never in a security guard's uniform designed for a man twice her size.

And never with handcuffs dangling from one wrist.

"What the hell is going on?" he demanded again, taking an involuntary step toward her.

Immediately, she took a step in retreat. And that, more than anything, told Dixon everything he needed to know. She didn't trust him. She was no longer certain of their partnership. She might even be afraid of him. And She-Wolf had never shown fear of any kind. That she should do so now, with him, was more than a little alarming.

She-Wolf had been assigned her code name by their immediate superior because that was the closest the woman could get to the word *bitch* and still stay within the organization's parameters. Most people at OPUS thought the moniker was appropriate. Including She-Wolf. Dixon had never been of that opinion himself, but his opinion scarcely counted. Although he'd never seen a softer side to his partner, he'd always sensed there was one inside her somewhere, beneath layers of emotional armor she'd spent her entire life erecting.

Dixon knew little of that life. But he knew a lot about She-Wolf, thanks to having worked with her for a half-dozen years. Although they didn't work shoulder to shoulder saving the world, they were in constant contact with each other when they were on assignment. Where Dixon's job was to assimilate, evaluate and articulate, She-Wolf's was to investigate, infiltrate and communicate. He couldn't do his work until hers was finished. But somehow the communication part never quite was. They met in person when and where they could, but more often they worked apart. Physically, anyway. Nevertheless, the trust and, yes, affection, they'd forged over the years ran deep in them both.

She-Wolf was smart and vigilant and resourceful. She played by the rules as long as they suited her and bent them to her needs when they didn't. She was a survivor. And she didn't take shit from *any*body. But she also felt things deeply. She had a keen sense of right and wrong. But Dixon had never known her to feel fear.

And he didn't know why she was here now, without warning, when he'd been told she'd gone rogue. Not that he'd believed any of that crap for a minute. But she had disappeared from everyone's radar—even his own. And that had troubled him. Seeing her here like this only compounded that concern. She was supposed to trust him no matter what, the way he trusted her. To realize she didn't… Well. She wasn't the only one feeling fear at the moment.

He forced himself to stay where he was, even though he wanted to approach her. He knew better than to touch her—she had real issues about being touched, even casually, and always insisted on taking the initiative there. So he stayed where he was and watched her.

"The last anyone heard," he said, "you were in Vegas burying your mother. You were supposed to be back at work by now. Instead OPUS has a price on your head."

"It doesn't matter where I've been," she told him. "But I need to be able to trust someone right now, Binky."

Dixon squeezed his eyes shut tight. Dammit. He hated it when she used his code name. She was the only one who'd ever used it and lived to tell the tale. Well, could he help it if he'd pissed off the guy in charge so bad during his basic training that he'd been saddled with such a code name? Just because of a harmless little panty raid? Through the commanding officer's bedroom? When he was entertaining his mistress while his wife was out of town? Thereby bringing every MP in a half-mile radius to the guy's house? Not to mention a half dozen television news crews? And a reporter for *Military Times?* Man. Some people had no sense of humor whatsoever.

Before he could say a word in objection, she corrected herself. "Oliver. I need to be able to trust someone right now."

Whoa. That bothered him even more. She'd *never* called him by his first name. Whatever was up, it was bad.

"You know you can trust me," he said. To emphasize that, he called her by her first name, too. "I'm always here for you, Lila. Always."

"You put our partnership before OPUS?" she asked.

"Yes," he replied immediately. Honestly.

She hesitated only a moment, then nodded slowly, once. To see if she meant it, Dixon took another step forward. She flinched a little but didn't move. So he completed another and another, until he stood right beside her. Close enough that he could have grabbed her if he'd wanted to and turned her over to their superiors. Not that he could have done that without a fight from her, since he and Lila were pretty evenly matched there. But where nature had given women an emotional edge over men that they could generally work to their advantage, when all was said and done, the physical edge the men had received usually won out. Had Dixon wanted to, he could have brought Lila in for questioning—or whatever else OPUS wanted to do with her. But she was his partner. He wouldn't have given her up for anything.

"Tell me what's going on," he said, making it an order this time instead of a question.

She inhaled a deep breath and released it slowly, then ran a shaky hand—the one decorated with half a handcuff—over her unkempt hair. "They lied to me, Binky," she said.

"Who lied to you?"

"All of them. Everyone at OPUS."

"Oh, well, color me astonished," he said sarcastically. "Golly, they always tell us the truth about everything."

"No, I don't mean about a case," she said. "I'm not talking about threat levels or the need-to-know stuff. I'm talking about *me*."

Dixon narrowed his eyes at her. "I'm not following you. How could they lie to you about you?"

She said nothing for a moment, then continued, "I have a sister."

Dixon wasn't sure why that was significant, other than that she'd never mentioned having a sister before.

When he said nothing, Lila clarified, "See, here's the thing. Until a few weeks ago, I never knew I had a sister."

Ah. Okay. But he still didn't know what that had to do with her going rogue. Or her appearance at the Nesbitt estate under cover of darkness. Or her appearance once she arrived. She was a mess.

"I'm not sure I'm following where this is going, Lila," he said.

She closed her eyes, inhaled another deep breath and released it as an impatient sound. "I'm an identical twin," she said. "I have a sister out there in the world, someone who looks just like me, and I never knew it. But OPUS *did* know about her. They've known about her for years. They found her when they did the background check on me before accepting me into the program. And they never told me about her."

"They probably just assumed you knew about her."

"She and I were separated at birth." Lila chuckled a little nervously. "Oh, God, this is going to sound so maudlin and clichéd."

"Look, just start at the beginning," Dixon said. "I

have no idea what a missing sister has to do with why you're here looking like this."

Lila lifted a hand, palm up, as if she were either groping for some way to explain or half surrendering to not being able to make herself clear. Finally, though, she said, "Okay. From the beginning. You know about my life in Vegas."

"A little," he conceded. "I mean, I know about your mother and the situation there."

And he only knew that because once, when he and Lila had had too much to drink after an especially grueling assignment, Dixon had told her about his father and she had told Dixon about her mother. About how she'd made her living as a showgirl and part-time prostitute and about the boyfriends and johns who'd wanted a piece of Lila, too. It was why she'd left home at sixteen and never returned. And it was why she was…well, it was why she was She-Wolf.

Lila continued, "After her death, I was going through her things—what few she had—and I found some letters written to her. By my father. I never knew who he was, Binky. When I was a little kid, I used to ask about him. But my mother would always answer me by saying that someday, when I was older, she'd tell me all about him and that I'd understand. Finally, when I was about thirteen and I asked her again, she told me she didn't know who my father was, that he could have been any of a dozen men. By then, I knew what kind of woman she was, so I didn't have any reason to doubt her answer. I figured I was the result of some one-night stand or some job she had, some guy whose name she probably didn't even know."

She licked her lips, and her voice was quieter when

she continued. "But when I was going through her stuff, I found some letters in a box in the back of one of her closets from a man named Elliot. There were only four of them. The first was dated a month after the day I was born. The last one was dated six months later. I don't think my mother replied to any of them, because Elliot mentioned in each one that he hadn't heard from her. Long story short, from what I gather, Elliot was my father and he and my mother decided that they would each take one daughter to raise, since they didn't want to marry but neither felt as if they could handle raising two kids.

"I don't know how they met or what their relationship was like," she continued, "but he *wasn't* some one-night stand. He seemed to have genuinely cared for my mother and for me and my sister. But he took my sister somewhere else to raise her. And OPUS knew all about it, Binky. But they never told me."

"Well, like I said, they probably figured you already knew."

She shook her head. "No, I told them during the initial interview that I'd left home before graduating from high school and rarely spoke to my mother. That I didn't know who my father was. That I didn't have any family. It was one of the reasons they were interested in taking me on. You know how they are about that stuff. They love it when we're mongrels with no family or friends. They love it when we don't have anything to risk except ourselves."

True enough, Dixon thought. The only reason he hadn't had a problem with that himself was because of his father's history with the organization. His father had been alienated from his own family and hadn't met Dixon's mother until he'd been an OPUS operative for nearly a decade. Since Dixon was a legacy, they'd taken him on.

Lila's voice grew a little louder and more animated when she started talking again. "But OPUS learned about all of it during their background check. They knew who my father and sister were and where they lived. They had the address, Binky. *And they never told me about either one of them.*"

"How do you know?" he asked. "Have they confirmed this?"

"Yes!" she said. "When I confronted them, they said they didn't tell me because it would have made me a weaker agent. They figured what I didn't know couldn't hurt me—or anyone else."

Dixon didn't know what to say. Certainly he would have been shocked to learn he had a family at this point in his life. But Lila had never seemed like the type who would care about something like that. In fact, she'd often made little jesting comments about Dixon's own apron strings and his ties that bind. Lila was a tough broad. *Hearth* and *home* weren't part of her vocabulary. At least he hadn't thought they were.

"I'm still not sure what this has to do with your abandonment of your OPUS responsibilities or your appearance here tonight."

"I didn't abandon my OPUS responsibilities," she said coolly. "You know me better than to even suggest something like that."

"I didn't mean it like—"

"You know, you're just like them," she said before he could finish. "You gave yourself over to them completely after your father was killed. They own your soul."

"No, they don't." *Not anymore,* he added to himself.

And only then did he realize that Lila's accusation was true. Or at least it had been true. He really had given himself over to OPUS after his father's murder. He'd devoted every moment of every day to finding out what had gone wrong with his father's last assignment and who had been responsible for his cover being blown. Once he'd discovered it was Adrian Padgett who'd leaked the information, he'd known he wouldn't sleep until he found the guy and ripped him limb from limb. Even on those sporadic visits home to see his family, Dixon had spent his time missing his father and seeing how his death had affected his mother, and reaffirming his conviction that he would find his father's killer and wreak vengeance upon him. OPUS had become his only means of doing that. So OPUS had become his life.

Until Avery.

He wasn't sure when or how the change had come about, couldn't pinpoint now the moment he'd stopped living his life solely to avenge his father's death and had started letting her creep into it. But at some point over the past couple of weeks she had more than crept into his life. She had become part of it. That night the two of them had made love so explosively had been unlike anything Dixon had ever experienced. He'd told himself at the time it was only because the sex had been so spontaneous, so hot and so raw. But now he knew better. Now he knew it was because he'd already started to care about her on some level other than the superficial. And it was in a way he hadn't cared about women he'd known far better than she. Or at least whom he'd *thought* he knew far better than she. There had been something about Avery from that first night onward that had connected to something inside him he hadn't even realized needed connection.

All along he'd been telling himself he only cared about her because she was his means to an end. But now he understood it was because he'd felt so alone. And being with her, he'd stopped feeling that way.

"You're still just like them," Lila said, pulling him out of his epiphany and bringing him back to the matter at hand.

Dixon shook his head adamantly. "No, I'm not. Not anymore."

"Then try to understand," Lila told him. "I have a family, Binky. You know what that means, to have people in the world who are connected to you that way, who care about you that way. I've never had that. But I had the chance to learn what it was like, a chance that was taken away from me right after I was born. A chance I might have found a second time. But OPUS took it from me again. Had it been up to them, I never would have found out about my father or sister. But they wanted me to be a better agent. So they never told me."

Dixon thought about that for a minute. About how he would feel if he'd been denied the chance to know his father and mother and sister. And only because someone had thought it would make him do his job better to be kept in solitary confinement for the rest of his life. Because by preventing him from feeling an emotion like love, they would make him a more effectively operating piece of machinery. A piece of machinery they needed in order to make their own jobs a little easier.

Yeah, okay, so that sucked.

"I still don't know what any of this has to do with

your disappearance and the reports that you've gone rogue and tried to kill the Big Guy and—"

"That's bullshit," Lila said. "Pure and simple. I didn't try to kill anyone. And I haven't gone rogue. I've gone AWOL."

Dixon arched his eyebrows. "And the difference would be…?"

"Going rogue means going over to the other side or out for my own purposes."

"And you're out for what—a sandwich?"

She managed a smile for that, but it didn't last long. "I just want to find my sister and father," she said. "And they won't tell me where they are. I even tried to blackmail them into telling me."

"Oh, great," Dixon said. "The last time anyone tried to blackmail them, people ended up dead." His own father among them.

"I didn't do it the way Sorcerer did," she said. "I have information about him, a few vital little tidbits OPUS needs if they want to find him. And it's stuff I haven't told anyone yet." She hesitated only a moment before revealing, "Not even you, Binky. Not because I didn't trust you," she hastened to add when he opened his mouth to object. "But because I couldn't get it to you at the time. But I won't tell you now, either. I told OPUS I wouldn't reveal what I know until they tell me where my family is. They refuse. They said any records they had of their existence were expunged the minute they realized I didn't know about them."

"Which is almost certainly true," Dixon said.

"I know," she agreed. "But the reason they won't tell me anything is more likely because I pissed them off. You know how they are."

"I do," Dixon agreed. If there was one thing OPUS hated more than anything it was not having the upper hand. Lila had it now. Which meant they'd act like a big baby and make up stories about her, and if you were her friend, you weren't their friend and you couldn't have any cookies, either, so there. "And *you* know," he countered, "that it can be very dangerous to piss OPUS off."

She lifted up the hand wearing the handcuff bracelet. "Yeah, I know even better now than I did before."

"And what's with that anyway?" Dixon asked, dipping his head toward the handcuff. "Not to mention your new wardrobe. You've never been one for uniforms."

"One wears what one has available," she said. "Especially if what one was wearing previously was extremely identifiable."

"And that's not?" Dixon asked.

"Well, it's a little less conspicuous than the bunny suit," she said.

"Easter Bunny or just generic bunny?"

"Playboy Bunny," she told him. "I had a tip about the Vegas Playboy Club."

Oh, Dixon would have given up every nickel of his retirement, his Keogh *and* his 401(k) to have seen Lila operating in a place like that.

"This," she added, sweeping both hands down over her attire, "and this," she said, holding up the handcuff again, "came about when the tip turned out to be a bogus one fed to me by an OPUS operative previously unbeknownst to me in an effort to bring me in."

"Let me guess," Dixon said. "The operative in question was the one who went in instead—probably in a body bag."

"Stretcher," Lila told him. "Not that I didn't try."

"I don't think I want to know the details."

"You're right. I let down my guard because of my state of mind. That won't happen again."

"But then, we were talking about this missing twin sister," Dixon said, getting them back on track again. Even if what they were back on track with was a runaway train.

"I'm going to have to find her by myself now," Lila said. She met his gaze levelly. "Or with a little help from my friends."

"You don't have any friends, Lila," Dixon reminded her. He would have grinned when he said it, but he wasn't kidding. Of course, Lila knew that. Then he added, "Except me." She knew that, too.

She nodded. "And you're better at what you do than anyone. And part of what you do is find people."

True enough, Dixon thought. There was just one problem. "They were telling you the truth when they said any record OPUS has of your family has been purged by now. If any record ever even existed to begin with. Do you have names?"

"Only the first ones," she told him. "From the letters. Elliot for my father. Marnie for my sister."

"Got any kind of geographical information?"

"Elliot's letters mentioned Pennsylvania. I don't know what city. There were no envelopes with return addresses or stamp cancellations or anything like that. But that was almost thirty years ago. They could be anywhere by now."

Dixon expelled a sound that was at once energized and fatigued. "Well, at least they're not common names.

And at least Pennsylvania is a starting point. We might
be able to dig something up."

"We?" Lila echoed suspiciously. "Who's we?"

Dixon hadn't even realized he'd used the plural
pronoun instead of the singular one. Funny that he'd
begun to think in terms of him and Avery as a unit
without even consciously making the decision to do so.

This time he did grin when he spoke. "No offense,
Lila, but I have a new partner."

"Yeah, I know. That little Cowboy upstart. Me, I
thought his code name should be Teletubby."

"No, not him," Dixon said. And then his grin broadened. "Lila," he said, "there's a new woman in my life."

HE THOUGHT SHE WAS HEALED.

As Avery sat in her bed two nights after her
parents' party, idly rubbing her fingers over the
downy fur behind Skittles's ear, she heard not the
cat's easy purring but Dixon's words from Saturday
evening. *Peaches, your scabs healed a long time ago.
What you can't seem to quit doing is showing off
your scars.*

How could he say that? How could he think she was
healed? She was more damaged now than ever. She'd
been living in the house where she'd grown up for two
weeks, and her family was still barely speaking to her.
Well, save Carly, she amended, who'd actually been
kind of nice to her the past couple of days. But that was
because of Tanner's entry into her life, not Avery's.
And, okay, there had been that brief exchange with her
father in the living room a few mornings ago that Avery
still wasn't sure she understood. That *could* have been
an attempt to build that bridge she'd been hoping might

materialize. And, yeah, there had been her father's insistence, too, that she be at the party, which she supposed in its own weird way might have been an effort on his part to let the rest of East Hampton know she was back in his sort of good graces. Maybe…

Still, even if her family was coming around—and she still wasn't convinced they were—it wasn't because *she* was "healed."

So what had Dixon meant?

She watched the Beziers screen saver as it tumbled leisurely across her computer monitor, its random curves changing from red to orange to yellow to green to blue. Staring at the elegant dance of color eased her tension some, and she was grateful for the scant light it provided to the otherwise darkened room. She hadn't seen Dixon since the party. He'd left immediately after Gillespie's arrival, and the two men had gone to the guesthouse to hook up to OPUS from Gillespie's equipment and find out what was going on with his missing partner. His missing partner who was obviously more to him than a co-worker. Avery just wished she could figure out what.

Where was he? she wondered, turning her watch toward the computer to read the time by the screensaver light. He had said they would go back to work tonight, and he was always here by ten-thirty. Now it was after eleven. If she didn't get online soon, Adrian was going to think she was a no-show and he might get suspicious. She still wasn't sure he'd bought her multinight absence of a couple of weeks ago. To have it happen again so soon would be a little unusual. Especially on a weekend, when regular business hours were over. He knew she never had anywhere to go on the weekends, when most people were out running around. He knew she did her running around on the Net.

Where was Dixon?

Maybe he'd fallen asleep, she thought. He and Gillespie had probably been working around the clock. He would have needed a nap or something before spending another night in front of the computer.

Oh, just go over and get him, she told herself. *He's right across the hall. It's not like you were sent to your room without supper. You can go out anytime you want.*

She laughed at that. Because she couldn't go out anytime she wanted. Though maybe the fact that she'd even thought such a thing was a good sign. She had seemed to be managing her anxiety and panic attacks better since returning to her parents' house. Which was odd, since it hadn't been long ago that the mere thought of having to confront her family would have sent her over the edge.

Resigned to if not going out, at least going across the hall, Avery scuttled off the bed and made her way out. She was lifting her hand to knock on Dixon's door when she heard voices on the other side. His first, then one she didn't recognize. It was a woman's voice, though—there was no mistaking that. Although the voices were too quiet for her to understand what was being said, there was an unmistakably intimate quality to them. And there was unmistakable affection, too.

Who could he be talking to? Especially this time of night? And how had whoever it was gotten as far as his room without Avery's hearing her go by?

Spy stuff, she immediately realized. Whoever was in there was probably someone Dixon worked with. His partner, she thought. The woman who'd gone rogue and who was wanted by the very organization she was supposed to be working for. The woman Gillespie had said was armed and dangerous.

Avery wondered what she should do. Was Dixon in danger? What if his partner really was armed and dangerous? Of course, he'd seemed to find the suggestion ludicrous, but who knew about these spies? OPUS had already set one crazy agent loose on the world. Who was to say they hadn't driven another one around the bend, too? Her mind surging, her heart pounding, Avery turned the knob and pushed the door open—

Just in time to see Dixon leaning forward to kiss a woman.

Okay, it was dark, so she couldn't see that well. But moonlight filtering through the filmy curtains threw into stark profile two people—one man and one woman—who were touching each other intimately. Dixon had taken the woman's hand and was lifting it for what looked very much like a kiss. Whoever she was, she was someone he knew well and someone for whom he cared deeply. Someone he knew better—and had known longer—than Avery.

"Dixon?"

His name was out of her mouth before she could stop it, and both he and the woman jerked their heads up to look at her. The woman started to bolt away, toward the window, but Dixon held her wrist firmly in his hand, and she halted. Avery waited to see if she would struggle, but she didn't. Judging by her posture, though, she was in no way comfortable at having been discovered.

"Avery," Dixon said, his voice low and tinged with apprehension.

Avery took a step forward, then stopped. "What's

going on? Who's that woman?" she asked. And she hated herself for sounding like a jealous wife who'd just walked in on her philandering husband.

"Go back to your room," Dixon told her. "I'll explain later."

She started to march into the room with the indignant demand that no, he would explain right this instant, but halted herself. He wasn't her husband. He wasn't even her lover. Yes, they'd had sex. Yes, they'd shared parts of themselves with each other that went beyond the physical. But she had no claim on him whatsoever. They were two people who'd been thrown temporarily into close quarters by extraordinary circumstances. But they owed each other nothing.

"I'm sorry," she said. "I didn't mean to interrupt. I just—"

Oh, God. Now she sounded worse than an angry wife. Now she sounded like a heartbroken schoolgirl. But she'd been a heartbroken schoolgirl, she reminded herself. And it hadn't felt anything like this. This was worse than anything she'd felt before.

"Never mind," she quickly amended as she stepped back into the hallway and began to pull the door closed.

But Dixon was there before she could complete the action, tugging it open again. "Oh, no you don't," he said. "You're not leaving here thinking what you're thinking."

"I'm not thinking anything," she said.

"The hell you're not."

"Oliver."

His name came not from Avery's mouth but from the other woman's. And it was the name she knew he shared with very few people.

"I don't have a lot of time here," the woman added impatiently. "I need to get lost. Can you take care of this or not?"

The woman lifted her hand again, and now Avery saw what looked like handcuffs dangling from her wrist. Whoa. Evidently she'd not only interrupted something here, she'd interrupted something really weird.

"I need bolt cutters," Dixon said.

Way weird, Avery thought. Way, way weirder than anything she'd ever heard about. And that was saying something, since she had e-mail addresses she used specifically to solicit spam for her work. But of all the S-and-M subject headers she'd read on porn spam, none had ever mentioned bolt cutters.

"I really need to get out of here," she said softly. "You guys are into something I don't want to know about."

The woman on the other side of the room expelled a sound of disgust. "Listen, Strawberry Shortcake, no one's mind is in the gutter here but yours." Then to Dixon she said, "This is her? This is the one you were telling me about?"

"This is her," Dixon said.

He'd told his partner-slash-possibly-weird-handcuff/bolt-cutter-thing-lover about her? Avery thought. Did that mean he thought she was special enough to tell someone about? Or did it just mean he was into those three-way-handcuff/bolt-cutter S-and-M things? And then she finally processed what the other woman had called her.

"Strawberry Shortcake?" she echoed indignantly. "What the hell is that supposed to mean? What, you can't come up with something more creative than that? I can think of a million things to call you right now."

Even in the moonlight she saw the woman smile. "Oh, okay," she said. "I see it now. For a minute there, Oliver, I was worried about you." And then, before Avery could say another word, the smile fell and she added, "Hello? Bolt cutters? Please?"

Dixon turned to Avery, but before he could say a word, she told him, "I have no idea if there are any bolt cutters around here. If anyone would know, it would be Jensen."

"Who would doubtless get suspicious if we asked him for some."

This time Avery was the one to smile. She still had no idea what was going on. Somehow, though, she didn't feel quite as bad as she had when she first entered. Dixon had some explaining to do. But for the first time since meeting him Avery began to think maybe he would answer most of the questions she asked. Now if only she could figure out what to ask him….

She shook the thought off. For now. "Jensen wouldn't get suspicious if I were the one doing the asking," she said.

Dixon's mouth hitched up on one side, too. "Peaches, I knew I could count on you."

CHAPTER EIGHTEEN

NOT UNTIL ALMOST AN HOUR after She-Wolf's departure was Dixon finally able to make himself relax. Not that he wasn't confident she could slip off unnoticed or take care of herself should someone discover her. But her appearance had put him on heightened security, and it always took him a little while to come down from that. He wasn't sure, though, why he'd gone on heightened security in the first place. It wasn't as though She-Wolf had been doing anything tonight she hadn't done a million times before. In fact, her coming to the Nesbitt estate to ask him for help and then leaving after getting it was pretty tame compared to most of the assignments she'd completed effortlessly and without consequence in the past. Ever since he'd sent Avery off in search of bolt cutters, though, Dixon's adrenaline had been pumping like an oil refinery.

Once he made that association, he understood. When Avery became involved, he had begun to feel fear. If Dixon had been caught helping She-Wolf, he would have been in a boatload of trouble, might have ended up behind bars with her. But that wasn't what scared him. That was part of the job. *His* job. Not Avery's. Had she been caught, she would have been in a boatload of trouble, too, might have ended up in prison again, one way or another. Hell, worst-case scenario, if things had gone wrong tonight, there could have been gunfire. Dixon and She-Wolf were trained to handle it. Avery wasn't. She might have been caught in the middle of it. She might have been hurt. Or worse.

And Dixon would have been responsible.

But as he watched her fire up her computer and take her seat before it as she had every night, he realized he'd been putting her in danger since the assignment began simply by pulling her into it. And now he was insisting she meet Sorcerer—a man even their best trained agents hadn't been able to capture—face-to-face. Of course, had it been up to Dixon, she never would have left her Central Park condo. But he was going along with instructions to ensure she made contact. He might have offered up some meager objection when his most superior superior had mapped out the plan, but he hadn't fought much. He tried to reassure himself with the reminder that at that point, Avery had been a stranger to him. He hadn't felt about her then the way he did now.

So just how do *you feel about her now?* he asked himself. And it bugged the hell out of him that he couldn't come up with an answer. Or maybe he just didn't want to come up with an answer. Which bugged the hell out of him even more.

"I've got mail," Avery said. "From Adrian."

Dixon leaned forward in his seat to read over her shoulder and, as always, was assailed by the fresh, luscious scent of her. Instead of asking her about her e-mail, he instead heard himself say, "What makes you smell like peaches, Peaches?"

She turned to look at him, obviously startled by the

question. "Lotion," she told him. "Is that why you call me that?"

He nodded.

She studied him in silence for a moment, her dark brows knit downward. Then, "Oh," she said softly, and turned back to look at the monitor.

Dixon wasn't sure what to say after that, so he leaned forward again—to see the monitor, naturally—and was again assailed by the intoxicating scent of her. Unable to help himself, he inhaled deeply, holding the breath inside him for as long as he could, until dizziness finally made him exhale. But even when he breathed normally, he was surrounded by her fragrance. And even when he breathed normally, he felt dizzy.

"He wants me to meet him Tuesday," she said.

"At the club where his alleged band is supposedly playing?"

She shook her head. "No."

"He must have been convinced then," Dixon said. "He must have believed you when you told him you couldn't meet him in a public place. This is good. He's buying it."

She turned around again and met his gaze, her eyes brimming with something that looked very much like fear. "Don't be so sure," she said softly.

"Why not?"

"Because he wants to meet me at Rockefeller Plaza. At lunchtime. When the place will be crawling with people."

Dixon muttered a ripe curse. "What's the e-mail say?" But even as Avery started speaking, he looked past her to read along.

Sorcerer started off with his usual platitudes, telling

Avery how much he missed her when they weren't together, then segued into the events of his day, most of which seemed to consist of working at a music store and teaching guitar to kids who didn't even recognize names like Eric Clapton, Jimmy Page, Greg Allman and Robert Johnson.

"Who's Robert Johnson?" Dixon asked.

"Only the greatest blues guitarist of all time, according to Andrew. I mean, Adrian."

"I never knew Adrian was into the guitar thing."

"Yeah, well, obviously when he scams someone, he does his homework first," she said flatly.

Which, of course, was exactly like Sorcerer, Dixon thought.

He read more of the e-mail, afraid to skim it, though there was nothing of significance until he came to the final paragraph.

I know you're scared to go out, he had written, *and I know you don't give out your address to anyone. But it might be a while before I get back to NY. We've known each other for more than a month now. You mean a lot to me, Avery. A lot. If I mean anything to you, couldn't we just meet? Please? Rockefeller Center's cool this time of year....*

There was more cajoling, more assurances of her importance to him, more wheedling, more sweet talk, more con.

"Why wouldn't he press to meet you at your place?" Dixon asked, thinking Sorcerer's insistence on meeting out in the open when he knew Avery was agoraphobic felt wrong somehow. "If he were going to try and convince you to get together with him, especially if he knows you're agoraphobic, why would he add to your anxiety like that? Why wouldn't he be trying to talk you into letting him come to your apartment?"

There was actually a very good answer to that question, Dixon knew. He just didn't want to think it was the right one. If Sorcerer was on to them, he'd want to draw Avery out where he could see her from a distance, to pick out anyone in the surrounding crowd who might also be watching their meeting. If he was on to them, he'd know that going to her apartment could easily be walking into a trap. But how could he possibly know Avery was working with OPUS? They'd done everything they could to cover their tracks, and Dixon was confident that even Sorcerer wouldn't be able to figure out what was going on. This had to be a legitimate request for a meeting on his part. It had to be a genuine attempt to meet Avery and pull her into whatever little intrigue he was hatching. But even then, why wouldn't he want to come to her place?

Avery had an answer for the question that Dixon liked better than his own. "I made a big deal early in our relationship about how I don't give out my address to *any*one I meet online, no matter what," she said, stressing it the same way Sorcerer had in his e-mail. "If I could get away with not giving it out to *any*one anywhere else either, I would. I'm a total privacy freak," she explained. "Unfortunately, my…condition…makes it necessary for me to give the information to a select few."

"Mohammed at Eastern Star Earth-Friendly Market, for instance," Dixon said.

She nodded. "Yeah, and look how that turned out."

He said nothing in response to that.

"I have features in place on my PC that make it virtually impossible for anyone to find me, even ordering online as I do."

"Yeah, I know," he muttered, remembering her homemade firewall.

"Even if Adrian really was Andrew Paddington, aspiring musician who truly loved me," she continued, "it would take a long time for me to trust him enough to tell him where I am. Even if it meant not meeting him face-to-face. But that was part of why I…liked him…so much," she added. "Because he knew all that about me and he was still patient enough to put up with it. He was going to wait for me as long as it took for me to get comfortable with him."

"No, he wasn't," Dixon reminded her unnecessarily.

"I know that now," she said so softly he almost didn't hear her. Then, just as they had the night before, her eyes began to fill with tears. And as before, she spun around quickly so Dixon couldn't see them.

This time, though, he understood. Avery Nesbitt, who was so whack no man in his right mind could possibly want her, had finally met a man who wanted her. And then she'd discovered that he'd been lying to her all along, that he didn't want her at all.

But she was wrong. There was a man who wanted Avery Nesbitt. Dixon wanted Avery Nesbitt. He just couldn't have her, that was all. Because the kind of work he did was too erratic and nomadic—and too dangerous—for a woman who couldn't stray far from home. If he got involved with her and someone decided to use his…affection…for her against him, she'd be a sitting duck. Firewall or no firewall.

Before he realized what he was doing, Dixon lifted a hand and began to move it toward her hair, to the black silky tresses she wore unfettered since having it cut. He stopped himself before touching her, though, curling up his fingers and returning his hand to his lap. It was pointless, he told himself. Yeah, maybe he cared more for Avery than he let himself admit, and maybe he'd overstepped boundaries both professional *and* personal since meeting her. But he was back inside those lines now, where he was supposed to be, where he intended to stay. This thing with Avery, whatever it was, couldn't go any further. In a matter of days they'd be saying their goodbyes. There was no reason to make it any more difficult than it would already be.

"I don't think it's weird that Adrian would be asking me to meet him somewhere other than my apartment," she said now, once again pulling Dixon out of thoughts he'd rather not be having—funny how he kept going there anyway. "He knows better than to ask for an invitation to my home. And if he doesn't meet me at my home, and since I told him I wouldn't come to the club, that leaves somewhere away from both."

"Meaning somewhere out in public."

Her back still turned to him, she nodded. "And in New York City, public is really, really public."

"Good point."

Dixon still didn't like it. It still felt wrong. He was about to say so, but a chime from the computer signaled Adrian's arrival online and a pop-up window in the corner announced an IM from him to Avery. Hey, Babe, it said. What's the forecast for Tuesday?

"What do you want me to do?" Avery asked, turning to look over her shoulder at Dixon.

Kiss me, he thought before he could stop himself. *Touch me. Make love with me. Spend the night at my*

*side. Wake up with me in the morning and then go some-
place with me where no one will ever find us. Be happy.
Be yourself. Be with me. Forever.*

"Reel him in," he said instead, his voice gritty and
low. "Do it slowly. Don't spook him. But reel him in,
Avery. It's time to put Sorcerer in the tank, where he
belongs."

ADRIAN COULDN'T HAVE CHOSEN a better venue for their
rendezvous. For *himself,* Avery thought as she focused
every last iota of her person on not turning into a
frothing-at-the-mouth wacko. This was the first time in
nearly a decade that she'd been out in the open this way
without first getting herself three sheets to the wind.
Their meeting time was still five minutes away and she
was already nearing meltdown.

All around her, people scurried to and fro, carrying
brightly colored shopping bags full of early holiday
gifts or armed with briefcases and backpacks that were
essential to their everyday living. The Rockefeller Plaza
Christmas tree soared up behind her, glittering in its
elegant holiday finery, even though Thanksgiving was
still more than a week away. Skaters glided past her
through silvery, softly falling snow, a never-ending ka-
leidoscope of dappled sweaters and Polartec. Tony
Bennett sang to her that she should have herself a merry
little Christmas, accompanied by a street vendor
hawking hot cider nearby, close enough that Avery
could inhale the faint aroma of apple and cinnamon
and clove.

On the next bench, a little girl was lacing up her
skates, two long black braids tumbling from beneath her
fuzzy white hat, her short pink skirt and sweater indi-

cating she was serious about the icy pursuit. A man who was clearly her father sat beside her tying his own skates, and the two of them were engaged in animated, intimate conversation. As one, they began to laugh at something the man had said, then they stood hand in hand and headed for the rink. A slice of envy knifed through Avery at the sight, so she made herself look away. And she tried not to panic when she realized how exposed she was in the crowd of people. And how very, very alone.

Truly, everything around her would be enchanting, she knew, had she not been so terrified of everything around her.

She closed her eyes and clutched with both hands what to the casual observer appeared to be a covered venti latte but which was in fact a quadruple scotch on the rocks. Hopefully those three sheets to the wind weren't far off. Dixon had at first nixed the liquor, telling her it was essential her mind be clear for this endeavor. She'd countered that without the liquor she'd be a doddering lunatic. She agreed with him that she needed to find another way to combat her panic attacks and work toward good mental health. Assuming, of course, she still had something remotely resembling mental health once this assignment was over. Until then, she thanked God for the almighty Glenlivet.

Maybe if she just avoided looking at the crowd and the buildings and the sky overhead, she'd be okay. Maybe if she didn't see the massive, sprawling horde of people and the staggeringly immense skyscrapers and the stark, infinite sky, she could function normally. Maybe if she forgot she was surrounded by millions of strangers who could turn on her at any moment and towering edifices that might come crashing down on top of her any second and a vast chasm of space that might suck her into the void if she wasn't careful…

Oh, God…

I have nothing to fear in this moment, she told herself as she lifted her drink to her mouth for a healthy sip. *In this moment, there is nothing to fear. I have nothing to fear in this moment. In this moment, there is nothing to fear….*

Again and again Avery recited the incantation to herself, until she was utterly focused upon it. Little by little, her heart rate slowed, her head stopped hammering, her body stopped trembling and her heated skin cooled. She took another sip of her drink and reminded herself she wasn't alone. Dixon and Gillespie were both watching her, even if she couldn't see either of them. She really did have nothing to fear in this moment. The people around her weren't here to hurt her. The buildings were perfectly sound. The sky was a place of magic, with the snow falling as it was. And in this moment, at least, Adrian Padgett wasn't around. Even when he showed up, she told herself, he wouldn't pose a threat to her. He didn't know she was working with OPUS and trying to lure him into a trap.

She hoped.

She tried to remind herself that if the situation had been genuine, if she'd been a normally functioning woman who had come here to meet a man with whom she'd fallen in love, this moment would be special and romantic. But then she remembered that she hadn't been a normally functioning woman for a long time now. And the man she was meeting was a menace to society. The man she loved was nowhere in sight.

She had no trouble admitting that now, at least to herself. She did love Dixon. Oliver. Whatever and whoever he was. She'd probably been in love with him since the night they made love. Maybe even before that. He just wasn't like other men she'd known. Not that she had such a vast, experience-filled history with men. Nor had she ever been a good judge of masculine character. But Dixon had a lot of character. He had even more masculinity. More than either of those, though, he had decency. He was a good guy. He'd treated her with respect and civility, even when she'd been at her most whack. He'd looked out for her. He'd championed her. He'd taken care of her. But even more important than that, he'd put her on the path toward learning to take care of herself, learning to respect herself, and learning to be her own champion.

She didn't kid herself that her life was going to be smooth and rosy once Dixon left it. She knew she had a long way to go. But with him at her side, she'd taken the first steps. In the short time since he'd entered her life, she'd left her home and gone miles away and lived to tell the tale. She'd become part of a dangerous assignment, something that generated real fear in light of her irrational ones, and she'd managed to carry it through to its conclusion—or would, once this meeting with Adrian was over. She'd reunited with her family, however tenuous that reunion had been. She'd forged an alliance with her sister—again tenuous but with potential—where there had never been one before. And she had fallen in love. Real love. The kind that when you lost it left you feeling melancholy instead of angry, wistful instead of vengeful.

She had begun to live life since meeting Dixon,

instead of exiling herself from it. For that she would always owe him. And she would always be grateful.

She wished they had more time together, wished that the other night, when she'd gone to his room to ask him about the healing remark he'd made at the party, he'd been alone. But he hadn't been alone. They hadn't had a chance to talk. And she'd never had another opportunity to ask him what he'd meant. They'd been too busy setting up Adrian for his colossal fall.

She lifted the heavy cardboard cup to her lips and pushed up the plastic lid to make it look as if she were blowing on hot coffee to cool it. "Dixon," she said softly into the microphone that was hidden in the heavy red muffler wrapped around her neck. "Are you there?"

"I'm here, Avery. Hold steady. It won't be much longer. Three minutes to contact. Sorcerer is always on time."

His voice came to her through the earpiece hidden beneath both her hair and the red knit cap she'd pulled low, to just above her eyes. She silently thanked the weather for cooperating today. The temperature hovered in the upper twenties and a light snow was falling, making it essential that she wear enough clothes to hide all the paraphernalia OPUS had insisted she have on her. In addition to the mic and earpiece, she was equipped with a cell phone, a global positioning device and pepper spray. Dixon had offered her a gun, but she'd laughed in his face. Literally. That was all she needed to do—shoot herself. Although her usual self-defense weapon of choice was a Louisville Slugger, it would have been a bit difficult to hide under her coat. She figured, hey, she was reasonably adept with Tabasco sauce, so pepper spray couldn't be too far a stretch. She also was wearing a minuscule tape recorder, in case she and Adrian somehow moved out of range of the surveillance equipment Dixon and Gillespie were manning.

She tried not to think about that happening. The only way Avery would move out of range of Dixon and Gillespie would be against her will. If Adrian for whatever reason figured out at some point during their meeting that she was setting him up—or if, God forbid, he already knew—he could harm her or anyone else nearby. In this crowd, in this weather, it would be easy for a man with his intelligence and depravity to commit a kidnapping or inflict injury—or worse.

She was sipping her drink before the thought even fully formed in her brain. "What if he doesn't show up?" she said into the mic.

"He'll show."

Just the sound of Dixon's voice calmed her some. She closed her eyes and sipped her drink again, visualizing him the way he had been when he'd wired her up earlier, his eyes filled with a genuine concern for her safety. He wouldn't let anything happen to her, she told herself. She was perfectly safe as long as he was around.

"But what if he doesn't?" she said, tucking her mouth into her scarf. "How long should I wait?"

"Don't talk," Dixon instructed her. "He'll show. He's got a lot of time and effort invested in you and he's convinced you're the best person to help him carry out whatever plan he has. He'll show. He may have just been slowed down by the weather and the crowd. Sit tight, Avery. I've got your back."

She almost smiled at that. He had a lot more than her back. He had every part of her, right down to her heart and soul. She hadn't meant to fall in love with him. And she still wasn't sure how she felt about her condition. It might be different if Dixon loved her, too. Or if there was some chance he might fall in love with her someday. But he wasn't the sort of man to fall in love. And she wasn't the sort of woman men fell in love with. Sure, she had a few things going for her. She was smart and she could be funny and she wasn't bad-looking.

But she had problems. And she was difficult. And she was weird. Most guys, when they settled on one woman, wanted someone they could at least take out into public from time to time without fear that she would go completely nuts.

Then again, Dixon wasn't the type to be overly concerned with convention. And he didn't much care about making a good impression. He probably wouldn't let something like phobia and panic disorder keep him from falling in love with the right woman.

So it was just that Avery wasn't the right woman, that was all.

More emotional baggage, she thought as she took another sip of her drink. Just what she needed. More psychological crap to stuff into the teeming closet of her subconscious. She was going to have to clean that thing out soon. Have herself a psychological garage sale. She wondered if eBay allowed listings like "Bruised Ego" or "Neglected Id." Hell, her Defense Mechanisms and Compulsive Behaviors were practically good as new. She'd have to check into it.

"Avery? Avery Nesbitt?"

The moment she heard his voice behind her, her brain skidded to a halt. Panic exploded in her belly and anxiety began to claw at her throat. Her mouth went dry, her face went hot and her hands began to tremble. Fog billowed into her head and all coherent thought threatened to flee. *Not now,* she told herself. *Not here. Not yet. Not after coming so far. Please, please, please, don't let me lose it now.*

I have nothing to fear in this moment. In this moment, there is nothing to fear....

She took a few seconds to calm herself, forcing down her panic to where it was—she hoped—manageable. Then she turned to look into the face of the man she had once thought might change her life. The man who could now, if she wasn't careful, end it....

CHAPTER NINETEEN

FROM HIS OUTDOOR SEAT AT a café-side table, where he'd been pretending to sketch the skaters and passersby, Dixon could only see Sorcerer from the side. But his head was turned toward Avery, making it impossible to see his face. Like her, he was dressed for the snowy day in heaps of clothing and a knit cap pulled low, but there was something about his attire that bothered Dixon. Of course, he wouldn't dress in a way that might draw attention to himself and he would dress in sync with the Andrew Paddington persona he had been feeding to Avery. Not that she'd ever buy the twenty-something age range when she saw the man claiming to be Andrew. But she'd been instructed to play along. Even in normal circumstances, when people met online they often fudged the details of their reality. Had this been a situation where Avery was actually meeting a man named Andrew whom she'd met online, there would be things about his reality that wouldn't jibe with her fantasy.

And why did even the thought of such a normal meeting bother Dixon? Why was the concept of her meeting a man, some nice, normal guy she'd hooked up with online, troubling to him? He and Avery would be winding this thing up soon, and he ought not to be thinking in such terms. She was finally in a position where she'd begun to tackle some of her problems, and it was very likely that with time and help she would eventually be able to function in society the way she had when she was younger. He ought to be wishing her well and hoping she *would* meet some nice, normal guy who would give her the love and respect she deserved. Some guy who deserved her, too.

But Dixon couldn't quite make himself think in those terms. The idea of Avery being with someone else just felt wrong to him. And then he realized how he had just worded his own thought in his own head. Avery being with *someone else?* By using the phrase *someone else,* he was pretty much indicating that right now he was thinking of himself and Avery as an item. As in, romantically involved. As in, she was his, and he was hers. As in, that was the way it should be. And once this thing was over, she'd be with someone *else.*

Someone else. Why did that sound so strange when all along he'd been telling himself she *should* be with someone else? And he should be with... Well. He should—and would—be with no one.

"Hi, you must be Andrew."

The sound of her voice, crystal clear and rock steady—*yeah, that's my girl*—came through his earpiece, jerking him back to the matter at hand. He could think about that *someone else* business later. When it was just the two of them again. He panicked for a minute when a woman stopped in front of him to rearrange her shopping bags and cut off Avery from view, but he shifted his chair to the left a bit until she was in sight once more. As was the man who had just joined her. But Dixon still didn't have a clear view of his face, especially when he rounded the bench to stand in front of Avery. So he studied everything he could see.

And it struck him again that there was something about the way the guy was dressed that bothered him. The snow was picking up now, making a study of details more difficult, but from where Dixon sat he could tell the other man was wearing the sort of too-big, too-sloppy jacket favored by younger men these days. His jeans in the back rested atop heavy hiking boots, also not unexpected for someone posing as Andrew Paddington, midtwenties musician. Still, there was something about the clothing that just didn't seem right....

No, not his clothing, Dixon realized as the man sat down beside Avery. It was his stance and the way he moved that seemed off. Not jerky or nervous or unnatural. Just...wrong.

"It's so great to finally meet you face-to-face," his voice came through the earpiece as the man sat down beside her.

And Dixon frowned when he heard it. He told himself it must be the equipment, that that was why Sorcerer's normal baritone had suddenly become a tenor. Or maybe he was deliberately trying to disguise his voice in an effort to throw off anyone who might be watching or eavesdropping. He was called Sorcerer for a reason, and part of that reason was his ability to change his appearance with fairly little effort. That meant changing his voice from time to time, too.

It was Sorcerer, Dixon told himself. It had to be. Because if it wasn't, then the last two weeks of his life—hell, the last six months of his life—had been for nothing.

As soon as the thought formed in his head, though,

he knew it wasn't true. He could never consider his time with Avery to be nothing. On the contrary, the last two weeks with her had been, in a strange way, more enjoyable than any he could remember spending in a long time. Because for one thing, Dixon hadn't spent those weeks alone, which was his usual way of existing. Even though he had a partner for his work, the nature of that work often required the two of them to operate apart. He'd found it surprisingly agreeable to spend time with another person. That the person had been someone like Avery, someone smart and resourceful and witty and brave, had only been a bonus.

No, not someone *like* Avery, he instantly corrected himself. The fact that it had been her specifically was what had made the time so rewarding. So exhilarating. So special.

But if the man talking to her now wasn't Sorcerer, then Dixon was back to square one. And if it wasn't Sorcerer standing where Dixon could see him, then Sorcerer might very well be somewhere looking at Dixon instead.

Dammit.

He focused on the man talking to Avery. It was Sorcerer, he told himself again. Who else could it be?

"You don't look like your picture," Avery was saying now, reaffirming Dixon's earlier thoughts.

"Okay, I have a confession to make," the guy said. "That picture I sent you? It wasn't really me. It was a JPEG I scored from a singles site. I was afraid you'd think I was a geek."

Avery managed an almost genuine-sounding chuckle at that. *Hang on,* Dixon encouraged her silently. *Just a few more minutes.*

"*I'm* the geek," she said. "The picture I sent you was totally me."

"I thought you were cute," the guy told her. "Just like now."

Something cold and unpleasant settled in Dixon's stomach. The guy still didn't sound like Sorcerer. But that wasn't the real reason he felt sick, he realized. No, it was because whoever this bastard was, he was flirting with Avery. Dixon swore eloquently under his breath.

"What? What's wrong?"

This time it was Gillespie's voice coming through the earpiece. He was wired in to Dixon for sound but not Avery. So she could continue to blithely small talk with her new best friend—well, as blithely as someone with panic disorder could small talk anyway—without being bothered by Gillespie's commentary. She had to have heard Dixon swearing, though, and she would hear what he said now.

"It's not Sorcerer."

"*What?*" Thankfully that was Gillespie, too.

"Whoever that guy is, Avery, it's not Adrian. Keep talking for now, but be careful."

She'd stumbled a bit over her words when he began to talk but regrouped beautifully—after a long, long sip from her alleged coffee, he couldn't help noticing.

"I, um, I was just expecting someone else," she said, making Dixon tense up for a minute, until he realized what she had said was perfectly in keeping with the conversation. Now, though, it just had a double entendre, whether deliberate or not.

"You're totally who I was expecting," the guy said.

And why, Dixon thought, did the innocent remark sound so sinister? Was he simply coloring it with his own suspicion and fear? Or was the guy a genuine threat?

It wasn't a risk he was willing to take.

Without even thinking about what he was doing, Dixon rose from his chair, discarding the sketch pad and charcoal as he did. He had a weapon in his pocket, but he didn't withdraw it. He only strode slowly and purposely forward, toward where Avery was sitting.

When Gillespie saw what he was doing, he squawked through the earpiece, "Dixon, what the hell is going on? Where are you going?"

Dixon said nothing in response because he didn't want to do anything that would alert Avery to his actions. She needed to just keep chatting casually with whoever this guy was, because whoever this guy was needed to be casual, too.

"Dixon?" Gillespie said again.

Dixon pulled the earpiece from his ear and tucked it into his pocket.

The distance between him and Avery was closing, but not as quickly as he wanted it to. He kept his eye, though, not on her but on the man seated next to her. This time Dixon was grateful for the man's back being turned to him. Because it posed no problem whatsoever in his approaching unseen and wrapping his arm around the guy's neck and jerking him up from the bench.

"Dixon!" Avery cried when she realized what was happening. She, too, jumped up from her seat, her big cup of scotch flying from her hand when she did so. Vaguely Dixon noticed that she didn't seem to notice.

The guy he'd just collared, literally, struggled hard to free himself, but Dixon had skill and years of experience—not to mention absolute fear for Avery's safety—

on his side, and he was able to keep the man pinned with no problem.

"Who are you?" Dixon demanded without preamble or explanation.

"Andrew Paddington," the guy said, gripping Dixon's arm with both hands. But he'd stopped trying to pull himself free and his body had relaxed a little. Obviously he'd figured out it would be useless to fight.

"You're not Andrew Paddington," Dixon said. Then he jerked his arm tighter. "Who are you?"

The man's fingers on his arm went rigid again, but still he didn't fight. "My name's Benny Culver."

Dixon jerked his arm tight again. "And?"

"And I'm a student at Columbia."

"How do you know about Avery?" Dixon asked. "How did you know to come here when you did?"

"Let me go, man," the guy said. "I'll tell you whatever you want to know. Just let me go."

"Dixon," Avery said softly.

And just the sound of her voice made him relax. She was fine, he reminded himself. She was safe. It was over now and she was okay.

Of course, *he* was over his head in trouble. If there had been any possibility of Sorcerer showing up here today, Dixon had just made sure the guy was halfway to the west coast by now. If this Benny Culver was someone Sorcerer had sent in first to test the waters, then Dixon had just managed to pollute those waters by coming out of hiding too soon. No way would Sorcerer show his face now. And now he would know he'd been under surveillance. Not that that would come as any great surprise to him, Dixon was sure. But it sure as hell was going to make it harder to catch him next time.

Funny, though, how that didn't really bother Dixon as much as it probably should. Because all he cared about right now was the fact that Avery was safe and that OPUS wouldn't be able to use her anymore.

He eased up his hold on Culver but didn't let go of him. He saw Gillespie behind Avery, his expression grim as he approached. But the other man said nothing as he joined the trio waiting for explanation. Of course, Dixon knew that it was he, and not Culver, who had the most explaining to do.

"Let me go," Culver said again.

"Not until you tell us who you are and why you're here," Dixon said.

"Hey, man, I could ask you the same question," Culver countered.

Dixon jerked his arm up again, then relaxed it.

"Okay, okay," the other man relented. "I'm doing a favor for a friend, all right?"

"What kind of favor?"

"A buddy of mine met Avery online and set up a meeting with her. But he asked me to go first and pretend to be him, in case she turned out to be heinous."

"Where's this friend now?" Dixon asked.

Culver looked across the ice rink and started to lift a finger to point. "Oh, shit, man, he was right there a minute ago."

And now he was gone, Dixon translated. He muttered a ripe expletive and repeated it a half-dozen times.

"My words exactly," Gillespie said.

And even though he would have been well within his rights to demand Dixon explain his behavior, he said nothing more. Dixon wasn't sure if that was because he didn't want to challenge a senior operative or if maybe, just maybe, Gillespie had figured out what was going on between him and Avery, since, hey, he'd had some goings-on himself with Avery's sister. Maybe Gillespie already understood Dixon's actions. Hell, he might even understand them better than Dixon did.

"Look, man, I don't want any trouble," Culver was saying now.

"Yeah, well, you've got it anyway," Dixon told him. "In spades."

Culver should take heart though, he wanted to tell the man further. Because he wasn't the only one who had trouble. Nor was he the one who had the most.

IT WAS AFTER MIDNIGHT THE next day when Avery finally got to see Dixon again. And just as it had been that first night, it was because she answered her front door to him. This time, though, she knew what she was getting into when she invited him inside. And this time, she was actually kind of hoping they *would* end up horizontal on her sofa. Unfortunately this time, it was doubtless out of the question. Because this time Dixon would be wrapping up the assignment, not dragging her into it. This time, she was sure, he would be telling her goodbye.

He said nothing as he entered, looking more tired than she had ever seen him. But then, he'd had a pretty busy couple of days. After instructing Gillespie to take Benny Culver in for questioning and assuring him he'd be right behind them, Dixon had driven Avery home—*home* home this time—and helped her get settled. There was no reason for her to accompany him to OPUS, and East Hampton was too far to drive when he had a suspect waiting for him. Plus, he knew she'd be more comfortable at home after everything she'd been through. Within minutes of their arrival, though, he'd been off again. And within minutes of his departure, Avery had known she would never be comfortable at home again. For some reason, home didn't feel like home anymore. It hadn't since Dixon had left.

Although he'd told her he was returning to OPUS to question Benny Culver, she knew Dixon would be questioned, too. He'd have to justify cutting short the meeting, something that had let Adrian Padgett slip through their fingers. She still didn't understand why he had done that, why he had revealed himself when she hadn't even been in any danger. Had he waited even ten more minutes, Adrian might have considered the situation safe and made an appearance. It didn't make sense for a man of Dixon's experience and expertise to do something so irresponsible and stupid. She'd told herself there must have been some danger she wasn't aware of, that maybe Gillespie had identified something about the situation that put her at an immediate risk. But Gillespie had seemed as confused as Avery when he'd joined them.

"Is everything okay?" she asked now as Dixon went straight to her sofa and collapsed onto it.

He was wearing the same clothes he'd had on yesterday—jeans and a sweatshirt under the leather bomber jacket he'd worn that first night. The one she had feared might hide a weapon—other than his hands, which she recalled thinking then might be more dangerous than any manufactured firearm. She realized now that she'd been right about that. His hands really were very dangerous. Just not in the way she'd first thought, that was all. She was back into her usual at-home attire of battered pajama bottoms—these printed with cartoon cats—and an oversize sweatshirt of her own. Slowly she crossed the room to where he was sitting and folded herself down onto the sofa next to him.

"No, everything's not okay," he said wearily.

"What happened with Culver?" Avery asked.

"I'm not supposed to tell you," he replied. "Your part in the assignment is officially concluded, so now you're not on a need-to-know basis anymore."

"The hell I'm not."

"Yeah, that's kind of what I thought you'd say."

"So what happened with Culver?" she asked again.

Dixon sighed heavily and told her, "We're reasonably certain the guy is innocent of any real wrongdoing. It seems he was duped by Adrian the same way everyone else was."

"Like me, you mean," she said softly.

"Like lots of people," he assured her. "He says he met Adrian at Columbia, where they were in the same postgrad class, and that they became friends because they shared an interest in a certain computer virus that was unleashed on the world some years ago."

Heat swamped Avery's insides. "Mine, you mean."

Dixon nodded.

She expelled an exasperated sound. "God, I still can't believe there are people out there who remember that thing and think it was so great. I'm never going to live it down."

Dixon said nothing, only continued, "You would have thought Culver had just met Paris Hilton, he was so starstruck by you."

Avery closed her eyes but said nothing. Would there

ever come a day when she could just be a normal, anonymous person? Oh, right. Of course not. She was too whack. And the world was too unforgiving.

"Anyway, he said Adrian told him he'd met someone online who had been badgering him to meet in person—"

"Oh, please!" Avery said, outraged now. "I badgered him?"

Dixon smiled. "I told you you were good at that."

She growled at him but said only, "Go on."

"Long story short, Adrian told Culver he'd pay him fifty bucks to meet you first, in case you turned out to be a nutcase, and Culver, being a broke college student, not to mention an ardent fan, jumped on it. Of course, we know Adrian offered him the money to do it in case you were being watched. Evidently he did get suspicious of your too-quick capitulation to meet. I shouldn't have pushed you to make contact so soon." He paused for a moment, then added, "I shouldn't have done a lot of things I did for this assignment. But I guess it's too late now."

Avery swallowed hard. *Here it comes,* she thought. *The big brush-off.*

"You're in a lot of trouble, huh?" she asked softly.

"Whoa, yeah."

"You didn't lose your job, did you?"

He shook his head. "No, but I got a nice diatribe from my boss that lasted a good forty-five minutes. And they're bucking me down a few ranks, which will limit my benefits and delay my retirement. And I'm probably going to keep hearing about this for the rest of my career. What's left of it anyway."

"I'm sorry, Dixon," Avery said.

He turned to look at her, meeting her gaze intently. "I'm not."

She arched her eyebrows in surprise. "Why not?"

"It's not the job I'm talking about when it comes to being in trouble," he told her. "I've been in trouble at work lots of times. My butt gets chewed for forty-five minutes at least once a year, and the bust in rank is mild compared to what they could have done to me. It's *you,* Avery," he added. "You're the reason I'm in a lot of trouble."

"I know," she said, her words touched with exasperation. "That's why I'm apologizing. Because I screwed up everything so badly."

"You didn't screw anything up, I did," he told her. "You were doing just fine. You don't owe anyone an apology. Not OPUS for the job. And not me for the trouble you put me in."

She eyed him suspiciously. "So then what kind of trouble are you talking about?"

He grinned. "Woman trouble."

"I'm not woman trouble," she countered.

"Peaches, you're nothing *but* trouble," he assured her. He lifted a hand and brushed a strand of her hair back over her shoulder, then dropped it nervously back into his lap, as if he feared some kind of reprisal for what he'd done. "But as anyone in OPUS will tell you," he added, "I love trouble."

Her heart hammered hard in her chest at hearing him say what he did. She told herself not to hope, that she must be misunderstanding. He couldn't possibly mean—

"I love you," he said further without one iota of uncertainty or frustration. And without another word, too, as if he were waiting to see how she would react to the announcement. As if he feared maybe she didn't reciprocate.

Men could be such idiots sometimes.

"You love me?" she said softly, still not quite able to believe him.

"I do," he told her.

"Even though I'm not…normal?"

He chuckled at that, and some of the tension she'd sensed in him seemed to ease. "Normal means common," he told her. "It's ordinary. It's routine. It's predictable. It's boring. Why would anyone fall in love with normal?"

"Why would anyone fall in love with whack?" she countered.

"You're not whack," he said softly. "You're unique. You're distinctive. You're rare. You're special."

Never in her life had she been called such things. Things similar, certainly, but never flattering. *Strange, bizarre, odd, peculiar*—those were words she had heard applied to her often enough. And those were the most polite. Not once had anyone said she was special. Not once had anyone thought she was special. Until Dixon.

"That night at my parents' party," she said, thinking now was her chance to ask him about that healing comment he'd made.

"What about it?" he asked.

"When we were dancing, you told me my scabs had healed but I couldn't stop showing off my scars," she reminded him. "What did you mean by that? How could you say I was healed? Especially since I'd just nearly had a panic attack."

"How can you not understand that?" he countered.

"Especially since when I said it you'd just successfully battled a panic attack?"

She opened her mouth to say something more, then realized she had no idea what to say.

"Look at you," he continued when she didn't speak. "How can you think you're *not* healed?"

"I do look at myself," she said. "I look at myself every day. I'm a mess. My life is a mess."

He started shaking his head before she even finished talking, even went so far as to chuckle at her. "No, Avery, you're not a mess," he said. "And neither is your life. Maybe you don't live conventionally, but you're not a mess. Your family—now, they're a mess," he said with a smile. "You…you survived that mess. You knew a long time ago how you wanted to live your life, what you wanted to make of it and yourself, and you went after it. In spite of them. In spite of everything. Maybe you didn't make it easy on yourself and maybe you stumbled a little here and there along the way, but, hell, who doesn't? That's what life is all about. You're a survivor," he told her. "Even with all the adversity you had to put up with—your family, prison, agoraphobia, seclusion—you've made a productive life for yourself. You have a job, a home, money in the bank. Hell, you've made more of your life than a lot of people without adversity have. And you did it all by yourself."

"But I'm terrified to leave my home," she reminded him.

He met her gaze levelly. "Yeah, well, that's something we can work on. And what, you don't think most people *aren't* afraid to leave their homes from time to time? You're just in a position where you don't have to, that's all. There are a million people out there who, if given a choice, wouldn't go out in this world. And frankly I don't blame them."

"But—"

"You're not perfect, Avery," he continued, not giving her a chance to interrupt. "But you're not a mess, either. You're a decent human being, and at the end of the day you can go to bed knowing you haven't hurt anyone. You haven't betrayed anyone. You haven't made anyone unhappy. Do you know how few people can honestly say that?"

She realized she wanted to keep arguing with him, then asked herself why she was so determined to. He was right. Maybe she hadn't lived a normal life so far, but neither had she led an empty one. Because she had found enjoyment in many of her pursuits. And she had learned from her experiences. And now she wanted to learn more. Wanted to be more. Wanted not to be normal but to be…unbroken. Complete. Whole.

She smiled at the thought. She was whole, she told herself. Because what she had been missing, she finally realized, was love. Someone to love and someone to love her in return. Now that she had both of those things, she could…

A feeling welled up inside her then that very nearly overwhelmed her, a potent concoction of happiness and well-being and hope and a certainty that everything would eventually be all right. It was unlike anything she had ever felt in her life, and for a moment she was nearly drunk with it.

"I love you, too," she told Dixon, exhilarated to finally be able to say it. To finally be able to acknowledge it. To finally be able to feel it.

She launched herself forward and into his arms, her

mouth finding his unerringly. For a long time they remained tangled in their embrace, reacquainting themselves with the feel and smell and taste of each other. And Avery was filled to near bursting with an exhilarating understanding that this was only the first of an infinite number of such embraces. She would never, ever be alone again. Because she would always, always have Dixon. And he would always, always have her.

When he pulled his mouth from hers, she murmured a disappointed sound and pushed herself forward again. But after one brief kiss Dixon placed his hand between their mouths and said, "There's something else I'm not supposed to tell you about the assignment. Something else you need to know."

And even though the assignment was the last thing Avery wanted to talk about at the moment, the look on his face made her pause. "What?" she asked.

He shifted their positions until they were seated next to each other, Avery cuddling at his side, one arm draped over her shoulder, their hands linked in her lap. "You need to know the reason we took the assignment to your parents' house."

"I already figured that out," she said, thinking it odd he would bring up something like that just when things between them were heating up. "To keep me under Adrian's radar."

Dixon shook his head. "No, that's what they told me, too, at first, but it wasn't that."

"Then what?"

His gaze found hers and held it. "It was because your father wanted you to come home, Avery."

Certain she must have misunderstood, she said, "What are you talking about?"

"My boss, the one who ordered me to take you to East Hampton, knows your father."

"What?"

"They went to college together," Dixon said. "He met you, in fact, when you were a kid."

Avery recalled that first night at OPUS, the man she'd met right after Dixon had taken her out of her restraints. "I knew he looked familiar!"

"He called your father when he realized you were involved with Adrian," Dixon continued. "Felt like he owed it to the guy, I guess. And your father called in a favor, using the opportunity to have you sent to East Hampton, thinking your coming home might start to mend the rift from ten years ago. He was hoping the assignment would take longer, long enough that you would be at the house over Thanksgiving. And he was hoping maybe the rest of the family, being together again for the holiday, would start to come around.

"He wants you to come home, Avery," Dixon said. "He wants the Nesbitts to be a family again. But he doesn't know how to do it himself. When he found out what was going on, he saw it as an opportunity to make it happen."

To say she was surprised by the revelation would have been a major understatement. That her father was reaching out in whatever way he could to bring her back into the family was nothing short of astonishing.

But all she could think to say was, "He wants me to come home for Thanksgiving?"

Dixon shook his head. "No. He wants you to come home for good."

"What about the rest of the family?" she asked.

This time Dixon shrugged. "Guess you'll have to find out for yourself, won't you?"

"What about you?" she asked.

"What about me?"

She smiled. "What are you doing for Thanksgiving?"

He smiled back. "It doesn't matter. As long as I'm with you. For Thanksgiving and Christmas and New Year's and Valentine's Day and St. Patrick's Day and Arbor Day and every other day of the year."

"Even if we have to spend them all here at my place because I'm too scared to go out?" she asked.

"Anywhere," Dixon told her. "I'll go anywhere with you."

And hearing him say that the way he did made Avery want to go everywhere. More than that, hearing him say it the way he did made her think maybe she could.

"I love you, Dixon. I love you, Oliver. I love you no matter who you are or what you are or where you are. And I will love you forever."

He lifted a hand to her face, cupping her jaw gently in his palm. "Binky," he said.

She narrowed her eyes at him.

"That's my code name," he told her, smiling. "Binky."

She chuckled. "Hence the reason why no one lives to talk about it after saying it."

"You could say it and live," he promised.

She lifted her hand to his face, too, brushing her fingertips over his rough beard. "Nah, I kind of like you as Dixon," she said. She smiled. "But who knows what I might cry out in a moment of heated passion."

He quirked up one dark brow. "We could find out."

She nodded slowly. "Yes, we could."

And in a moment of heated passion—several moments of heated passion, in fact—they did.

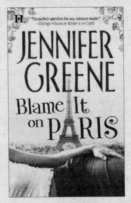

Thoroughbred *Legacy*

Launching in June 2008

A dramatic new 12-book continuity that embodies the American Dream.

Meet the Prestons, owners of Quest Stables, a successful horse-racing and breeding empire. But the lives, loves and reputations of this hardworking family are put at risk when a breeding scandal unfolds.

Flirting with Trouble

by *New York Times* bestselling author

ELIZABETH BEVARLY

Eight years ago, publicist Marnie Roberts spent seven days of bliss with Australian horse trainer Daniel Whittleson. But just as quickly, he disappeared. Now Marnie is heading to Australia to finally confront the man she's never been able to forget.

The race begins in June, wherever books are sold.

REQUEST YOUR
FREE BOOKS!

2 FREE NOVELS
FROM THE ROMANCE/SUSPENSE
COLLECTION PLUS 2 FREE GIFTS!

YES! Please send me 2 FREE novels from the Romance/Suspense Collection and my 2 FREE gifts (gifts are worth about $10). After receiving them, if I don't wish to receive any more books, I can return the shipping statement marked "cancel." If I don't cancel, I will receive 4 brand-new novels every month and be billed just $5.49 per book in the U.S. or $5.99 per book in Canada, plus 25¢ shipping and handling per book plus applicable taxes, if any*. That's a savings of at least 20% off the cover price! I understand that accepting the 2 free books and gifts places me under no obligation to buy anything. I can always return a shipment and cancel at any time. Even if I never buy another book from the Reader Service, the two free books and gifts are mine to keep forever.

185 MDN EF5Y   385 MDN EF6C

Name	(PLEASE PRINT)	
Address		Apt. #
City	State/Prov.	Zip/Postal Code

Signature (if under 18, a parent or guardian must sign)

Mail to **The Reader Service**:
IN U.S.A.: P.O. Box 1867, Buffalo, NY 14240-1867
IN CANADA: P.O. Box 609, Fort Erie, Ontario L2A 5X3

Not valid to current subscribers to the Romance Collection,
the Suspense Collection or the Romance/Suspense Collection.

Want to try two free books from another line?
Call 1-800-873-8635 or visit www.morefreebooks.com.

* Terms and prices subject to change without notice. N.Y. residents add applicable sales tax. Canadian residents will be charged applicable provinãal taxes and GST. This offer is limited to one order per household. All orders subject to approval. Credit or debit balances in a customer's account(s) may be offset by any other outstanding balance owed by or to the customer. Please allow 4 to 6 weeks for delivery. Offer available while quantities last.

Your Privacy: Harlequin is committed to protecting your privacy. Our Privacy Policy is available online at www.eHarlequin.com or upon request from the Reader Service. From time to time we make our lists of customers available to reputable third parties who may have a product or service of interest to you. If you would prefer we not share your name and address, please check here. ☐

BOB08